Test Patterns

Pesice, Duane (*ed.*)

Published by Planet X Publications

First Edition. 2017.

Vacaville, California, USA.

planetxpublications.blogspot.com

Dedicated to the members of the Weird community,
without whom this book would not exist.

Cover Art by Nick Gucker
Cover Design by Michael Adams
Interior Layout & Design by AW Baader
Proofreading by James Russell

ISBN: 0692999981
ISBN-13: 978-0692999981

TEST PATTERNS

CONTENTS

SUMMONING SPIRITS

by Michael Adams

Another dreary shift ends and you leave the sunlit, workaday world behind. You seek the comfort of home and your familiar easy chair. There you will spend an evening transported to unknown worlds, ancient times, possible futures, and other planes of existence.

You embark on this journey with the aid of sophisticated electronics, but nothing as exotic as a spaceship or time machine. No, your journey through the spheres is taken via television, and the ultimate destination is within your own mind.

The fuel for this voyage will be unique, though. As you make yourself comfortable you produce from your shirt pocket a small glass vial. What's inside it shimmers and shifts in black and white like television static.

You take the requisite amount in the prescribed manner and begin your trip.

Alone in a room, shrouded in darkness save for the monochrome glow of the television, you focus on the shapes and sounds before your eyes, absorbing as many of the outré and otherworldly images as possible. There in the twilight, you are taken to your limits, and find yourself moving beyond.

Sometime after the creature features and midnight movies, you begin fading in and out of conscious reality until you wake at last to find the broadcast day is done, the station has signed off for the night.

A standard test pattern glares out at you from the screen.

Disappointed your trip didn't take you farther into those outer reaches of consciousness, you begin to debate the merits of finding your bed when you begin to notice… changes… in the image.

There is something else there, something just past those familiar predictable graphics and gradients, another vestigial transmission trying to break through… it's there, past the surface of the screen, and if you stare long enough, focus deeply enough, you'll see it, the programming that rides in the interstices of the carrier wave. You are on the precipice of discovery; the television has become the medium in a great electronic summoning.

Then it all changes, a great electronic eye opens in the center of the screen and you begin to understand, you have become the transceiver, and now the TV is watching you.

You know you can only be dreaming, but that couldn't matter less. The lines between dream, reality, and hallucination have all fallen away. You begin tuning into new stories in the dark and the dead of night.

These are some of those stories…

THE STARS ARE BLACK

by D. L. Myers

Above me there is only the indigo sky with its flare of dying twilight bleeding away into the endless vacuum of night. In the spreading darkness beyond the reach of day's lost light, multitudes of kaleidoscopic solar spheres, a myriad of pulsing, ever-changing color, grows steadily brighter as the light recedes. I peer sharply into the sparkling dome of the heavens feeling the weight of my body suddenly slip and then slide away like a billowing shroud, leaving me weightless and adrift in the blackness that reaches for me from above. In the now ebon sky, tendrils of essential night stream down from the spaces between the stars, enveloping and penetrating the wraith I have become. All around me, great arms of black undulate and serpentine like sargasso in a nocturnal sea. A burning cold seeps into my being from the crawling web that surrounds me, and then I am drawn into the starry depths, torn by cosmic forces from the familiar bounds of earthly sanity, and hurled into a realm of utter and eternal darkness. Bereft of light and form, drowning in a claustrophobic terror that teeters on the verge of madness, I drift through viscous blackness for a measureless span until my strained nerves sense that I am approaching things vast and yet unknowable in this sightless space. And there is a sound, faint at first but growing ever louder, as of a great cataract plunging into stygian depths. And then with a stunning suddenness, I pierce the veil of uttermost darkness to see that I am surrounded by black orbs shrouded in clouds of ebon dust that swirl and surge in the dark energy that bleeds endlessly from their black surfaces. The sound seems to arise from the constant flow of this force streaming into the void, and I can feel it pushing me like a wind-blown cloud back toward the veil of darkness which seems to feed on this outpouring of nighted energy. I again approach the veil which seems like a sable curtain studded with glittering jewels, and I pass through it with the hissing sound all around me.

I come back to myself on the couch in my darkened living room. The sound has followed me from that inexplicable realm, and for a moment I again see those vast sable spheres pouring their blackness into the void. Then all I see is a swarming wall of black-and-white which slowly resolves into the image on my television. I press a button on the remote and the room is plunged into black silence.

THE WOMAN IN THE
FORGE OF SATURDAY NIGHT

by Joseph S. Pulver, Sr.

Slipper-quiet steps down the carpeted stairs. Slowly. Streetlight, no moon, lighting her way. Pausing. Avoiding the third stair's long groan. Across the floor of the dustless foyer into the shadow-colored family room. Slender fingers that know books and how to dazzle with culinary skills and long rows of numbers and how to beautifully arrange fresh-cut flowers, turn on the new RCA color television set. Careful fingers adjust the volume, keeping it listenably-muted. Above her, behind the thick door to their bedroom in the rear of the 5-bedroom/3-bath Victorian house (on a heavily-wooded 5 acre lot bordered in the rear by Vale Cemetery), her parents tucked into their dreams. A lustful film of desires, of *wild self* taking and tumbling, losing fortune's quest, fills her eyes.

The Creature Zone, Susan's secret fare every late-night Saturday night (after mother and father had retired at a respectable hour) for the last two years was gone, taken off the air, no reason given. For three weeks after her monsters vanished Alfred Hitchcock films, Vertigo, The Paradine Case, Spellbound, played on Saturday Night Late Cinema. Mother, daughter of a senator and a concert pianist, wife of a man who was the Dean of Faculty at one of New York's foremost preparatory schools, (a Sunday, church-going woman), did not approve of Hitchcock; too lurid, "saturated in blasphemies and wickedness", and "wholly degenerate". Not once did Susan tremble with the pleasures of seeing monsters or alien invaders darkening the conventions of the mundane world when The Creature Feature was replaced by Hitchcock and the month-after-month of old, black and white noir films.

Susan missed the grainy activities of evil astrophysicists with special plans ready to confront and destroy civilization, missed the soft-blur of the crab-clawed blobs and the eerie shambling of the robot demons from the Insanium of Professor Terror. Night of the Robot Crabs, Devil Girl from Mars, Beware the Teenage Zombie Scarecrow, Ship of Monsters,

The Astro-Vampires From Prison Planet M, When Orrgo Runs Amok, Queen of Outer Space, Invasion of the Zuggtarr, The Man from Planet X, Fire Maidens of Outer Space, The Man Who Did Not Believe in Ghost Stories, gone.

The Hunchback. The Phantom of the Opera – Chaney, Rains, Lom. Frankenstein. Kong. The Mummy. The Wolfman. Storms in the black sky and in demented hearts. The Creature from the Black Lagoon. Spooky houses on spooky streets. Metaluna. Ray guns. Vincent Price. Spaceships, and headed toward mankind, the deadly space-rays of strange invaders. Nights of cursed moon. Boris Karloff. **TERROR! MENACE! MARS!** Gone. Gone. Graverobber's shovel mining cold ground. Cannibals. Apes and omens, rites, and devils, and ghouls. Godzilla. **THEM!** Lon Chaney. Gone. Two years of dark joys. Two years of being outside of Mother's rigid parameters while madness and terror owned late-night Saturday during The Creature Zone. Two years that let the hungry inside her breast frolic, gone.

Into the family room of 39 Green Manor Dr., Schenectady, New York, WKVI (Channel 13 Schenectady, New York) beams tonight's old, black and white noir.

Story from the secret corners of the night.
Low lit.
Shadows.
Lipstick. And legs. The big con. Flesh, older, no less hungry than the young femme fatales. Sitting pretty as a plated-up pork chop, but the gravy is poison.
Booze. Watered-down beer. Cheap gin. Cheaper whiskey. Dirty glasses.
A 4-fist riot. The tornado with the small, clumsy fists loses a fair amount of blood.
Failure and paradox. Forgot every word in Mama's Sunday-come-to-meeting Bible.
Black ball in the corner pocket. Loser eyes the door.
Six chamber ace-in-the-hole.
The grammar of desire. It always looks like Hitchcock had his hands on it.
Suspicion. Greed. Suspicion.
Suspicion.
Suspicion.
Thoughtless fear.
Suspicion.
Eyes dismembering the displays pinned on faces.
Dime a dozen drunk, just a little. No rhyme. No reason. He looks like Richard Widmark, psychosis, desperation, in need of a shave. They all look like Richard Widmark.
Sirens in conversation.
Rain. It always rains.
Transactions.

Bar on the corner next to the drugstore and the barbershop. Pint of whiskey in a paper bag and tramps. There's always a tramp turned pro last week and a fool, and a no-good two-faced rat. Each has its own particular stench.

Sour grapes.
Anger.
"You always were a whore."
"You're still a bastard. And a liar."
Coils. Cigarette smoke and ominous music. It always sounds like Bernard Hermann.
End-of-the-rope.
Dead end.
At close range: this ain't gonna work out. Nothing ever works out in these bleak stories.
Tears. Someone, failing to find The Dream, always cries.
Barbara laughs at spineless. The chastisement of cold blue steel. Blood.
Oblivion drinks up and goes home.
Midnight exits the streetcorner.
Vertigo.
The final commandment: *some gonna lose.*

Fifty minutes into the show, Susan yawns. *Have I seen this? Why do all of these seem the same?* She yawns again.

We're experiencing TECHNICAL DIFFICULTIES – Please Stand By appears on the screen.

Susan sits on the floor in her blue bunny-print, cotton PJs and waits. The flicker of jealousy and despair and running back to pain and the blood of enemy-self does not return to the screen. As WKVI ceases the day's broadcasting without correcting their technical difficulties and posts the RCA Indian-head test pattern, Susan begins to drift off. Headlong… forgetting prevalent day tick-tocking precisely, into inner focus. Wanting her own language enacting the exhibits of night, she unwraps her secrets.

MEMORIES ON THE CORNER OF 16TH & NIGHT
STARRING
SUSAN DOUGLAS
and
JACK STEWART
SPECIAL GUEST STAR
KEN NORDINE (as Book, the narrator)
PRODUCED BY
H. M. TELOTTE
WRITTEN AND DIRECTED BY
RALF SCHATTEN

Night does not give a reason (no left or right or highest branch) for its philosophy – it cares not if your tongue boasts, or is burdened by funeral songs. October (autumn with no flowers in its mouth) brings a river of rain filled with distressing hindsight.

Night and October come. Shuttered within their industries, people will often wonder how they came to be prisoners.

Norton Furniture Company. ¼ mile (and a smidge) long parking lot (long walk to the bus stop at 11 pm in the cold October rain.)

Susan (single/lives at home/31-years-old/shoulder length black hair, straight cut with choppy bangs/neatly-trimmed short nails, no nail varnish/ no lipstick or eye make-up) is the manager of the Norton Furniture Company Credit Department. She knows where 22-year-old Jack Stewart lives, read his employment application, ran a credit check on him, checked his references and for an arrest record. She's observed him in the lunchroom, knows what he eats. Knows what brand of cigarettes he smokes. Approvingly, she's noted the paperback books he sometimes reads during breaks and at lunch; DUNE, The Left Hand of Darkness, Stranger in A Strange Land, 1984, This Perfect Day, I, Robot, A Canticle for Leibowitz – she, too, has read them.

Susan's black Camaro zipping across the parking lot toward the bus stop where Jack stands out in the cold autumn rain.

(She's looked at him – there, shivering, thought to stop – 10 times – more, pick him up and give him a ride. Driven home wondering why she didn't. Driven (with her fears and longing) by the string of motels, neon VACANCY in her headlights. Cigarette in her lips. Whispered: 'I am shame and boldness. I am shameless; I am ashamed. I am strength and I am fear.' In reply to Gene Pitney's "Only Love Can Break A Heart" on the radio, whispered, 'I am shameless.' – 'I am strong… and I am afraid.' – 'I am the substance and the one who has no substance.' – 'I am she whose wedding is great, and I have not taken a husband.')

Susan, shamelessly warmed with thoughts of Jack in her arms, chooses oneness over the smallnesses of never. "Strength."

The Camaro stops. "Get in."

She hands him her pack of smokes. "Light me one, too." Points her black Camaro in the direction of Jack's cramped apartment.

Seven days later; Saturday 11:30 pm *Saturday Night Late* Cinema. No monsters. Not a single creepy crawly or reanimated cadaver, and certainly, no menagerie of multi-tentacled, giant bugs telepathically controlled by a Venusian Cruella de Ville decked out in a satiny mini-dress and knee-high anti-gravity boots. No devil girls or men from Planet X. No Lom, or Frankenstein, or MARS, or October shadows, come to turn the clock back. What Susan gets, again, is a black lagoon of hard-boiled sound and fury, the consequences of social malaise and legs (hell-bent on sin) and double-crosses.

D.I.V.O.R.C.E.D. From (despicable) Ron. One year ago (after eighteen months spiked with irritants and arguments that threatened to go nuclear). Two-timed her. Lied. Took money from her purse and her bank account. Came out, he spent it on strange – some Barbara or Cheryl, and booze and pills.

Staggered in one Sunday morning, reeking of some Barbara or Cheryl. WORDS. HOT! HARD! *Poison!* His right hand became a fist. She found herself on the kitchen floor. The next day she had a black eye. A week later, reeking of cheap whiskey (and some Barbara or Cheryl), he backhanded her. Broke her right wrist when she fell to the hardwood floor.

Ron's cleaned out her bank account and her purse and had gone out on her. Tonight he slapped her hard, cleaned out her purse again, told her he was going to find some strange. She's standing at the dresser. Crying. Opens the top drawer... there, among his socks, is, his revolver –

30 minutes into tonight's feature the crises and illness, undeniable lies at breakneck speed, have stopped happening –

We're experiencing TECHNICAL DIFFICULTIES – Please Stand By appears on the screen.

Susan sits on the floor in her bunny-print, cotton PJs and waits for the coffin of struggles to reopen. Pulling a blanket tight about her, she's nodding, modifying reality, as WKVI (Channel 13 Schenectady, New York) ceases the day's broadcasting and posts the RCA Indian-head test pattern. Susan shifts from staring at the numbers, and drowsy, plunges headlong... into

BLAME THE MEMORIES
STARRING
SUSAN DOUGLAS
and
JACK STEWART
SPECIAL GUEST STAR
LILY DRACO (as The Blue Bunny)
PRODUCED BY
HENNING SCHATTEN
WRITTEN AND DIRECTED BY
RALF SCHATTEN

Eyes. Screen of single eyes. 5. 23. Too many to count. Floating. Open. Blinking. Closed, some with eyes painted on them. Dark eyes. Her own eyes staring at her.

A mouth appears. Opens.

November. Wednesday. Twenty minutes back 11pm died. Jack Stewart, waiting (in the cold rain/chilled to the core) for the bus. He just put in a grueling double. Susan's Camaro pulls up purrs. "Get in." Purposely-slow ride home. Tosses Jack her hardpack of smokes, "Light me one." Westbound, Camaro's heater healing the night. Bob Seger's "Mainstreet" on the radio. (In the backseat, the Blue Bunny sits silently, smiling.) Camaro pulls up to his frontdoor. When he gets out Susan gives him another smoke and her telephone number, winks (to warm his dreams).

Seven days later; *Saturday Night Late Cinema.* No BOO! Sons-a-bitches. Femme fatale, refused, rejected, not even scraps to swallow, clinging to the only solution, murder. In the middle of it all, a losin'-side wretch (trying to grab the handle, missed too many boats to count) and a detective (with more than one ghost in his past). One (head full of ideas, goin' for broke) just took the dare. Come midnight one's going to get erased.

We're experiencing TECHNICAL DIFFICULTIES – Please Stand By appears on the screen.

Susan sits on the floor in her blue bunny-print, soft-cotton PJs and waits to see if the cinematic metropolis of paranoia returns. Minutes pass between her yawns. After yawning a fourth time, she drowsy, now lying on the floor, as WKVI ceases the day's broadcasting and posts the RCA Indian-head test pattern, falls into slumber and yields to the oncoming dream.

WITH ONLY THE NIGHT BEHIND YOU
STARRING
SUSAN DOUGLAS
and
JACK STEWART
SPECIAL GUEST STAR
KEN NORDINE (as Book, the narrator)
PRODUCED BY
HENNING SCHATTEN
WRITTEN AND DIRECTED BY
RALF SCHATTEN

A late November night of fat, wet snowflakes falling in a lonely world. A woman and a man with an appointment in a room far from the string of motels they pass.

He's nervous. Likes her eyes.

She's nervous, too.

The Burt Bacharach/Hal David song about lovers wanting speaks for them.

He's thinking – (not for the first time), soon she'll close her eyes and he'll make promises neither can resist.

Flying within her, thoughts of the first kiss… and the closer to you that comes after.

Another ride home (something she does when the weather is bad/fairly often these days). Jack sits in the passenger seat (smoking a cigarette she has given him). Susan beside him, driving, hoping her profile offers him faith. When she arrives at his place, she walks into his apartment and goes to the bedroom. Opens her overnight bag. Takes out three candles, places them (one on each bedside table, one on the dresser) and lights them, their flames begin to spin like pinwheels. 50 stuffed blue bunnies surround the bed. She lights a reefer cigarette, takes a toke and hands it to Jack (still standing in the doorway – telling himself, he's finally free of the rain)… and slowly unbuttons her PJs.

Seven days later; *Saturday Night Late Cinema*. Heat in their faces, each telling a story in predator shorthand. The lips of Crimelord of the Sewers' jigsaw face move. He says, "No." Reaches into his vest pocket –

Please Stand By - We're experiencing TECHNICAL DIFFICULTIES appears on the screen.

Susan, in her bunny-print, dream-hide, lies on the carpeted floor of the family room and waits. Susan yawns a 3rd time. With her stuffed, blue bunny beside her, Susan continues to stare, as WKVI ceases the day's broadcasting and posts the RCA Indian-head test pattern. Peering, she's tempted to wave at the Indian chief. Moments later, her focus moves from number to number – 20-25-30-30-35-35-45-30-30-20-35-30-30-25-20 – before her eyelids (weakened by the tugging of drowsy tides) go heavy.

ANGEL IN A TOMBSTONE DRESS
STARRING
SUSAN DOUGLAS
and
JACK STEWART
SPECIAL GUEST STAR
DAVID MCCALLUM (as Ron)
PRODUCED BY
HENNING SCHATTEN
WRITTEN AND DIRECTED BY
RALF SCHATTEN

Warm July night, as far from winter rearing its creature as you can get. Moon observing the night gardeners (boys who'd agree to anything/girls who want to know they're in a real relationship before there's any talk of third base or home) drink tequila, beer, smoke their smokes, hunt for sign. Banks of the Mohawk River, across from the old American Locomotive Works, River House Bar. Susan's with Ron, 2nd date, only accepted for something to do on a kind-of-blue Saturday night. Having a cold one in a longneck bottle on the newly built patio facing the river. Surrounded by Nancy and Rosie and Barbara, Edna, too, all with their furnaces burning for Ron. Looks up sees Jack; he's nervous (and trying not to let show), thinking Now? Should I? The current she transmits to his lovelight wins, he comes over. They (sparks and shyness) talk briefly. Susan (wearing a tombstone-gray dress with her mother's name and D.O.B. on it) introduces her date, Ron. Jack smells shark doesn't shake hands (with the creature in the Indian chief war bonnet). Disappointed, Jack leaves. At home, again searches for her phone # – she gave it to him, but he lost it. He looks for it all the time.

Seven days later; 11:15pm slippers on the stairs; should her beloved creature features return to television, she doesn't want to be late. No, what ought to be fills the television screen; *Saturday Night Late Cinema.*

In a large room (with a door to the backalley) at the back of Vernon's seamy billiard hall, in the Professor's office: consul at midnight, a forest of stormy faces. Hooper snaps, "He's out of tune." Points his accusatory trigger finger at Bloy. Bloy, the rat that played stud (claimed, he was born for the role), the (parasitic – according to Hooper) rat from L. A. that Hooper never trusted, the rat who talked too much, the lowdown rat who burned the tables on his partners. Smith & Wesson out of its shoulder holster. .38 no BANG – misfires. The clearout; the rat wriggles out the door into the alley. Round a corner, running through the neon-lit business of the crowd – bursting – timeslip – enemies hungering at his heels – no post war.

We're experiencing TECHNICAL DIFFICULTIES – Please Stand By appears on the screen.

Susan's camped on the floor in her bunny-print, warm cotton PJs, waiting. As she drifts through the maze where rapture and impatience intersect, Gort and Tobor the Great, Chani and Robby, too, consume her. Smiling, she whispers, "Klaatu barada nikto." After 43 minutes, she places her hand over her mouth and softy yawns into her palm. The telecast about cold sleepwalkers that want to live (their wounds sweat as they begin seeking any dry destination) does not return to the television screen. When WKVI ceases the day's broadcasting, Susan probes the RCA Indian-head test pattern. As every circle on the test pattern revolves, each in an opposing direction and at diverse speeds, and the numbers begin to wink out, she, with a last, drawn-out yawn, yields to slumber.

A QUICK HAZARD
STARRING
SUSAN DOUGLAS
and
JACK STEWART
SPECIAL GUEST STAR
PATRICIA LAFFAN (as Mephistaphilis)
and
THOMAS BROWNE HENRY (as the Reverend Mr. Perkins)
and
WALTER PIDGEON (as the Blue Bunny)
PRODUCED BY
HENNING SCHATTEN
WRITTEN AND DIRECTED BY
RALF SCHATTEN

Susan parks her Camaro in a dirt and gravel parking lot full of Mustangs, GTOs, and Chevy pickups with rusted beds; pair of Harley Davidson Panhead FLH choppers bookending a '46 Knucklehead chopper and a Triumph T100c.

A long-stemmed sparrow awash in hope, she's through the bar's heavy oak doors. The place is a kabuki stage of complex décor; every player, face painted and costumed, a ronin or bushi or lord, or geisha – hands soft as lilies, glaring demons elbow about with shy virgins, romantic heroines, ghosts and birds of prey. Senses forward, every ribbon of the puzzle is decked out in a panorama of fanned-out colors sailing. Her desire to find Jack in this throng, searching the bar; angle-turned eye and footfall on and around the clocks and speeding lamps – the missing, and the parade-unmodulated. Susan's dark eyes quickly adjust to the beer-trumpeted and pleasure-scented displays and dramas, as the performances blow from contender-hopeful now to the sorrow-frosted rust of turned down winter places.

Last Thursday of August: ladies night; perfume and cleavage chum the bloated testosterone tides of trick-or-treat-Charlies.

Moonlight lovelight.
River House Bar.
Patio.
Someone's birthday bacchanal (spirals of indiscreet high school talk) (laughing alcohol-frenzy loud, dancing, panting – amorous clearing the ground for kissing) (with fangs bound to happen and not a wise mouth alive in the pack) spilling out of the bar and on to the left side of the large, outside wooden deck.

Jack's been going to the River House, a lot, searching for Susan.

Susan's been popping in as often as she can for the same reason.

Jack sees Susan scanning the assemblage. Quickly decides she's alone. Smoldering, his heart rate heads for in your arms.

Susan sees Jack. Starts moving toward him.

The shape of a future island of wonderful moments between them, tonight the briar-crowd is the enemy keeping them apart.

Edges showing; there's no soft click warning with liquor and it doesn't offer you terms. A pressure burst, tumbling on the canvas. Savage swells, the breath of riot moves passed outline to gallop.

Breathing the experience into the phone, one of the barmaids calls the cops.

Susan closer. Hard to imagine 10 feet is that far away.

5' 10" 34-24-24 in a deluge of front-line weather, Susan goes down like she was shanked.

No weight-in. With a right hook, Jack lays out the brawler that shoved Susan to the deck.

Sirens. Flashing cherry tops.

A heavy bank of clouds turns off the moonlight lovelight.

Nine in handcuffs.

Jack cuffed, and put in the back of a police cruiser.

Jack sees Susan cry as the cops take him away.

Mephistaphilis stands next to the Blue Bunny leashed and seated to her left. From her purse she produces a pair of scissors made entirely of fire, while smirking darkly at the Reverend Mr. Perkins.

Exactly seven days later; Saturday 11:30 pm *Saturday Night Late Cinema.* The author of a bestselling crime series that includes 11 novels, two of which have been made into B movies by Shadow House Pictures, is between two worlds: on his desk there's the manuscript of his newest novel, unfinished, awaiting an ending, and there's a revolver in his hand and the body of a man he does not know on the floor by his desk. The body shot twice at close range. CUT TO: the other side of town, a lifetime-night of windows and ghosts that won't sleep. Loneliness trapped behind closed curtains in a cheap hotel room. Her twin sister Uta is dead and somewhere out there in that throng of gothic shadows and anything can happen urges Uta's murderer is now searching for her. Panic has ripped sweet from her face.

SORRY! We're experiencing TECHNICAL DIFFICULTIES – Please Stand By appears on the screen.

Another Saturday night lacking heaven-sent, Susan, deep in the backend of the midnight hour. Feet in the air, propped-up on her elbows on the soft ornamental carpet in the family room, in her cotton, blue rabbit PJs. Waiting. The grainy film from 1953 about the weight of night with no allies does not come back on. Susan, after yawning four times in a row while staring at the RCA Indian-head test pattern WKVI (Channel 13 Schenectady, New York) posted when it ceased the day's broadcasting, she (in a slow tug-of-war with drowsy) drifts, as blooming impressions pull her state of mind to and fro. Covering her with a cloak of deepening slumber, drowsy wins. Behind her sleep-sealed eyelids, a dark dream delighted to have an observer brings it lonesomeness to the stage.

MEMORIES OF RAIN
STARRING
SUSAN DOUGLAS
and
JACK STEWART
SPECIAL GUEST STAR
DAME JUDITH ANDERSON (as Mother)
and
ALFRED HITCHCOCK (as Dr. Wald)
with
JAMES MASON (as the Blue Bunny)
PRODUCED BY
HENNING SCHATTEN
WRITTEN AND DIRECTED BY
RALF SCHATTEN

She sees Jack (having just come in from the downpour, he's soaking wet) going in Proctor's Theatre, a former vaudeville house, as she enters the Carl Co. department store with Mother to shop for a new dress. She's also seen him go into the theater when she was with Mother at the Carl Co. to buy a new pair of shoes two weeks ago, watched Jack buy this ticket while Mother exchanged pleasantries with Dr. Wald. On a third occasion Susan's seen Jack enter Proctor's Theatre when she was with Mother at the Carl Co. to buy a new raincoat last month.

In the movie palace, Jack turns to the Blue Bunny seated beside him and says, "No, I've never been to Akron."

* * *

Nondescript receptionist in simple, light-gray business attire, no jewelry. One midsize window looking out on Glass Street and the main branch of the post office. Eggshell walls. Wall art: three impressionistic, watercolor paintings, woodland fields of yellow flowers, painted by Dr. Wald's 2nd cousin's wife. A single non-flowering, wide-leaf plant. Floor lamp and two end table lamps; characterless. No magazines. Sonatas composed by Francis Poulenc flow at ambient levels from the speakers installed in the white interlocking tiles of the drop-ceiling. Susan sat (upright, rigid, still wary of what the quartet of ceiling-mounted surveillance monitors might reveal) in the outer waiting room of Dr. Wald's office.

She was in recall mode, scanning the Mother/Father/Susan interactions of the last three months. Mother must have called Doctor Wald and reported an issue, as it was 83 days until her next scheduled annual assessment. But rapid-scanning revealed no issues that could have given Mother any cause for concern.

Susan fears Dr. Wald will clear "dream mode, sections of her identity narrative, and her short-term memory arenas" with his machines before she can discover a way to remain with Jack.

She's been watching hard, *nobody* wins B black and white flicks on *Saturday Night Late Cinema* (films her parents do not like and do not want her to watch. When they discovered they could not have children, they bought a *nice girl*, one suited for white picket fences and garden parties, not the arms of mad dreamers – penniless warehouse workers – from the wrong side of town. Mother would not approve. Susan is expected to exercise suitable mannerisms, to dream of linen and colorful floral bouquets, beaus from the *right* families, and weddings, Donna Reed happy homemaker dreams). Susan believes during her television dreams the Test Patterns connect her to Jack's dreams, as, she's certain, Jack views the same movie and they both enter dreamtime and the same dreamline at the identical moment.

Survival depends on what his searchlights observe.

Sit still. Be calm, do not offer him contradictions. If his probes are stirred, he'll see my soul, all I have absorbed. With a glance he'll see my dreams.

The chrome and gray plastic chair in front of Dr. Wald's desk has always been uncomfortable; Susan can well imagine nail-biting and nervous tremors and tears occur on it. Today is no exception.

Crunch time: poised, Susan sits, ladylike, in the patient chair in Dr. Wald's office. Dr. Wald wears black horn-rimmed glasses, a dark gray suit, and chain-smokes. His anti-affable guise mirrors Alfred Hitchcock's corpulent form, and his phrasing and tone twin Rod Serling. Dr. Wald's every remark is delivered in a manner suggesting a judge's analysis of the rites and duties of the species. Pinned to her chair before him, she always feels like an animal reined to his questions, only protected from blindness and extinction by appearances. Susan offers his scalpel eyes a polite smile befitting Mother's prize ornament and awaits his questions, the calculating questions that attack her yesterday and dissect her forward with anguish, smugness, and loathing. One by one, precisely leveled, they come from Dr. Wald like the poisonous secretions of a malicious behemoth.

Susan's dressed in a simple, knee-length, blue cotton print dress, a white sweater, and flat shoes; all recently purchased (while shopping with Mother in the Carl Co). She wears no makeup and no jewelry. She hopes her display speaks of quiet and well-adjusted, normal.

Susan tries not to fidget. Protectively places her hand upon her small, inexpensive-leather white purse. What if Dr. Wald wants to examine the contents? He hasn't before, but should he; he'd see the paperback novel she bought in Cavanagh's Card Shop five months ago. The book (secreted away) she keeps rereading. Do Androids Dream of Electric Sheep?

Susan remembers her previous sessions with Dr. Wald, every question, every guarded reply. She fears today's inquisition will be harsher.

Dr. Wald: (*not looking at Susan; intently cleaning his eye glasses*) Can you recount, to me, the contents of the last dream you remember?

He is after my dreams. She tries to remain poised, appear calm.

Susan's tempted to offer something not cocooned in the shadows and ceremonies of her hidden place, something old, perhaps a mixture of two or three dreams would keep the doctor from prying secrets from the hours she spends pleading with the isolation of persona. He's not looking at her; he might not be listening too closely.

Over the wall of sleep and through the wood, beyond the black-faced sheep, come down from the moon on rainbow-colored dragon ships, to the matryoshka picnic on the giant blueprint quilt, where characters from Alice's Wonderland eat bite-size cakes that were shaped like bats and sang nonsense songs to characters from various Dr. Seuss books. Would that deflect his inquiry?

She instantly decides, *Keep it simple.* He'll frame and dissect the definition. *It's safer that way.*

Susan: It was back and white. You've seen those old noir films on television; it looked like one of them.

Dr. Wald: Susan, you've previously mentioned that some of your dreams began with screen credits. Can you recall if this dream began like a picture show, with credits?

Susan: Yes, it did. It was called; The Last Fact Weights 700 Lbs.

For control purposes Dr. Wald was recording the session.

Dr. Wald: Please, continue.

Susan: …

Dr. Wald: (leaning forward in his chair) Is there anything else you can tell me?

Susan: That was last Saturday. The mermaid (part exotic apparition/part long-eyed visionary) (under the Chagall-veil) in the small lifeboat told dream-Susan that is what the mirror-river revealed – "Sorry, Little Ishmael, that's how I read the clouds tonight". The next morning dream-Susan could not find that date on her calendar, the calendar pinned to the mast of her crow's nest in the chickenshack. Standing there, dream-Susan understood, that left no room for decisions, or goldfish.

Dr. Wald's fountain pen is pressed to his lips. His cold gaze discloses no impulse or expression.

Susan (trapped in disquiet and wanting to run from the room) sits in the chrome and gray plastic hardback chair in Dr. Wald's office for 12 minutes, as he writes a page-and-a-half note to her mother and seals it in an envelope. "Please give this to your mother, Susan. I'll see you on–"

EVIDENCE OF ABSENCE

by H. S. Graves

Sometime after World War II, a group of Georgia and Carolina veterans from various military branches got together and called themselves the Pinetop Ramblers, their objective being to go hunting, fishing, and camping any time they wanted, "as long as pine needles are green".

None of the original club's membership is around anymore, and members come from all over the country these days, but we still follow their lead. They had a working relationship with their families, which was that they did all the work and the wives, children and girlfriends all promised to have a good time if they came along on their outings. This kept the peace so well it's still in effect today. We leave out early to set up in the field, and they come around a little later for the fun. I figure it works because of the essential give and take, and it ultimately leads us to practice the same discipline it takes to be war dogs in the pursuit of acting at least halfway civilized.

So we always stick to their plan, and raise a toast to the Old Guard.

We are actually a fairly wholesome group, all things considered, and nobody gets too far out of hand, except for The Colonel. He is always what you might call marching to the beat of his own drum, and to be taken with a grain of salt – preferably with a shot of tequila. By my estimation, his attitude is mostly due to his upbringing in the wilds of Kentucky, but getting blown out of the sky over the DMZ in Viet Nam and making it back – past a Cape Buffalo and what he always refers to as "ungodly hordes" of Viet Cong – seems to provide him with a permanent adrenaline boost none of the rest of us have. Or want, actually.

As he puts it, "After the Cape Effin Buffalo the rest was your basic Sunday School Picnic".

That is cleaning up The Colonel's standard terminology considerably, as you might imagine. Cape Effin is a particularly rough piece of geography to negotiate.

This particular evening The Colonel finished reeling off an outrageous and convoluted tale set in some unpronounceable Chinese desert where he "wasn't supposed to be", dealing with representatives of what he called "an extinct human culture", the upshot being that after a dispute involving whether or not The Colonel was going to give up his sidearm, "everything exploded into a white light and I don't know how long we were on the run." The next thing he remembered was being in an expensive hotel in Thailand, taking a "good cussing and dressing down" over the phone from the Secretary of State.

Supposedly.

The rest of us would not be privy to that highly classified conversation, and as usual nothing came of it.

"But if word got out about those shenanigans," said The Colonel, "I wouldn't be here, now would I?"

Like I say, we all give The Colonel plenty of latitude with his anecdotes, and a couple of us in this bunch are ex-Rangers and such who are not prone to skipping out on details or stretching facts.

Richie "Rich" Ramirez, who I had first met way back in Panama, sat a big steel wash pot of corn on the cob beside the campfire and said, "Was that before of after I saw you in Noriega's basement, Colonel?"

"Oh, now you never seen me there," says The Colonel. "Must of been somebody who looked like me."

Everybody laughs, no matter how often he says it, there is no mistaking The Colonel for anyone else on the planet.

Camp is all set up proper as twilight creeps in and shadows are filling up the Linville Gorge down the mountain from the spot where we've gotten situated. Steaks are marinating, beers are coming out of ice chests, sounds like a little jazz playing from a truck radio. "Might be a good night to see the Brown Mountain Lights," somebody says.

"Well, as far as that goes, we know what we know, and sometimes we know for sure what we don't know," I offer. "As many times as I've seen them come out across yonder I have no theories."

"No telling, but we've all seen 'em now", Richie replies. "Man, last time we were up here it was a serious light show. Ain't no car headlights reflecting off the mountainside looks like that."

"Especially not back in the eighteen-forties," B.P. adds, dropping a double armload of dead wood to the side of the fire. B.P. stands out as a big, BIG man, even standing among these big biscuit-eatin' boys, and I would hate to be among those who suddenly saw B.P.'s face and it was the last thing they ever saw. "You know that old song about the lights being lanterns carried by the ghosts of slaves, looking for their master lost in the Gorge. They never made it back, either. Might say they never came back. If they were my ancestors, gentlemen, they followed the light from those lanterns all the way up to the Free States and said the hell with Ole Massa."

"Damn right!"

"Oh Hail-to-the Yeah!"

All's easy around the fire and B.P. sits himself down on rock big enough to suit him, looks around at the dozen or so of us loafing for the moment, glances up over to the high ridge beginning to dim with early darkness and proceeds to relate an experience as only he can.

B.P. has possession of several degrees in what you'd think are unrelated subjects, and he made his first million in computer applications some decades ago. But his real talent is his way with words. It's more than hypnotic. You feel like Moses might have felt, listening to the burning bush. I can't even describe what it's like. But I will do my best to relate his tale the way I remember it, and as close as I can to the way he told it, even though there is no way I can lay it out like he can, like you are right there in the middle of it all.

When I finished my last tour, (he began) I came back home to a very stagnant job market, and we know how that goes. I was mainly concerned with getting set up in my own business, but that would take a little while to line up investments and things of that nature.

I had my master's in math, so I hustled on that. Opened up doors, you know. Turns out math teachers are always in short supply, so I took a position at MHS down in the city, just to keep finances in order for a bit. Makes sure you can afford everything money can't buy.

That meant teaching everything from Consumer Math and Algebra to a Trigonometry class. Now Maxwell, as some of you all know, is a very old school, and long established in the community, so we had the full range of students from the roughest street chaps to the upscale kids. I saw them all, and got situational awareness on their ways and how they looked at the world, and they all knew how to get into the same kind of trouble regardless. You hear about kids being "at risk" – well, they're all at risk, whether they think they are affluent or dirt-poor. We had a quite a few bad actors, and one of the worst was named Jaime. He wanted to be called "Dakar". but nobody ever knew why. He did not come from there, or have relatives or ancestors from the region, because I asked him about it. He looked at me like I was stupid. Probably he thought it made him sound *bad*.

Here's a young man with opportunities, a high school sophomore who should have already graduated, with no real reason to fail at anything. He's intelligent enough, but not thinking ahead, carrying a bellicose air about him, getting his little bit of dope-money "street cred" together since that was his idea of having respect. Now all that was a purely materialistic, concrete notion, but that's how it was. These children…

I called them children, and I was barely thirty… were all showing out, acting out, talking about money and power like they knew something nobody else could possibly know. All that mattered to a lot of the kids, as far as that went, was having the right clothes. And *shoes*.

(Men muttered and nodded. Some lit cigarettes, and exhaled slowly.)

"Yeah, I know". B.P. continued:

Kids were getting killed over stuff like jackets and sneakers, trying to be ruthless like these glorified crack cocaine dealers made out to be movie stars. Jaime – Dakar – wanted that attitude, and affected it. He was always on with it, repeating trash talk like he invented it, not passing a single class, and plainly not intending to. You can do a lot with a young mind that's motivated, but not if it's that kind of motivation. I worked with a good team of teachers, too, and we all tried to talk to him, but he would never show you his real face.

"Nothing, nothing you could do. He wouldn't let you in." Pausing for a moment, B.P. looked over into the shadows gathered in the woods and I thought I caught a glimpse of what's sometimes called the thousand-yard stare. Then he shook his head and went on:

I would see Jaime talking to other kids and he would put 'em down, say the opposite of everything they would say just to be contrary. He would say day was night and night was day if he thought it made him look smarter than they were. That was his *thang*. And it really was that noticeable. Basically, he was sociopathic, or at least getting close to it, and you didn't need a M.A. in Behavioral Science to see it.

The end of the year came around, right before summer break, and Jamie failed everything, like he was set on doing, and I figured I'd see him back in Consumer Math in the fall.

My summer was spent on the move, Houston, Chicago, St. Louis, up and down both coasts, anywhere I could connect with business, industry, military contractors, anybody and everybody looking ahead to major updates of their computer and communications systems.

I don't believe I spent a full two weeks in town. I knew my apps would bring in some cash, but I badly underestimated demand. I went back to Maxwell in August, as planned, figuring I would be teaching for a least another year or two. I did not even imagine I'd be going to full time production status by Christmas. It was a busy time all the way around, extremely so.

Anyway, I'm sitting in my classroom looking at a dot-matrix print-out and recognizing names I had in Consumer Math taking Algebra I, then others who did not pass that would be back to try to learn how to make change and figure percentages. That might have been one of the last years that kind of math class was even offered at a high school level – kids literally have to do better than that now. But there's the name of a girl who left to have a baby, and a couple others who didn't get cut it for one reason or another, but no Jaime – no Dakar. That did not necessarily mean anything, because students come and go, in and out at odd times, and I figured I would see him again if he had not transferred to West or somewhere else. Sometimes kids will do that when they mess up like he did, just to have a new start or try to play the system.

School started and I forgot all about him, with a whole roster of new individuals to sort out. Then one afternoon a few weeks into the semester I am standing in my doorway during class change and there are Shanique and Tonya, who had passed Consumer Math with me back in the spring. We just chit-chat, you know, "how's it going" and "fine". Then it crossed my mind to ask about Jaime.

"Where's Jaime? I have not seen nor heard of him since we got back…"

"D'kar? You talking about that Jaime?"

"The very one," I say, and they both look at me for a minute like I just landed back on Earth from Mars, and then they cut loose with a barrage of jibber-jabber till they were just about out of breath, all about the boy getting his self shot, and the two of them witnessing it happen, right up the street here in the middle of the day, and everybody in the neighborhood locking doors and having all their guns out right at the kitchen table, and the Po-lice standing on the street corners with them big old huge rifles and:

"Mr. Petty," Tonya looked me right in the eye. "Do you believe in The Devil?"

You do not lie to a child. "I have seen his work," I said to them, and I could see a subtle change come over their faces. They calmed down then.

"Are you gonna be here after school?"

"Can we come by and tell you about it?"

"Most definitely I will be here. Now you got to get off to class before you get locked out."

Off they went, and when I got a break I strolled up to the main building and poked my head into the SRO's office. Our campus cop was an Officer Bridges, a good guy all around. He had been an Air Force S.P. and we had good rapport, he'd done some heavy lifting. For a change he did not look too busy, but that was not going to last. I took advantage.

"Bridges," says I, "What's this about one of our kids getting killed up the street here, back during summer break?"

Again I get a look of amazement. "Brother, how in the world did you miss all that?"

"Out of town the whole time. What kind of 'all that' do you mean?"

"Just about the worst kind you can think of. Step in here and close that door."

I had a seat and he gave me the run-down. "Jaime Clayton. You had him in class? Yeah, that's him. No surprise, Coroner found thirty two grams of crack in his pocket. I got a little frustrated with him from time to time. Just a little frustrated. I don't even know if the boy was capable of a straight thought. He strictly acted on impulse, all the time, and even if I had him sitting down right there in that chair you're in he never heard a word. Just sat there cutting his eyes toward the door. Waiting on the next impulse to strike. And every time he opened his mouth he lit somebody's fuse. There's no excuse for it, but I had to bite my tongue more than once dealing with him. Done ruined for anything is what he was. Completely spoiled."

"Spoiled?"

"Spoiled rotten, man, rotten. He didn't go without nothing. His daddy's a college professor. His momma 's got some job with the School Board. You didn't know that? Any regular kid doing half of what he did here would be in class behind barbed wire at Buxton. You were not here when he was… nah, he's just as bad now. Well, he *was*."

I waited for him to go on while he rubbed his forehead, then he said:

"Everything finally died down in the papers, but his folks really had things stirred up for a while, and they never let up on us till the FBI came in and took charge of it. Then it got quiet, after that."

I guess I just looked curious while he rested his elbows on his desk top and bumped his fists together a couple of times.

Then he smiled. "It's really a cut and dried case," he went on, "Perp walks right up to the boy and busts a cap in him, right across the street from the Mini Mart up here. Bam, it's done, but the problem is it's an unknown subject, and an unknown weapon, too."

"Couldn't find the slug?"

"If there was a slug. I was in here clearing out files and heard it. Loud, and I mean *loud*. Then all the screaming. I got out the door and on scene in a minute, less than a minute. Screaming girls running up to me, and there he's laying, spread out all over the sidewalk. A mess. I'll tell you how bad it was, so bad we got a memo not to talk about it. There was a briefing put together for the press that was "official", and after that an "unofficial" briefing for everybody in the field that day that basically said to shut the hell up on the case and let the Feds do their job – if you don't want to be answering to the Feds. That took care of it. But really, that day, all we knew was we had bad trouble, man. That sound I heard so loud? Did not even sound like a gun. Didn't echo like gunshots do around here, either. A sound like… now I know this don't make sense… you ever heard a big industrial boiler vent steam? Like that, man, so loud it hit me in the gut. A big impact, like something rusted shut busting open. That's what led to the FBI taking over, see. No ordinary Glock blew that kid away. That was some extreme firepower. How do we know it's not something Soviet, East Bloc, Russian Republic, whatever you call 'em now? There's no way Yeltsin's got anything under control over there yet. No way."

"Some knucklehead got his hands on something heavy," I said. "Intimidating problem, tense situation."

"We were very busy, Quite busy. We couldn't exactly keep a low profile. The south side was locked all the way down. Took three days before we got things halfway back to normal. But that was it. I mean, I read an editorial in yesterday's paper about the threat of unsecured military tech in Russia – even nukes getting loose – anything could be out there. But around here, things are just about the same as before. No worse. No better, for sure." He laughed. " My bet is we'll never know what gun killed that kid. But you been talking to Tonya and Shanique."

"Of course," I said. "That's why I figured I'd better check in with you." We both laughed.

"Yeah, Bix," Bridges said. "You never want kids to see a homicide, and not one that bad, and they were both perfectly good witnesses as far as that goes. Told it straight up, and exactly the same. Old Jaime Clayton comes down out of that patch of woods up there, down that embankment, acts like he don't even see them. Big dude just comes up the walk and blasts him. Done deal. At least we had that much, but that's it. Clerk in the Mini Mart heard it, but said she didn't see anything, and nobody but her in the place. But, you know, those two girls were rightly hysterical. Didn't have much in the way of description or which way the shooter went. Anything else you hear from them," he concluded, "Is what you and I might call *overactive imagination*. You know what I'm saying."

Of course I did. And at that time it was not unheard-of for drug gangs to have access to hired enforcers of the most elite kind, use illegal ammo, "cop killers", mercury-filled bullets and such. There's a reason they call those days the time of the crack wars, to be sure, and no reason to think they wouldn't use any kind of exotic weaponry they could get their hands on coming up out of the black market, Soviet-made or not. Would not be surprising at all.

Tonya and Shanique were in my classroom before the last class emptied out at the end of the day.

"Mr. Petty, the Devil got Jamie and we seen it happen."

"Whoa, whoa, let's not get too quick to judge on something like…"

"But we seen it!"

I left the door just slightly ajar and got them into desks. Then I sat down as Tonya said, "But you said you believed in the Devil". I could hear an edge of frustration in her voice.

"I stand by that," I told them. "I don't have any reason to lie to you. Or not to believe you".

"My great-grandmomma said when she was a little girl she saw the Devil come out of a coal pile and run around in the snow till he disappeared," Shanique said. "He didn't have no horns and no tail, but she knew it was the Devil".

"Well, you know the Devil is a symbol of evil," I said, just wanting her to think it through.

"That's what my aunt says. But she says that's all it is. She says stuff like there is no such thing as bad people, just good people who do bad things. That don't sound right".

"I don't see it that way either, but you have to think for yourself. I'll tell you what I think, but it's still for you both to decide. From everything I've ever seen, it's out there, it's evil, and you can call it the Devil or anything you want, like Satan, Old Scratch, Beelzebub…"

"My great-grandmomma calls him the Father of Lies".

"And the Lord of the Flies," Tonya added. "We read that book".

"He puts the lies in your mouth," Shanique continued. "Then you say 'em, or you fight him. And It's real hard sometimes."

"That's what I'm talking about," I said. "Evil is a force, and you can see it. But I believe it acts on its own accord, for nothing but destruction and ruin. It thinks for itself, and if you go too far into your own bad nature, whether it's from selfishness, or meanness, or even ignorance and stupidity, you open that door wide enough and that force, that Devil comes in. And takes over." I surprised myself saying that. Never really put it into words before. Never had a particular reason to, but it made sense to me then, and still does.

The girls turned to look at each other. Tonya spoke. "That's how he got D'kar. But he came on out and got him his own self.

"Listen, Mr. Petty, now listen, this is how it happened, and why it happened. Here school is about to be out for the summer, and we are in English class reading this story, "The Devil and Daniel Webster". And old Ms. Davis says, 'That's what happens when you make a deal with the Devil'. It's a cautionary tale, she says."

Shanique picked up the story. "And then Jaime just shouts out, 'They ain't no such thang as the Devil! They ain't no Devil!'. He just went *off*! Well, it's a metaphor is what Ms. Davis says, and the bell for class rings and he goes out in the hall cussin' and carrying on."

"And he slams his book in his locker, and he's saying, 'They ain't no Devil! I'll prove it! I sell my soul to the Devil right now! Right now!' And I should not have said nothing, but I did."

"What did you say?"

"I said you got to sell it for something, fool!"

"I was standing right there," Tonya adds.

32

"Well, I feel bad about it," Shanique continued. "And then he say, 'I sell my soul to the Devil for *fifty cent! Fifty cent or a Baby Ruth candy bar, it don't matter!*' And he goes stomping off. I don't think he even came back to school no more after that. I never saw him in class after that."

I told her, "That's bad, but it is not your fault. He was just showing out, like always."

They sat in silence for a long moment.

"School wasn't out a week and me and Tonya was just hanging, you know, and grandmomma wants me to walk up to the store and get her a newspaper, says we can get whatever we want with the change, so we went walking up the street. We get up two blocks to the stop light and look, and here comes somebody down out of that track of woods up there."

"It's Jaime ," Tonya says. "Now it's already hot, *so* hot, and he's sweatin', and he comes down out of the woods and walks right across the street towards us, didn't even look for cars or nothing, and we say, 'Hey D'kar' and stuff, and he walks right between us like we ain't even there, just walks right between us, sweat running down on his face."

"And we turn around and holler some mess at him," Shanique continues, "Just as this man comes up of a sudden right on him."

"Tell him what he said. We both heard it."

"He say, HERE IS YOUR CANDY BAR, BOY!" Shanique gestured wildly with her hands, and so did Tonya.

"BAM!" They said.

"I never heard such a awful noise"

"I thought I was gone deaf!"

"Blue smoke all over the place!"

"And the air full of ashes!"

"And Jaime, Jaime is blowed in two!"

Now I'm just about dumbfounded. "What are you saying?"

"He was blowed in two! He in two pieces on the sidewalk, Mr. Petty, and his hand is twitchin'!"

Tonya closed her eyes. "Oh my Jesus, child, hush. That is well enough."

Shanique mutters, "Candy bar laying on the ground. Little old Baby Ruth."

"Yes, yes it was."

B.P comes back to his own voice. "So I ask, where's the shooter? What happened to this man? And they say he's gone. Just gone. Like he was never there. Well, what did he look like? Just a man, a big man. Big as me? Bigger than you, they say. They say his face was a shadow, and that's the only way they could articulate it, even to me, so they told the detectives he was a black dude. This happens at noon, remember. No horns, no pointed tail."

Somebody yells, "Yo! Women and children on deck!" There is a brief flash of headlights. A big custom R.V. pulls up to the edge of the campsite and B.P. stands up smiling and waves at his wife. The various other wives, kids and lady friends disembark with a burst of chatter and activity.

Up over the valley on a distant ridge a ball of dim light brightens into a pale, pastel blue and arcs above the treetops, followed by another, and then a smaller red-orange one. I point it out to The Colonel.

"Well," The Colonel says with a wry look, "There are things we know we do not know, and then there are those others… the ones we don't even know we do not know."

I AM BECOME DEATH

by William Tea & Ron Gelsleichter

TO: Major General Leslie R. Groves, Jr. USAC

FROM: Colonel Richard C. Hamner USAC

Enclosed are the copies you requested of the items from Sergeant Edward S. Rodman's personnel file and from Site Report TZ-59. All items are classified under "Elite" level clearance.

* * *

Document A (a)

Summary: Document A (a) is a photograph taken by Sgt. Rodman at the "Little Boy" Strike Zone on 10/24/45. Photograph depicts a city street cluttered with miscellaneous refuse. Roadway is relatively intact but sidewalk tiles are shattered. Four metal streetlamps are visible. Three have been uprooted completely and lay on the ground near their bases. The top of each pole lays pointing in a southwesterly direction, indicating the blast came from northeasterly. A fourth streetlamp remains standing but is bent at the halfway point at an extreme 90 degree angle, also in a southwesterly direction. All surrounding structures have been reduced to rubble, making differentiation between individual buildings problematic.

Document A (b)

Summary: Document A (b) is a photograph taken by Sgt. Rodman at the "Little Boy" Strike Zone on 10/28/45. Background of photograph is dominated by the skeletal façade of a large four-story building. All door and window frames are empty. A significant portion of the roof in the right-hand corner has collapsed. Preliminary research identifies this location as an elementary school. Notable in the immediate foreground is the presence of a bare and blackened but otherwise intact tree of indeterminate genus. Nearby metallic remains appear to resemble segments of a children's swingset and/or jungle gym.

* * *

Document B

Summary: Document B is an excerpt from Recording Transcript No. 173-3601. Impertinent sections omitted. Session Date: May 8, 1946. Doctor: Beaumont, Gerald. Patient: Rodman, Edward.

(00:11:39 – 00:46:08)

BEAUMONT: So, why don't you tell me what brings you here today?

RODMAN: Didn't they tell you?

BEAUMONT: They?

RODMAN: My superiors. Lieutenant Matheson. Colonel Hamner.

BEAUMONT: Ah, that "they." Of course they contacted me, but between you and me I'm not overly concerned with what they have to say. They only think they know why you're here; the only person who really knows is you. So tell me, please, in your own words, what brings you here today?

RODMAN: Alright. What brings me here is a recent pattern of disruptive behavior which affects my effectiveness as a soldier and which may or may not be a response to recent emotional duress suffered in the line of duty.

BEAUMONT: Those aren't your own words, Ed. Can I call you Ed?

RODMAN: Alright.

BEAUMONT: Wonderful. Ed, all you're doing is repeating what they've said. You're telling me what they think, but I've already heard what they have to say. What I want to hear is what you have to say. To me, you're not Sergeant Rodman. You're just Ed. And I'm Gerry. I'm not your superior officer. There are no hurdles you have to jump here nor standards you have to meet. I'm not demanding your report from you, I'm asking for your honest thoughts. I sit here without judgement or expectation. So, one more time, without you trying to tell me what you think I want to hear, what brings you here today?

(long pause)

RODMAN: I'm here because I don't know who I am anymore.

(pause)

BEAUMONT: Well, who did you used to be?

RODMAN: (laughing) I don't know. An American. A Christian. A soldier. Someone trying to do the right thing, protect his family, put the boots to the bad guys, all that jazz.

BEAUMONT: And what's changed?

RODMAN: (sighing) Everything.

BEAUMONT: Is this about your recent assignment in Japan?

RODMAN: No. Well, yes. Not Japan. Japan's still a place. Japan still makes sense in context of the world. This is about Hiroshima. What I saw. What we did. Hiroshima doesn't make sense anymore, not in any context.

BEAUMONT: You were assigned there as part of the occupying forces?

RODMAN: Yeah, as a photographer. Since the Japs are playing nice now, I was sent in to document the effects of the bomb, bring back some pretty landscape shots so the boys in white coats can get an eyeful of their handiwork. So they can study it, I guess. Probably help them figure out how to the make the next thing even nastier.

BEAUMONT: You've photographed war zones before, haven't you?

RODMAN: More times than I can count, but this was different. The scale of it, for one. I mean, you could stand right smack dab in the center of Hiroshima and look out in every direction and not see nothing but craters and gray wastes all the way to the horizon. It's like being on the moon, except every now and then you find a half-scorched mailbox or something weird and wrecked that you realize used to be a car. Hell, sometimes you even find a little hut or something, maybe half a house or one of those – what do they call them? – shrines? Little relics standing despite everything else getting pancaked, something to remind you this was once a place people lived.

BEAUMONT: In all fairness, Ed, we're not just talking about any people. We're talking about the enemies of America. Lest we forget, these are the same people who attacked us at Pearl Harbor.

RODMAN: No, that's not quite right. These were families, not troops. Japs, sure, but women and kids and old folks. I know because I saw their shadows. It was the damnedest thing; frozen on the crumbling walls and all these jagged jutting ruins that used to be homes, I saw shadows without any bodies to cast them. It's like the fire burned so hot and so bright it vaporized the people and seared their outlines right into the concrete. (sniffing) Shadows twisted with their arms up in front of their faces, clinging to each other, as if the people they belonged to were still standing there, dying forever.

(sobbing)

BEAUMONT: Ed –

RODMAN: (sobbing) Little shadows holding hands with big ones. Little baby shadows, all black and flat.

* * *

Document C (a)

Summary: Document C (a) is a photograph taken by Sgt. Rodman at the "Little Boy" strike zone on 10/28/45. Photograph depicts the side of a building believed to be same location identified in Document A (b). All door and window frames are empty. Silhouettes of civilian casualties stain the building's wall. Analysis suggests these are the result of nuclear radiation bleaching the structure's surface. Foreign bodies intercepting said radiation during the initial blast would result in these "silhouette" areas appearing darker. Forty-six individual silhouettes are counted, the majority of which measure around three feet tall, with the exception of a trio of larger silhouettes measuring between five and six feet tall. Body language of silhouettes indicates civilians involved in athletic activity at time of blast.

Document C (b)

Summary: Document C (b) is a photograph taken by Sgt. Rodman at the "Little Boy" strike zone on 10/31/45. Photograph depicts a wide stone stairway ascending a small hill. At the base of the stairway, on both sides of the first step, are stone statues of unknown figures. Identification is problematic due to the condition of the statues, which have had large chunks broken off and most of their features eroded. At the top of the stairway is a large archway whose architectural design indicates the location previously functioned as a Shinto shrine. Entire area appears to have undergone bleaching similar to that depicted in Document C (a). Stairway is stained by the darkened silhouettes of two civilian casualties, both measuring between five and six feet tall. Body language indicates civilians were embracing at time of blast.

* * *

Document D

Summary: Document D is an excerpt from Recording Transcript No. 173-3615. Impertinent sections omitted. Session Date: Aug. 14, 1946. Doctor: Beaumont, Gerald. Patient: Rodman, Edward.

(00:29:01 – 01:03:52)

BEAUMONT: I know we talked last time about the insomnia you've been suffering. Any improvements there?

RODMAN: Not really. Nausea's been making it worse lately.

BEAUMONT: Nerves, perhaps?

RODMAN: I guess. The thing is I, uh, I don't even like it. Sleeping, I mean. Turning the lights off; hell, I don't even like closing my eyes. (laughing) I'm scared of the dark, is what it is, like a kid. Even the little bit of it I get when I blink.

(pause)

BEAUMONT: What is it about darkness that bothers you? A sense of disconnection? The world becoming abstract? For some of my patients, I know, darkness makes things feel distant or unreal. You lose the little details and –

RODMAN: It's not that. If anything it's the opposite. It's not what isn't there that gets me; it's what is there. It's what's there in the dark that isn't there in the light.

BEAUMONT: And what's that? What is in the darkness?

(long pause)

RODMAN: Can I show you something?

BEAUMONT: Of course.

RODMAN: Something crazy?

BEAUMONT: Ed, you know I don't like that word. There's no such thing as "crazy" in this office. If there's something upsetting you, it's perfectly valid for discussion.

(pause)

(zipping, shuffling)

RODMAN: Here.

BEAUMONT: What's all this?

RODMAN: Photos.

BEAUMONT: I can see that. Quite the stack. What exactly are these supposed to be pictures of?

RODMAN: You tell me. Go on, look.

BEAUMONT: Hmm. Well, I see a lot of things. People at the beach. What looks like a dinner party. A child blowing out candles on a cake.

RODMAN: That's my niece, Anna. Just turned eleven this year.

BEAUMONT: How nice. When was her birthday?

RODMAN: May 29th.

BEAUMONT: May? That's when you first started coming to see me. You've had these pictures all this time and you just now bring them to me. Why?

RODMAN: Because I didn't notice at first. It wasn't until I started looking at all them together that –

BEAUMONT: No, Ed. I don't mean why didn't you bring them sooner; I mean why have you brought them at all? What's the problem here? Honestly, looking at these pictures, despite all the issues we've discussed, it seems to me that you are a stable, well-adjusted individual living a normal life, complete with loved ones and trips to the beach and –

RODMAN: Don't you see them?

BEAUMONT: See what?

RODMAN: The shadows.

(pause)

BEAUMONT: I'm sorry, I don't understand.

RODMAN: Look. Just look at this one from the birthday party. Look behind her head, in the background. Count the shadows on the wall.

BEAUMONT: One, two, three, four –

RODMAN: There's twelve.

BEAUMONT: Okay.

RODMAN: There were only nine people at the party. Here, look, you can see my niece and her parents, and her two cousins. Her grandma and grandpa and her aunt and uncle, they're with me behind the camera, but you can see their shadows plain as day because behind us was the big patio screen-door with all the daylight streaming in. So who the hell are these three over in the corner?

(pause)

RODMAN: Ed, surely you, a photographer, know all about the way light from different sources can throw multiple shadows in different directions. Why can't it be that? Or some furniture that you caught at an angle that simply makes it looks like the outline of other people?

BEAUMONT: But what about this photo? Or this one? Keep looking. Go through the whole pile. This is every photo I've taken since I've been back on American soil and they're in every single goddamn one, shadows that don't belong.

RODMAN: So what are you saying? You're being followed? Someone's stalking you? Someone always just out of sight, evidenced only by their shadow? Who do you think is after you?

BEAUMONT: Aren't you listening? The shadows.

RODMAN: Whose shadows?

RODMAN: (shouting) The shadows themselves.

(long pause)

BEAUMONT: Ed, calm down –

RODMAN: They followed me home.

BEAUMONT: Okay, let's take a minute. Slow it down. Deep breaths.

RODMAN: Here, here, here. Look at this one.

BEAUMONT: Ed, relax.

RODMAN: Just look. This is me at Coney Island, by the pier. My friend Clay took this one. See, there's nobody around, but look behind me; do you see the long shadow between mine and Clay's. You can tell that one is Clay's because his silhouette is holding the camera. All three are coming from the same direction, because the sun was at our backs. You know what else was at our backs? The fucking ocean. I was there, eyes fucking forward, and there was no one behind him. There was no one to cast that shadow.

BEAUMONT: Ed.

RODMAN: No such thing as "crazy," huh?

BEAUMONT: Ed, please.

RODMAN: No such thing as "crazy."

* * *

Document E (a)

Summary: Document E (a) is a photograph taken by Sgt. Rodman at unidentified location, date unknown. As indicated in Document D, photograph appears to depict a birthday party. Location appears to be a room in a civilian residence. Visible furnishings include one linoleum kitchen table with four matching chairs. Chairs are occupied by three pre-adolescents (two male, one female) and one male adult. A female adult stands behind the female preadolescent, captured in mid-clap. Female preadolescent is hunched over table with pursed lips in the direction of a frosted sheetcake decorated with ten lit birthday candles. All visible individuals wear pointed party hats. As indicated in Document D, there are twelve distinctly humanoid shadows visible on the wall in the background. Analysis suggests all shadows cast by a single light source located behind the photographer. Only three of the shadows do not appear to be wearing pointed party hats. Cause of anomaly not yet determined.

Document E (b)

Summary: Document E (b) is a photograph taken by unidentified individual dubbed "Clay" at location purported to be Coney Island, date unknown. As indicated in Document D, photograph depicts Sgt. Rodman in civilian attire standing on a beach. To the left is the base of a pier whose length extends diagonally out of frame. Photograph appears to depict an exceptionally sunny day with clear skies overhead and relatively few areas of darkness in proximity. Likewise, no foreign bodies appear present in proximity. Behind Sgt. Rodman three distinctly humanoid shadows are visible on the sand, one corresponding to Sgt. Rodman, one corresponding to the photographer, and one whose correspondent is unidentified. Analysis suggests all shadows cast by a single light source located behind the photographer. Cause of anomaly not yet determined.

* * *

Document F

Summary: Document F is an excerpt from Recording Transcript No. 173-3625. Impertinent sections omitted. Session Date: Oct. 23, 1946. Doctor: Beaumont, Gerald. Patient: Rodman, Edward.

(00:02:20 – 00:46:13)

BEAUMONT: Ed, where have you –

(fabric ruffling, metal scraping)

BEAUMONT: What are you doing? Be careful with –

(loud crashing)

BEAUMONT: (shouting) What the hell, Ed? I haven't seen you in weeks. You skip your last three appointments and now you barge in here and tear down my curtains?

RODMAN: Too dark in here. Got to stay in the light.

(pause)

BEAUMONT: Jesus, you look like hell. Sit down, please. Everything's okay now. Sit, sit. When was the last time you ate?

RODMAN: I don't know. I can't, uh, can't keep anything down. Keep throwing up. And my teeth, look.

BEAUMONT: My god.

RODMAN: They've been falling out. First, just the one, in the morning one day when I was brushing. Then another one a couple days later. Then a couple more. Hair too. Just coming out in clumps in my hands. (sobbing) I'm wasting away.

BEAUMONT: What did your doctor say?

RODMAN: (sobbing) I didn't go. I can't. I won't.

BEAUMONT: Ed, this is serious. You're not well. You need to go to the hospital. Let me call –

RODMAN: (shouting) No.

BEAUMONT: You said it yourself. You're wasting away.

RODMAN: I can't go to a hospital. They'll put me in a bed in some prison cell of a room with the shades drawn. And when the sun goes down they'll keep me there. In the dark.

BEAUMONT: Sit down, Ed. What are you doing? What –

(fabric ruffling)

RODMAN: Look. Look and see what I'm becoming. Bony as death. And my skin…

BEAUMONT: Good lord, are those burns? What happened?

(pause)

BEAUMONT: We need to get you to a hospital, Ed.

RODMAN: I didn't come here for help. I came here for confession. I need someone to listen. I need someone to know.

BEAUMONT: Know what? Ed, you know you can tell me anything.

RODMAN: Can I? Yes, I can. Can't I?

BEAUMONT: Always.

RODMAN: Alright, but you can't tell anyone. Not until it's over. No one.

BEAUMONT: Nothing you say with me ever leaves this office.

RODMAN: Alright. You know those photos I told you I took, the ones from Hiroshima?

BEAUMONT: Of course.

RODMAN: You know the reason I never showed them to you is because I can't, right? They're censored. Classified. I shouldn't have even told you about them, I guess.

BEAUMONT: Nonsense. In here, you can speak freely in full confidence of your privacy.

RODMAN: Maybe that's true. I don't know. Even still, I didn't tell you everything. I didn't tell nobody, but all those shots I mentioned, the ones of the smashed-up buildings and even the ones with those fucking shadows; that's nothing compared to what I saw at the hospitals. I didn't just document the bomb's effects on the city, but on the people too. The ones that survived. The ones who didn't get hit with the blast, but were close enough to feel it. Those photos were the worst. Those are the ones they really don't want anybody to see. Don't want the American people to know what we really did, what that looks like. Might make them question themselves. Might end up like me.

BEAUMONT: Is that what this is about? Have you been hurting yourself as some kind of penance? Trying to put yourself through some approximation of what the Japanese people suffered? Did you burn yourself, Ed?

RODMAN: No. God, no. It's the shadows, the ones I brought home. They're punishing me.

BEAUMONT: Ed, listen to what you're saying. Just –

RODMAN: No, you listen. But first, you promise me I can trust you.

BEAUMONT: I already said –

RODMAN: Swear to me.

BEAUMONT: I swear. You can trust me.

RODMAN: I understand what I got to do. I got to show people the truth. Matheson doesn't know it, but I kept copies. I always keep copies. Later tonight, I'm meeting a guy from the Times.

BEAUMONT: Hold on, you're what?

RODMAN: A reporter. People need to know, they need to see. Not just the little pieces the higher-ups deem acceptable, but everything, the real face of this thing we did.

BEAUMONT: Why are you telling me this, Ed? It sounds almost like you're unsure about it. Maybe you're hoping I'll talk you out of it, hmm?

RODMAN: (laughing) You couldn't if you tried.

(pause)

BEAUMONT: Then what? Why are you here?

RODMAN: Because there's nowhere else to go, no one else to tell. Least not yet. Not until I meet this Times guy. But I can't keep it inside. I been doing that too long, and they know. The shadows know. Spilling my guts is the only thing that keeps them at bay, like daylight pushing back the dark.

BEAUMONT: There are no shadows to be afraid of, you know, except the ones in your mind, Ed.

RODMAN: (laughing) Maybe that's true. Maybe that's where they hide when the lights are on.

(footsteps)

BEAUMONT: Ed, wait.

(door opening)

RODMAN: See you around, doc.

(door closing)

(long pause)

(footsteps, door opening)

BEAUMONT: Meredith, get Lieutenant Matheson on the line.

* * *

Document G (a)

Summary: Document G (a) is a photograph taken by Sgt. Rodman at a Red Cross Hospital located outside the "Little Boy" strike zone on 11/11/45. Photograph depicts a female Japanese civilian aged 10-12 sitting on the edge of a cot, her back turned to the lens. Her robe is pulled down to expose the upper back and shoulders, which are thick with dark, cracking, cross-hatched radiation burns. An unidentified white-gloved hand extends into the frame from the right side, pulling aside the female's hair to reveal melted flesh on the lower part of her left cheek and mandible, fused to that of her neck and left shoulder. The rest of the female's face is not visible.

Document G (b)

Summary: Document G (b) is a photograph taken by Sgt. Rodman at a Red Cross Hospital located outside the "Little Boy" strike zone on 11/11/45. Photograph is a wide shot depicting an unspecified wing of said hospital where two visible doctors and four visible nurses administer care to an indeterminate number of civilian patients. Patient overflow has resulted in cots lining the hallway outside the primary treatment areas and scattered medical equipment is piled up in all available free spaces. All cots are occupied by patients bearing radiation burns similar to those depicted in Document G (a), with more patients crowding the doorways. The tight quarters and severity of the burns makes differentiation between individual bodies problematic.

* * *

Document H

Summary: Document H is an excerpt from the Incident Report for 10/23/46 filed by [REDACTED] regarding the arrest of Sgt. Rodman at his residence at [REDACTED]. Impertinent data omitted.

Report: Upon receiving clearance from [REDACTED], [REDACTED] and myself approached Sgt. Rodman's home and requested entry. Met with no response, we initiated forceful entry only to find Sgt. Rodman unconscious on the floor in the living room. Attempts to rouse Sgt. Rodman were unsuccessful and medical assistance was summoned. While waiting for medical assistance, [REDACTED] and myself executed a thorough sweep of the residence and recovered numerous classified documents, including a large cache of photographs and film rolls secreted behind a removable panel in the bedroom closet.

Of note in Sgt. Rodman's residence was the unusual dearth of furniture and other accoutrements, and the excessive presence of lighting equipment, both civilian and professional grade, found in every room of the house. All lights were plugged in and turned on at the time of our entry.

Sgt. Rodman was later admitted to [REDACTED] where he was declared comatose. He is now being treated for symptoms which physicians [REDACTED] and [REDACTED] tell us are consistent with a preliminary diagnosis of severe radiation poisoning. Symptoms cited include low red and white blood cell counts, hair and teeth loss, severe malnutrition, inflammation of the mouth and throat, and the presence of numerous malignant tumors in the thyroid and lungs. Sgt. Rodman has been placed in a private, guarded room as we await further updates from [REDACTED].

* * *

Document I

Summary: Document I is a Certificate of Death for Sgt. Rodman issued by the state of New York on 10/31/46. Cause of Death is listed as Acute Radiation Syndrome. See attached.

* * *

Document J (a)

Summary: Document J (a) is a photograph taken by [REDACTED] on 10/23/46. Photograph depicts Sgt. Rodman in civilian attire entering his listed residence approximately thirty minutes prior to the incident detailed in Document H. Close observation reveals a second shadow trailing Sgt. Rodman's own despite [REDACTED]'s claims that no other individuals were in proximity. Presence of unidentified individual may indicate an ongoing security concern. Further inquiry recommended.

Document J (b)

Summary: Document J (b) is a photograph taken by [REDACTED] on 10/23/46. Photograph is completely black. Presumed operator error. Photograph included here at the insistence of [REDACTED].

* * *

TO: Colonel Richard C. Hamner USAC

FROM: Major General Leslie R. Groves, Jr. USAC

After reviewing the documents, I hereby order everything in Sgt. Rodman's personnel file and everything in Site Report TZ-59 expunged. All transcripts and recordings. All recovered pictures. Even the death certificate. Copies and originals.

Burn it all.

THE JUDGE

by Philip Fracassi

Chris pulled into the parking garage underneath the concert hall, the cool shade of a concrete tunnel giving his hangover reprieve from the obnoxiously bright sun he'd been fighting all morning. Of course, if he hadn't left his sunglasses at the bar, he would have had a little extra protection against the Los Angeles sunrise hitting his face like a flaming spotlight the entire drive downtown. And (of course), had he not stayed out until two a.m. drinking an inordinately obnoxious amount of gin and tonics while trying to sweet-talk the very attractive woman he'd met into coming home with him, he would not be feeling as god-awful as he did, he'd still have his favorite pair of sunglasses, and this early morning drive into downtown would have been, overall, much less unpleasant.

But no. Chris just had to get the girl. Had to get laid. Sure, he did. Even after his buddies patted him on the back and headed for their respective Ubers right around midnight, wishing him luck but not willing to wait it out (like a good wingman would have, he thought bitterly), he hung on, hoping that this one time fate would shine down on him, let him have just *one* night with the extremely cute girl he'd managed to splinter from a very lame gaggle of bachelorette attendees (*Come on, how cool could they be to throw a bachelorette party on a Sunday night?*).

But no.

Fate fucked him again.

One minute, the two of them were kissing at the bar, her friends already slowly melting into the night, one-by-one, each vanishing bachelorette attendee increasing his odds *ever so slightly* that his girl would be needing a ride home and, hey, maybe they could share a ride and, hey, maybe they could have a nightcap at his place or, better yet, at *her* place. The next minute, however, she excused herself to go to the restroom, and the bar flashed the "we're closing" lights before turning the dim bulbs to a proper bright white that revealed the depravity and ugliness of the formerly shadowed flaws of the tavern interior. The bartenders gave one more shout of last call while the doorman amused himself by walking through the remaining patrons and warmly reminding them that "they don't have to go home, but they sure as hell can't stay here."

And so he'd waited, having paid for *both* their drinks (not a cheap tab, btw), because in his mind it was really more of a first date and less of a chance meeting with a stranger, and he was pretty positive they'd had a rare connection and that she was super into him and he, for one, felt *really* strongly about the odds of him finally catching just the littlest, tiniest break from the sex gods above and that within the hour he would have the girl (Cindy? Sheri?) on her back and undressed in her potentially very sweet Santa Monica apartment where she (potentially) lived while finishing her doctorate at USC because her dad (likely a prominent surgeon from Marin County, where she grew up wealthy and liberal) wanted her to be a doctor just like him, but in Chris's fantasy she was instead opting for a career in pharmaceuticals because she enjoyed the science of medicine more than the hands-on physical aspects of human biology and the base average salary of such would allow her (them) to cruise the Mediterranean once a year and spend the remainder of her time in the lab while he pursued his own career doing, well, whatever it was political science majors did.

All of this was spinning gloriously through Chris's head right up to the moment a pronounced tapping on his shoulder caused him to lift his head – yeah, it'd been drooping a bit – and turn to find the witty, boisterous doorman looking at him with a smile that was aggressively joyful and came nowhere near his deep-ocean blue eyes saying, "hey buddy, time to hit the road." And it was at *that* moment that Chris realized – with much confusion, then realization, then pain – that the bar was practically empty except for him and three other guys near the back who looked like maybe they knew the owner or something because they didn't appear ready to leave at all and were likely fueled by cocaine in addition to what had been consumed from the half-empty bottle of Petron sitting at the hub of their outwardly spiraling, currently benign shot glasses.

What was *not* in the bar, nor on the sidewalk outside, nor around the back alley of the building, nor on any of the nearby streets or even further down toward the ocean and its ethereal nighttime crashing… was the *girl*.

He knew this because he'd checked. For an hour. Give or take.

It was only when a neighbor yelled at him to "shut his fucking mouth" because he was sort of stumbling down a dark residential street in Venice Beach yelling out both "Sheri" and "Cindy" rather loudly in the hopes she would emerge from a hedgerow or the front door of a nearby bungalow, the whole "leaving him behind" thing a complete misunderstanding and "wasn't it lucky he found her because as it turned out she'd been actually looking for *him*" kind of hysterical irony, that he knew he'd better go home. Which, it turned out, was an adventure unto itself involving a pissed-off German Shepherd and a poor Uber passenger rating, but not one worth recounting in his mind this very bright morning as he lamely showed his Jury Duty paperwork to the bespectacled parking attendant, who waved him indignantly through the entry with vague mumbled instructions of how to proceed from the parking garage to the street above and, hopefully in the next seven-to-ten minutes according to his dashboard clock, the courthouse, where he was due to be, punishable by possible fine or even jail time, by 9 a.m.

* * *

Chris rode the escalator up from the parking garage. The walls of the tall corridor that enclosed the escalator veins was painted a bright blood-red. An art installation hung overhead – milky-white cloud-like plastic structures the size of school buses that emitted calming electronic bell-like chimes as lights danced within their confines like kicking lightning, pre-birth.

He'd only been to the concert hall one other time, a disastrous first and only date with his then-roommate's younger sister, Ashley. He'd been a bagger at Trader Joe's at the time, working for minimum wage and accruing part-time hours while waiting to hear back from one of the hundred career-oriented positions he'd submitted applications to post-graduation. He'd blown a week's pay trying to impress the very smart, very funny Ashley and acquired tickets for "A Night of Casablanca" which featured the film accompanied by the LA Philharmonic Orchestra. The show was astounding and afterward he'd convinced her to have drinks with him at the nearby pub. They'd had more than a few, maxing out his sole credit card in the process and actually made out a bit in his car before she'd left him broke, sexually frustrated and incredibly more familiar with the orchestral movements which accompanied *Casablanca* than he'd ever thought possible.

The proverbial shoe fell the next morning when he woke up, penniless, creditless, and with the horrifying realization that his car was completely out of gas, forcing him to walk the four-and-a-half miles to Trader Joe's for an eight-hour shift with a lunch consisting of a customer-broken-open bag of Sweet 'n' Salty Trail Mix and a stolen bottle of Pellegrino, before making the four-and-a-half-mile walk back to his shitty apartment where his dickhead of a roommate informed him, with an appropriate amount of disdain and shame, that his sister Ashley wasn't interested in seeing him again because – wait for it – her high-school boyfriend, some douche named Rodger (yeah, with a "d"), was moving out to Los Angeles to be with her, and she was pretty god-damned confident he was going to propose and therefore, obviously, not dating anyone, including his penniless, creditless, Trader Joe-bagging, nine-mile roundtrip walking, minimum-wage making, Sweet 'n' Salty Trail Mix stealing sorry-ass roommate Chris. And despite the fact that the music-making cloudy plastic art installation that hovered above the escalator was in Chris's opinion actually kinda cool, he still thought in the back of his mind that the concert hall could kindly go fuck itself, as if the inanimate, womb-like, acoustically fabulous hollow embedded within the building's deconstructionist architecture had anything at all to do with the fact that Rodger the high-school sweetheart (that's Rodger with a motherfucking "d") was moving his stupid cock-blocking ass to Los Angeles to steal back the only girl Chris actually thought might be someone he could fall in love with, which, given that they had only been on the one date, was pretty fucking lame of him to begin with.

Reaching the apex of the final escalator in the series that brought him from Parking Area C to the Ground Level, Chris banged through the glass door which led to the sidewalk and sulking city beyond. The infernal blast of heat, ambient highway-accentuated soot and eye-stabbing sunlight physically assaulted him to the point that he forgot all about his tragic dating life and focused instead on finding out where the hell 888 Flower Street was located, as he now had approximately five minutes to get himself there, signed in, and ready for a quiet day of sitting in a plastic chair with a dumbass juror badge clipped to the only clean dress shirt he had in his closet, the buttons of which he was just now noticing didn't match up, giving his collar a tweaky sort-of slanted appearance, and making him feel, if it were at all possible in this moment, like an even bigger disaster than he had already, sadly, credited himself.

* * *

"Have a seat and be sure to listen for your name to be called," the woman behind the Plexiglas window said, handing him a plastic-shielded badge through the small slot at the window's base, like a bank teller pushing through a withdrawal.

Chris turned to face the large assembly room. He was still sweating from his run to the building, and his sour stomach was knotting and unknotting like a twisted ball of slippery eels. The coffee he'd had that morning before running out was a day old, and acid was spitting up into the back of his throat, adding to the plague-like feeling of nausea he was already embattled with due to the previous night's hard drinking. Despite the pressing heat and waves of sickness, he had found the building easily enough, but his summons had informed him to check into a room on the 5th floor, which he'd done, arriving just before nine a.m. after his quick-walk / jog from the parking structure. Room 512 had consisted of four long lines of depressing humanity, all tethered to separate check-in windows. But he recognized no one carrying the jury duty summons, and he saw no seating area where other jurors were patiently waiting to be called. When a haughty older man in a rumpled cream-colored suit passed by him on the way out, Chris noticed the man holding paperwork similar to his own in one tightly-balled fist.

"Excuse me," Chris said, showing his own paperwork, "are we not in the right place? I feel like I've made a wrong turn somewhere."

The man who turned to regard Chris was bald and short, stocky as a barrel, his white dress shirt collar tinted yellow at the fold, contrasting sickly with his pitted pale skin. The harsh lighting of the room created a glistening crown on his sweat-dappled head. "No, this is bullshit. Looks like they screwed you, too."

The bald man told Chris they needed to be in the Jury Assembly Room, which was on the *first* floor at the *opposite* end of the building, nearly a block away. "This room is if you lost your summons, but it's written out so stupidly I made the same mistake you did and came here first. Now we're late."

"Shit," Chris said under his breath, re-studying his summons closely and realizing that, yes, the fine print did say "only if a new copy of your summons is needed."

"Shit is right, it's past nine already," the man said, and hustled onward, his cheap black briefcase tapping the side of his knee as he walked out.

Chris stood there another moment, studying the summons, desperately looking for the correct room number... *there*. Jury Assembly Room. First Floor. Room 102. Chris turned to beat it out of there, stumbled into a massive beast of a man with a blue skin-coating of tattoos crawling up his neck toward his ears and chin, like a disease closing in on the last bastion of remaining humanity; in this case a scowling, mustached face with sunken brown eyes and a coarse dome of shaved hair.

"The fuck," the man said in a gravelly baritone, leaving Chris to apologize and quickly move around the beast and all but run out of Room 512, into the white marbled hallway, and trot toward the bank of elevators before diverting to a set of wide stairs, his heels pounding each worn step as he jittered down four flights in a frantic race for time. At the bottom, he nearly plowed into a skinny dude in a faded blue janitor uniform and hefting an oversized black backpack who had seemingly appeared from nowhere. Chris apologized heatedly once more without waiting to hear what curses janitor-guy might throw his way, then entered the main lobby again, searching desperately for signs pointing the way to Room 102.

After questioning a surly security guard and then a coffee vendor, he finally arrived at the assembly room at quarter-past nine, waiting for the lady behind the glass to tell him to go home while informing him that a million-dollar fine would be sent to him in the mail along with instructions for payment. To his surprise, however, she had only, sullenly and without preamble or emotion, punched his summons with a rubber stamp (haphazardly and vehemently enough to give Chris the impression she was killing a bug that had crawled onto his paperwork), printed a badge from her station, and told him to sit his sweaty ass down. In so many words.

And now, as he faced the sea of strange faces that dotted the breadth and length of the large room like passengers huddled together on a massive lifeboat, heads bent and solemn, he looked for a dent in the humanity, preferably at least three seats wide, where he could sit and let his rumbling stomach settle, his aching feet rest, and allow the running sweat trickling down the back of his neck and moistening the hair at his throbbing temples to dry.

He walked down the middle row, passing two men talking loudly and animatedly in Spanish, a knot of old women who had somehow gelled together in a unified mass of advanced age and bickering prowess, and the bald man from Room 512 (who had apparently arrived safely and even gave him the slightest nod as he walked by) before finally settling into a row that had two middle seats clear. He gladly dropped into them, relieved at having finally gotten through an extraordinarily dismal morning, and could now, at least, have a few hours of delicious, air-conditioned reprieve.

After sitting hunched over for a few minutes, breathing deeply and willing his empty, acidic stomach to settle down and for his rapidly beating heart to mellow, a soft voice came from beside him.

"You okay?"

Chris, startled, sat up and turned his head. He had been so occupied on finding the empty seats that he hadn't noticed the very attractive brunette sitting in the seat adjacent. *She's like me*, he thought, as if the other strangers in the assembly room were somehow all part of a society or section of humankind that was genetically and behaviorally different than he and the young woman. And although, in Chris's mind, she likely circulated amongst a higher class within said genus, at least she was similarly composed on a biologically modish level, if nothing else.

"Oh," he said, some part of his subconscious hitting the brakes on the output, keeping the words minimized until the rest of his brain could catch up and quality-check each blurp of verbiage before it escaped into the ether, never to be taken back. "Yeah," he continued, the mind's intricate series of security checks allowing the single word clearance for departure.

The brunette smiled, kind laughter in her blue eyes. "Okay, just checking. Thought you were having a heart attack."

"No," Chris said, sitting straighter, thankful he'd spent a moment re-buttoning his shirt on the walk to the courthouse, getting everything aligned properly. "I was running late, and then they sent me to the wrong room, or, rather, I didn't read the paperwork correctly. And by correctly, of course, I mean at all."

She laughed, and he smiled.

Well, I'll be damned, he thought happily, and continued to carefully talk to his fellow, alarmingly attractive, juror, noting with what he felt was incredible mental dexterity (especially given his current physical state) that the name on her juror badge was Jennifer Wagner, an identity which was only a few minutes later shortened throughout the course of delightful conversation to the moniker Jen, a name Chris thought would pair, quite nicely, with his own, as in *Chris and Jen are coming over for dinner*, or, *Make sure we invite Chris and Jen*, or even, and why not dream, *Did you hear about Chris and Jen? They're engaged!*

Chris nodded and laughed as they talked, comparing movies and music and social media stories and all the other wonderful things that life offered the young and moderately well-to-do, but it wasn't until she allowed him to buy her a coffee at the small newsstand in the courthouse hallway that he felt secure enough in his standing to make the resolution of asking for her number before the day was out.

* * *

"If I call your name come to the front of the room to await further instructions. Please bring all personal belongings with you as we cannot be held responsible for the security of your items while in the assembly room."

It was mid-morning, nearly two hours having passed since Chris's arrival to the Jury Assembly room, the time having gone by in a flash thanks to the incredible good fortune of having met Jen, who seemed – astonishingly – as excited about having met Chris as he was to have met her.

"Wow, day's clipping along," he said, glancing at his watch.

"Oh god, I hope we don't get called," Jen said, sitting up to listen more attentively to the woman at the front of the large room.

That makes two of us, he thought, and divided his attention to also listen to the announcement.

"Beltross, Cadivan, Charles, Davenport, Fredericks…"

Chris tensed as she made her way up the alphabet, toward the R's… toward *Ross*. She did not disappoint, and Chris had to physically restrain a curse when she called his last name out.

"Reznick… Ross…"

"That's me," he said quietly to Jen, who was still perked up and listening closely. He was already thinking of a way to ask for her phone number in the next sixty seconds without it sounding desperate or pathetic, but she only waved a hand at him in a "shut up a second" motion…

"Wait," she whispered, watching the roll call woman with almost exaggerated attention.

"Tillman, Vance, Yakomoto. If you heard your name please come to the front of the room now for further instruction. If you did not hear your name please remain in…"

Chris tuned the woman out, fascinated with Jen's body language, the way she slumped when her name was passed over, as if she was actually disappointed to *not* be called for juror selection.

"You dodged a bullet," he said, the words sounding lame and cold to his own ears.

"Yeah," she said, and gave him a small *(sad?)* smile. "Well, good luck. Maybe you won't be selected and, you know, they'll let you back into purgatory."

He forced a small chuckle and stood to leave. His mind raced, his heart thumping, and he felt himself sweating all over again, despite having exerted himself no more than rising from the molded gray plastic seat to a standing position. "Well…" he started, already knowing he was going to chicken out, making him hands-down the biggest loser on the face of the planet. *Will I regret this forever?*

"See ya," he said, and started to shuffle past bent knees toward the aisle.

"Chris!"

He turned, his swelled heartbeat now so loud that he would swear the entire room could hear its pulsing bass thrum.

Jen was smiling, holding out her phone. "We should trade numbers, you know? In case you… um…"

He nodded numbly. When he pulled his phone from his pocket, he was mortified to see his hands trembling. *Get a grip, dude!* "Do you want to give me yours…"

The air around them vibrated with their excitement, their budding potential. Jen relayed her number. He called her while simultaneously typing J-E-N into his phone's contacts field. "Great," he said. "I'll give you a call… this week?"

"Cool," she said. "I'd love to hang out."

"Okay, me too," he said, feeling more awkward with every passing moment. "I better go."

"Have fun," she said cheerily, and gave him a wave as she sat back down.

Cheerfully dismissed, he sidestepped his way into the aisle and walked to the front of the room. He tried to keep the wattage of his smile down to reading lamp strength but it wanted to burst out of him like the sun. He barely heard the instructions as the woman told the gathered group of potential jurors what courtroom they were to report to, how to get there. When the others in the group began to file out, he simply followed, dazed and happy.

He turned back only once as he reached the door, but didn't see Jen in the sea of bored faces, and then he was past the doorway and stepping into the hall. Something bumped his elbow, and the bald man blew past him huffing, heading for a set of stairs. Craig saw half the crowd heading to elevators, another large group taking the same set of stairs as the bald man. Feeling much better now, he decided walking up a few flights might do him some good, and as he hit the first step he was already thinking about the lapsed gym membership he would be reactivating the second he arrived home that evening.

* * *

Five flights later, Chris saw a small brass placard screwed into the white and gray marble frosting-swirl of the wall, indicating that Court Rooms 23-49 were straight ahead. At the top he recognized a group of people wearing juror badges streaming from the elevators nearby, and after a quick glance down the long stretch of hallway he spotted the bobbing bald head of the man he'd followed up the stairs. He continued searching faces in the thickening crowd and identified one of the loud Latino men and one of the old ladies from the assembly room, plus a few others he noted in passing that were definitely familiar. Confident he was in the right place, he followed the stream of jurors down the long hallway.

As he walked, he noticed the interactions of the hallway's many other residents. After passing by a few of these clusters, he made a game out of who was a lawyer, a defendant, or a plaintiff… or just maybe a distraught family member there to lend moral support for Uncle Ed's drunk driving charge, or a hot-tempered husband's barroom brawl. As he studied the faces – distraught, bored, angry, scared – he felt increasing relief to be here as a juror, and not a defendant. It almost gave him a feeling of superiority, until he thought how shitty it was to think that way, especially when these people were obviously in such turmoil. He looked at the faces in a new light, saw the sadness, the despair, the mad hope. And there were so *many* of them, the hallway jammed with people of all different stripes, and yet ominously quiet, respectful. Chris, feeling a small knot of shame coiling in his chest, ended his guessing game, lowered his head and kept his eyes forward.

He continued past the midpoint of the long hallway, passing a dozen sets of heavy wooden double-doors, feeling exposed beneath the bright ghost-white lights nestled within deco-style ceiling fixtures. The heavy scuffed marble floor and walls gave the passage a psychological weight, a *significance* that only an old, big-city courthouse like this one could muster. He felt the judgment seeping through the walls, its invisible tendrils pressing and sliding along every warm body, deciding their worth, their degree of guilt, their punishment. His group had stopped and were circling around a small black woman with darting, intelligent black eyes and a whiplash smile that he found immediately endearing. "Okay folks, come on, come closer… I ain't gonna bite ya. The judge might, but not little ol' me," she said, loudly and clearly, an obvious veteran.

A few folks chuckled, relieved and perhaps a bit nervous now that they'd arrived outside the courtroom. Despite himself, Chris found himself listening with rapt attention to the woman as she talked, afraid (now that he was here in a more official capacity) to miss some piece of vital information he might need once they entered.

"My name is Ms. Evans and I am a court deputy," the woman said with experienced patience. "When we go inside you will take a seat in the viewing area of the courtroom. There should be just enough seats to accommodate you all so please file to the end of each row before sitting. Once the juror selection process begins, you will be called upon…"

The deputy continued talking, and Chris listened while studying the other prospective jurors in his group, wondering if he would be chosen or released, debating whether he should try and shape his answers so that he *would be* released, allowed to go home, where he could begin thinking about calling Jen, and, even more terrifying, planning what they should do together that weekend. He felt his excitement rise again, and he smiled as the deputy finished her spiel and opened the heavy wooden doors of courtroom forty-three.

Chris was near the back of the group. He waited patiently as his fellow jurors began to file inside.

"Miss?"

Chris looked to his left and saw a tall, skinny man wearing tan khakis and a blue denim shirt. The man was smiling and lightly touching the elbow of the deputy. People continued to file slowly in through the doors.

"Someone left their backpack," the tall man said, pointing across the corridor. Chris turned, saw a black backpack tucked beneath one of the wooden benches that lined the hallway. The top of the bench was empty.

"I'll ask about it when everyone's seated," the deputy said, and continued to monitor the jurors entering the courtroom.

"I don't even know if it's one of ours," the tall man said, "I just noticed it had been left."

Chris put his hand into his pocket, felt the solidity of his cell phone. He thought about Jen's number being stored inside. He took a half step forward, then something tingled at the nape of his neck. He looked back once more at the backpack sitting beneath the wooden bench.

By doing so, he was able to see it explode.

The detonator attached to the four pounds of C4 triggered, and the force of the detonation – combined with the canisters of fuel and armload of nails, screws and other shrapnel packed within the bag – ripped apart flesh, wood and bone in an erupting blast of fire and metal that consumed the length of the entire hallway within seconds.

There was no time to wonder *why*. Regardless, there would have been no response.

The world concussed and went mute as Chris's body disintegrated in a flying wall of flame and superheated metal shards. An inner part of his mind, long-hidden, watched helplessly as the veil of reality tore apart and the chasm opened beneath him – an infinite, gaping black maw of fire and eternal damnation eager to consume. He was vividly aware of the moment his consciousness was ripped from this dimension and pulled hungrily into the abyss.

The screams of the dead followed his soul down as it fell.

* * *

The explosion outside the sixth-floor courtroom killed more than two hundred people, including many standing outside the courthouse who were crushed by the falling debris of concrete and steel as it propelled outward into the blue Los Angeles sky. It left behind a charred, blackened chasm that burned and smoked as the survivors on the floors below made their way to safety, the injured and elderly escorted by those with better fortune, all of them crying and screaming in primal fear and despair for what had happened.

It was later reported that the Honorable Frank W. Morris, a senior member of the Superior Court's prestigious resident judges, was also killed in the blast.

THE SNAKE BENEATH MY SKIN

by Sarah Walker

As the day drifted into afternoon, he wondered at the sudden quiet. Normally, the street here in Mexico was full of sound and color, its hectic organization making it seem more urban than this area really was. Earlier, circling above the town in the small private airplane he used to fly in from the coast, he thought the town looked more like an anthill than a collection of adobe buildings. It's like an unknown Amazonian species, he had thought. Maybe they're down there using their tiny bodies to build elaborate structures hoping to reach some distant uncaring god.

"Another cerveza, Señor?" his waiter asked, breaking into his reverie.

He nodded. The waiter disappeared into the dark of the small restaurant's kitchen, a magician vanishing off a stage. He was alone again. He noted that the vanished throngs moving by a few moments ago had also disappeared. Maybe they are all taking siestas? More likely they are in church, he told himself. Opportunities to pray in this damned country never seemed to be ignored. At every chance, the natives headed into the giant stone cathedral at the center of town. He looked over to the church with its great dark spires. Those spires cast black shadows that stretched and seemed to have tendril-like fingers elongating, seemingly trying to reach him with their cold touch. He scooted back a bit, back into the Southern sun.

The church had been built by the literal blood and oftentimes death of the indigenous people when they were conquered by the Spanish centuries ago. It disgusted him.

He took another sip of beer and let his mind wander again. He had once asked his boss Gonzalez about the locals' preoccupation with religion in Southern Mexico. Gonzalez had been a good man but sometimes slightly disturbing to deal with. His abnormally long canines would catch the light when he spoke, spit glinting off white daggers in the afternoon sun. He had been a top general in the Mexican army, was university educated, and quite worldly. But the pull of the drug business had been too strong, the money too tempting when compared to the meager stipend the members of the army received from the government, and Gonzalez had left, just as many of the other soldiers had, hoping to make a better life for his family and for himself. He had worked his way up through the cartel and now ran it, his penchant for violence always present, an undertone that resonated deep and foreboding. Samuel had watched his boss after asking the question, and at first had worried he had somehow offended the man. But finally, Gonzalez had turned slowly towards Samuel and said in a strangely low voice,

"You Americans rarely understand these things. There are forces in the world, forces that must be…" He stopped for a moment, as if listening to some distant conversation. When he turned back to Samuel, a strange look had come over his grizzled features and his eyes appeared black and distant.

"Sí…" he muttered softly, as if responding to someone Samuel could not hear. Suddenly he shook his head fiercely and began to speak in his normal voice.

"You see, Gringo, there are forces that must be placated. Like anything living, Gods must be fed." The old drug dealer stopped speaking, grinned and took a long drink of his probably now luke-warm beer.

Samuel had laughed at this show at first, thinking he was being messed with again. He knew Mexicans loved to tease the Gringos, and his blonde hair and light skin certainly identified him as one. But when Gonzalez did not laugh along with him, Samuel stopped, resulting in his making a stifled noise that vaguely embarrassed and then angered him. Damned stupid peasants, he thought, looking down at his glass.

Gonzalez hadn't seemed to notice, but his lined face took on a look of a deadly seriousness. When he spoke, his voice was soft now, even whispery. "There are things going on under what you see here. There are layers within layers, even realities within this one. We Mexicanos here know this, and we accept this. You Americans, you fight it, and that's why you are so miserable. That is why you do the drugs. That is why you come to Mexico to party and have sex. You simply refuse to see. Sometimes what is beneath the skin is what defines a man. And yet sometimes the skin itself is the answer."

"Ha… um… OK. If you say so," Samuel answered.

The old drug dealer nodded and then fell silent as if he was now contented with what he had just said.

That night Samuel returned as usual to his small hotel room, walking past the many boutiques set up for the tourists. One store had caught his eye. Flyers of dance competitions plastered the walls near the large plate glass window, the colors and bold letters vying for the attention of tourists walking by. Inside, stacks of local artists' works were piled in huge towers. Hand blown colored beads and small neon painted animals that may have jumped out of a Dali dream made the window appear a door into a surreal world. He shook his head. What a lot of cheap shit. He started to walk away when his eyes caught one small set of sculptures.

Something about the figurines made his stomach turn. Was it their faces and their hard clay eyes that bothered him? At first he had thought they were simply men, warriors from the distant past, but something looked askew. He leaned down to get a closer glance and realized that though they were men, they were draped in skins. He had heard of this practice from other natives, who told him that in the old days the Aztecs would sacrifice their greatest warriors to the gods so that their crops would be plentiful. The ceremony involved peeling the skin off the living man and then the priest would wear it, symbolizing the new earth that came when spring had arrived. It was completion, a circle finished and begun anew.

"Barbarians," he muttered underneath his breath.

He believed violence was necessary sometimes, but only for money, for a reasonable purpose at least. This legend was disgusting. He didn't understand why these modern people, though "modern" might be putting it too nicely, would still make figurines of such an awful myth. He shook his head. Someday, when he had made enough money, he would return home, set up a little store, and get away from these people. But for now, he had to do his job. He would remain quiet, and use them, and then leave. He took one last glance at the sculptures and headed to his home away from home.

* * *

Back in his room, Samuel drank a beer while sitting on his bed. He thought over the figurines and tried to grasp what exactly it was about them that disturbed him so much. He had seen extreme violence many times. He was not new to the world of war and brutality. But as his mind wondered, it kept going back to the little clay eyes staring blankly out at him from the store window, their expressions those of a person who has seen something not meant for humankind.

"Jesus, get a hold of yourself," he muttered and guzzled the last of his beer. Exhausted, he did not bother to turn off the bedside table lamp. His eyes closed and he began to snore.

* * *

Two days later, the strange beliefs the sculptures had hinted at were the least of his problems. Gonzalez had not called and his cell phone appeared to be shut off. Samuel had a feeling that Gonzalez hadn't lasted long as the boss after he had seen him. After he hadn't heard from him for several days, he had to admit Gonzalez was not coming back, ever. He wasn't sure how to proceed. He knew the worst thing to do would be to panic, so he simply waited, drinking at the cantina and hanging around near the dilapidated hotel in hopes someone would come and clear up the situation.

A day later, two Federales appeared at his hotel room, banging on the door in a way that communicates the presence of the police in any city in the world.

"You will no longer deal with Gonzalez. You will deal with us," the shorter of the two hissed at Samuel.

He was a man so small as to seem unimposing until one really looked at him. A long scar ran across his neck, puckered and darker than the rest of his flesh. His eyes were very hard, black and glittery, and though he smiled at Samuel when he told him Gonzalez had disappeared, those eyes stayed black and impenetrable. Samuel did not want to deal with these men. Gonzales was the man his brother Frank had insisted he deal with, and now Gonzales was gone. He wasn't sure what to do, but he knew he should not show fear, though everything in his gut told him to get the fuck out, just leave. But the money... he needed the cash too badly. He also knew it would be foolish to argue. These men would not take no for an answer.

He took out the cash he had been sent to purchase product with and paid the men. The little man counted it once, then twice. He looked up and motioned to the other Federale, a quick and almost unconscious gesture that most others would not have even noticed. It was as if the two were telepathic, and Samuel knew that came from being on the frontline of something bad, a war even if it was a secret one. Yes, blood was indeed thicker than water.

Samuel took the package they proffered, not even checking to see if it was quality or even real. He knew if he tried to open it, he would fumble it, his hands shaking with adrenaline and fear. Still holding it, he had shown the men the door, but once they had gone he had finally calmed down enough to carefully open it.

It had been real, in fact some of the best cocaine he had found in his 20 years as a drug mule. One part of him argued that he should stop and go home now, but another part said wait. If they had been able to produce such a fine product once, they could probably do it again. And, he told himself, dealing with crooked cops had its advantages. There was no need to worry about being busted now. But always in the back of his head was that fly of doubt and worry, buzzing around, disrupting any prospect he had of feeling peace in this foreign land.

He thought back to that day.

Where had Gonzalez gone?

He knew Gonzalez had been high up in the organization, but that hadn't seemed to protect him. His brother Frank had told him not to ask about things; opaqueness was the nature of their business. But still… he wondered every time the later shipments were delivered efficiently and quietly by the two Federales.

However, weeks later, one of Gonzalez's workers delivered the ordered package to his room instead of the sociopath policeman and his larger sidekick.

He tried to hide his relief at seeing someone he recognized but Gregorio knew and smiled, patting Samuel on the back.

"It's ok. Everything is ok," the Mexican man said.

They had drunk a beer together, and after a time the conversation had died down. He had better ask now… now or never, a voice added in his head.

"Gregorio, can I ask you something?" Gregorio seemed to sense what Samuel wanted to say even before he said it.

"One thing I can tell you, Gringo, is never ask anything here. Some things must remain unknown if one wants to stay whole."

At this he had waved his brown hand at him, showing that the top two joints of his index finger, as well as the top of his ring finger were gone, leaving only scar tissue and empty space.

"You see this? Like my fingers, he's gone, so leave it." And with that Gregorio left.

* * *

Samuel bought the pure coke again and again. He was now living like a king, even after setting up the transfers to his brother and his cohorts. And he kept quiet, keeping to himself and staying out of trouble. But Gonzalez was never far from his mind. He couldn't lose the memory of the missing fingers on Gregorio's hand and reports of more bodies found in neighboring Chiapas: headless, tortured, burned, dismembered, knives stuck in every inch of a person's body. All this kept swimming back and forth behind his eyes. He could only quiet his fears by thinking of the profits he was making, the cash he was quietly accumulating, the success of his business.

A few months after the visit from Gregorio, he had gone to his favorite cantina for a beer and some food and was sitting quietly by the door when his stomach lurched. He knew instinctively that someone was watching him. He could sense danger even though the cantina looked as quiet and dull as it had when he came in. He downed the last of the beer the waiter had just brought, opening another immediately, hoping to drown the fear congealing in his gut, but it had no effect. He had lived with fear for so long, had seen so much here, that it had become an unwanted companion, always present, patiently waiting to take control, a ghost haunting him.

TEST PATTERNS

Sarah Walker

He turned to see who was looking at him, and he saw the two policemen coming towards him. The smaller one, the sociopath, "The Sadist," as he had nicknamed him the afternoon they met, carried a large, semiautomatic machine gun. It glinted in the late afternoon light.

"You need to come with us."

Samuel knew to hide his fear. And, he also knew it was unlikely they would mess with him. His brother worked in the border patrol, and he regularly fed information to their boss about who was talking to the Americans, as well as who was going to be busted. His brother had many friends. Samuel took a deep breath.

"Sure, but after I finish my beer."

He wished he hadn't drunk the first one so fast earlier, and he tried to look uninterested in the violence emanating from these two men. He swirled the beer around in the bottle, desperately trying to buy some time to think. After a moment, the taller man spoke up.

"Senor Gonzalez needs to speak to you now."

Samuel looked at this younger man's face. Pockmarks covered it, and his skin was rough and worn despite his obvious youth. His eyes seemed less hard then the smaller man's, and Samuel saw something within those eyes that confused him. The man was frightened. Something was bothering him on a level that Samuel could not untangle despite his almost psychic ability at reading people.

He drank the beer quickly though it burned painfully as it went down his throat, trying to appear as nonchalant as he could. After a moment, he knew he couldn't put this off any longer.

"OK. Let's go. Vamonos."

Samuel walked calmly to the men's car despite the anxiety that was weighing on him. Their Mexican army jeep was parked at an angle near the small Bodega where he had been drinking. Another officer sat at the wheel. He silently started the car after the two men ushered Samuel into the passenger seat and then took their place in the back. It roared to life, showing it had clearly been souped up by the cartel as most government vehicles rarely sounded so clean or smooth.

They drove in silence for a long time. Samuel glanced at his watch and saw that an hour had passed. The cityscape had dissolved into the barren Mexican countryside as the night began to press on the warm day, pushing the light back and overtaking the landscape with broad strokes of indigo and purple until only blackness remained.

Samuel watched the locals flash by as the jeep sped to wherever they were headed. Indigenous women walked along the sides of the road, their goods from the daily local market piled on their heads making their shadows look like weird beasts creeping across the cracked and weathered blacktop, mutating as the light faded into twilight. They all averted their eyes from the jeep, as if by refusing to see them, the jeep and its occupants didn't exist in their world. They kept about their business, intentionally blind to the American in the apparent custody of the Federales. Once, a small Indian child aimed his finger at the truck and made a strange motion. An old woman, perhaps his grandmother, grabbed his hand and yelled something in Mixtec and then clearly made the sign to ward off the evil eye.

* * *

After over two hours, and a segue into an unpaved side road, the men stopped the vehicle. Samuel could see nothing around him, but he tried to push the flutter of panic that was rising in his chest, secretly looking for a hastily dug grave nearby and trying to plan an escape. But he needn't have feared his captors. The driver of the jeep nodded to the two men in the back who then got out. They walked over to a clump of dry bushes that appeared no different than the others, and began pulling on something that Samuel could not see.

A small side road that climbed crookedly into the darkness appeared. The two policemen who had moved the bushes did not get back in the vehicle, but instead lit cigarettes, the flames of the tips glowing like two orange eyes in a vast, now totally black night as the remaining two occupants drove up the steep mountain road.

Samuel watched closely as they drove, looking for landmarks in case he had to run through the countryside. Nothing indicated what was going to happen and the driver would say nothing.

After a time, their destination appeared looming in the dark as they rounded a dark bend in the dirt road. He was relieved to see it was a giant hacienda much grander than any he had ever seen. It was sprawled on the hillside, a large and beautifully wrought wood deck wrapping around the front of the mansion offering vistas of the lower hillside below.

They pulled into a small driveway, and the driver simply sat unmoving and silent. Samuel waited but becoming impatient, he began to ask what he was supposed to do when he heard Señor Gonzalez.

"Samuel, up here!"

Relieved, he saw that Gonzalez was indeed alive! He seemed to have grown younger and become healthier. His hair was now a dark black and his clothes a stark white against his umber skin.

Samuel walked up the long staircase, almost tripping in the dark a few times but finally arriving safely at the deck.

"How is my good amigo, Samuel? Mi policía weren't too rough on you, were they?"

Samuel attempted a sickly smile at this statement, and shook his head. "No, no! Everything is fine."

"And the product? Do you like it?"

The old man held a whiskey in his plump hand, the ice cracking lightly against the side of the carved glass. He motioned to a shadow in the darkness that moved into the light. Once she moved away from the shadows, Samuel could see she was a young Mexican girl, maybe 16 years old, in the dress of a servant. She stood there motionless and silent, waiting. He glanced at her, thinking with a house like this you'd think they could afford to hire a better class of servant.

"Una bebida para mi amigo."

She nodded, and disappeared into the cavernous house to get Samuel his drink.

Samuel smiled, feeling a bit better that things seemed to be returning to normal.

"Yes, great in fact. No complaints."

The girl returned quickly, and silently handed Samuel a glass brimming with golden colored whisky. He thankfully took a deep slug, letting the expensive liquor burn blessedly down to his belly, making the earlier chill and fear seem distant and unreal.

As he took another swallow waiting for Gonzalez to explain what it was he wanted, he noticed something strange. Though Mexico was quite warm, Gonzalez rarely sweated. He had remarked upon it once when he had first arrived here, amazed at how cool the man seemed to stay despite the pounding summer heat that year. But as he now looked at Gonzalez, he could see a single droplet of sweat that moved sinuously down his cheek and dropped unnoticed into his glass. Samuel's stomach turned slightly. Old warning systems he had tuned in Iraq and then later in San Quentin were screaming out that something was not right.

"Are you OK, Señor Gonzalez? You seem…"

And then he felt it, a glassy, smooth feeling. Whatever they had drugged him with, it was hitting fast.

His logical mind tried to grasp at something to disentangle the problem and find a solution to the unsolvable. Over the slippery motion in his brain he heard Gonzalez' voice, quiet and flat.

"Don't fight it, Señor Gringo. Once the door is open, once the way of the snake is decided, you cannot turn back. Once the skinless one has chosen you, you cannot run. I merely do his bidding. I have no choice, you see. They picked you; he picked you, as you picked them. You must join them."

"As we all will," said a small female voice in the night.

The old dealer stood as two large bodyguards appeared. His face was invisible now that the light for the deck was behind his shapeless form. Their movements looked surreal, the drug making the forms grotesque, a shadow play formless and vast. Samuel imagined himself jumping up, punching the one guard and then kicking the other. But as he tried to act this out, his legs fell beneath him, crumpled and useless. He lay on the floor as ineffectual as a broken mannequin. His eyes wandered as the light grew dim and the drug began to fully take control and smother him.

The deep sky above echoed the spinning feeling that overcame him. A few distant stars that he could see were shining. Though burned out long ago, the light from the stars blinked and flickered, like small bugs being electrocuted as they flew too close to a light. He knew now that their promise of light was a lie because the darkness was complete. Their light had been extinguished as by an eclipse in slow motion, a sweeper that eats the sun, leaving only darkness at the end. He heard nothing, saw little, but he could feel the smooth and desert dry hand of the girl touch his face before the black engulfed him.

* * *

A sound.

The dripping of water.

His eyes slowly and painfully opened, and his blurred vision tried to focus. Gradually a rock wall became clear, and then a stream of water which ran down the green speckled walls, painting the mosses and tiny plants clinging to the roughness in a bright green, reflecting light from an unknown source.

His head ached terribly and his mouth was dry. He tried to lick his parched lips but even that seemed a Herculean effort. The cold had claimed him, sucking the little heat his body produced into the ground's endless depths, its hands of rock bracing and cradling him, an icy mother for a prodigal son.

He turned over and looked up. He realized he was somewhere underground.

A cave?

Flames lit up the walls like some Paleolithic dwelling. Grotesque drawings, tall and distorted, of Mayan, or perhaps Zapotec priests, slitting their own throats in a final act of obedience to a forgotten god were depicted along the roughly hewn walls. Despite their obvious great age, they brightly decorated the stone. He tilted his head back at the feeling of a breeze, realizing that above him an opening into the night hung promising escape. As it was barely lighter than the dark grotto, he couldn't make out whether anyone was up there.

He thought of calling for help, but quickly discarded that idea. Gonzalez had wanted him dead.

No, if he wanted you dead, you would be dead, his inner voice admonished him, and he knew it was right. But he couldn't imagine why in the hell old Gonzalez would have drugged him, and then dumped him here. His mind thought back to the carrier whose fingers were gone.

Never ask anything.

Yes, that seemed wisest. Though hung over from the drug, and freezingly wet and sore, he was still alive.

I need to get out of this fucking cave. I need to get home.

He rolled over again and slowly managed to rise up on his weak legs. They were shaking badly from the after affects of the doping and the icy water that had been leaking down his pants.

Yes, definitely time to get the fuck out of Dodge. I will get the hell out of this God forsaken place, get the fuck out and never return. Just get me out of here. Please God, please, just get me out, and no more drugs. No more I promise!

He normally did not pray, being a life long atheist, but this was a bad situation. Not only had someone taken his shoes after dumping him here, he was clearly out of his league with this man. The why of this occurrence wasn't important at the moment. He just needed to act and act fast. He was finally standing upright, but still had to lean on the walls. He took a breath to try and get his mind to work more clearly.

Think, goddamn it, think. How the hell am I going to get out of here?

He looked around and suddenly realized the obvious through the drug haze. Someone else must have been down here with him as there were three torches fixed to rudimentary holders that lit up the cave. As his eyes became accustomed to the dim light, he began to realize what exactly he was in. Piles of ritual pottery objects littered the pool he had been passed out next to, the darkly beautiful water shimmering in an unreal indigo color along the clay faces of the idols, their devilish expressions looking grotesque on the moving torch light. It was a cenote, a sacred cave used for rituals by the indigenous people here long ago.

"What the fuck? What the hell is this place?"

He whispered this under his breath, unconsciously picking up some secret signal that the chamber seemed to emanate, that this was indeed a place of sacredness, of ghosts, of long dead demons, or even gods, which demanded silence. The strange idols grinned and glared at him in their watery graves, the slight current making their faces seem to be alive and moving despite the impossibility of it. He carefully leaned his still-swimming head down to look closer. Among the greens and blues reflected onto the anthropomorphic sculptures, he suddenly realized what he was seeing.

Bones were scattered along with the figures, hundreds of them, maybe thousands; skulls, femurs, finger bones, old bones, newer ones, whites and tans all blended into an almost incoherent mess. Though his life as a criminal had left him unusually resilient to the sight of death, a shudder rippled over his body, as if he had never seen death before. He felt he should know this spot, that he had seen something similar long ago on TV maybe. But it was ungraspable, and his mind refused to give up the memory. It lay hidden.

And then he heard it.

A shuffling, slipping noise. It was the sound of painful walking, the footsteps those of someone who was more than ancient, joints creaking audibly, painfully moving. He turned and saw that in the darkest of corners there was in fact a tunnel, and out of this tunnel came a shape.

The fear that Samuel was trying to suppress erupted and Samuel began to shout.

"Hey, I haven't done anything! I haven't talked to the cops! I don't know why you are doing this but my brother is on the border patrol. Just let me go, and nothing will happen to you! I just want to go home!"

The words flew out of his mouth, embarrassing him and adding to the panic that rose like bile threatening to pour out of his unconsciously grimacing mouth. At the sound of his voice the shape stopped for a moment, and then it turned and as if honing in on him began to move, no longer slowly but very, very quickly.

Samuel tried to jump over the pool and then climb up the walls, but it was pointless. There were no footholds, and rock had purposefully been broken away in the parts where they might have once been small ledges that could be used to get out. As he stared, desperate to find a path out, he finally saw the blood on the walls and scratch marks in the rock.

The form had reached the light now, and Samuel's mind refused to grasp what he saw. It was a man, or had been long ago, but now it was something unnatural, something which should not be, something greater than a simple man. A memory of one of his experiences in Mexico came back, illuminating the form and filling him with terror. It was of the sculptures of the old pagan god sitting in that shop window, the god of misery, of death, of rebirth through pain, of being fed, and of feeding.

The skins of the many sacrifices hung on this creature like ill fitting suits, draping its corrupt ancient form with the skin, and the being, of those many lost souls who were now found inside this ancient God. They had been reborn in the image of bloodied dirt, of darkest obsidian, black, sharp, and made in fire. It grinned at him, the piles of flesh moving despite their state as dead things.

Do not be afraid. He heard a deep voice clearly in his head.

What is happening? He tried to yell, tried to speak, but he could make no sound. The living embodiment of the great God myth, the legend still worshipped in secret, stood before him, and it wanted him. He would become unseen. He would join.

It leaned down, the eyeholes showing nothing at first, only pitch, all meaningless death by the thousands. A slight movement inside caught his eye though, and then he saw them, thousands of maggots swarming in the empty sockets. It grabbed him. The grip was of a child playing with an insect. He could feel the supernatural strength in that grip and knew it could crush him with one single movement. It was indeed a God, an old God, the true God worshipped throughout the world. It was a god of blood, of death, of the rise and fall of the seasons, of darkest summer and of coldest autumn, and of payments too terrible to be named. Its being promised a fruit that could only be obtained through sacrifice. The blood that grew the maize, the blood that protected the cartel. It ran through the ground here, veins in the earthen body of the ancient land. Blood must be spilt. Even Christ had to die to be reborn, he thought fleetingly, lost in hysteria now. He understood as the thoughts flashed through his head in one bright explosion. He quit fighting.

The creature pulled him up, causing his feet to no longer touch the cave's floor. It stared at him, and he saw. He saw sacred caves, cenotes, dark watery pits where the ancient people dumped their offerings, like the one where he had been dumped to feed this God by Gonzalez and his cohorts. He saw the centuries go by, the Spaniards killing millions, the temples torn down, and replaced with the crucified god called Christ, but always this true God of the earth and of blood waited beneath, immortal and unknowable; he was the dark snake sliding beneath the surface of the light.

A set of alien hands the color of ebony, unreally long and thin and tipped with claws, slid out from beneath the layers of skin. Without hesitation, despite his babbling pleas, they reached into him sharply. He screamed, the pain indescribable and unending as his skin was separated from his flesh and his soul was torn through his eye sockets. His head fell back and above he saw the stars spinning, the dead moon rising and falling, and the heavens which sat watching his meaningless death. There was no mercy. There was no savior... there was only the cycle. Only rebirth through death.

He began to black out, the searing of his skin being torn away too much for his frail human form, but the god would not allow him to sleep. Distantly he heard screaming, high pitched and piercing as it echoed off the caves walls, bouncing back and forth as the sound joined the ghosts of the others who had left their bones here in the icy pool. The great God's claws slipped and pulled harder. Distantly Samuel heard the sound of Velcro being torn open. He realized as the blood stung his eyes that the sound was his scalp being torn off, the god expertly removing this encumbrance to reality.

As he felt himself separate, his pain suddenly ceased, the old self known as "Samuel" falling to the floor in a chaotic heap as the God placed him among the others. He could feel the wetness of the other skins touch his. But it was not unpleasant. He was now complete. And as he was reborn into death, a dark light the shade of a million exploding suns beckoned to him. Samuel answered the clarion call to be reborn into eternity.

THE HANDS OF CHAOS

by Ashley Dioses

Into the cosmos astral beings burn,

Their flames, their weaving flames, fair fatal fae.

In swirling rhythms, fiery bodies turn

Like sparkling marbles; Hands of Chaos play.

THE NOMENCLATURE
OF
UNNAMABLE HORRORS

by Pete Rawlik

In a small, windowless cell, in the heart of the very last asylum, Doctor Ambrose Dexter sat listening to the woman who occupied that dread room. He sat there and listened, and tried to keep from screaming.

"I appreciate what you have done for me here, this position has been one of the most productive I have ever known," she said, "but my writing is complete, I need to go to press."

Doctor Dexter tried to be objective. It was perhaps a mistake to have taken this particular case, but given the situation, he had little choice. It was his job, his duty, and he was most fitted for it. There were other doctors, younger doctors, but he would not wish this work on any of them. Besides he didn't trust them. For the last five years he had attended the woman, and had seen her grow with the times. She was in a way, voluptuous. He did not want to say attractive, because he did not find her so, and he knew what she truly was, but he knew others might find her so. Her hair was dark black with a streak of gray over her right temple. Her eyes were bright and smoldered with intensity. Her long legs were smooth and curved in all the right places. In her lap, her delicate hands gripped a thick conglomeration of papers that had been assembled during her stay using a variety of sources. It was an assemblage of mismatched papers, not of one color, or size, or stock, but rather of whatever she could have laid her hands on at the time. Thus, there were loose leaves of photocopy paper, pages torn from notebooks, sheets of drafting paper, salvaged pieces of gift wrap, and even endpapers torn out of books from the hospital library. The makeshift binding of her ragged conglomeration was made from used cereal boxes, glued together quadruple thick, but not with much thought to alignment or orientation. Underneath her thumb Dexter could make out where she had inscribed a name on the cover: Merci C. Noonon. He had to suppress a shudder; it was best if she didn't see weakness.

"Merci," Dexter addressed her informally when he could, it took away her a sense of authority, even if just for a moment. "Merci, tell me what you've been working on, please."

Her hands reflexively gripped the book in her lap a little tighter. A smiled crossed her face. It was obvious that the question pleased her. When she finally opened her mouth, she spoke with the voice of authority, one that Dexter wished she didn't have. He still wondered where she had learned it.

"Human beings have an inherent need to name things. This practice is built into the very core of most languages. The few linguistic systems that lack this characteristic are fundamentally primitive, and are almost immediately supplanted by whatever more precise, more complex system that is encountered. The more complex the world is, the more complex language is, and the more complex and more important names are. For example, in primitive, isolated societies the word cow might be sufficient, but as the society expands and becomes more complex, cows become divided into types of cows. Dairy as opposed to meat animals for example. Then when new breeds are introduced the word cow is replaced with more specificity, one that might embrace breed, origin, appearance, diet, condition and usage. But as the language becomes more complex all this can be embedded in a proper noun." She paused and smiled nervously. "Traditionally this has been an organic process, and different names have been assigned to the same thing by different cultures. For example, the sportfish known in Hawaiian as mahi-mahi, is known in English as dolphin or dolphinfish, and in Spanish as dorado. On the island of Malta, they are known as lampuka. For the most part, the use of these common names by local societies creates no issues, save for the occasional tourist. However, for scientists there became a need to standardize the name of the animal, or more specifically the species. Thus, Bauhin and later Linnaeus develop the binomial naming convention that we now use for animal species. Today the nomenclature – the rules – for the naming of animals is administered by the International Commission on Zoological Nomenclature. It is important to note here that the ICZN only establishes and manages the rules for naming, it only rarely gets involved in the actual taxonomy of a species or subspecies."

Dexter nodded, he had heard her explain the concept many times before. He knew all her beats and where he could prompt her to move in the direction he wanted. "But Merci, you're not a biologist, you're a professor of literature. What's your interest in such things?"

She bounced her head excitedly. "Only as a model for what can be thought of as a pseudo-taxonomy of literary monstrosities. Dr. McNally has done a comprehensive job of examining both vampire legends and literature, and developing a system for classifying the various tribes. Professor Lai has done something similar for serpent men, tracing their origin and transformation in literature through Lovecraft, Howard and Long. He's done something similar for monstrous pachyderms as well. I've attempted to go through the literature of the last two hundred years and develop a nomenclature of the creatures that dwell within weird fiction. It is immensely helpful, at least for literary critics, to be able to track down potential influences between one writer and others, particularly since some authors tend to try to conceal their borrowings."

"Could you give me an example?" Dexter knew that to get the information he wanted he would have to go through several steps. It was slow and methodical, but if he tried to push her too hard she would retreat, go silent for days. They could not afford that.

"If you look at what some of these authors have done, it's quite sublime. They've created monstrous things, inhuman, non-anthropocentric creatures that defy space-time, that defy logic, that defy biology and physics, and yet the one thing they have in common is that they are driven to give these things names. Bierce used the term the Damned Thing, Lovecraft coined the term the Unnamable, and Koontz used the phrase the Ancient Enemy. They gave these unreal, unspeakable horrors terms that could be used to identify them, proper nouns if not proper names. And this is where they were quite clever in their understanding of the scope of cosmic horror and what it truly means. What need would such things have with names? As if they needed them, as if they would communicate them to us. Does a human introduce himself to an ant?" She paused, but I knew the question was rhetorical. "It should have stopped there, but it didn't. Lovecraft and the others took the next step and did assign proper names to the monstrosities they created."

"Monsters with proper names?"

She paused for a second and then leaned back into her chair. "Lovecraft's Cthulhu." She seemed almost smug when she said it. "But that wasn't enough. Lovecraft may have invented Cthulhu, and even coined the name, but his literary heirs spawned dozens of copycat monsters, the spawn of Cthulhu so to speak. They include creatures like Tulu, Katullu, Kutullu, Cathulhu, Cthul, C'thlu, Ktulu, Icthultu, Uhluhtc, C'Thun, K'Chu, Char Gar Gothakon, Hydra-Stat, Pf'legmwad, Dagomon, and of course the sublime Kraken. There are numerous others, but these are the most important ones, and all of them are simply variations on the original. Under my system of nomenclature, they are known as Cthulhidae, alien squid gods."

"You have a system of nomenclature," Dexter interrupted, "for unnamable horrors?"

"There has to be a nomenclature," she insisted. "You can't just name things however you want. We need rules, without rules we would descend into chaos." She leaned forward and her eyes narrowed. "The names have all been assigned, terrible alien names. Where do you suppose they come from? Who names such things? Who would dare?"

She was beginning to ramble, to become lost in her own chaotic philosophy. He had to drag her back. "If I gave you a description of one of these monsters, do you think you could identify it? Merely as a test for your nomenclature."

She leaned back in her chair as a smug look crept across her face. "Almost certainly." She tapped her book. "I've built a kind of cladistic key into this." She flipped the faux volume open. "Ready when you are."

Dexter closed his eyes. "What about something described as a rolling bag of jelly."

Merci nodded and flipped through the book. The pages fell one after another as she searched for what she wanted. She mumbled as they fell, but it wasn't a mumble, it was a song, or at least a tune of some sort. Then with a sudden snap of her neck she looked up. "Something in the Shoggothiformes, I think. Tell me, do they whistle and fly?"

"They whistle, but they don't fly."

She nodded. "So not any of the polypidae. Do they produce inky black tentacles?"

"No, no appendages of any kind."

"Not a tsathaqquan then, and not that evolved either." She flipped a page and ran her finger down it. "Does it leave a trail of acid?"

Dexter moved to the edge of his seat. "Yes, and it devours everything organic in its path."

"Shoggothus brennani, a proto-shoggoth. They can grow quite large."

"How large?"

Merci consulted her notes. "Vast. The word titanic is often used."

Dexter sighed. "Do they have a weakness?"

"Electricity and fire will slow it down, but cold, extreme cold, will freeze it in place. I would avoid explosives of any sort. The explosions would only tear it into pieces that would then grow independently. You wouldn't want a whole army of ravenous little blobs swarming over your town." She slammed her book closed. "Also, according to the literature, the original creature is only semi-intelligent, reacting almost entirely on external stimuli like heat and movement. As it devours organic material, particularly animals it may develop a rudimentary intelligence. Absorption of large numbers of humans can result in a kind of malevolent, gestalt consciousness."

"Thank you, Merci," Dexter stood up and walked towards the door, "Thank you very much."

"What about my request for a transfer?" There was a sadness in her voice.

Dexter used a non-committal tone. "I'll see what I can do. In the meanwhile, keep working on your nomenclature. I think it's a very important piece of work."

Given a modicum of praise she beamed. "Thank you, Doctor Dexter, I do my best."

The heavily reinforced door closed behind him and one of the orderlies handed him a clipboard and a pen. "Did you hear any of that?" He eyed the orderly suspiciously.

The orderly was nervous, it was a standard question, routine, but he still didn't like it. "No sir. The white noise generator was flipped on just after you entered. Only she and you know the full content of your conversation." The end of his reply had a tone to it.

"You have something to add?"

The orderly looked down at the floor of the hallway. "She screams, Dr. Dexter. Mostly it's unintelligible, but sometimes I can understand her, the words – I think they're words. What do they mean? Who are these people she talks about? Lovecraft, King, Machen. It's all just nonsense, isn't it? She's just mad, right?"

He signed off on the log sheet and then scanned for his last entry. He had last been there three days earlier. He took a card and wrote two words on it SHOGGOTH and COLD. He tucked the card into his shirt pocket. "Yes, of course. She lives in an entirely made up world of monsters and maniacs. Mad doesn't begin to describe what she is." He paused and looked at the orderly. "Your name is Blake, isn't it?"

"Yes sir." He shuffled his feet nervously.

Dexter dug around in his jacket and pulled out a bottle of pills. "You're doing good work, Blake. Fine work. Important work. Merci is one of our most important assets. By keeping her safe, the human race just might survive." He shook the bottle and listened to the pills rattle. "Tonight, before you go to sleep, I want you to take all the pills in this bottle. They'll help you with the anxiety you feel in dealing with what you hear down here."

"Thank you, sir. I appreciate it."

"Not at all Blake, it's my job to make sure patients and staff are looked after." With that he excused himself and walked down the hall to the waiting elevator. The dull brass metal creaked as he ascended five floors, but Dexter hardly paid attention. He had other things to worry about.

On sub-level three the doors opened and he stepped out to be greeted by his personal assistant, Gedney, and Doctor Marsh. He took the card from his pocket and handed it to Gedney. "Take this to General Orne, and whatever you do, don't read it," he warned her. She nodded and nearly ran down the hall to the war room.

Marsh was looking at him in a very clinical fashion. "You all right?"

He shook his head. "No. I had to give my pills to Blake. He's beginning to hear her more clearly now, beginning to see her too I think. The psychic impression is just too massive. We're going to have to rotate him out soon."

Marsh nodded. "It's getting stronger then?"

Dexter nodded reluctantly. "The book looks twice the size as last month, and the letters on the cover are all there. I'm losing my grip. She may be growing stronger, or I may be growing weaker. Maybe both." He took a step and nearly stumbled, catching himself against the wall. "I need to forget."

Marsh produced a small vial of pills. "How long?" He seemed genuinely concerned, almost sympathetic.

"A week, maybe ten days." Dexter took the bottle and shook three pills into his hand. "You have no idea, Marsh. When she speaks it's as if she is opening your brain and forcing information into you. Each word is an encyclopedia, each sentence a world of information. If it wasn't for the pills…"

Marsh raised his hand. "I'm sorry, Dexter. I don't want to know. I can't afford to. The entire human race, twenty thousand people, depend on me staying sane and keeping you functional." He paused and let his colleague relax. "Take your pills and get some sleep. I'll brief you when you wake up, get you up to speed."

Dr. Ambrose Dexter, Chief Neurolibrarian for the last human army, watched Dr. Marsh rush away. Eventually he made his way toward the barracks and found his cot. There he waited for the pills to do their work. He didn't want to think of the trillions of people who had died as wave after wave of things had emerged from subterranean lairs, and seeped down from space, or risen from the ocean. He didn't want to think of the things that clambered outside the walls of the last city, the last asylum for mankind on Earth. They were things that crawled, and fed, and seethed with hatred. He didn't want to think of the woman in the cell below. Sometimes he regretted using the procedure, scanning the book and then encoding it into an organic data node. Sometimes, but then the pills took his memories away, and he no longer had to think about the unnamable thing that pretended to be a woman – and had even named herself. The name was wrong, of course, but the letters were there, almost, so close, so very close.

Thankfully, the nannites he had swallowed would soon begin to disassemble some of the RNA in his brain. In time, his memories of such things would cease to exist. He wouldn't have to remember, to know about the Nomenclature of Unnamable Things, the Book of the Laws of Naming the Dead, Merci C. Noonon, the Necronomicon - whatever she called herself. There were some things man was not meant to know. But in a moment or two he wouldn't even remember that. And for that, some forgotten part of him was grateful.

GOLDEN GIRL

by S. L. Edwards

I

Zack's favorite puppet was the one covered in gold. Kevin, however, found the thing distinctly unsettling. It had a bulbous, uneven head. Concave in some places, perfectly round in others, its only normal feature was its little chiseled face which looked just like a baby's. Its small mouth full of glinting tooth-fragments, some jagged and some square, but all of them yellow and rotten looking. Its absurdly round cheeks were painted gold to match its shimmering medieval clothes, face and clothing alike adorned with glittering, swirling patterns. Its eyes, however, were what transfixed Kevin.

They were a light brown, flecked with varying shades of light and dark greens. The milky whites around the green were lined with red silk-thin veins that seemed to have just the right amount of blood in them. The eyes darted irrationally up and down as the marionette bounced on the stage in jerking, animated cartoon motions. They did not seem painted on; more like the puppeteer had stuck glass orbs into the hollow wooden head and let them hang loose. While the puppet was small, the eyes were human-sized and gave the creature a haunting, diabolical look. Kevin thought the puppet belonged in a ghost town pawn shop, not in a children's show.

The stage was small, a three-foot-long, four-foot-tall structure with the jet-black curtain of a morbid kissing booth. Behind it, just poking above the edge of the curtain, were the head and shoulders of the puppeteer. Their shoulders were covered in something that looked like snow, while their face was covered in a mask just as disturbing the puppet's face.

The mask had, at one time, almost certainly been blank. Now it was covered in black and green glitter splotches; purple, pink and red heart stickers and streaks of yellow paint. It looked like a first-grade art project, made with all unreasoning recklessness of a child just discovering its own creativity. There was a thin red fabric that covered the mask's eyes and gave the puppeteer a bloody, feral look.

The puppeteer, in their strange regalia, gave each of their puppets a variation of the same awful screeching voice:

"I can do whatever I want! I am the Golden King and I am more powerful than anyone in the world."

The gold puppet's voice was grating, two pieces of shipwreck metal rubbing together along the bottom of an ocean chasm. Kevin was absolutely lost in the spectacle of the grotesque, nonsensical puppet show. Maybe that was all it was supposed to be, a spectacle for the kids. The juvenile audience sat around in a horde, a thick semicircle of folded hands in laps covered in jackets of all shades and textures. On all sides the vast semicircle was watched by a periphery of cautious, nervous adults.

Zack laughed and howled and pointed with all the other kids as more disturbing, distorted puppet figures leapt and danced on the black stage. There was a red dragon with centipede feet, a purple woman whose white face was painted with all the chaos of the puppeteer themself, along with various children and animals who gave stupid, irreverent lines that only contributed to the macabre insanity of the show. Each puppet had an unsettling mix of realism and absurdity that made Kevin cringe; human ears with all the fleshy irregularities, noses with nostrils of believable and unexaggerated curves, cheeks that looked like smooth little bee-stings. Innocence and a certain cherubic happiness were carved into the glistening tooth-smiles of each of the little puppets.

He looked up at the other parents, moms, dads and grandparents who also smiled uncomfortably at the stage. The plot, if there was any to speak of, was written in the magic of a madman who understood what it took to gain and hold the mesmerized attention of children. Adults, however, looked at the play, with its eerie dolls and black curtains, and saw only the deranged absurdity that existed only on the fringes of unrestrained art. Their smiles were pulled tight across their faces as they hissed in winter air between locked jaws. Their hands fiddled with hidden keys in pockets, and occasionally one would turn to the other and give an uncertain shrug and half-smile.

Kevin heard his little brother's laugh louder than the rest and smiled. He was happy he brought Zack to this thing.

Neither Kevin nor his mother had heard Zack laugh for months. When their dad died, Kevin had transferred to the local college. He planned to stay here a year and then transfer back. But mom couldn't give up work, couldn't be there as often as Kevin to help out with groceries, cleaning, and make sure that Zack was happy. Everything had been good until some little shit at Zack's school started picking on him out of the blue. Like a kid with autism and a dead dad didn't have enough problems. Kevin took a breath in, once again suppressing the fantasy of going down to Zack's kindergarten and telling his brother's teacher to cut the crap and do their job.

Bullying, coupled with the loss of their dad, pushed Zack into a morose silence that made him listless and unable to enjoy any aspect of life. Zack could spend days without saying anything, and whole nights crying without words. Kevin hated the familiarity of his brother's crying, the half-angry, half-tortured screams of a child who feels cruelty but does not understand it.

The gold puppet, Zack's favorite, held up a sign: The End.

Kevin sighed with the rest of the parents. The boys and girls clapped, chattered and yelled out in excitement as the puppeteer held up each puppet at a time so it could take a slow, unseemly bow. Lastly, the puppeteer stepped out from behind the curtain and took a bow themselves.

Herself.

The snow-colored shoulders revealed themselves to be part of a shining, pearl-colored dress that gleamed in the grey December sunlight. It was almost a gown, with little ribbons of different colors attached to it like ridiculous homecoming mums. The multicolored streamers were matched by a gigantic multi-colored necklace that hung around her neck like a Mardi Gras trophy. Kevin felt an involuntary nervous smile as he realized the metallic orbs around her neck were a rainbow of metal shrunken heads. The expressions on the heads were tight, dry and sour; as if they had been lifted straight from the pickle jar, dipped in acrylic paint and placed around her neck.

Despite the awful mask, the random streamers and the ghastly inappropriate head-necklace, Kevin could not stop the butterflies in his stomach. The kids seemed to like her too. She was short, but clearly built for the strange, over-the top dress that cut off just above her knees to reveal thin, ballerina-swan legs

She took off her mask.

Kevin felt blood numb the spot just behind his face, smiling out of reflex and surprise. She smiled too, with bright red lipstick and long, curly blonde hair that probably reached the V between her shoulder blades. Her smile… completely happy, so absorbed in a joyful moment that even the skeptical and grouchy grandparents smiled back at her. How young could she be, to be so unrestrained and strange? He clapped too, hoping not to get her attention, but simply caught up in the euphoria of children.

But, he clapped louder than he meant.

She looked into him and he felt something slide through his chest. Her eyes were blue, the color of the sky seen through a sheet of ice on a frozen lake. The kind of blue the fish must see in the winter; mesmerizing, freezing cold and alluring all at the same time. Her eyes could have gone on forever. Kevin reached up with his hand, scratched his head and pretended not to notice.

When he looked up, she smiled slyly with her red lipstick and perfect teeth, then looked down with unbridled enthusiasm at her adoring crowd. They were clamoring for her. She turned her attention to the kids, and Kevin breathed a sigh of relief.

He wasn't sure if he wanted to talk to any girl, he didn't want a reason to linger in town any longer than his family needed or wanted him there.

There were too many ghosts.

So as soon as he could, he persuaded Zack that they needed to go home. But he looked behind him as they left they left the park.

The puppeteer smiled at him, and he picked up his speed.

II

His nightmare was an uneven hell and paradise.

He could not see his own feet in the foggy, half-formed landscape that he dreamed in. He was walking on hills of grey gravel that he couldn't see, but he felt and heard tiny little rocks sliding under his feet. Fog wisped and curled around his feet like smoke snakes, ethereal tentacles reaching out from the darkness-soiled earth and licking him for just-a-taste. However, he was only disoriented, not frightened.

He walked forward, slowly and unsurely towards some unknown goal out there in the black. There was something in his flesh and in every joint that compelled him to move forward despite every rational inclination to do otherwise. He knew there was danger on this path, in this eerie dreamscape that was horrifying in how dismal and how big it was. There was something comforting in it too, like he was taking a walk somewhere in his past, or that this was the walk that he had been working for his whole life.

It was a walk that could end all his troubles.

Then the fog cleared, and Kevin stood face to face with the Gold King.

The puppet loomed over him; his bulbous eyes replaced by normal little brown ones lined on a pulsing, beating face. His entire head was throbbing like a purple, oversaturated heart. There was a wet, sloshing sound as a mouth opened wide to show fragmented, broken teeth that grinned against fat, gold-painted lips. Clawed, wooden-raked arms reached out and grabbed his shoulders.

A long, throbbing tongue lolled out of its mouth, and he could feel hot breath inches away from his face. He felt something scraping in his lungs, the ghost of a scream he was too paralyzed to make. There was a snake crushing his windpipe, his body shut down in a reflexive reaction against mortal fear.

He closed his eyes.

The hot breath went away. The long claws stopped tearing at his shoulders.

He opened his eyes. The puppeteer was there.

And her mask was her face.

III

Kevin's second time seeing the puppet show wasn't any less disturbing than his first. The park was full of wind, knife-biting cold rushing from miles away, shaking black-bone trees while maple brown leaves fell like rain onto grey, dirtied pavement. The kids bundled up in heavier, puffier jackets and sat and rioted in laughter around the dreadful black stage.

The puppeteer wore the mask again, the crazy hodgepodge of color and morbidity that had made a strong enough impression to leak into Kevin's dreams. He wondered though, her face was pretty, one of the prettiest he had seen in months. Why couldn't he dream of that instead of her mask? He shrugged the thought off; happy enough that Zack wanted to go again. It was hard to find things his little brother liked, and if the consequence was that Kevin was a little unsettled, so be it.

There were more puppets that day. There was a little boy in blue overalls and a feather hat, freckles painted on with a mix of orange-brown-red. There was woman in a long, black dress that melded into the curtain. Her mouth was wider than the others, the teeth more jagged like rough rocks swept by a tormented ocean. Her hair was taped on.

Then came the Gold King.

He seemed bigger this time; his crown had grown longer and more pointed like a stove-pipe hat with little bead-jewels on the tip. In some way that he couldn't define, Kevin thought the puppet looked older. The texture of the wood seemed marked with darker lines; his mouth seemed a narrower and his clothes greyer than when Kevin had seen the day before.

Then, the puppet looked at him.

The Gold King looked Kevin in the eye the entire time it was on stage. The eyes did not bounce and jostle like they did the day before, but stayed focused and level with inanimate curiosity and hatred. Kevin looked around; none of the nervous parents or bewitched children saw the intensity, the canine hunger in those eyes. They were redder than before, and as he observed this Kevin saw the little black centers get smaller. He shivered, unable to look away or even think while those dark, blood-brown eyes were fixated so rigidly on him.

Somewhere in the quiet outside of Kevin's existence, the play had ended. Snapping back to awareness, he watched each of the puppets take a bow. The red-faced children laughed and chortled while parents forced themselves to shrug off the uneasiness the play so easily inspired. Zack was slapping his hands together across a crossed lap and laughing in the almost forgotten chaos of childhood abandon.

Kevin looked to the stage.

Her mask was off, and her icy eyes were staring at him with the same intensity that her puppet had. He stood again, for all of the world feeling like he was crumbling apart. Nervousness, attraction, and a bit of fear boiled right beneath his throat. Her eyes weren't like the puppet's. They were the smiling, amused razors of someone playing with their food; something which knew, beyond the shadow of a doubt, that her funny little prey would never be able to get away.

* * *

Zack was loud, howling his sentences because he had trouble controlling his voice (especially when he was excited). He was practically jumping up down, reveling in the special attention that the puppeteer was giving him, asking all sorts of questions about where the puppets came from and what their lives were like off the stage.

She leaned against her stage relaxed, looking attentively at Zack for intervals and sneaking glances and smiles at Kevin when she could. Zack's questions had more than once ventured into the realm of ridiculously childish. But she had fantastic answers like, "They live in castles," and "Oh yes, they are married." Each puppet had a story and life off the stage like any other actor. The puppeteer clearly had an unbounded imagination, and it was this that must have echoed so well with the children when they watched her show. Restrained, stunted and worn by life, Kevin and the other adults could apparently only see a fraction of what she called "Art for children."

Finally, Zack asked a question that could be answered in grounded reality:

"How do you make them so real? The noses and stuff?"

The puppeteer grinned. Her lips were sweet-apple red, her teeth wickedly white, waiting to tear and rend between those soft, shining lips. Her mouth was half-cruel, half-playful as she put a hand on Zack's shoulder and answered: "They're real. I use spare people parts."

Her voice was serious but soft, a mother calmly lecturing her child to sleep.

Zack looked up at her, a little paler and a little quieter, "You hurt people?"

She laughed, "No, the people don't even miss them. It's like getting your appendix taken out." She poked at his stomach and his eyes lit up in terror, glinting over to a glazed embarrassment.

"Oh."

She lost his attention as he suddenly spun off through the crowd, shaking some kid in a black-puffy coat on his shoulders until the boy turned around. Zack talking to other kids… that was good.

"Thank you for talking to him. Zack is…" Kevin struggled, not wanting to people to unduly pity his little brother before they even gave him a chance, "A little different from other kids. It's been hard for us to get him laughing. So, thank you."

She quirked her head a little, a puppy confused at a new noise. "Every kid is different, but they all laugh at the same things."

Kevin was sure there was something profoundly artistic in that statement, but he did not want to look like an idiot trying to figure it out. He felt that instinctual, desperate pride a boy feels when he wants to impress a woman who is only half-interested; the desire to be as concise and intelligent as possible in fear of creating a conversational stumbling block that could bring down him.

"That was a cool trick," Kevin changed the subject "Making the eyes follow me the entire time. How did you do that?"

Her smile got a little wider, as if it couldn't get more genuine and happy, "The Gold King doesn't like me looking at other boys… especially when they have prettier eyes than he does."

Kevin was caught off guard.

"My eyes?"

"Yes…" she stared into them, and even though she did not raise a hand he felt a soft, warm palm against his cheek; drawing him in and forcing him to look back into the star-scattered lights of her blue eyes. He felt weaker, using everything in him not to move an inch while she kept speaking, "They're this beautiful grey-green… like aged jade… a very rare, very beautiful color of eye… one I haven't seen many times before… you must get that a lot."

Women liked his eyes, but rarely had they made him feel this unsure about them. He didn't know what to say; somehow her description sounded like the most poetic thing he had ever heard.

"Umm… thanks… you must be a good judge of eyes then, having such a good pair yourself." This, he felt, was the single stupidest thing that he had ever said.

He felt all the discomfort, jitteriness, anxiety that ended a long time ago with puberty. Primal adolescence was clawing at the back of his mind, and he hated every moment of it. Silently, mentally, he began hoping that God or Nature would intervene before he made a fool of himself.

Luckily, she didn't give him an opportunity, "You're a student?"

"Yeah, how did you know?"

"The only people in this town my age are students… the rest of them just apparently disappeared, an entire generation." Before he could fumble with another observation she added, "Because of this, I really don't have anyone to show me around my last night here."

"You're leaving?" There was only a little dismay and surprise in his voice.

"Two days from now, the morning after next."

"Well, I know there's a great Chinese restaurant…"

"Great, I'll be ready at 8 p.m. tomorrow night!" She said it with the mild enthusiasm of someone masking deeper, stronger emotions.

"Umm… great, see you then."

She did not turn around to acknowledge his last remark. Instead she turned away and began packing up her stage and puppets as if her sentence ended the matter conclusively. He liked that. While he chatted with the parents of whatever kid Zack talked to, he watched her carefully, lovingly put away her puppets into their little cases and folded stages.

She picked up the Gold King. The puppet's head dropped, tilted, and glared back at Kevin. She seemed surprised, putting a hand to her mouth and jumping a little before turning her own head to smile playfully at Kevin.

One wink and she turned back away.

His face was tingling.

If he had looked in a mirror, he would have looked just like one of her puppets.

IV

He couldn't sleep.

Kevin hadn't really had a relationship of any sort since his dad died. That had been eight months ago. He had thrown himself back into helping his family, taking Zack to kindergarten, finding part-time yard work on weekends to put a little money back into Christmas or doctor funds. He didn't want to take the time to think about himself, to worry about himself. It was easier to worry about others than for him to face the fact that he may be having a harder time than his little brother. After all, he had known dad longer than Zack had.

He was aware that he had regressed, turned back to a younger age when a girl would flutter her eyelashes and his insides would flutter back. He at once liked and hated this, not wanting to be a fool but also liking how innocent… no… how happy feeling this way made him. He wished he could have just had the date tonight, gotten it over with and taken whatever poisons or pleasures it would incur. Instead, he was restless in his bed at 2 a.m.

So, he would wait. He would wait until finally, somehow he managed to sleep. He would try to think of anything but her. Anything but the next day.

* * *

It felt like there were little hooks in his joints. He felt a burning pull behind his knees, in his shoulders and elbows as his arms laconically dragged beside him. Something held his eyelids open, peeled the all the way back so he could not miss a moment. He had gotten up from his bed, accepting that he was in a dream and not second-guessing his impulses, and half-dressed himself in boxers and a t shirt. With minimal movement he padded softly at the wooden stairs, opened the door slowly, and went out into the hours between night and dawn.

The world was different, vast and clouded so that he could only see a few feet in front of him. The ground was wet beneath his feet, grass and soil spotted with moisture that slid along under his soles like so many crushed night crawlers. He was cold, but not bothered. There was something for him at the end of this dream, something that would keep him warm.

Through the glinting of streetlights, he saw little stream-lines that walked and moved with him in the mist. They were fateful, tiny strings that moved next to him like all the friendly ghosts he so desperately missed. He felt hooks at his mouth and let a smile be pulled out of him. The painful hooks, the strings, he had accepted these things as good in his half-formed dream logic.

The mist was gone, and Kevin was in the park.

There was a trailer, a small and dingy white-and brown compartment from the 1980s attached to a red truck that kept on going despite all the age holding it back. There were smiling cat stickers on the trailer door, little rainbow puppies that said "Come in, come in," as Kevin went up the rough carpet stairs, pulled the door handle and walked through the bright threshold.

So many people were there. A woman in purple with a big smile, a little boy with freckles, another woman with a long black dress. They all were so welcoming; Kevin felt a pull at his wrist as his hand waved at them. A voice that was not his own fluttered from his lungs, "My name is Kevin, I am most pleased to help."

"Hi Kevin." The audience said back. "We are so glad to have you."

His head turned to the side, and Kevin saw the Gold King.

He was tall and gaunt now, head craned down close to his face so that the King's unwieldly crown would not scrape against the top of the trailer. The King's face was frowning and empty, with tar-bleeding eyeholes that wanted to swallow Kevin whole. The happiness, the easiness of the dream suddenly left him as the King craned away from the darkness that surrounded him, rattling and snapping with each lifeless movement It made. The light of trailer became darker, more dimmed and subdued as the King's face contorted into that of a vengeful torturer.

A cruel, evil smile hurt worse than any bite ever could.

Kevin fell down, backing away from the smiling faces of the onlookers as the King came closer and closer. He wanted to scream, but there was no string at his lungs to help the air escape. He felt warm all over, blood leaking from every part of him as the dream became worse and worse.

Without strings, he turned his neck around to see if there was any way out.

There was a dark, cavernous room. She was in there. Her white face was covered in glitter, hearts and streaks of ceremonial paint. She held something vaguely x-shaped in each of her two hands. Her arms were impossibly long. Her eyes were shadows.

Kevin managed to scream before something crushed his throat.

* * *

When Zack's mom took him to the puppet show the next day, she didn't seem too concerned about Kevin. She thought he "finally went out" and said, "He'll be back when we get home. He's just at school," and because she was confident about it, so was he. After all, she had the day off and really wanted to see what all the fuss was about. He had been frantically telling her about the show all this time, and he was happy to have his mother by his side. Not that he didn't love his brother, but Zack knew he was sad.

He could just tell.

Zack waited, static blood running through him and jolting his nerves to hyper-awareness while his mom sat with him, stroking his back lazily with her gloved hands. It was even colder today, but Zack didn't care that his nose was already numb.

He wanted to see the Gold King.

When the puppet came out, his mother stopped stroking his back. She was just like Kevin, he guessed, and couldn't understand why the play was happening to begin with.

But there was something different about the puppet today. Its clothes were brighter, paint more glowing and crown more regal than it had ever been before. There was something else too, a change that was lurking just behind the new paint and clothes that Zack didn't see but felt.

Until the Gold King looked at him.

Until it looked at him with sharp, grey-green eyes.

SCENES FROM A FORGOTTEN DIORAMA

by Brian O'Connell

1. – "one: dinner (1)". – (the first snapshot. a standard full-color digital photo, evidently taken fairly recently, with a black sharpie caption reading "one: dinner (1)" (hence previous – .). the image has some scratching/dusting, which leads to conclusions that a) they were added digitally b) this is a photograph taken of an original instead of being the original itself. image is otherwise surprisingly legible – :)

A scene of what we may presume to be a dining room, with four occupants engaging in relaxed household pleasures.

The diorama is occupied primarily by a long table. At first glance it appears this table is carved of actual wood, though we cannot be certain. A doily, or a doily-type object, is draped over it as a tablecloth. There are two chairs, one at the right head of the table and one at the left. At the right extremity of the diorama, behind the high-backed chair (wood again?) there is a large, plain door. There is a single window, and behind it is a drawing of a great forest, with thin black strokes for trees.

The green-yellow wallpaper has what we might assume to be a rough Fleur-de-Lys pattern, though determining the exact nature of the shapes – is – difficult. A light source, presumably coming from behind the camera, illuminates the four figures in stark relief.

At the left head of the table sits a female figure. We shall call her the Woman. She appears to be some sort of miniature doll, with a shining white face and little black ovals for eyes. If we look closely, we can see the dainty curve of a nose. The carving of this figure is that of a master. There is no mouth or lips. She wears a plain dress, probably made of lace, with little ornamentation. Her hair is long and auburn, and she wears a large black bow in it. There are joints at her elbows, which rest on the table, her left hand artfully placed on her cheek. She looks directly across to another figure sitting at the right head of the table. We shall call this figure the Man.

As opposed to the relative realism of the Woman, the Man seems to have been designed with slightly more "cartoonish" features. He is taller than the woman, with a long thin neck and a subtly hunched back. His face is a large oval, with a clear pointed nose and the same two black ovals for eyes, but there is still – no – mouth. His head is given no hair. He wears a tuxedo-like outfit and looks back at the Woman. His hands are placed one on top of the other on the table.

In front of the dining room table, towards the front of the diorama, are two small figures. One is much like the Woman, save she is smaller and has dark brown hair (we shall call this figure the Girl), and the other is also carved much in imitation of the Woman – though, while again smaller and with dark brown hair, the length of this figure's hair indicates that it is male. We shall call it the Boy, and he is dressed in a childlike sailor's outfit. The Girl and the Boy are crouched on the ground, playing with tiny toy blocks. The Boy (who is towards the right) seems to be reaching for a block, while the Girl (on the left) has her hand hovering over a stack of three.

Were it not for the somewhat exaggerated shadows rearing against the walls (undoubtedly caused by the warm lighting of the scene – presumably meant to affect candlelight), the diorama as it appears in this photo seems to depict, with charming efficacy, the quaint domestic life of a bygone age.

* * *

2. – "two: waiting (1)". – (second image. much like first in quality, dusting and scratching, &c. somewhat overexposed (see: – :). the black sharpie captions reads "two: waiting (1)" (hence &c.). – :)

The scene has changed somewhat from that described in "one: dinner (1)".

The doily-tablecloth has been removed from the dining room table. We can see it in the corner, folded. The lighting is brighter, perhaps meant to imitate daylight (as opposed to the candlelit atmosphere of "one: dinner (1)".

The Woman has pulled her chair from the previous scene's "dinner" in front of the table and is now facing forward. She is ever so slightly overexposed by the light, lending her a somewhat ethereal glow. She has a small, snowflake-like doily in her lap. Her right hand is raised gently in the air, the fingers pressed together, while her left hand rests on the doily. This, presumably, is meant to pantomime sewing or needlework.

There seems now to be something sad, or lonely, in her aspect – but – this is impossible, for the expression has not changed.

Still, the solitude of the scene gives off a sense of resigned isolation, broken only by the toy blocks still strewn on the ground, like discarded memories.

* * *

3. – "three: return, with the [illegible]". – (image number three, again, is much like the others in quality. caption reads (see prv.), but the last word seems so hastily written that it is illegible. guesses from close examination of both writing and the diorama scene depicted have given rise to guesses of "heartache", "mandrake", or (most probably, given below – .) "snowflake". – :)

We are back to the set-up of "one: dinner (1)": the doily-tablecloth, the candlelight-esque lighting, and the presence of four characters. However, there is a singular difference in the action of the scene.

The Woman sits in her usual place, and the Girl and the Boy crouch on the floor with their wooden blocks, but all attention is directed to the Man. He is literally entering the diorama through the open door at the right, one slender leg jutting out cartoonishly into the room, the upper half of his body leaning in. He wears a small hat (possibly a fedora) and his right hand, which is just beyond the door, seems to clutch onto something – possibly a briefcase. But in his left hand, the terminus of a long thin arm, he clutches a black – object – of some kind, looking to be cut out of cardboard or cardstock paper. It appears to be a large snowflake design of some kind, fairly simple in pattern, but obviously unusual in color and size. His stance gives off an air of surprise, probably something of excitement as well. The Boy and the Girl are looking at him (the Girl seems to be in the process of rising) in wonder.

The Woman, on the other hand, is quite different in attitude. While she, too, is surprised, there is nothing excited or joyous in the way her left hand delicately touches the space where her mouth would be. If anything, it gives off the impression of grief, shock, or alarm.

* * *

4. – "four: pre-coitus". – (see previous notes for comments on quality, caption is as – , &c. – :)

We are no longer in the dining room. While the wallpaper and positions of the door and window remain the same, it is quite clear that this is a different setting than that of the previous scenes.

The window reveals a large full moon, and this presumably provides the pale, ghostly lighting of this scene. There is no table nor tablecloth, but in the far-left corner there is a small bed, one with an ornate (real wood?) bedframe, a white sponge for a mattress, and sheaves of cloth for sheets. There are no pillows.

The Woman's bow had been removed, as has her lace dress. Her hair lies disheveled about her shoulders. She wears a large doily around her neck in affectation of a nightdress. We can see through the holes the shining curvature of her doll's body, sexless and smooth. Her legs are spread wide and obscene, her left hand tracing the edge of her thigh.

In the front center is the Man. He is naked, and faces the Woman. His body is featureless and white. There is no detail applied to musculature, curvature, or bodily organs. A curve of his leg hides his genital area from view. His tall frame is somewhat bent to avoid hitting the ceiling.

The Man and Woman are looking directly into each other's eyes, which (though they of course haven't changed) seem to harbor a touch of innocence mingled with hunger. Effects of shadow and light seem to exaggerate their forms, make them something grotesque.

It is hard to see in the half-light but on the floor, as if tossed there, is the black snowflake from the preceding scene. Its presence is incongruous in the context of the scene, almost jarring. One can only wonder why it was placed in the scene, and why in such a haphazard manner.

The single door is ever so slightly ajar, and, if we look very closely, we can just see the figure of either the Girl or the Boy peeking through the crack, observing the event unfolding in the dark room.

* * *

5. – "five: DREAM". – (radically different image quality than preceding images. red-tinted, the image is heavily distorted with a large black spot (see below – .). it is unclear whether these are issues with the original image or the digital image taken of the original (if the digital isn't the original itself?). it seems, however, more like photo manipulation than anything else – though why this would be done is unclear. image quality is profoundly less legible than in previous images. – :)

We are in a room.

It is unclear if this room is the same one depicted in the "bedroom" set of "four: pre-coitus", though the title suggests it may be so. But it may be prudent to assume that we are in an entirely separate room from any we have seen depicted before.

An impenetrable mass of blackness swells from the bed towards the window. Anything caught in its path is blotted out and impossible to view. It swallows the whole of the makeshift bed – indeed, most of the left side of the image – and some of the wall. The rest of the image is tinted a dark red and heavily distorted. Through the haze we can make out the contorted shape of the window, beyond which lies a moonless and starless night.

Towards the right of the picture is a hazy blur which we can vaguely identify as the Woman. Her arms are seemingly raised in the air and her head is thrown back, her hair disheveled. She is naked. It is – hard – to determine with the blur and the lack of expression, but it seems she is in some state of extreme terror, or perhaps exultation.

It is just at the door, now an impenetrable black hole, that we can make out the crouching, fetal figure of the Man, a dark object (presumably the snowflake) at his side, his face upturned in childlike curiosity or wonder at something just beyond the door.

* * *

6. – "six: terror". – (and we are back to standard image quality. title written as described, &c. – :)

We are back in (were we ever gone?) the bedroom set. The bright lighting, and lack of moon outside the window, show us that it is morning in the household.

The door is slightly ajar, but there is no sign of the Girl or the Boy. The snowflake lies on the ground much as it did in "four: pre-coitus", but it seems to have moved – somewhat – closer to the bed.

The Man and Woman lie next to each other in bed – the Woman on the right, the Man on the left – but their attitudes are much changed. The Man is sitting up straight in bed, his head turned directly to face the Woman. He appears very calm, almost taciturn.

The Woman, however, is evidently in a state of shock. Her arms are raised up in the air, her hands spread wide – we can assume this is the stance she took in "five: DREAM". It looks as if she is about to leap out of the bed.

Her alarmed state is probably due to the appearance of the Man. His eyes, you see, have been utterly whited-out, to the point of it being hard to distinguish if they were ever there in the first place.

* * *

7. – "seven: waiting (2)". – (quality as before, caption written as before, &c. – :)

A grim dawn in the "dining room" set of our first three scenes – particularly like that of "two: waiting (1)", perhaps explaining the similarity in "title". Grey light washes over everything, perhaps in imitation of a cloudy day. The doily-tablecloth is folded in the corner; the Woman sits in her usual seat, facing forward. She is still in her nightdress. There is no small doily in her lap, and her hand is not raised to indicate sewing.

She is instead hunched over, her head in her hands, as if she is sobbing inconsolably.

The Boy and the Girl are lying on their backs on the floor. The Boy is on the right, the Girl on the left. Their hands are joined. The blocks lie in between them, unused.

Through the window we can see the white, behatted head of the Man, still lacking in eyes, standing out starkly against the thick black brushstrokes of trees. Is he engaging in some activity outside? Is he watching the Woman, Girl, and Boy through the window? It is impossible to determine. It is – perhaps – notable, however, that, for the first time since its initial appearance in "four: return, with the [illegible]", the snowflake is entirely absent from the scene.

* * *

8. – "eight: return, with a snowfall". – (a curious merging of qualities that must have been the result of some manipulation. the left & center of image are standard, but the right is somewhat distorted like the fifth image. it is red, somewhat hazy, with little black flecks. caption as before. description provides better articulation, as always, of photo manipulation. – :)

The Woman is standing in front of her chair from the previous scene, both hands clapped over her mouth in an attitude of shock. The children's heads are turned towards the open door at the right extremity of the dining room set, which is wide open. Stepping through it is a figure which is identical in all respects to the Man, save that his frame has been painted ebony black from head to toe.

His stance is much like that in "three: return, with the [illegible]", but here he is surrounded by a dark red tint like the one that coated "five: DREAM". His figure is slightly distorted, like a mirage, waving in the heat. Little black flecks, possibly representing snowflakes, float about his legs. It is impossible to determine what he is thinking or feeling or doing. His right hand holds some type of long, thin pole, while his left is reaching over the table, fingers spread wide, like the hand of some dark, unnamable god.

9. – "nine: dinner (2)". – (radically different from any other images. while most had a crisp, if somewhat "transferred" (see comments on 1. – :), look to them, and two had a photo-manipulated aspect, this image is shot in a stark, gritty b&w. contrast is high and there is little midtone. scratching is less present but those distinctive black flecks from preceding image, possibly dusting, are. black sharpie, &c. – :)

We are in the dining room.

The scene is hard to make out, due to the harsh black-and-white. The door, and the surrounding area, is completely dark. Likewise, the window is entirely indiscernible. It is impossible to determine whether it is day or night.

The table is covered with the white doily. All other furniture is gone. There are two blocks placed at either end of the table, their arrangement bizarre, their purpose unknown.

Three objects have been placed at the center of the table. The only thing that we can determine is that they are round. Little doilies, about the size (perhaps a little larger) of the ones the Woman appeared to be "sewing" in "two: waiting (1)", have been placed over the objects. There is blackness hiding behind the holes, but what it conceals we cannot determine.

Two of the objects have been placed further back than the central one, which leans forward, rearing up like a half-remembered sheet ghost from childhood, a veiled bride.

At the right extremity, if we scan along the bright white floor, we can see a pointed object, like a foot or a shoe. It is connected to a long thin stalk, like a leg, before being absorbed into the darkness about the door. Is it the Man? What is he doing, and what has he done? What is he waiting for?

Such guesses are useless, in the end. There is an inky blackness swallowing the photograph, and the darkness beyond the door is impenetrable.

* * *

Some Closing Notes

– The digital photographs described were circulated around the Internet from about 2005-2007. We cannot determine who originally posted them, but it [...more...]

– By sheer coincidence, a woman found the (original?) photographs in her suburban attic in 2013, in a box labeled (with the distinctive black sharpie we have mentioned in our notes) "DO NOT [...more...]

– A search into the history of the house in which the digital photographs were found proved most fascinating, and more than a little disturbing, when viewed in context with (the photographs of) the diorama. According to our source, the house was once occupied by [...more...]

YOU CAN'T GO WRONG WITH GRASS-FED BEEF

by Jill Hand

Frank Rooney wrapped a flank steak in white butcher paper and handed it over the counter to Mrs. Ellis, whose hair was worn in a style that might have worked on someone twenty years younger but which wasn't doing her any favors.

"What else can I get you?" he asked her.

Mrs. Ellis looked up from her phone. "I was thinking about a rub. Casual Cooking magazine had something about rubs but I never tried one before."

Frank pursed his lips and thought about it. "You're grilling, right?"

Mrs. Ellis nodded. "Bill is."

Bill was her husband. From Labor Day to Memorial Day, weather permitting, he liked to cook outside on a hulking stainless steel Flame Pro gas grill that was nearly the size of a Volkswagen beetle.

Frank was a big, broad-shouldered man who wore his white hair in a neat ponytail. With friendly blue eyes behind little steel-rimmed glasses he resembled a jolly, beardless Santa Claus. He'd been at the Val U-King so long that he seemed as much a part of the place as the walls and the floors. Mrs. Ellis had known him since she was a Girl Scout selling cookies from a card table outside the store. Like all his longtime customers, she considered him to be almost a part of the family. It wasn't unusual for his customers to show him sonogram pictures of their yet-to-be-born babies, or to ask for his opinion on the pluses and minuses of in-ground sprinkler systems, or whether they should take out a loan to remodel the kitchen.

Frank straightened his bright blue vest with the nametag on the front that proclaimed him to be FRANK ROONEY, MANAGER.

"There're two kinds of rubs: wet and dry. For a flank steak, I'd recommend going with a dry rub. They're made of spices, like garlic powder, chili powder, cayenne pepper, oregano and so on. Do you guys like your meat spicy?"

"Bill does, I don't care for anything too hot," Mrs. Ellis told him, frowningly examining her iPhone. He daughter Olivia kept texting her, asking if she could borrow the car to go to the mall with her friend Shanna.

Mrs. Ellis texted back NO U DIDN'T CLEAN UR ROOM LIKE U SAID U WD.

"Okay, in that case you want to go easy on the chili powder and the cayenne pepper," Frank advised. "You'll find some complimentary recipe cards in the spice aisle. As I recall there's one for a rub that goes good with flank steak."

Mrs. Ellis put her phone away, having said all she was going to say to Olivia about letting her borrow the car so she and Shanna (who wore too much makeup and had a smart mouth on her in Mrs. Ellis' opinion) could go to the mall and flirt with boys. Her phone kept pinging insistently, but she ignored it as she listened to Frank's instructions for grilling a flank steak that had been massaged with herbs and spices.

"Once you're done rubbing it in, put the steak in a Ziploc bag and refrigerate it 'til about half an hour before Bill's ready to fire up the grill. Take it out and let it sit so it gets to be room temperature, then grill it for about four minutes on each side, depending on how rare you like your steak."

"Thanks, Frank, I'll let you know how it comes out," she told him, and rolled her shopping cart in the direction of the spice aisle.

* * *

Frank Rooney peeled off the clear vinyl disposable gloves he used to handle Mrs. Ellis' flank steak and threw them in the trash, feeling glad to have been of service. Gary Esposito returned from his break and Frank turned the meat counter over to him.

"Any word from Tyler?" Gary asked as he struggled to tie the strings of his red apron around his considerable waist. Tyler Mikovsky was the assistant manager at the Val-U-King. He was a young up and comer with a degree in business management. It had looked like he'd be taking over as manager when Frank retired, but he hadn't shown up for work for three days now.

"Nope. Not a peep out of him."

"You think he's sick or something?"

Frank shrugged. "Who knows? Like I said, he didn't call."

"The rules say you gotta call if you're not coming in," said Gary, who was the local representative for the meat cutters union to which the Val-U Mart butchers belonged. Gary wouldn't have brought up that point to Frank, who was management, and therefore on the other side, but he didn't much care for Tyler, who'd chewed him out for parking his truck in front of the store instead of out back, on the cracked and pot-holed patch of asphalt where employees were supposed to park. If there was a black mark next to Mr. Eager Beaver Mikovsky's name, it served him right for being such a tight-ass.

"You gonna notify corporate?" Gary started shoveling crushed ice from a plastic bin with a silver-colored metal scoop into the display case where the crab legs and lobster tails were arrayed.

"No, I'm gonna call the cops and suggest they drag the lake."

The scoop halted in mid-plunge and Gary's thick eyebrows shot up toward his hairline. "Really?"

Frank sighed. "No, Gary," he said patiently. "I'm not calling the police. It just looks like he quit without bothering to give notice."

"You had me going there for a minute," Gary said, and went back to shoveling ice around the crustaceans.

Frank strolled toward the front of the store. On his way he picked up a fallen bag of pretzels and placed it back on the shelf. He directed a distracted-looking woman with a red-faced, screaming toddler riding in her shopping cart to where the frozen pie crusts were. As usual when he was at work, Frank felt a deep sense of satisfaction. He liked the familiar routine and how the place ran smoothly under his command. He'd started out in the grocery business when he was a kid, working in his father's store, where he learned the intricacies of cutting up cows and pigs and chickens into edible portions. He'd worked there until it closed, in 1976, when the gleaming new Val-U-King opened its doors and edged homely little Rooney's Family Market out of business. Frank was one of first employees hired at the new supermarket.

Three years later he was named assistant manager. Six years after that, he became manager when Art Buckhalter retired. He planned to remain as manager until they rolled him out on a gurney with a sheet pulled over his face, having dropped dead while selling lottery tickets, or while in the process of showing some green young cashier how to bag groceries the right way, so the bread didn't get squashed and all the heavy stuff wasn't in the same bag.

He went behind the customer service counter, where a cashier named Kimberly who'd recently come back from maternity leave was explaining to an irate man in a NY Yankees warmup jacket than the coupons for a dollar off a carton of Breyers ice cream were one per customer. Kim was looking frazzled (the baby had kept her up all night) so Frank stepped in and smoothed things over, confiding in a lowered voice, as if he were letting the man in on a tremendous secret, such as the location of the Lost

Dutchman's gold mine, that he could go out and put the ice cream he just bought in his car and come back in again and use the other coupon he'd been waving at poor, tired Kim to purchase another.

That done, he went into his cluttered office and closed the door. He had a phone call to make to corporate. It looked like his assistant manager had quit.

* * *

"But why can't you retire? I thought we were going to go on that Alaskan cruise with the Silvermans," his wife Marlene wailed that night, when Frank told her he was going to be staying on at the Val-U-King.

Frank loathed Wendy and Bruce Silverman, a retired couple whom Marlene had taken up with after she retired from working in the better dresses department at Shantz's department store a few months previously. Wendy never shut up, nattering endlessly about the weather, her bursitis, her youngest grandchild's toilet training, or whatever else came into her head. Bruce was intensely competitive and wore Frank out by aggressively comparing his car's gas mileage to Frank's, as well as the size of their respective flat-screen TVs, the cost of their snow blowers and every other item that he discovered both he and Frank owned. The idea of being trapped on a cruise ship for ten days with them while Wendy yakked and Bruce got out the retractable tape measure he carried with him everywhere to show Frank how his cabin was slightly larger than Frank's filled him with horror.

"I can't leave. There's nobody to take over. The guy who was going to do it quit," he told Marlene over the shrimp scampi she made for dinner. She'd wanted Frank to bring home some flank steak and was disappointed when he told her there wasn't any more. He'd sold the last piece to Mrs. Ellis.

"Can't they get someone else?" Marlene turned her gaze to a northern brown shrimp, which she angrily speared with her fork and conveyed to her mouth.

"Eventually, but for now I have to stay on," he said calmly, thinking how he'd dodged a bullet. The Alaskan cruise would be bad, but it wouldn't end there. The Silvermans were enthusiastic cruise-goers. There would be invitations to accompany them on trips aboard some gigantic floating beehive packed full of loutish, drunken hordes and their screaming children to see the Norwegian fjords, or the wonders of the Mediterranean or to experience Carnival in Rio de Janeiro.

Frank had neither liked nor disliked Tyler Mikovsky, his former assistant manager. He had no reason to kill him, other than the fact that he didn't want to retire. If he eliminated the young man who was going to take over his job he'd have to stay on. It was as simple as that.

He didn't think he could bear an endless string of days when there was nothing to do except wait for the mail and tag along with Marlene when she went shopping. He definitely didn't savor the prospect of bus trips to Atlantic City or to go leaf-peeping in New England that were sponsored by the senior center.

Tyler lived alone in a rented condo downtown. He'd confided to Frank that he was, as he put it, "in a relationship" with a woman who lived in Germany. They'd never met in person. Their interaction, whatever it consisted of, was carried out solely over the computer, leaving Frank to conclude that dating had changed radically from what it was like when he was single. He hadn't exactly been the Sheik of Araby, but he'd had personal contact with women whom he knew for a fact were real, and not some person inside the computer who might not even be a woman.

Tyler took the bus to and from work, so there was no problem of having to deal with his car being left in the employee lot behind the supermarket. Frank asked him to stay after closing, telling him only that there were some things that needed taking care of. He turned off the security cameras and walked him back to the meat department, talking casually about this and that. Tyler hadn't suspected a thing when Frank pointed underneath the shiny stainless steel table where they cut the meat and asked him to bend down and take a look.

The cleanup had been the worst part. Frank didn't mind the sight of blood (he'd grown up helping his dad cut up sides of beef, after all) but there had been a lot of blood when he whacked Tyler on the back of the head with a mallet, aiming for the spot where the young man's dark brown hair grew in a spiral. Some even got in Frank's mouth. He stoically spat it out into the stainless steel sink and went about turning Tyler into cuts of meat. He ground up what was left over into hamburger then got out the mop and bucket and bottle of industrial strength disinfectant. When he was done the meat department was sparkling clean, not a drop of blood anywhere, and Tyler Mikovsky was ready for consumption by Val-U-King's carnivorous customers.

That chore over, Frank changed into a clean white shirt he kept in his office. He balled up his blood-stained shirt and apron and threw them in the dumpster behind a nail salon that he passed on his way home. The whole thing took a little over two hours. He did not put in for overtime.

Murder, to his surprise and relief, was a whole lot easier than he thought it would be. That was good, because there would be another assistant manager sent to take Tyler's place and Frank was now certain he would be able to dispose of him, or her, just as competently. All it took was careful planning, a steady aim with a mallet, and some sharp knives and a meat-grinder.

"How'd the rub turn out with that flank steak?" he asked Mrs. Ellis the next time she came in.

"It turned out good, nice and tender. Bill said it was the best steak he ever ate," she said.

"You can't go wrong with grass-fed beef," Frank told her. He smiled, picturing Tyler down on all fours in a field with a herd of cows, chomping on grass. "What can I get you today? We've got some nice ribs."

ABETTOR

by Ruth Asch

The boxer's face is cracked
in a permanent half-smile.
He dresses the other to match it
 – mostly; a cheerful guy:
smaller than me
but he walks with the swagger
of one who has nothing to lose
            much to win.
Slings a black leather jacket
over his shoulder and grins
wider than usual.
"Won't be pretty" he warns
"But I won't beat him too bad."
"Promise?"
"Promise."

My dress is happy.
I keep my hoodless coat
held upon my head,
though the rain has stopped;
it puts one eye in darkness.

Has he noticed,
my smile awry –
    like his?

I want to flee,
but I'll need his strength
in the soot-smudged building
where a thief sleeps
toes twitching from his socks…
Up and up
the dust fringed staircase.

Among his hoard
is buried my flute.

A WORK GROUP

by Peter J. Carter

The Collective stood quietly as a modern marvel. The Collective was composed of over 500,000 minds linked together in a gestalt that through "collective thinking" had solved all of man's problems. For not only did it contain the sum parts of minds linked together to form a formidable quantitative calculator, it used those bodies linked to it to perform tasks to benefit mankind.

A member of the Collective stood to one side of the courtroom. His/her ashen skin and bald head made their birth sex long unidentifiable. It stood ramrod straight on the black circle set aside for them. Its eyes, a hue of hazel, didn't move, but blinked at precise intervals and its skin was cold and hard like a piece of alabaster in the snow.

"This hearing is called to order. Will the accused, Charles Edmund Arbeider, please stand?"

"I am speaking to you Mr. Arbeider. Please, stand up." The judge, a slightly overweight septuagenarian, turned a slight color of pink.

A skinny man, whose thinning brown hair splayed across his eyebrows and threatened his eyes themselves, lounged back with his feet upon the table and had been looking at a blonde woman a few rows behind him. She had decided to cut her eyebrows off and replaced them with neon purple glitter and affixed some type of orange plastic box to her head. He was deep in thought about what compelled her fashion choices and not listening.

Now firmly in the judge's focus, he turned and pointed a lazy finger to his own chest.

"Yes, you, Mr. Arbeider, please stand up."

He pulled his shoes off the desk, leaving a mud caked edge behind, and drew himself up to his 6 foot five height.

"Mr. Arbeider, you stand accused of public sedition, social unrest and endangerment. How do you plead?"

"Okey-dokey, but that remains to be seen." A bright white smile splayed across his face.

The judge let out a small gust of air from his lungs.

"I'm sorry, the rules of the court demand that you plead either guilty or not guilty, and if you cannot or will not answer one way or that other, I will find you in contempt."

"Can I take that one?"

"Which one are you referring to?" The judge asked.

"I'll take the contempt one. It seems much better than the other two choices. 'Asides, contempt is closer akin to how I feel."

"Your feelings have nothing to do with this hearing. You have refused a court appointed representative, is this correct?" The judge gripped his gavel with whitened knuckles.

"That fella you sent to talk to me was kind'a skittish and seemed, I dunno, like a few of his marbles leaked out of the sack."

"You, Mr. Arbeider, made Mr. Golden feel quite bad and you left him in a somewhat emotional state." The judge released his death grip on his gavel.

"Somewhat, Judge? He was crying like a day old kitten. He told me that I was a bad person for what I did to those people and to throw myself on the mercy of the court, so I just asked him what his maw would think about him today, knowing mine would be proud of me."

"Questions about parental lineage were banned as hate speech twenty years ago. It looks as though you also refuse to use the prescribed skin toner, is this correct?"

"Well, this is the skin that God gave me. Darker than most, but suits me just fine."

The judge snatched the gavel from its well-worn spot on his desk and beat it down upon a hapless piece of maple.

"MR. ARBEIDER! You will refrain from using some fictional being from this conversation. Understood? It's been scientifically proven that God doesn't exist!"

"Did anybody tell him?"

"Who?"

"God. That He doesn't exist. Although, He is a pretty forgiving fella."

The Judge held up his thumbs and forefinger. "I'm this close to having you gagged, even though I will be removed from this bench."

"I'm beginning to think that your mom didn't give you any hugs either."

The judge emptied his lungs in exasperation and sat back in his chair. He sat quietly and tapped fingers on the arm of his chair.

"I'm sorry, Judge. I apologize for causing you grief. You seem like a good man."

After what seemed like minutes he spoke. "Alright, allow me to ask few questions and if you could answer me directly, I would appreciate it, Mr. Arbeider. I think we can get through this if you are honest with me."

"Yes, your honor."

"Do you think that you've done anything wrong?"

He scratched the top of his head. "No your honor, I don't rightly feel as though I have. I'm just acting how I was raised."

"Fine. Please enter in the proceedings that the defendant has entered a plea of not guilty. Now, Mr. Arbeider, if you could answer some questions for me, I think that we could maybe get to the bottom of this. On May 16th, did you use the men's room in Pryor's Square?"

"Why, yes sir, I did."

"You do know about the Transgender Bathroom Act of 2030?"

"Yes sir, I just kind or forgot. I live way out in the country farming. Out there we don't pay much attention to such silliness. Whoever came up with the idea for men to use the woman's room and women to use the men's room?"

"The Transgender Bathroom Act was initiated to make sure that everyone felt comfortable in the bathroom, transgender and historic alignment alike."

"Yeah, just always seemed silly to me. We only have one bathroom back home."

"If everyone has the same level of discomfort, it's equal."

"Why don't you fellas just leave the lights off? That'd make the blind people feel O.K. too."

The gavel smashed down.

"Let's just stay to the pertinent facts and save the diatribe."

"Who? I never bothered no Indians."

The gavel smashed again.

"It's Indigenous Homo sapiens. I meant commentary. Mr. Arbeider, there was a report that came in from commuter station nine that a young man was expressing his political opinion and that you interrupted him to disagree."

"Well you see, your Honor, he was going on about pets being slaves back in the day. I was telling him that back when we were allowed to have them, they were like partners and part of the family. I remember one time back in '03, a fire started in the back-house and our dog, Rick..."

"Stop! Mr. Arbeider."

The judge placed both hands firmly against his eyes before releasing them.

"Did you know that it is against the law for you to offer an opposing political view within 30 feet of another person?"

"Yessir, I just thought that he should know that it wasn't always a bad thing."

"The last complaint we have is the most heinous of all, rape. Did you or did you not assault a diverse gender individual on May 30, 2062?"

"Helping that woman up? I was walking through city square and this lady steps on one of those super kelp leaves you folks eat and she goes ass over teakettle and lands straight on her butt. I ran over and took her arm and helped her straight up. She looked at me like I was from outer space."

"You took her arm? I've heard enough." The judge banged the gavel twice. "I have no choice to find you guilty. You will be added to the Collective. Do you have anything to add before sentence is carried out?"

"Is that the place where all those people are kinda linked up and they speak their mind to each other?"

"It is, Mr. Arbeider."

"Well, I don't rightly fit around here anymore since you guys took my farm and put them robots on it, let's go."

The scientists at Worcester Poly Tech had to been waiting for fifteen months to submit their question to the Collective;

"In regards to our second generation poultry design, we have been using length-variant STR alleles to typically separate and genotype our comparison on an allelic ladder. Our hypothesis contains a newly devised library of cloned STR alleles. This library will cover alleles X and Y for the sex-determining locus and 163 other alleles for 13 autosomal STR loci. New primers already designed will be mapped for all these loci to construct recombinant plasmids so that the library retains core repeat elements of STR as well as 5'- and 3'-flanking sequences of ⊚500 base pairs. Since amplicons of commercial STR genotyping kits and systems developed in laboratories are usually distributed from 50 to <500 base pairs, this library could provide universal templates for allelic ladder preparation and ensure maximum output from future generations. What would a reasonable increase in production for the next ten generations, based on an 8-14 percent efficiency increase in design."

The Collective's answer was,

"Don't count your chickens until your eggs are hatched."

THE CLIFFSIDE TAVERN

by Sean M. Thompson

I pull the SUV to the side of *Old King's Highway*, and try to wait the heavier rain out. The drive's been treacherous, and I'm breathing heavy, keyed up with worry. I'm very glad I didn't drive the damn car into the guardrail blocking the road from a large drop into jagged rocks and a violently thrashing Atlantic ocean.

"Tony, babe, I love you… but you're a fucking asshole."

I give Greg the finger. It definitely wasn't a good idea going out in this weather, but God we were so stir crazy cooped up in that quaint little seaside hotel. Plus, we only have a few days left of our vacation!

The fault lies with yours truly, as I was the one who proposed we drive to Wellshore, even knowing the storm was only supposed to get worse.

I'd read about the township on an absolutely wonderful travel blog I kept up with: breathtakingly beautiful seaside cliffs, a few wonderful restaurants (serving, what else, seafood) but the town also has a rich history. Plus, it was only a half hour from the hotel.

I'm kicking myself; I think Greg was in the mood to fool around. That's probably why he's throwing such a hissy fit. He can be such a brat when he doesn't get his way.

"Calm down, we'll just wait until the rain eases up a bit, find a restaurant, grab food, then head back."

"Yeah, if you can get us back to the hotel without killing us."

"Oh shut up, I said I was sorry."

We wait for twenty minutes, Greg doing his usual passive aggressive routine, checking his phone. He doesn't make eye contact. I stare out the window, realizing the rain might not let up anytime soon. That's when I notice the old looking tavern, complete with hanging wooden sign, though the visibility's too poor to make out the name.

"Think you can wait a minute to eat."

"Why?"

"Because I just found a place."

"Oh yeah, and where's that?" Greg says, eyes still glued to his phone.

"Roughly three hundred feet away."

Greg finally looks up, squints. He scoffs, then smirks.

"Yes, sweet Jesus, let's go. I'm so fucking hungry I could kill someone."

I carefully navigate to the tavern's parking, an unpaved lot which doesn't a have a single other car. I can make out what the hanging wooden sign says now: *The Cliffside Tavern*. Greg's got a big dopey smile on his face. I love it when he grins like that. It means he's genuinely happy.

"You have an umbrella, right?"

Greg's smile falters a bit, and I answer him by reaching under the seat, and pulling out the navy umbrella I keep in the SUV for just such occasions.

"You're wonderful."

"Oh? What happened to me being a 'fucking asshole.'"

"You found me food, that's what happened."

He leans over and kisses me, tongue lightly caressing my own. His hand moves up my thigh. I stop him before he reaches the intended destination.

"Not here. Let's eat. When we get back to the hotel, then we can have some fun."

His face slides into an exaggerated pout.

"Okay. But I'm holding you to that."

"You ready?" I ask.

"Ready as I'm going to be."

I open the door, and hit the button on the umbrella, unfolding the nylon that snaps against the wind, threatening to buckle. Greg shouts something I can't make out over the howling gale and crashing surf. He finally points at the tavern, and we rush over to the entrance.

I open the old wooden door, weathered from years of moisture. Once inside, I fold the umbrella, and rub the rain out of my eyes.

"What we're you saying?" I ask.

"I was saying 'let's hurry up.'"

With time to catch my breath, I notice the tavern is pretty dark, lit only by candles, and a fire crackling inside an antiquated fireplace of stone. There's no patrons, save a bartender who looks to be in his eighties. A large grey beard stops at his chest, and his eyebrows are bushy over eyes dark blue. His hair is to his neck, a lighter grey than the beard, which he's tucked under a weathered, black fisherman's hat. I notice a peacoat, navy, just as beat up, hanging off a large fishing hook attached to a warped wooden beam. There's a strange look to the man, like he's surprised to actually see people inside the tavern. He very well may be on a day like this.

"Welcome to *The Cliffside*, gents. Look like ya could use a drink."

I'm about to protest, when Greg answers for us.

"Absolutely we could! Do you have any brandy?"

"Jesus Greg, really? I'm not made of money, you know."

The old bartender chuckles, his barrel chest heaving.

"Not too expensive here. I charge a fair price."

We walk over to the bar, and sit on wooden stools. The bartop is an enormous piece of driftwood. The bartender brings over a bottle of brandy in an ancient glass bottle, pulls the cork free with a pop. He proffers the bottle to Greg.

"Have a sniff of that, lad."

Greg leans in and inhales. His eyes close, and he sighs with pleasure.

"Oh, I'm definitely going to need some of that. If I have to, I'll pay you back tomorrow when I can hit an ATM."

"How much?" I ask, looking around for a drink list, a menu, anything that might hint at the prices at *The Cliffside*.

"For the brandy, the cost is six shillings."

Greg throws me an incredulous look, and I shrug my shoulders.

"So how much would that be in modern day dollars?" Greg asks.

"I only know shillings," the bartender says, and smiles without showing his teeth. There's a menace to the expression, like we've offended him somehow.

"Hey, Greg, over here one second," I say, and motion away from the bar.

Under my breath, I whisper, "This might be one of those historically accurate places where they don't break character. Just play along. We'll figure it out at the end. I have five hundred in cash on me, and I can't imagine it'll cost much more than that."

"You sure you don't want to confirm the prices?"

Greg looks concerned, and he shouldn't be. I remember I haven't told him about my promotion at work yet, and decide to keep it a secret until later.

"This'll be fun, come on. Let's stop being 'landlovers.'"

"I'm questioning your judgement after saying that."

I tickle his ribs, and he giggles. I know Greg hates it when I tickle him, but I think it's cute, so I do it a lot. We sit back on the stools at the bar, and I grab the old bartender by his beefy shoulder.

"Set Greg here a glass of that brandy!"

Right away I can tell I've really fucked up, could actually tell right as I touched the bartender and felt the muscles in his shoulders tense. His whole demeanor darkens, brows furrowing, eyes narrowing to slits. Even Greg, he so often aloof, senses the change and leans back from the bar.

"You're not going to want to touch me again, lad. Things don't go well for people who set their hands on me."

I'm debating grabbing Greg and just bolting from the place, when the bartender breaks into a big grin, exposing a mouth full of crooked and missing teeth.

"Oh, you should have seen your face, boy! White as a nun's ass ye was!"

The man laughs so loud I nearly fall off my stool. Greg is outright slapping the bar, tears streaming down his face. I can't seem to find any humor in the joke, myself. Something about the old man seemed very genuine when he was angry. I'm probably just being paranoid. My nerves are probably still on edge from the drive.

"Why don't you give me a glass of brandy while you're at it."

"Comin' right up, lad."

I catch a quick glimpse of the aggression underneath the old man's facade; a vulpine snarl as his eyes are shadowed. He turns from me, and I glance around the rest of the tavern. A painting of a boat on rough seas, waves crashing white foam under dense coal-dark storm clouds. A grey cat sits on the sill of a window which overlooks the steep cliff, and the tumultuous sea.

"Any chance we could sit at the table by the window? Seems like a great view."

"Not a problem, gents. I'll bring your drinks over."

Another flash of the predator beneath the friendly demeanor. I try to push my apprehension away. The view aids in distracting me quite nicely.

If anything the storm is way worse than I thought it was, the clouds above so grey they might as well be black. Almost as dark as the clouds in the painting.

The cat rubs against my leg, startling me, and I flinch. The cat hisses.

"Just Gertrude. Don't mind her. She's just a sour old thing, like her owner."

Lightning cracks across the sky, a few moments later thunder rumbling, cutting through the sound of the storm.

"You know, my grammy used to say thunder was the sound of God cracking his knuckles. She was always a bit touched, though. Used to sit on her rocking chair on the front porch during storms like this, cackling to herself, for what reason we could never rightly say."

Greg spins his index finger around his temple, and I kick him in the shin to get him to cut it out. This is hardly the time to be pissing off the old man. Especially when we're the only other people in his establishment.

"You have any menus?" I ask.

"Nope. We only serve four things. Fish, fish chowder, clam chowder, and clams."

"What kind of fish?" Greg says.

"Whatever the hell I catch," the old bartender says, and winks.

"So, like a white fish, or-"

"Haddock today."

"How's it prepared?"

"How I prepare it."

I take a tentative sip of brandy. It burns my throat terribly, and bites inside my stomach. A warm fuzzy feeling quickly fills my head, silencing the pain in my belly.

"I'll have the fish, and the fish chowder," I say.

"Good choice, lad. And what'll ye be havin'?

"I'll have the clam chowder to start, and the fish for a main course."

"Can we start with the soup?" I ask.

"Sure can, lad. Excellent choices, the lot. I'll be off to get your soups."

The bartender (who seems to obviously also be the owner) wanders through a door to the left of the bar.

"Shoot. I have to pee," I say.

"Hurry back, sexy."

I turn around, and slap my ass. Greg hoots, and laughs. We're such idiots sometimes.

I walk to the opposite end of the tavern. I find a door, unmarked, try the handle, and see it isn't locked. Find the bathroom is lit by a single candle. There's a crude wooden bowl, and from the sound it's clear the waste simply falls through a hole.

"A little too authentic," I say, but when in Rome.

I can't find a sink. I hope I haven't touched too many germs, and cross my fingers. I remember about the hand sanitizer in my raincoat, and apply a liberal dose to my palms.

Back to the table, I notice Greg is looking towards the kitchen. He seems really nervous.

"What's wrong?"

"I heard him scream back there."

"Who, the bartender?"

"Yeah."

"Maybe he cut himself, or saw a rat. God, I hope this place doesn't have rats…"

This time I hear it. A distinct scream, and it doesn't sound like the old man is in pain. He sounds positively furious. Maybe he injured himself, and deals with pain by yelling.

"You think we should go?" And just then the old man comes from the kitchen, two bowls of steaming soup in his hands.

"Okay gents, one fish chowder, and one clam chowder. I'll be off cooking the fish. If you'd like a refill, just holler."

With that he ventures back to the kitchen. I wonder what kind of setup he has back there if the place is going for authenticity. I take another sip of brandy, and try the fish chowder. It's easily the best I've had in my life. From the noises Greg makes, the clam chowder is equally delicious.

"Oh man, Tony, this is incredible. How's yours?"

"Also incredible."

We eat our soups in ecstatic silence, too wrapped up in flavors to talk. We've been dating for six years, besides. When you've been with someone long enough, you can go long stretches without speaking without it being awkward.

God, this soup is so good. I've lived in Massachusetts my entire adult life, have eaten seafood all over the state, and I think this is still the best.

I try to look up the name of this place on Yelp on my phone, to leave a glowing review. But I can't seem to find the tavern listed anywhere. I Google it, and still get no results.

This isn't really all that surprising, considering the bartender and presumed owner is older. It's easy to forget sometimes not everyone uses the internet, let alone review apps. But wait, if he had any customers, one of them was bound to write something about the place, especially with food this wonderful.

Another scream from the old man in the kitchen.

"Tony, you heard that… right?"

"Yeah. I did."

Both of our soups are sitting comfortably in stomach, and I'm quite torn. This place is really starting to creep me out, the owner in particular with his constant screaming. But this is seriously the best seafood I've ever eaten.

Greg bends down and pets Gertrude, who yowls in the manner of all elderly cats: a bit shrill, and exasperated. I sigh, and Greg downs the rest of his brandy.

The pervasive gloom truly sinks in now that the rush of being safe from the storm has ebbed. All at once this tavern is entirely too dark.

"I'm going to go in there and check on him," Greg says.

"What? No, don't."

"He sounds like he's having a hard time, maybe his wife passed recently or something."

"I didn't see a wedding ring," I say.

"Well maybe he took it off."

I've got the terrible sense something awful is in the kitchen. I can't pinpoint an exact reason for my premonition, yet every fiber of my being screams to leave a hundred on the table, and drive off. Go back to the hotel, maybe even get a bottle of champagne on the return trip. No food, no matter how delicious, is worth the tremors in my arms, and the pit opening in my stomach, which has nothing to do with digestion. Hairs on my forearm stand up like wind-rustled grass, a phantom fingernail tracing its way up my spine.

A heavy thud comes from the kitchen. Greg, who's been walking towards the room puts his hand to his mouth. He hurries to the table, grabs me by the arm.

"What? What is it?" I ask.

"There's blood coming from under the door."

The old man screams again, and there's no mistaking the rage now. Blood pools under the threshold, darker than the fake stuff I've seen in movies. Thick burgundy liquid oozes across the aged wooden floorboards. A copper tang permeates the air.

"I don't care if it's his, let's fucking go."

I grab Greg by the arm, and we run to the front. Heart palpitations seize in my chest. Greg grabs the handle, yanks the door open in a frenzy. Rain whips at us, as howling wind assaults our skin.

The door wrenches out of Greg's hand, and slams shut.

"Oh lads, ya haven't even had your main course yet."

I clutch Greg's hand tight.

The Old Man's eyes are white as lightning, corneas and pupils gone. His flesh is bluish grey, the pallor of a corpse ravaged by unforgiving salt sea. His hair is missing in patches on a rotting scalp, seaweed and barnacles attached to the remaining tangled strands.

"Afraid I haven't aged very gracefully, gents."

Greg turns and tries the door again, yells in frustration when it won't move an iota.

"Let us go," I say.

Greg's hyperventilating. I don't blame him.

"Come back and sit down, lads. I've already had a bit of a row with my last patron."

The old tavern owner grabs us by the arms, and drags us to the table. Empty bowls and half-filled cups of brandy litter the wood like lost skeletons. The old bartender/ owner/ whatever the fuck plops down onto a chair he drags over, and I hear the sodden squishing of what I pray are just wet clothes.

"What are you?" Greg asks. He's voicing the very question on my lips.

"Why, I'm the owner of this tavern. What else would I be?"

"You're a ghost," I say.

"Ah, that's where you're wrong. I am corporeal. Observe."

His palm slams across my cheek with a liquid smack. Rotting, water-ravaged skin sticks to my face from the impact. Everything momentarily filters in and out of focus. As my equilibrium recovers, I rush a hand to my cheek, retch and wipe chunks of the old man's putrefied flesh from my face. With sheer force of will I keep from vomiting.

Greg's crying, doing his best to stay calm. I lock eyes with him, tears streaming down my face, and wish I could figure out a way to escape.

"Now, now, boy-o, no use blubberin'. Would you like some more libations?"

"I don't–" Greg begins to say.

"I SAID DO YE WANT SOME MORE FUCKIN' ALCOHOL?!"

"Yes, yes, that would be fine," Greg says, his voice cracking with raw emotion.

"Oh, boo hoo to you, you're like a wee baby, lad. Worse than my mum, how she always blubbered on. Fit to be on the stage, that one. You know, I once caught her carrying on with a dead fella in the barn when I come back from a few months at sea?"

I have no idea how to respond. I don't want to die. This is supposed to be our vacation!

"It's downright disgusting, ya can say it. Ma's dancing a jig in Hell, probably polishin' the Devil's knob for a good Irish whisky and pipe tobacca. But ya can't pick your family, that's for damn sure."

The old man squelches off to the bar, and grabs the bottle of brandy. When he's turned I notice his shirt is riddled with holes, crabs scuttling in and out of his ocean-ravaged flesh.

He whips his head around, a crazed expression on his rotting gray-purple face. A quick burst of fear vocalized as our screams echo in the tavern. Blinding white eyes squeeze in mirth, then the old carcass does a sort of half dance towards us, his elbows rocking back and forth. The bottle's clutched in a drippy fist, fingers with bones exposed curled about the glass.

"Lot of folks don't understand the ocean is as enigmatical as a lunatic. I was a ripe old age, tavern was doing well. All I could ever want, I had. A place to feed folks, give 'em something to warm their guts… I was content to die a happy man."

He punctuates this by refilling our glasses, tips the bottle to his lips and glugs down the rest. Amber liquid siphons out the lower half of his shirt.

"A storm come, worse than this. Much worse. Wind so strong it threw horses clean across fields, tore the roofs off houses. Was closing the tavern, desperate to make it home, make sure my house was still in one piece. Anyway, I'm cleaning up when this gentleman comes in, looks like a sailor. Old fella, oldest man I've ever served. Man tells me he wants a drink. Fella's got a weird disposition."

The old man turns to Greg.

"You really should drink that, it's good brandy."

Greg hesitates, raises the glass slowly to his lips. The old man moans, and puts his hand under the glass to tip the brandy into Greg's mouth. He sputters out the first few sips, then gulps.

"That's a lad."

Liquor finished, Greg gasps for air, coughs. His eyes are blood-rimmed, full of sorrow like a beaten dog. I wish I was stronger, braver, just more in general.

The old man puts his decaying hand on my shoulder.

"I have to do the same to you, son?"

I swallow deeply, cringe as the booze burns my esophagus. Fight down the acid in my stomach as it threatens to organize a walk out.

A jellyfish falls out a fissure in the old man's cheek, and thumps to the floor.

"Well for fuck's sake… thought I'd got rid of them jellies."

"Please, let us go," I say.

"I'm not done with my story, boy. Don't interrupt me again. Got my favorite fish-guttin' knife in me pocket."

The tavern owner grabs each of our hands. What veins are left in his arms glow white hot fire through his dead muscles. Ocean water dribbles out his blue lips.

"Now this man, he tells me there are places the ocean goes living men can't. Says durin' rough storms, the sea opens up ways of terrible egress darker and deeper than those known. Tides which churn outside time, carryin' wayward souls from this world on black waves to hungry abominations that claw from haunted fathoms. The things I've seen, lads. Ya think the beasts in the Atlantic are terrifying, ye can't imagine how much larger and stranger such devils are in those shadowy depths. When the wind howls a banshee scream across the Lost Ocean, babies die in their mother's arms, and lovers make suicide pacts. Men flay themselves to bloody bone to chum the surf, longing to sink to the depths of a doomed sea, where abhorrent beasts dwell, too awful to view without succumbing to howling red madness."

The candles all burn out at once, the only light the dead tavern owner. Lightning traces him in the gloom, as he squeezes our hands tight as a constrictor. The wind screeches like prey in the death throes. The roof of the tavern rips off, the furious gale shrieking through belting rain.

"Lads, we're going to have so much fun," the old man shouts.

Black waves smash against Greg and I, knocking us to the floor, all the tables and chairs smashing against what remains of the walls. I blubber and swallow down seawater, try to grab Greg, but the water is too rough.

The old man laughs wildly, still clutching our hands as we're all washed off of the cliff. The free fall pulls my cheeks back, and as I stare at the approaching obsidian sea, my last living thought is:

At least we're dying together.

ONE EVENING IN WHITBRIDGE

by Scott Thomas

Whitbridge, Massachusetts, was anything but a cheery place, gray and faded as it was, and you might easily have thought it forgotten by the greater world beyond, for few people ever went there, and fewer still ever left. It was connected to the outside more by television signals and phone calls than by roads, for no one had bothered to make any major highways in the area. There had been no reason to. There was, of course, no airport, not even a train station, though tracks skirted the border. But the residents seemed resigned to their measure of isolation, content to sit in drab homes, penned in by dull November woods. They listened to the rumbling of passing trains without any desire to ride away on them.

Martin and his father Gabe lived on Turner Street at the western edge of town. The house, a modest thing built at the turn of the last century, had once been sound and painted white, but storms had plucked at the roof shingles, and the clapboards had weathered to an ashen shade. It was a magnet for mice. The nearest building was two-minutes distant by foot, an abandoned boxy structure with blank black eyes and a discolored sign that read: Grigg's Auto Repair.

It was Sunday, a chill afternoon that promised rain, and the two residents of the little house on Turner were busy tidying. They were to have company. There were few visitors now that Martin's mother was gone, and housework generally got away from them. Father and son were like two busy ants scurrying from room to room, the older one muttering curses as he battled cobwebs and dust.

Martin, who was seven, was sweeping. He hated sweeping or anything to do with cleaning, the dishes especially. He stopped and gave his father a pleading look.

"Does she have to come?"

Gabe was gruff. "Yes, she has to come."

Martin said, "But I don't like her. She has a stupid laugh, and her perfume makes me sick."

The father narrowed his eyes. "If you do anything to ruin this for me you'll find yourself in the shed."

Martin shrank. His gaze dropped to the floor where a spider, dragged out from hiding by the broom, was staggering out of a puff of dust.

"I'll be good."

The shed to which Gabe referred was a shabby upright rectangle of loose boards that a good wind might have kicked over. It was set back from the house there on the hill it shared with the larger structure. Down the scrubby slope, hidden behind leafless weeds and tangles of birch, railroad tracks stretched along the town's edge and curved off into mist.

Soon the house was in order and looked as handsome as a widowed plumber and a boy who hated cleaning could possibly make it. It was actually rather cozy, the whole first floor warmed by the smell of the homemade spaghetti sauce gurgling in the kitchen. The dining room table was set with three plates and even some candles that generally only saw use when thunderstorms or winter wrath knocked out the electricity.

Martin sat quietly, glumly, anticipating the dreaded sound of a knock on the door. He stared mournfully at the photograph of a 30-something woman hanging on the wall between two windows. She was pretty in a soulful way, her eyes a caring brown, her soft autumn hair curtaining pallor. The lips were set in a shy little smile. He remembered that mouth singing him to sleep when he was very small, comforting him on those nights when the close sound of passing trains woke and frightened him, sounds like a stampeding line of metallic bison.

"Why did you have to go and die?" Martin asked, but his mother did not reply.

* * *

It began to drizzle shortly before May Peregrine arrived. She parked by Martin's father's pickup in the dirt driveway, and trotted up the walk to the front entrance holding her purse over her head like an umbrella. Gabe spotted her out the window and ushered his son into the front hallway to join in greeting her. But something occurred to the man before he opened the door, and he dashed back into the dining room for a moment. He returned, took a deep breath, and gave Martin one last warning look before reaching for the knob.

"Hey, boys!" the woman gushed when the door swung open.

May came in like the bright, flowery season she was named for, an incongruous force considering the season. November, with its impassive gray face and patient expectation of snow, didn't know what to make of the woman. Neither did Martin. It was hard to say which was more jarring, her laugh, her perfume or the red of her dress.

Gabe was one big smile. "May, come in! My, you look pretty!"

It wasn't really a bad assessment. The features beneath the copious makeup were fairly appealing, though they lacked softness of spirit. Her hair was dark, done in a professional sort of helmet cut with severe bangs. The dress – announced more vividly when Gabe took her coat – evoked the sexy-enough business look Martin would have expected to see on a realtor. But that was fitting, because May, whose projecting disposition suggested that she had recovered well from her most recent divorce, spent her workdays selling used cars. Today she was, in a figurative sense, selling herself to the handsome widowed plumber.

Martin almost cringed when this loud, ambitious gust of a person turned her attention toward him. She mussed his hair, one of her scary plastic nails scraping his scalp. Close as she was, her perfume came upon him in a wave; insidious chemicals pretending to be flowers.

"So, how's my favorite little man doing?"

Martin mumbled, "Okay."

May looked over at Gabe and beamed. "Oh, he's crazy about me!"

* * *

Whitbridge in November had little use for the sun. The light seemed to tire easily, and it didn't last long enough to do much warming. There were no growing things to benefit from it, after all, and so it skulked off early in the evening, perhaps in search of some more appealing locale. The sky had dimmed noticeably by the time Gabe and Martin and their guest were seated at the table in the dining room.

Gabe may have been lacking in some domestic skills, but he was an able cook, and the sauce he had pained over proved as rich and hearty as its scent suggested. One would have mistaken the trio for a family the way they looked gathered about the meal in that homey scene with their faces warmed by candle glow, that same glow making little gold ghosts of the steam rising from their plates.

May never stopped talking, though Gabe didn't seem to mind. He never stopped staring. It was embarrassing, Martin thought. May might as well have been carrying on a conversation with herself, or doing a sales pitch. Every so often she would punctuate her monologue with a laugh that went into Martin's ear like an icicle. He wished that she would take her perfume and her laugh and just go away.

A low rumble came on the air and vibrated through the floor and walls, building as a train approached. Wine in glasses jiggled perceptibly and old windows rattled. The roar of the train – in a hurry to be somewhere other than Whitbridge – was not enough to drown out May's voice.

"Oh, you should have seen his face when I told him the price!" May said, punctuating shrilly.

Martin rolled his eyes and sighed. He looked over at the windows, at bleak November beyond, at a sky the color of drowned slate. His gaze fell on the picture hanging on the wall between the panes, and his mouth dropped open. The picture showed a younger version of Gabe clad in an army uniform, smiling handsomely with his hands on his hips. Martin slammed both fists on the table and flew up from his seat.

"You took her down! You took my mother's picture down!"

Now Gabe shot up from his own chair. He barked, "Shut up and sit down!"

Martin did not sit down. He shouted back, "I hate you! I hate you!"

Gabe pointed his finger as if it were a pistol and growled, "You're going in the shed!"

May, in a moment of uncharacteristic silence, watched bewildered as Gabe dragged Martin away by the arm.

* * *

Dimming air draped sullenly around the old house and the barren woods that hid the little town from the world outside. It was chill, clammy, the dead leaves underfoot more soggy than crisp. A softening jack-o-lantern squatted at the base of the shed watching their approach. Its withered grimace expressed sadness rather than menace, and its eyes were full of mold that could have passed for smoke. The shed loomed in the dusk like a vertical coffin.

"No, please! Please! I'll be good!" Martin begged, but dragging his feet and pleading proved futile.

Gabe was too angry to speak. He tugged his son across the yard to the shed, flicked up the eyehook, and wrenched open the rickety batten door. Hinges squealed. The interior was revealed, its tight confines suffused in shadow, the space vacant but for an old kitchen chair and a vague figure standing opposite it.

"No, please!"

Gabe released the boy's arm, and Martin staggered, nearly fell into the darkness that had been waiting for him. The door slammed shut with such fury that it was a wonder the shack didn't topple over or that some of the weary boards didn't drop off. Martin began to weep when he heard the familiar sound of the eyehook being latched.

* * *

Martin sat rigidly in the murky confines of his wooden dungeon, alone with a nameless shape. While he had been allowed to put on his winter coat, the moist atmosphere and even the stiff piece of furniture felt cold against him. The chair was a battered thing from the 50s with tubular metal legs. The red naugahyde of its seat and back had split in places, and a dulled viscera of padding showed in the wounds. Temperature and dampness and chair conspired to provide a measure of misery, but none proved as dreadful as his companion.

The effigy was a cruel work of art that Gabe had assembled when Martin became troublesome in the months following his mother's death. It stood as high as a man and was largely comprised of a grandfather's long black overcoat fitted over a wooden frame that was basically a cross on an x-shaped base. Its fingers, cheap steak knives drilled through the handles and fastened with wire, dangled from the limp, moth-worried sleeves. The worst of it was the head.

In truth there was no actual head but for the face, and that, reminiscent of a demon mask from a Japanese Noh drama, was painted black and had a hideous fang-crowded grin and metallic eyes that glared from under malevolent brows. Gabe, harkening to the muse of his desire to punish, had taken the time to paint tooth and stare in glittering supernatural silver.

The wall on Martin's right bore the shed's only window. It was small as windows go and filmed with webs like the ghosts of curtains. Enough light got in to show the awful figure, but at that hour of the day, and considering that it was a cloudy evening in November, the shadows were expanding by the minute. Almost purposefully expanding. Perhaps they had been whispering with the clamminess and the chilliness and the harshness of the chair and were eager to get in on the tormenting of their visitor. Martin wondered how long it would be before the voracious shadows entirely swallowed the little illumination that remained.

It's just a scarecrow, Martin thought, his eyes fixated on the thing standing against the opposite wall. But he was no more effective in getting himself to believe in the innocuousness of the figure than he had been the other times he had been sentenced to spend time with it. Denying what it was did not change what it was, because he knew it to be more than a ghastly oversized puppet, much more than simple painted wood and an old coat. It was the embodiment of all that was unfathomable, all the horrors of the unknown, the desolateness of death and loss, all that is menacing and malicious gathered into a monster with midnight for a heart and broken stars for teeth.

Martin told himself not to look, but how could he not? If he took his eyes away for a moment the horror would advance. So he sat there with his trembling fists held up against his chest staring at the glowering face as the multiplying shadows hid more and more of it, made the eyes glow more eerily against the deepening contrast. He wondered if he would die of fright before the monster had a chance to tear him apart with its metal talons.

Sound now joined the darkness and the dank air. It was distant at first, something between a rumble and metallic rasping. Knife-fingers began to clink against each other in an icy dance. The demon looked like it nodded, smiled wider as the earth began to hum palpably beneath Martin's feet. It was trembling, and it appeared closer, the shiny talons jangling. The noise grew louder and louder, a rusty roar that shook the shed and made the figure shake with fury. It was moving forward.

"No," Martin cried. "No!"

An unbroken rush of thunder filled the air, the vibrations so powerful that the demon swayed dizzily on its stand. At last it lunged, like a great raven swooping down toward the boy. Martin sprang up with a cry. He hit the door so hard that the eyehook gave and it flew open, the shrill voice of hinges a mockery of his own. The monster engulfed the battered red chair.

Martin ran panting, the night a blur of dusk and tears. The clamor of a train was everywhere, the lights of passenger car windows blinking behind the snared trees that tottered on the hill above the tracks. Martin pounded through dead leaves and crippled weeds, fast down the slope to where the line of silver-grey cars shrieked. He stopped short of the dark gravel mounded about the rails.

The boy stood breathless and teary as the last of the train came along. He looked up at it, felt the oil-scented heat of its wind pulling at him. The train was so very close that Martin could see into the lit compartments, close enough for him to see a 30-something woman with her face framed by the last window. She was pretty in a soulful way, her eyes a caring brown, her soft autumn hair curtaining pallor. Her sad gaze caught his for just a moment, and she waved with a pale hand as the train coursed away on the dusk-immersed tracks that led somewhere better than Whitbridge.

THE VELVETEEN VOLVO

by Nathan Carson

The streetcar spit Chip Jenkins onto a sidewalk littered with spent grey gum, then rolled away in a disgusted huff. Scents of Chinatown rode the summer night air, delicious sodium vapors on a bed of garbage with a garnish of urine. Chip ground his molars, hunched his shoulders, and dug his knuckles deep into his pants pockets. It had been a long day of honest work and he wasn't made for it.

The first check wouldn't roll in for another week and change. A single twenty burned a hole in his wallet. That bill had two potential fates: a cab ride most of the way out to deep Gresham where he lived with his girl and her ma, or a quick celebratory puff. After the day labor he'd endured, a metabolic cry for relief sent twinges through his lean muscled forearms.

Five minutes later he was flaming up a tiny rock in an alleyway and hoping light rail security were taking the night off since he could no longer afford the three-dollar fare. Buzzing now with eyes wide and pupils pinned, he started marching toward the tracks. He crisscrossed a parking lot full of weekend warrior rides, and stepped onto a dark street walled off by one long warehouse. From inside his shoulder bag came the muffled ringtone he'd grown to hate. Was it Ren or Stimpy? Only one way to find out.

He rolled his shoulder; the bag strap dropped into his sweaty palm. He unzipped and dug around, saying, "Yeah yeah," as if it was a baby insistent for a bottle, or his parents riffling through his room to steal back the pills he'd stolen from them in the first place. Finally out came the black plastic Tracfone. The screen read "Wren."

"What's up, baby?" Chip answered. He could picture his girlfriend's bug eyes popping from her skeletal face, her over-polished teeth chattering out of their receding gums.

"Are you fucking serious?" he asked. She was. Her ma was the landlady, and she was hauling his things out into the front yard. Chip called Wren Ren and her mother Stimpy because the latter was three hundred pounds and dumb as a set of truck balls. "Alright, alright. I'll get there as soon as I can. Just don't let anyone run off with my shit. Yeah I luv you too."

The meth surged in his system, crossing streams with a dose of adrenalin that left him sweating through his already stained wifebeater. Chip peered down the street, vision telescoping four long blocks to the MAX stop where he'd have to take a train and two separate buses. It was a forty-minute ride if everything panned out just right. Longer if it didn't. And a strong likelihood of being busted by transit cops along the way.

But there was another option. Chip cast his gaze along the block. Parking lot on one side. Warehouse on the other. Not much light. No people close. No cameras that he could see. Then he started scanning for cars. Too new, too new. He didn't have one of those mystery boxes that cracked security on anything modern. Too new, too new. Then he spotted it and started to smile.

Chip had grown up spoiled in Lake Oswego. Before his folks lost everything in 2008, they'd been big-time auto enthusiasts. Chip spent several summers in their four-car garage tinkering with his dad on European motors. That's why he recognized the Volvo 780 coupé for what it was.

To most, that car wouldn't look like much. It was a boxy 1990 sedan. Sure, the wire mesh wheels were a bit of a giveaway, but the red pearl metallic paint had been fading for twenty-seven years. The gas door was missing and so was the Bertone plaque. But cosmetics be damned, it was a turbo. Fast enough for Chip's purposes. The only question was if its antique security system still worked. He was willing to bet that it didn't.

Chip slipped a slim jim and screwdriver out of his shoulder bag. Casual. He leaned against the car like it was his own. Cool glass and metal against his back. A group of young Friday night scenesters in miniskirts and khakis howled down the next block. But none were looking his way. He slipped the lockout tool through a crack in the window and went to work. In seconds he was digging his bony ass into the velvety leather two-tone bucket seat and wrenching at the ignition with his screwdriver.

When the Volvo fired to life, so did its stereo set, blaringly loud. Chip's head jerked up in such a panic that he busted his nose open on the wooden dash inlay. He angled the rear view to get a look at himself. Red gushed down the front of his white shirt. Fuck.

It took three full revolutions of the volume knob to get the sound down low enough so he could think. He hit eject, and the old tape shot out into a pile of others, all of them covered in pentagrams and skull-faced demons. That total grandpa guitar rock that Chip always hated. He flung the tape out the window and stomped on the gas.

The Volvo was groggy at first. She'd expected to sleep for several more hours. No matter. She loved her owner and he loved her and she took him wherever he needed to go whenever he wanted to go there. Something seemed off tonight, though. Why was it so quiet? Where was the music that serenaded the neighborhood with the Sturm und Drang of her Swedish homeland? With each shifted gear she felt fear of the manic and irrational touch of a stranger. She was so afraid that she just drove wherever he steered.

Chip cruised over the Steel Bridge, constantly scanning for red and blues. For a beater with rust spots and a cracked dash, the car ran smooth and the turbo did its job. He figured whoever left it parked downtown might not come looking until bar-thirty. If Chip were lucky, the owner would be buzzed enough to wonder if he'd forgotten where he parked it in the first place.

Soon Chip was blasting through a residential neighborhood en route to the I-84. By now the Volvo was on to him. He tried to turn the wheel left toward the onramp but something went wrong with the steering. As he battled for control, they hopped a curb and clipped one of those big glass garden spheres. It shot like an eight-ball into a corner transformer, which erupted with a spectacular burst of electrical ozone outrage, leaving the wooden pole burning like a matchstick, thirty-foot tall.

"Jesus!" Chip cried. He kept trying to steer but it was no good. The car had its own agenda. The brake pedal wasn't working either. In no time they were cruising back up Burnside toward the bridge. Downtown where he'd come from was exactly where Chip did not want to go. He tried to open his door but the lock pinned down. He tried to roll down the window but it rose higher of its own accord, sealing him inside, emphasizing an unrepaired exhaust leak. The Volvo swerved and Chip's face smacked a blood smear onto the inner window. The obstacle they'd dodged was a school of boring silver fish economy cars waiting at a red light, which glowed unholy through the window's sheen of plasma.

The Volvo wanted nothing more than to return to the spot where she had been patiently waiting for her owner. If he got off work and she was missing, what would he do? Could he ever forgive her? Would he finally buy a new car and leave her for the junkyard? Break her down for spare parts? It was all so horrific and unthinkable that she raced up the bridge, heedless of the fact that it was starting to rise.

Chip felt like he was in a Robitussin nightmare. The dream went from bad to worse when the car's frontend shot sparks and clunked up the incline. The drawbridge was steep, but not too steep for the turbo to blast them both up, up, up, and finally right out into the yawning chasm of night sky.

He reached again for the door handle. This time the lock clicked up. The door swung open and Chip stared down into the abyss of the Willamette River far below. He slammed the door closed and tried to keep his stomach from doing vertigo carnival ride backflips. The car was hovering in the sky, wipers waving in fury, emergency flashers twinkling like a beacon. Chip's phone started ringing again. He reached for it, but his hands were now so slick with nose blood that he dropped it unanswered onto the floor of the back seat out of reach.

Helicopters were circling now. Searchlights revolved around the city skyline. The radio blared back on with the sound of midnight metal at maximum deafen. Out the back window down the long wing of the trunk, he thought he saw an AMC Gremlin creeping up from behind. The only thing Chip could think to do was turn the fucking car off. As he had no keys, he reached into the wire mass left hanging from his funky hotwire job and gave a solid tug. The engine died. The music stopped. And the car plummeted from the sky.

Chip locked his jaw and planted his feet on the ceiling, braced for impact. When it came, he found himself sitting on the sidewalk on the same Chinatown street where he'd first found the car. Nothing seemed changed. He looked down at his shirt. No blood. His phone rang in his bag. He was so confused that all he could do was answer it.

"Hello?" It was Wren, giving him the same spiel about Stimpy tossing all his shit out onto the lawn. "I'll be right there," he said, then hit the bitch button and tossed the phone back in his bag. The Volvo sat quiet in its spot on the dark street. Its window was still cracked just enough that he could easily fit his slim jim through.

His second trip didn't go any better.

When he found himself back on the same sidewalk, his phone rang. He answered, shouting, "I know I'm on my fucking way!" then hung up. He leaned against the Volvo to catch his breath then sprang back as you'd jump barefoot off hot desert asphalt. Time to find a new ride, he figured. He craned his neck to look up and down the block. Matching red pearl Volvos lined both sides of the street far as he could see. His vision blurred like the wavy lines in an old oscilloscope. He was having trouble controlling the horizontal and the vertical. Finally he stomped across the road and took one of the Volvos from over there.

The third trip went just as poorly.

When he opened his eyes he was back in the same spot. Before his phone could ring he pulled it from his bag and flung it, plastic shattering on the brick warehouse wall. "Fuck all of this," he said to himself and whichever Volvos might be listening.

Chip stormed off toward the MAX track. His fingers clutched in the air. The meth was dwindling in his system and there was nothing left to replace it. It was going to be a long ride out to Gresham, and he looked forward to nothing about the trip or what might be at the end of it. The Blue Line was rolling up just as he got there. A teenager dressed in black denim stood waiting with his ticket in hand. Chip never broke stride, muttering to himself while he plucked the ticket right out of the kid's grip. The teen started to protest. Chip crossed the track toward the Blue Line just as the Red Line plowed into him with the fury of a thousand vintage Volvos scorned.

ON

"Outre Non-limitations"

by Frederick J. Mayer

Inside bone covered in skin,
flesh wet so within;
floats upon grotesqueries,
realms of tainted sin

Inn corporeal without,
found sanity no doubt;
fine outer source purities,
mindless its about

Intercoursing skewed tissue,
folds embraces pew;
finite whorls monstrosities,
swirl Nunnery view

In holy out abjection,
ejaculation;
la petite mort heave,
death benediction

Inner Eye ON down mortal,
carnal pall vital;
fresh penetration heady,
boney sepulchral

Insight orbs cavern coves gate,
sleep dream die their fate;
science tells brain niceties,
peregrination state

Innocent grotto terra,
Massa damnata;
skull obscenities,
drain etched veve viscera

Inlaid jaded fair icons,
Plato's cave wrong gone;
strange limitless zone beauties,
exquisite beyond

Incognita lunacy,
undiluted be;
uptorn blood imageries,
cracked embalmed dome free

Infernal self-portrait bore,
finger paint ichor;
sacred offal nymphec seas,
await on you for…

THE KUMIHO QUESTION

by Frederick J. Mayer

> "Once upon a time, back in the
> beginning of an era… There was no one
> but you and me. Time after time we
> have been separated… I still believe
> in your flexible beauty, though you no
> longer have figure existing." – THE RED FOX

She was an Asian queen.

"'When The Tiger Smoked The Pipe', who can tell me what might be used for this opening in the 'West'?" was asked of the school-aged Korean children hunkered down silently around a young Westerner, tall with a well-built frame, healthy glow of a tan, blue eyed and ever so bland of a man; prytaneum for the slightly wavering flames within a near frigid winter's realm.

"'Once Upon A Time'", regally responded a sotto, reserved voice of an eidetical 13 years old obviously maturing girl, whose oversized eyeglasses reflected a looking glass clearness of the campfire's individualistic flames from the whole as if they were all trapped inside a magician's mysterious preternatural prison cells of prism crystal; all the while making her pretty eyes seem a rich cerulean hue. "Sunny" (her required selected English name) was constructed athletically like a ballerina with extra developed lean sculpted muscles in her thighs, upper arms and torso. Yet, she maintained an air of natural looseness of a perky kit.

The remains of this developing young thing appeared swallowed by a hungry living black space, the ancient stalking, encircling, encroaching Namsan evening maw… verges of darkness' uncoiling fog, moving pale seminal white carnivorous thick tendrils through bleak underbrush and sinisterly attractive barren limbs, looking much like "witches"of yore articulated, gnarled digits long yearning for lust fetishes not sated. But, the sky was brilliantly twinkling despite a stark robust moon and the inky vastness' cold embrace.

The Canadian trying desperately to be a star theatrical teacher, Todd Bennet, was adorned with a tad too large, little used rabbit outfit whose pelt revealed moth larva eating effects like active maggots to dying forgotten skin; and his "creative" attempt for the gathered students only made the fresh and shiny new instructor come off akin to someone who had flayed with crude cutting instruments the old carcass of "Harvey the Puka", while putting forth a pedestrian stab at wearing the faux hide.

"Who knows whom offered the traditional cured, long bamboo pipe to the tiger?" asked Todd. A smallish adolescent boy whose pimpled, puckered face reminded many of a puffed-up "Puffer fish" (to digest is poisonous) proudly announced, "'Tokkei', the fabled rabbit in the moon!", while pointing his pulpy baby fat still filled middle finger stiffly erect into the celestial bodied night. "See!"

Todd and the ever looming "living" group of bodies were part of a "Winter English Language Learning Camp" and one of its most appealing activities is spending an overnight stay in the Namsan ("South Mountain") woods. The mountain itself stands straight and alone in dead center megatropolis Seoul… places like tourist trap infamous "entertainment" providing Itaewon, the traditional/historic huge marketplace Namdaemun and other business/sports spots seem as malignant cancerous growths about its base. However, once above these continuing expanding, rising "civilized" physical domains, there exists its famed and, surprisingly, haunting, day or night, copse of wind-whipped grotesqueness of seemingly in death throes elongated boney trees; the night time seeks to hide, sequester the whole into a phenomenal pertinacious phantasmal place of beauty where the substances for faery tales reside.

The spectral twilight gleam was ushered out, replaced by a garish, sparkling, prurient aged, nocturnal neon hot allure; even the massive puree of fungal smog infested low-lying clouds could not dim it. This was notorious Itaewon-dong ("district") at "night"; merriment thrumming with mixed sensations of plain, basic, evermore, decay and vitality of Art.

> "…neighborhood has been terrorized by the depredations of certain but still unidentified animals of a blood-sucking propensity… there is a burrow like that of some fox or other like-sized animal." – OFFSPRING OF THE GRAVE, Clark Ashton Smith

"She's got claws, she's got claws, she's got claws / She makes me nervous / …with dreams in cold storage," the chilled wind carried with crystalline clarity a Gary Numan techno-pop, neo-classic's lyrics that were gushing out of THE BIG ELECTRIC CAT club and cascading over the customers of the STARLITE cafe/restaurant just down the way. Amid the smog tainted fog billowing, enshrouding that neighborhood nearest the eros of scatology brownish Han river and situated at the foot of South Mountain, the flapping of insidious chimeric things softly twirling in their flight within the light shadow of darkness; penetration, intercourse, entrance torn into the air-borne waspy paper wings by a pure silver stiletto sharp impaling point that sprang from within a delicately carved Asian folk tale dragon's cleft.

"Still another brutally savage, heinous serial slaying," came the dispassionate voice of outre Artist/Author Joseph Gordon as his Korean fir cane stylishly descended, polished to near shimmering serpentine-shape behind, retaining its piercing of the front page sheet of a popular Korean ilbo and the pleasant patio lighting of Starlite shown onto the newspaper's sordid red headline: "Namsan Ripper Reaps Another Liver!" Gordon's imported Chinese cigarettes, "Septwolves", smoke sensuously left from his flared nostrils and sardonic macerating orifice going upward to seemingly perform the ballet movement "Pas de Deux" with the thick steam arising from his tasty "bosintang" simmering inside the shearing flesh hot traditional stone bowl before him. "Perhaps, it's merely an augur doing his/her thing."

"Joseph! My niece is in the Namsan woods this very evening," in a particular striking protective paroxysm form, arose from his dinner partner Ryu Rei-ho. Gordon, whose thinning, wispy hair and balding scalp made his facial features and head resemble characteristic charcoal drawings of an aged Charles Baudelaire, took advantage of the pregnant pause he created and calmly sipped his cooling in the growing breeze "Suk Cha" tea (ancient Korea's version of the Decadent/Romantic 19th century poets' drink of choice), then stated, "According to all publically allowed accounts, the 'victims' were all males, not counting the several gutted of their vitals and partially devoured rabbits spewed about each slaughter site."

Changing the subject, Joseph mused about the deprecating virility of Itaewon's existing condition, "It's slightly nostalgically sad how this once gleefully wicked area seems to have a darkening shroud tightening, slowly wrapping around the eerily sultry old genius loci of the dong to the point of virtually smothering it… (Orison) 'let's pass through the grime, let's coruscate through the slime, roots suck the lesser spirit, let itself die for the greater clime'… can colors' verity be sense seen for their birthing greyness, growing sickly aura of mordant extenting outer morose reality?" Gordon's sudden sullen seriousness gained Rei-ho's complete focus. "The sublime odours of the dripping cleavages' and thighs' sweat perfume of bodies back to back, face to face on long standing meet/meat markets' dance floors, such as the nefarious KING CLUB, and of the freshly sliced, bleeding beef and melting fat broiling on irregular, small, white hot rocks and jagged smoldering purgatory coals of outside foodstands have become the double helix and dying genes of the sickeningly sweet Itaewon body."

Joseph didn't stop his observational rant, "The sullied air along its central drag no longer holds any scent of esoteric epicurean sexuality (the neighborhood never was a true "red light" district) and sybaritic, phlegmatic suspense of manifested danger, violence, even killing… 'Juicy bars and girls' shrivel as spent penises to the STARBUCKS' spores collecting about the original Itaewon strip as places where the creatures meet… the once 'backstreets' where true Korean eateries could be found have yielded to white collar Western worker upscale eating/drinking venues on the mountain side off the center thoroughfare, building yaw, stretching, retching evermore with their delectable flesh and blood fare towards the Namsan peak… the hideously beautiful flora of the South Mountainside house various things hidden, beings of the mountainous soil whose raison d'etre is to 'feed'; appetizing humans are on these secretly awaiting, horrible lurking secretory shadows, bestial connoisseurs' menu."

"She's not a shape shifting were-creature totally 'evil' fox-spirit unique to Korea!" reiterated Sunny as she and her classmate cum best friend "Ally" strove with a smooth, supple animalistically strong gait toward the pup-tents set-up for their Namsan experience. Ally's sleek, gymnastic physique made her physically similiar to Sunny, though, the glasses-less, moonless night colored eyes, precocious girl with emerging embonpoint, consistently had a relaxed composure while her girlfriend was Yin and Yang, a somewhat threatening pleasing two-in-one demeanor, much like her celebrity aunt. "I agree with you, you know that… Mr. Bennet didn't doubt you either. He simply was re-telling the KuMiHo ("Nine Tailed Fox") folk legend as it has been recounted by our ancestors for aeons before us and to them she/it (can be a male) was considered a 'monster', manifest evil, after all, she is the only Asian fox-spirit that eats a part of their human target."

Sunny stopped dead cold in her tracks, the wind wildly fingered her "Betty Page" bangs and appeared to actually to bare her canines, "How could she be thought evil? Buddhist lore says this creature achieved its status as a nine tailed fox because it had lived for 1,000 years and, consequently, is considered a divine 'celestial' fox. However, instead of ascending to 'Heaven', she chooses to remain on this earthly plane." Ally nonchalantly stared at eye level straight back, "Yes, but does she stay to help others of her kind? No. KuMiHo craves to become 'human' in flesh, blood and spirit; one of the two ways allowed for it to happen is to eat 100 human livers raw without her real nature being discovered." Ally displayed a racy grin. Sunny, "Ever eat a rabbit?" The two (often called as a pair, the sun and moon in tandem) interlocked their arms affectionately and strolled off whistling with the ebb and flow of the rising gusts of wind the melancholic theme of the South Korean television's hit limited series: FORBIDDEN LOVE, "KuMiHo."

The GRAND HYATT SEOUL hotel squats just below the permitted camping portions of Namsan territory and on many an evening the elegantly expensive hotel's (location is everything) noxiously loud man-generated sounds could drown out to a lesser or greater degree the natural aural emissions of the mountain's forest. It seemed only the country's legendary, black and white, message-bearing (in Korean faery tales) magpies' cawing could be heard above the temporary residents grand housing complex's din. A protesting of the housing establishment's un-natural existence within the birds' eternal residence on the mountainscape. It has been said that to hear the magpies' rackety song in the early morning hours brought good fortune and tidings to those who heard it or, at times, even a herald of sorts. Ironically, this cousin of the raven and crow sang a few days before for only the bleeding sans liver corpse that originally came desirously to the Hyatt's late night party scene and ended up laying upon soiled ground under one of the "magical", vociferous birds' tree top nests/home. So it all began.

Pedagogue Todd sat yoga style before the dying flames forming images of splattering blood as crimsons, scarlets and varied rubian tints, almost in slow-motion, exploded as in windy invisible fists, clenching and releasing in masturbating squeezes; so perceived the male educator's mind's eye. Coming, at this same moment in time, noisily in cut arterial-like spurts, depending on the strong palpating breezes' direction, the Hyatt's current purely "copy" band, which like others of its party hard till puking/dropping soundtrack ilk that made the "Asian Hotel Circuit", was incessantly pumping out music and sung lyrics. The language camp was partially awash, sprayed with a Jimi Hendrix classic, "Foxy, Foxy Lady / ...comin' to get ya!" Todd did not hear the words nor felt the sonic pounding beat. He was too engrossed with his ponderings caused by what some of his more outspoken students stated during the discussion/palavering period that came after his telling of one of the most arcane, endearing "Korean" legends, whose prime character's existence still was very much alive within the social belief fabric of the culture.

"KuMiHo, a malignant fox-spirit?" Sunny demanded accusingly with a vicious, almost virile snarl, "Would such a so-called monstrosity, given a choice, between achieving their centuries old goal, all consuming desire, passion, by eating the still 'alive' liver of their last required human being or letting that corporeal body live because she 'loves' him, hence, having to start her quest all over again, freely select the latter?" Ally, however, added, "A KuMiHo has no compunction to kill whatever may be a perceived threat to her or threatens to reveal her real vixen-self. Perhaps, it's the terribly nightmarish obscene means she remorsefully relieves her quarry of their livers that helped give rise to her more common horrid visage?" Todd vividly envisioned how KuMiHo could appear as a young wholesome attractive girl not much different than some the older ones in his group. Then, knowing the camp was in the excellent hands of the well-trained Korean teachers working with him, he stood, still in his threadbare rabbit suit, and, oddly, found himself going for a walk, as the night's coldness continuously got colder, midst the trees of Namsan at 3AM in a mindset that perambulated into an "enchanted forest" to encounter what awaited inside for him.

"The two shall be one,
and the outside
as the inside,
and the male with the female
neither male nor female"
-SCOND EPISTLE TO THE CORINTHIANS,
Clement of Rome

Ryu Rei-ho is formally South Korea's top nude model, first of her profession university degreed ("Modern Dance"); as the "Rei" in her name implies, she has an consanguinity who were part of the royal Tcho-Korean bloodline connected, supposedly, to the legendary Grand Queen Zee Rei and truly Gordon's soulmate, his "Other." Rei-ho's most striking feature nowadays is her hair, which is black as the fur of a Korean red fox's "socks" and it reaches down to her prime muscled haunches braided tight like a leather whip until near its end where it is divided into nine smaller braids like a cat-o-nine-tails (though she refers to them as her "nine tailed fox look") with an exquisite single animal painfully sharp talon attached to each; when a writhe whirling wind kisses them, they are melodic as the most dainty of Oriental wind chimes.

"Have you noticed," started Ryu, simultaneously her left hand's index finger released, as some feline paw, an acute pointed and forever lethal nail (a throwback to her Tcho-Tcho side of the family tree) that she cleverly used to ream the fleshy center of a still exuding life, brackish sea urchin whose fright riddled puckering was a simulacrum of an anus opening to her. Catching Gordon in mid-sentence, she slid the succulent sea creature into his gape, thus succinctly halting his flow of verbiage. As he munched, Rei-ho continued, "that as the juicy bars are on a financial decline, at least those who cater to the 'straight' set, the transgender establishments have been reaching outward like predatory suckers on sinewy cuttlefish tentacles off the euphemistically named 'Hooker' and 'Homo' hills onto the main drag of Itaewon, such as STARBUTTS?" As if precisely on cue, "Xanadu" (aka C. Vixsela Foxx) sidled up smiling at the now masticating couple.

"Livers," the exalted designer, Lord Scott B. Smith, currently residing in New Zealand but on vacation in the Republic of Korea, was slatheringly extolling the merits of their meal to his wife, Lady Jean Elizabeth, and some unseen audience, "at GECKO TERRACE (one of the more newly arrived marvelous thriving restaurants flourishing on the sidestreets, to Itaewon's mainstreet, that clung to Namsan like a promiscuous, deadly prolific poison ivy) are incomparable! They're so absolutely fresh and raw, a seemingly drooling suety blood and oozing interior fluids as liquid excrement. Perfection of ever so slightly grilled meat with cut and harvested a moment ago vegetables and copious helpings of deliciously whipped Korean potatoes to a rabid-like foam intermingled with potherbs, and sliced homemade butter floating, no, make that bleeding slowly from the/inside a distinct depressed crater."

The eloquent Lady Jean noted, "The potato 'design' reminds me of Jejudo's stunning formation 'Sangumburi'", while her well developed pinky in an assiduously adroit circulatory motion entered into a tantalizing spun tumulus from tubers in yellow, a gliding digit ascent arrived in the anticipatory spouse's mouth; there was too a thread thin rivulet over Scott's protuberant lip. "Do you recall our honeymoon on that mystically romantic isle? We stayed in Pyosan-si." Over suckling sounds of her mate, solidly and curvaceously built Lady Jean thought aurally, "It occurs to me that the multitude don't appreciate livers because of its odious odour when overly cooked." Gecko's gifted, unorthodox head chef Kim Rei-suk, whose specialties were the Smiths' liver offering and sundry exotic meat dishes, eased over to the couple's electric candle-lighted indoors table and, with a salacious salivary glint to her dark adapted eyes, gracefully inquired, "Enjoying the liver?" They embarrassingly nodded. The luscious legged woman in an immaculate white uniform of her profession, "Delightful. We got it just this morning." Kim politely departed; the Smiths soon followed suit, not quite corporeally satiated, for their Seoul Hyatt suite fearlessly and, no doubt due to the aphrodisiac effect of particular livers, feeling like frisky pups. "You look…""Good enough to eat?"

"Look what the dog dragged in," (Joseph murmured "cat") humorously spoken by Ryu as she stabbed with an ornate custom-made wooden toothpick the abdomens of several in their infancy "bungdaeki" sluggishly thrashing in a shallow porcelain bowl by her firm right hand. Xanadu glanced, "Those little buggers do stink," as she gently laid a rare 1st edition hardback of Gordon's premiere volume of verse, WHERE DOES THE REAL GO WHEN IT'S GONE?, down for him to autograph. She placed her August Rodin model's figure straight as a Kitsune phallic tail into a chair between her two comrades, bosom buddies. Xanadu's sleek artistic finger tapered with an acupuncture needle sharp nail languidly traced Ryu's nicely pronounced cheekbone (that and her ample, nutritious breasts harkened back to her Mongolian, pre-Korean line), "Most can't understand, but I know why you are so attracted to this small statured fellow…" Ryu inched up a cup of some boiling hot "Tazo Chai" tea (a rich blend of such spices as black pepper and star anise "in the style of the hill dwellers of the Himalayas") to her dear friend, "This will take the chill out of your bones' marrow…" "It's his 'Romantic' poetry, it sets free the female animal deep inside." The growing voracious winds seemed then to begin to howl.

"Please Xanadu, indulge yourself in some lovely tenderized Korean tits found on Namsan itself", mumbled Joseph as he continued to gnaw away on uncooked ginseng, swished in local red chili pepper laced with minutely diced slivers of numerous Oriental fungi paste. "Odd," reflected the renowned poet, "This mythical health root believed in a human form lacks a 'head'." Xanadu's shapely skull's sockets that held her almondish eyes, along with her, depending upon the light, ruddy dark skin, led many a South Korean to believe her of Asian stock. Actually, she was mainly of Native American lineage, the Pequot tribe (the "Fox People"); the tribal owners of the largest gambling facility in the world. She remembered how their FOXWOODS RESORT AND CASINO dubiously procured her a start to international stardom, "almost like a perverse faery tale come true."

> "There is no better way to know death
> than to link it with some licentious image."
> -M. DE SADE

"What's she doing?" Ryu with apt use of her hereditary index fingernails had with veteran butcher's skill skinned, dissected and dismembered a live cuttlefish with amazing aplomb. Now, she had several wiggling tentacles within her upwardly poised mouth, leisurely sucking them in and out; the waving forlorn looking items seem to wave good-bye as they were dispatched to their gastric finality. Joseph simply shrugged, "It's her Lloigor imitation." "Blasphemy?" "Not if you have a sense of humor," issued from Ryu Rei, even though she was, at the moment, drinking her beloved organic beverage." "A chaser?" came the Artist's quietly sardonic voice. Ignoring him, Ryu smirked and pointed out to the puzzled Xanadu, "Ever noticed those Lloigor and Zhar 'devil poles' are always in pairs and 'smiling'?" The former top nude model continued, "I'm the guest 'Star' (making the quote sign with her strong but willowish expressive fingers) hostess for the formal annual "Brotherhood of the Star Treader" gathering, which is being conducted this year at the famous Itaewon juicy bar RED FOX." Here Rei-ho passed with alacrity a metal bowl of Korean cold wheat noodles still moist and having a cuttlefish's form of liver, bladder, heart and ink sac, interestingly different for they sloshed slightly on top, to her close friend…"Some whisper in very hush hush tones, it's a front for an exclusive homosexual filiation club," the entertainer articulated clearly despite she had some sepia hued fluid drool down her left jaw. "No," came out of Ryu's subtle yet sublime in movement grin, "They're basically pan-sexual or asexual with male leanings. Dagon and devotees have their E.O.D. while Lloigor's followers have the Brotherhood."

"And the tales of unbridled objurgational lust for human sacrifices?" Rei-ho's second eyelids shot up revealing eyes, like polished black gem stones of the grave at midnight sans moonlight and stars, that bore straight into Xanadu's contacts that made hers seem as florid flaming glass from sherry red orbs… both locked in laser focus at each other's cranial caves. Joseph was still working on his peculiar root, though by now, he was roughly about just below where hips would be in human anatomy, when he broke in, "Xanadu, how's the Starbutts gig going?" Eye contact broken, she re-calculated her thoughts, then spoke, "Quite well, since 'Diamond Dogs' (name taken from the immediate album after David Bowie ended his Ziggy Stardust personage) became the house band, the clientele more than doubled and the place changed from a so called den of iniquity to a popular neighborhood hang-out that lures both the hip 'Straight' and 'Kinky'…

"As you probably know, the main bar and dance floor is situated in its cavernous basement grotto with the shadowy jet walls and ceiling being accruals of mainly Hannes Bok-ish and Gigeresque murals, some even explicitly executed by your friend "Koonude" (aka Stephen K. Morrison). We would always start with the club's regulars, flagitious gorgeous drag queens, sumptuously attractive female impersonators and in various stages trans-ops, crowding the front of our raised chrome performance platform that was thoroughly buffed with softest of shagreen. They would get most of the newbies, sweet young things, into their near hidden booths; it was like observing trap-door spiders snatching their prey in slo-mo." Some of those new comers were seen nevermore. Of course, there were forever the dancing souls lost onto themselves upon the Alicean mirror floor."

Shortly after her narrative and obeisance, "The 'Dark' is young and to be had!" androgynous Xanadu ambled through the swarming "fields that never die". Joseph, "My how her eel-skin boots effectively showcase her deliciously sexy shanks." Rei-ho had on her ankle length coat, a gift Dr. Koh Rei-am and his identical twin sister Ms.Koh Rei-mi, Esq., expressly had made for her; its inner lining was a magnificent blend of Arizonian hares' winter fur and extremely rare jackalope hair, while its outside covering was superbly tanned Occidental flesh with broad lapels and cuffs done with Asiatic skin that was embroidered with gold floss that created outrageous tantric arabesques of Zhar. "Sorry, my love, I must bid you adieu, but I do have an early morning rehearsal tomorrow." Ryu sauntered with a royal grace toward her home NAMSAN MANOR that was verily a set of multi-leveled Korean "villas" on the mountain slope, which she shared with her niece, sometimes others of her extended clan. Gordon couldn't hear the melodious tinkling of her braids due to the blustery winds, yet did hear the din again debouched from the Electric Cat club; snippets of lyrics of a Doors tune of old, "She's no drag, just watch the way she walks / She's a '21st' century fox."

The poet for a brief melancholic moment mused, "Will there be any 'Lived Happily Ever After' before daybreak?" Winds coldly churning, he was kept cozy by his jade green (like his long jaded eyes) wool turtleneck sweater, matching corduroy pants and East Indian gore boots. Abruptly the air as if entwined tendrils funneled down extinguishing, upon his particular table, the lit sandalwood scented candle inside a crystalline brandy sniffer. Thereafter, Joseph Gordon sat in the dark.

The woods' atmosphere was still as if the seconds ago March Hare winds just self-aborted. Rabbits abounded and laid mangled picturesquely about, unmercifully used to slake a gluttonous appetite. The largest, costumed Todd, was unceremoniously plopped into the rough bark crotch of an old double trunked Namsan tree. A hand with nails keen as a mad sotted surgeon's scalpel easily tore through the Canadian's attire to his up-ended rear and was in through his anal canal… twisted like a corkscrew within vitals to locate the liver… quick as pain was out, yanked along the entrance path now much widened aperture… two bites and gulp the black blood-sodden internal organ was swiftly gone as was the penetrator. Todd released a slow suggestive moan as he not as swiftly bled to death.

Heaven's golden eye arose as red and black ants, large and small, with other such carnivorous insects were entering, eating orderly inwards at any wet opening; little miners. The loving mother magpie regurgitated portions of a blue-eyed eyeball for her perpetually ravenous, shrieking offspring. Todd forevermore the proper environmentalist felt one must always "see that it's an organic two-way highway and one must give as well as take." That dawn of another "Land of the Morning Calm" day, the sun and moon could be seen together… like twin children, the duo gazed upon the abominable tableau, setting below.

"This may all be part of an ominous portentous depravity that is, perhaps, a sacrificial ritual," offered officer Won Dae-il, a slender, young yet with a dignified bearing male who is the top aide to the senior detective assigned the gruesome Namsan case, Inspector Park Ser-im, "Sir, we may be dealing not with an individual lunatic, or as the Americans are wont to say, 'One sick puppy', but a 'group.'" Park, a fortyish still in excellent athletic condition, who otherwise is a typical South Korean man that wouldn't stand-out in a normal Seoul situation/mob, "Great, just the logical speculation I need to hear," Park uttered in his strident voice. Then, came a tentative, but matter-a-fact professional vocalization through the Inspector's workroom door opening, "Sorry to intrude on you sir, but a Lord and Lady Smith have something directly affecting your immediate case, something I think you should hear straight from them." "Please escort them in with all proper protocol."

"We encountered a dreadful, macabre, nearly darkly burlesque scene at the crack of dawn today," said the normally staid Ladyship, "that was so deplorably debased…" she held herself with an unquestionable authoritarian stance, however, her facial muscles twitched as if caught in a blunt and unexpected gelid blast of air. "It was carrion, male, whose self had some craven eunuchist operation of the type typical of Scandinavia, performed horribly most foul." "Pardon?" Scott entered the conversation, having steadied Jean by having his arms tightly looped assuringly around his wife's waist, "What my dear partner is meaning to convey is quite a few ghoulish magpies had already had their way, circumscribed the poor fellow's corpse enjoyingly cawing and gormandizingly crude swallowing into their gullets the grisly delicious gourmand fowls' repast of his more tender, exposed parts, including the genitals. Unfortunately, one of them gliding directly overhead accidentally dropped a prized piece of gonad onto her uncovered head; my Jean first felt it was merely some glop of bird dropping… on closer inspection, it turned out to be a section of testicle matter that was similar in texture to mushy phlegm tainted with, dripping fresh rosy red blood that was meshing, sticking to her breeze-elongated hair." Lady Jean barely choked down rising tangy but also tastebud disgusting bile in her constricting repulsing throat. "How distasteful."

"The Lady Smith is being tended to as delicately as permissible in our officers' ladies' lounge" came Won's diplomatic disarming statement. Jean's pallor was becoming more degenerate and appearing sorely akin to rancid melted tallow; she couldn't rid her senses of the vile gore of a natural orgy by feathered feasters at a bountiful banquet. Such was the impact upon the dedicated voyeuristic ornithologist. Park asked in now perfunctory perfect English, "Why were you two up so early inside the Namsan woods?" "The best time to observe those divine Korean tits whose abode is Namsan is just as the sun assails the horizon." "Various fully grown tits are, by many, considered a delicacy. And, the Korean Master Chef Kim Rei-suk is internationally renown for her unparalleled ability to titillate even the most discerning/decadent or decorous palates with her unique meat concoctions."

"Oh yes indeed! We had the pleasure last night to savor one of her liver delights at Gecko Terrace, not to mention, meeting her personally." "Wonderful. So you were at that restaurant and met their head chef Kim?" "Until early morning and she never boasted, let her creation speak for itself, as they would say." "It's her special culinary talent to blend sauces and to keep mysterious what are her sources of quite exotic pieces of eatable flesh to the point of the diner loving the taste while never suspecting what the meat was in its once living state." "Truly you say?" "True. Take those tits of hers, her chef d'oeuvre; she prefers to emulate the exquisite French fine cuisine dish where they force feed another aerial creature till it's about to literally explode. Chef Kim does that to the tits you so love to watch here, however, what she keeps very secret is what exact kind of meat she overly stuffs into the birds. 'Old family recipe' she claims." Park with a grin liken to that of a cat who caught the proverbial canary continued, ""She originally hails from Jeju Island and the 'Rei' in her name signifies that, so it is believed by the islanders, her parentage bloodlinks descend from the Grand Queen Zee Rei… in past ages, the chef would have probably been a real life queen, hence, Kim's sobriquet: 'Asian Queen of Asiatic Cuisine.'"

"Curious," …Lord Smith had departed to help give some solace to his suffering consort and was informed, when everything settles, which encompassed Jean's particular innards, the female officer calming and cleaning-up the Lady's vomiting escapade with the porcelain goddess would transcribe the couple's statements for them to eventually sign… "There's a time discrepancy." Won postulated, "There is the Hyatt's guest who viewed the couple prancing and copulating in the buff or, as he quaintly expressed it, 'naked as Jay birds', around 4 a.m., thus the accounted for time could easily be that they discreetly went back to their rooms after their 'discovery' before getting in touch with us instead of themselves." "Performing a pagan ritual/fertility rite with a 'sacrifice,' like those 'Druids' in England?" "Don't believe so, sir. The Smiths are nudists who take pleasure in bird watching a la natural. Lady Smith simply can't reconcile holy serene savagery and the grotesque in beauty's gentleness; other animals don't possess a Snow White faery tale version of the nature of what is to be found in a sylvan environment… no duality, killing and loving/sex a whole, just is." "Very existential of them." "Sir?"

"The original plan for tonight. With help from the United States Armed Forces, main military base is conveniently right by the mountain, by allowing us to utilize their expertise and 'manpower', we are going to strangle Namsan. Our people will be unseen and nothing on two legs goes in or out without us being aware of their presence. By the book, no escape circumstances for this monster." "Sir, it's the 'Night of the Tokkei Moon.'"

"When you wish upon a star, makes no difference who you are," C.V. Foxx sang wistfully and low, in a voice whose vocal cords had encountered imbibed soju shots for far too many years. "A shooting star, quick make a wish," Foxx whispered softly to her partner in darkness' emotion for that night's revelry. So her nameless one did. "Ah, my sweet pimpollo, I always get a kick coming up this Namsan pathway to a very elite spiritual retreat because on the archway over its entrance in bold lettering it says, 'A place to get closer to god.'" "So?" "You don't know? Under it, from dusk to dawn, the ageing 'ladies of the night' ply their legendary ancient trade to those in passing cars." "Well, for me, you are my Sylph, a fabled ' faery of the air.'"

Binary star system, two as one as a lustfilled topological curiosity, an erotical double helix of pliable forms… Loviatar was the guardian spirit of the lovers entwined, porphyrians of lust and rhymes, sleek in sweat, suppurating spume, undulating licentiousness of the final orgy, connubial death, mystified obsession. 'Tis how they laid, attractive youth's clenched jawbone and C.V.'s now lubricated hand, serpentine motion along curvature of spine, entranceway, ecstatic convulsive convolutions, exploring your fingertips as snaken tongue rhythmically crawl into anal grotto aperture. Out again amid Namsan arboreal cove dripping blood, "A virgin… welcome," smoothly soothing came the words,"to the world of amorous 'fisting'." Blast of brightest light.

"You are under arrest"… "We're consenting adults, officer"… "For the Namsan deaths"… Inspector Park sighed, "Lucky me. I get one of the few on record female serial killers." Won, "Sir, 'she' was once physically a 'he'."

And so it ends? A slinking taut bulk observing contemplating feral eyes within shadows of trees and an artificial light, "Why do I so desire to be Homo sapien?" Rustling rabbit prey and an extraordinary large canine pursuer, fox.

I'VE LIVED IN THIS PLACE A LONG TIME

by Candace Wiggins

I've lived in this place a long time.

It's the perfect town for me, a university town, full up with sweet tarts and beefcake. Nobody notices me because the crowds are big enough for me to blend in. There are thousands of kids, children from all over, many of whom I resemble, almost all of them little more than fatted calves, full of Daddy's money and blue blood.

Myriad support systems are available for everything and everyone now in this li'l ol' Southern cow town. There are the arts – movies, culture, sports. Lots of sports. You're familiar with that song, "We built this city on rock and roll", aren't you? Well, it's the same thing only athletics is what built this place, trust me.

Museums. Bars, naturally. Coffee shops. Clubs. The boutiques catering to those sweet little college girls come and go like seasonal flowers. Some stand the test of time, some don't – just like those girls. There's nothing much more monstrous than a cheerleader in the autumn of her life unless, of course, she has married well.

Nobody notices me and I like that. When I go into the town itself, into the markets, the ubiquitous chains like Barnes & Noble, I go at odd hours so nobody sees me, nobody sees a pattern. If you look for me, nine times out of ten, I'm not there.

I always dress the same. I maintain a gray exterior – gray like an overcast sky and who notices that? Gray sweatshirts, gray tee shirts or, to switch it up and throw anyone on a possible trail off said trail, dark shirts and black jeans, a long scarf, a shapeless coat, a hoodie. I look like anybody else.

My hair isn't long, it isn't short. I don't wear anything on my white face that could be considered makeup, don't do anything that would attract real attention.

That's what I'm not about – attention. But sometimes, no matter how I give it the old college try, it's depressingly unavoidable.

I've lived in this place long enough that when certain older people see me, we recognize each other. It's inevitable. I see their fading eyes on me, recognition close to dawning in their now-ruined faces. Then, I can practically hear their internal conversations come to the proverbial ass-grinding halt as they tell themselves and then each other that I simply look familiar. I sense the palpitations as they convince themselves that I'm a member of some family that's lived here forever and ever, that family that's always been here, always will be here, someone from church, from the shops, from the neighborhood.

And as they turn away from me, I feel their sadness even as they talk themselves off that ledge, as they ignore that tingling of the spine, that first deeper whisper – the ol' what's wrong with this picture. Of course they know me.

They've been here all their lives and so have I. So have I. I've been here all their lives, too. But that very thing is often my salvation.

Who -? Who –? I can always feel their confusion – hell, I can see it – as they try not to stare. But they don't always manage that courtesy as their floundering mental state jacks up their blood pressure. That can't be her. Must be a relative. She's a type. She just looks like – her.

Oh yes, her. Her being me. That long-ago sweaty fumble in an alley between bars, that first experience in a dimly lit dorm room, that little experiment in the sorority house, that one-night stand, that spark of attraction that didn't seem to go anywhere, a date they can't quite remember. Or, if the fog of a memory rolls back in, they manage to convince themselves it's not real, it's a false memory, a messed-up memory, it was the alcohol, it was the drugs, it was – something else.

It wasn't me and I'm not her. I couldn't be, they tell themselves, they tell each other. Otherwise, they would soon find themselves staring into that abyss Nietzsche warned them about so long ago in some long-dead professor's class, only it wouldn't be the abyss staring back into them.

It would be me, ready to finish what I began so long ago. Ready to drain any one of them dry if only to relieve them from the rising gorge of horror that something unspeakable once held them in its arms, once clutched them in a bone-dry embrace. Something wrapped its limbs around their supple smooth warmth to top off its own cooling cup of existence. And that something was me.

Odd, isn't it? People yakkity yak about immortality like it's a given for those like me, whatever I am. Some say only gods and monsters are immortal and then only as long as they have followers. Here's the this about that.

You can forget religion and you might as well forget philosophy, too. Immortality isn't what it's cracked up to be. God or monster, you have to work damned hard to stay in this gossamered condition, a state of being that withstands the equally eternal threat of exposure and destruction.

Because, surprise, sugar pies, I could die, just like anyone else. I could die in a car wreck. But I doubt that I will. I could die in a fire. That's probably an even bigger not going to happen, but I'm not keeping score. I could be decapitated or even staked by some lucky bastard who, so far, is not even a blip on anyone's radar. If you can see your monsters on Svengoolie, why look for them anywhere else? That would take real work.

After all, I don't really exist. Rather, what I am, whatever that is, doesn't. Yet, here I am.

I don't get lonely. I don't boo fucking hoo over anything. I don't have regrets. I don't form bonds with others of my ilk, and what a stupid word that is.

Because if there were someone of my ilk around here, that ilk wouldn't last long, trust me. Territorial disputes would take care of that. Like an Old Testament god, I will allow no others before me.

And trust me when I tell you that I have found it necessary to go that god one better. I allow no others around me at all.

Plus, I don't need to keep people on a chain to take care of me, unless by taking care of me you mean they feed me.

I don't worry about anything but assuaging my hunger. That's what I live for, that's what I am really about, that's what I tend to on a daily basis. My hunger. Better than scratching what some call a terrifying itch, better than sex, better than chocolate. Appeasing that sensation, and then resting only to rise again to satisfy that eternal emptiness and resting once more before the next onslaught crashes down on me is my life, ad infinitum.

Do I regret it? No. Do I hate this whatever I am? No.

Why would I? I'm having a wonderful time.

Dogs do not fear me, they don't try to stop me or warn others of my presence or the dangers I trail in my wake – if anything, they love me because they know I love them. Cats ignore me but that's always been the case. If you don't feed them, you don't matter. You barely exist. How I understand that little truth. Survival, baby.

Garlic does not stop me. No matter how many times that story is spun, garlic does not stop me. And not only does the sun not stop me, I cast a reflection and I cast a shadow.

If I want something, I smile and before anyone can say no, before a single question is posited, before anyone's head clears, it's mine.

If I want to go into someone's home, I don't have to wait for an invitation. I break in just like any other thief. I float through the rooms like I belong, like I have the right to be there. It's a given, like the air. Like the temperature. The fine – or shabby – furniture.

If I show up while they're there and awake and they do invite me in, fine. Like I said, I look familiar to them. Where do I know her from? That girl from that family –

But I sidestep human interaction whenever possible. Can you blame me?

Because people are messy. They're nasty, full of conflict and confusion, brimming with the pus of manufactured melodrama which twists into very real problems for everyone involved. Humans drain me as much as I drain them, if you know what I mean and I think you do.

What do I do with the bodies? There are no bodies, sugar pie. How do you think this really works?

Come closer. I'll be happy to show you.

THE WHITE TERROR

A Weird Tale of the Victorian Age

by Frank Coffman

My name is Reginald Motherspaw, late of the Queen's Own Corps of Guides, Punjab Frontier Force. I had been commissioned with the rank of 1st Lieutenant Guides Cavalry straight out of Sandhurst and had taken command of a company of horse. I had been in India for several years, initially doing my part in the Second Afghan War. At the time of the occurrences I am about to relate, I had been elevated to the rank of Captain by field promotion at Ali Musjid while serving under General Charles Gough. My unit saw heavy action again later at Fattehabad and Sherpur.

But those are stories for another time. The following tale takes place years later in the autumn of the year 1896, prior to the fierce actions at Malakand and Landaki in '97. It might seem a small incident in itself, since relatively few lives were actually lost – and my report of the events also seems to be lost, or, perhaps, was never forwarded to the high command. Nonetheless, I will swear on my honour that the events of the story I am going to relate are true, amazing though they will seem.

We were stationed at a post just outside Lahore, and word came down that a detachment of horse was needed to proceed at once down the river to near Khairpur. Now this place is in the Sindh region south and west of the Punjab – although still in the Valley of the Indus – but it was extremely unusual for such a mission so far afield. After volunteering for the task, the only words of explanation given by Major Trevathan in his curt Cornish way was, "Some bad business down there. Reports of three dead. Curious circumstances. Report back promptly. Be back within a fortnight – unless there's something serious."

That order left scarcely a week at the outpost to have time to get to the place, investigate the matter, and return. I received a few more details from the major's orderly, Lieutenant Grimes, who could only add that three sepoys had, evidently, died in most unusual circumstances, and the commander of a small garrison had sent urgent messages requesting aid. What kind of aid was unclear.

I selected three of my most trusted men to travel along in this excursion: 2nd Lieutenant Dylan ap Griffith, a young officer who had proven himself worthy and a man of courage, Sgt. Major Alfred Smythe, who was as brave and tested a soldier as I have ever commanded, and the Jemadar of my company, Sandeep Singh. We led a group of twenty cavalrymen, more than half of whom were natives. The natives were under Sandeep Singh, who also acted as translator for the troops who knew little to no English.

The journey to the encampment which lay between Khairpur and the river, indeed within a short walk from the Indus itself, took three days of steady riding over not always the best terrain. I imagine my little troop looked splendid – at least at the beginning of our journey thence – in our khaki uniforms (the Guides had been Her Majesty's first unit to wear the new drab) trimmed with scarlet and our helmets adorned with puggarees in twists of an intricate pattern of light blue and gold, the turbans of the native troopers in the same bright hues. But we did not feel so very splendid. In the days, the heat was well over 100 degrees, and nights brought an amazingly sudden drop in temperature and a chill to the air, autumn being well underway.

When we arrived, the commanding officer of the garrison, a Lieutenant FitzGibbon, was immediately there to meet us.

"Thank God you've come!" he said, with the most perfunctory of salutes. "You won't believe what's happening. You'll have to see it for yourselves. I can't explain it. I've never seen the like."

"Slow down a bit, Lieutenant. And at ease," I answered, for the young man had realized his lack of decorum and was holding a second salute, seemingly without any intention of dropping his arm. I returned the salute again, very crisply so that he would desist, this having the desired effect. "Let us go over to your tent, and you can explain the matter fully. I understand there have been some deaths?"

"If you please, Sir, not my tent, but what serves us as a field hospital tent instead. I think you must see the bodies to understand the full gravity of these killings."

"Killings?" I replied. "Has anyone been apprehended or arrested?"

"There's no one to arrest, Sir. At least no man. And in trying to, as you say, "apprehend" the one responsible – I've lost two more men in the process," the Lieutenant responded.

"Two more men?" I replied, "How many are dead?"

"Five, Sir, five in all – so far – and one near death having lost an arm at the shoulder. But here – come! – you must see for yourself."

Upon entering the hospital tent, Lieutenant ap Griffith, Sergeant Smythe and I were confronted by the horrific enough sight of five blood-soaked sheets, clearly covering the bodies of the slain. One man was moaning softly on a cot in another corner of the tent, evidently, the one who had been maimed. Lieutenant FitzGibbon and the surgeon, a medic named Chambers, worked quickly to uncover the corpses for us to examine. Immediately, the young Welshman had to leave the tent. I could hear him becoming ill just outside.

But I do not fault the Lieutenant for his reaction. Both the sergeant and I each had to keep back our gorge at the sight revealed before us. Two of the bodies had seemingly been torn nearly in half, huge portions of their torsos removed past their rib cages and breast bones and into the remaining rib structures beyond. The body cavities were seemingly devoid of organs. One that had been a man was merely a torso and upper body, the legs and everything up through the hips having been, somehow, torn away. One body was missing the head and the right shoulder and arm. The last of the five dead, the one that Lieutenant FitzGibbon told us had briefly survived, had a gaping wound, a ghastly deep gash more than two feet in length, piercing deep into his chest and down through the abdomen. Upon this last corpse being turned partly over, it could be seen that a similarly huge deep gash had been cut into his back below the shoulder blade and down to the buttocks, exactly paralleling the wound on the front of his body.

"What the bloody Hell!" I exclaimed, cursing as I was not usually wont to do.

"Indeed, Sir, bloody Hell it is," replied FitzGibbon. "But it's almost twilight. We might be able to see the Thing again if we hurry to the river. It seems to appear – or arrive at least – when it's near dark. Mayhap we can kill it this time."

"It, Sir?" Sergeant Smythe questioned. "Exactly what is IT, if I may ask?" These were my thoughts exactly, and directly parallel to the question I quickly followed them by.

"I swear on my mother's grave, Sergeant," he answered, "there's no name for it. Captain, I have no idea. I've never even heard of such a thing or had any nightmares that come close. Come, let's go to the river."

I was – up to the point of seeing the bodies – at least hoping that there would be some rational explanation for these deaths. But this was inexplicable. Nothing in my experience could come close to imagining what could have caused such destruction – such total devastation to experienced fighting men as these five had, most assuredly, been. The dead looked worse than the victims of direct artillery fire, except that the horrific wounds were "cleaner" if one could use that word.

Upon nearing the Indus at a place where the river ran exceedingly wide, we could see an armed group of no fewer than two dozen soldiers, including, prominently, several dismounted lancers, although most of that company were armed with rifles. A lone junior officer stood with cavalry sabre drawn.

"Has it appeared again?" Lieutenant FitzGibbon shouted out as we neared.

"Nothing so far, Sir," the young officer replied. "And hope to God it won't. Except for what it did to my two men yesterday – except for what I saw – I still can't believe it. But if we can be ready for it at all, I think we must be this time."

The whole company on the shore scanned the waters of the Indus in the near and middle distance for what must have been only a few minutes, but which seemed like a much longer time. Suddenly FitzGibbon shouted out, "There! There off to the right – about 100 yards."

I strained to see what he might be referring to. And then I saw something. It was moving downstream, but faster than the current of the ancient river. And it was coming closer and closer to shore. As it closed, I could see what appeared to be a white, seemingly solid shape breaking the surface occasionally, then diving below, then surfacing again and undulating slightly as it moved closer and closer to the shore.

"Be ready men, be ready!" FitzGibbon commanded. "Let's kill the damned thing this time! Lancers to front! Rifles, fire at will."

Volley after volley of fire from the Martini-Enfields ripped the waters of the Indus and, seemingly, all around and, indeed, into the white form that swept closer and closer upon the waves. As soon as another cartridge could be reloaded into the breech, each rifle was swung into action and fired again. I have never seen any infantry fire, reload, and fire again with more rapidity and precision than these men did that night in the autumn gloaming along the shore of that storied stream.

Yet the creature came on. For creature it was, but from what creation or by what creator I dare not think on very deeply – even to this day. It was, indeed, a ghastly white in color, like the bodies of the dead in pictures of corpses. Awfully, it was a non-human white, for no flesh of man was ever of that pallid a hue – even in death. In truth, it seemed to have a sort of strange light from within, making it even starker white against the waters of that waning day.

When no more than a dozen yards from shore, the head of the thing arose from the water, and all our small company gasped in horror and amazement.

In length, the thing had to be more than thirty feet, and at least three feet in girth. It was, for want of a better term, an enormous worm, but no worm has the mouth, the eyes, and the teeth that this monster quite clearly had.

It exposed a gaping maw as wide as its enormous head. Three rows of two "eyes" were situated above that mouth set at differing distances apart, growing wider in between as they went back from the mouth. The eyes were of the deepest black – like onyx or obsidian, glowing like polished stones, but showing no iris or pupil. But the most appalling and disgusting thing about the beast was the teeth! There were only two, one upper and one lower, but each at least two feet wide. Quick as thought, my mind raced back to the wounds on the one soldier who had briefly survived an attack from this being out of Hell. Quick as thought again, I was back in the present, staring in awe at that hideous thing. The "skin" of the beast appeared to be beslimed and glistened in the half-light. (Dear Reader, my description above cannot hope to do justice to the horrific appearance of this creature. Its image is burned into my memory, but words must fail in any attempt to truly capture the experience. I hope I have done something to come close to the horror of the occasion of first seeing this monster.)

When it was within twenty yards of the shore, three brave lancers strode forth seeking to advance upon and impale the thing. The riflemen had hurriedly split into two small groups and moved outward left and right to the flanks so as to have clear lines of fire at the creature without shooting past or into their own men. Other lancers followed, and the brave Lieutenant FitzGibbon plunged into the water with his sword brandished high. His subordinate officer had collapsed to his knees blubbering, "It can't be real! I'm going mad! Oh, God!" He then fainted dead away.

Lieutenant ap Griffith and I had drawn our sabers, Sergeant Smythe was firing his new Webley Mark 1 revolver into the thing – aiming "at its head and down its throat," as he told me later.

Then, the worm rose up, or at least the front part of its segmented body did, and – though pierced by no fewer than four lances by this time – it dove down onto the screaming head of one of the lancers, a native Dravidian. And in one hideous chomp of those awful teeth, the upper part of the poor fellow's body was gone, quickly swallowed by the great worm, as the lower part of the body fell away! At that point, most of the men who had waded out into the river turned and fled as quickly as they could, leaving only the brave FitzGibbon and one lancer in the shallow waters directly before the beast, although ap Griffith, Smythe, and I were wading in to assist, and the riflemen on either side kept up their frenzy of fire.

Then, in one more swift movement – more quickly than one would have thought the great bulk could maneuver – the worm, angling in from the side, engulfed the torso of the gallant Lieutenant in its jaws. An instant later, I was holding what remained of FitzGibbon in my arms, his body, like two of those before, bitten almost in two by the beast. Horrible to see, he had not breathed his last quite yet, and he attempted to scream, but the sound was feeble. In a last whisper, he gasped out, "...must kill it! Mother!", and then he was gone.

The thing too was going, it's white back could be seen swimming off to the left and downstream. The rifles kept rattling. I had to give the order to "Cease Fire!" and then repeat it before the enraged soldiers stopped. The waters near the shore were slick and reddened. Some of the entrails from the two dead men floated on the gory surface near the shore. A full moon hung in the sky, and the waters appeared blacker and blacker as twilight gave way to a darkness bejeweled by a million stars. The beauty of the heavens was in stark contrast to the horrors that had just transpired below them.

Taking full command, I led the men back to the encampment and posted perimeter guards. Who knew but that maybe this monster could crawl also about on the land, as more familiar worms could. We had to be ready. I called ap Griffith, Smythe, and Singh into my tent, having taken the one previously occupied by poor FitzGibbon, to plan how we might proceed.

It seemed, as the events of the previous few days were related by the men and translated to us through Jemadar Singh, that the first three deaths had occurred as the soldiers were simply bathing in the shallows after the intense heat of the day. They had waded out yards from the shoreline and were calling to others of their troop who were planning to join them and were approaching the river. Suddenly, first one, then another, and then quickly the third were victims of this awful worm; the last attacked from behind as he was nearing the shore, the worm grabbing and ripping off his lower body and quickly departing with another morsel of its ghastly meal. This last man had cried out in Sindhi before the monster had him, "Dapa Dandu! Dapa Dandu!" I had only a slight familiarity with Punjabi, and knew nothing of the dialect of the Sindh, but I was told by one of the men who also knew some English that this meant something like "Terror Teeth" or "Terrible Teeth." If that was its meaning, it was most fitting.

According to their account, at twilight two days later, guards posted by the shore saw the creature well out into the river. It was decided that it might frequent the area, seemingly around sunset or late evening. It had returned to the spot, perhaps sensing that there might be more prey. The last two fatalities prior to their arrival had been the following evening, the day before our arrival. The junior officer, Lieutenant Edmonds had been posted by the river with a handful of soldiers on watch for the beast. It had arrived, come close again, and quickly killed two of the men who were shooting at it and throwing cavalry lances like harpoons.

"Do you have a plan, Sir?" asked Sergeant Smythe.

"I'm working on some ideas, Sergeant, but I'd welcome any thoughts. I'm still more than a bit shaken."

"My God!" said ap Griffith "What the Hell are we dealing with here? I know that the thing was hit by literally hundreds of rifle rounds. We saw it pierced by four or five lances, and poor FitzGibbon got in one slash with his saber that I saw."

"Indeed," I answered. "It seems a very worm in truth. Like the small ones of the earth, there must not be much that is vital within its spongelike form – or at least we haven't found such yet. But," I continued, "there are differences. It clearly has a defined head, but more importantly, it has eyes – and there are those monstrous teeth. In those ways, this is no worm."

I thought for a bit more, then suggested to my compatriots, "It is a thing of the water, it seems, and therefore I am hoping it cannot abide fire. We might try to burn it somehow. It is a thing that sees – and, seeing, one of its banes might well be loss of sight. But it has six eyes!"

"I follow what you are saying, Sir," said Smythe. "Also this thought, if you'll permit me, Sir?"

"Of course, Sergeant. You know I value your opinion. How could I not, you having saved my life at Ali Musjid and on other occasions since?"

"Thank you, Sir, but I'm a thinkin' if we can't kill this beast from the outside, maybe we can kill it from within – so to speak," Smythe replied. He reached into his rucksack, brought forth, and held up a Bickford grenade, pretending to light its varnished jute fuze. "There are two cases of these in the ordinance shed, Sir," he added. "I did a bit of searching about." It was somewhat surprising that these were available, the grenade having been relegated to the role of, primarily, a weapon for defense of reinforced positions, the long range of rifles having made throwing distance warfare from the earlier century days of musketry obsolete.

"Of course!" ap Griffith and I answered almost in unison. "That's a brilliant idea, Sergeant!" said ap Griffith. I agreed, and over the next half hour, we worked on the specifics of a plan.

"Then it's agreed, gentlemen," I said to my cohorts. "Let us see what befalls tomorrow evening, but I believe we have the answer – at least a plan to enact. If you three are as beastly weary as I am from the journey and today's awful events, I'm sure we won't have too much trouble sleeping."

* * *

I had been wrong about the sleep. At least in my case. The night passed fitfully and full of nightmares. Worse than the nightmares and the cold sweat were the waking thoughts sitting on the edge of my cot, wondering to myself how little, after all, I knew of the world I lived in.

The next day saw the funerals of the men who had been killed, including FitzGibbon and the other most recent victims – the maimed survivor had also succumbed during the night. The native members of the combined companies did what they could to preserve the funerary custom of cremation for most of the fallen. FitzGibbon was interred. I had said some final words over the dead. We gave the fullest honors that were practical in the situation of this outpost, then a gun salute and moments of silence. There was one piper in my detachment whose pipes screeled out "The Fallen Hero" as we stood at attention, saluting. What more could we do?

As evening came on, we made the preparations. The riflemen had left their rifles behind and were each equipped with two grenades. If the thing returned, of thirteen lancers, ten were to divide: five to the left and five to the right of it – four of those flanking my Jemadar, Sandeep Singh, two on either side. The plan was for them to attempt to evade it by flanking and then impale it from the sides – whilst three central lancers, Smythe, ap

Griffith, and I would approach the beast directly. The grenadiers were to commence hurling their explosives when the thing was within the range of their skill. But I had given orders for them to throw, at first, beyond the beast so as to drive it shoreward. Smythe and ap Griffith each had a lit punk and a grenade. If it got close enough, I was going to have at its damnable eyes with a lance if the chance permitted.

The twilight returned. And so did the worm. We could see its horrid, pale form undulating upon the waves, sometimes beneath them, coming down the river, closer and closer to what it must by then have sensed – for I cannot ascribe thought to it – was a feeding ground.

As it came within about forty yards of us, the men with the strongest arms began throwing their explosives beyond the monster. Great spews of water burst forth up from the river behind the thing, the waves from each explosion helping to propel it closer, as I had hoped. As it came within about twenty-five yards, the grenadiers threw again, this time attempting to hit the beast – or at least come near it. Many of the fuses in the grenades fizzled and the weapons did not explode, even though the improved fuses were better in the wet than previous models. But some did their job, and some came close to the beast. I was appalled that these blasts so near the thing seemed to have no visible effect. One would think the shock alone must stun the creature.

It came nearer and nearer the shore. The lancers had divided and were seeking to flank the animal. Two on the left, the downriver side, simply let the current move the beast onto their lances, the other three on the left drove or harpooned their lances home. Singh and the lancers on the right, moving in, did the same.

Suddenly, the creature squirmed and undulated its body in such a way and with such rapidity and strength, that Singh and two of the lancers holding their lances on the right were catapulted entirely over the body of the beast, landing in the water fully ten yards on the other side – immediately coming up for air, gasping and sputtering.

Then, moving forward, the central three lancers, ap Griffith, Smythe, and I closed in upon that hideous head. One of the lancers drove at the creature, only to suffer the same fate as the poor man the evening before. He was engulfed by the giant maw, his head and upper body disappearing. The other two threw their lances and retreated, screaming. I pressed on with Smythe and ab Griffith on either side. The Lieutenant threw his grenade, attempting to throw the device down the gaping maw of the beast as we had planned. But it glanced off of the creature's hideous upper tooth and fell into the water directly to the left of the monster.

At only forty feet or so, the concussion of the blast stunned all of us a bit, and it knocked ap Griffith unconscious. But his grenade had had some effect. There was now a large, gaping wound, on that side of the beast, as if some of the stuff of its grotesque body had been scooped out by a huge spoon – there was no apparent bleeding, no organs visible. At this moment, the creature made the only noise that we ever heard from it

– a loud, high-pitched moan. No other animal in my experience makes a sound that even approximates what we heard. But it came on.

I moved forward, the lance extended to full length and struck at the eyes. I pierced one and then swept the blade across slicing out the other eye on that parallel. I was seeking to sweep again at another row of the eyes when Sergeant Smythe pushed past and ahead of me on the right. As the huge mouth opened to consume him, he threw his grenade directly into the monster's hideous maw! But in trying to turn away, the giant plates of the teeth crunched down, removing the brave man's arm up past the elbow. Smythe had the presence of mind, even in his agony, to fling himself back onto me, thus knocking us both into the water and away from the blast as his grenade exploded.

All of our company were dazed for the moment. Then, my ears ringing, pushing myself up from the shallows, I began to hear, very muffled at first, a rousing cheer from the men.

What was left of the thing was floating near the shore, but drifting out into the river. It's hideous head, that awful mouth, those hellish eyes, those abhorrent plates of teeth – all were gone. Pieces of what had been the forepart of its grotesque body littered the nearby shoreline, initially glistening in the pale moonlight. But, most remarkably, perhaps due to the explosion occurring inside its monstrous body, not only those few remains on the shore, but also the bulk of what was left of the creature that floated upon the waves suddenly burst into flame and began burning with great intensity. What was left of the thing was immolated before our eyes. Accompanying this awesome spectacle were a thick black smoke and a noisome stench – so awful that it sickened several of the men, cutting short their shouted "Huzzahs!"

Our plan had succeeded – but again at great cost.

Ap Griffith had been saved from drowning by two of the nearby sepoys and the quick action of brave Jemadar Singh – living up to his Sikh name as a "lion" in battle. The shock from ap Griffith's grenade had left the Lieutenant senseless and face down in the water.

We had to care immediately for the brave Sergeant who had once again saved my life and, almost certainly, the lives of many more. I quickly placed a tourniquet on his stub up near the armpit. Amazingly, my friend looked up at me as we stretchered him to the hospital tent and said, "Well done, Sir," saluting with his remaining left hand!

* * *

Of course, I filed a full report of these amazing incidents and told the full story to Major Trevathan upon returning to Lahore. As I have noted above, my initial written report of the incident seems not to have survived. I believe now that the Major did not deem it prudent to forward the report – due to the nature of the events described – even though he appeared to believe me and the several witnesses from my troop who attested to its veracity. I also recommended commendations and honours for Smythe, ap Griffith, Singh, and several others – even recommending the Victoria Cross for the Sergeant and, posthumously, for FitzGibbon. But, it seems clear, these recommendations, along with the report of the incident itself were never forwarded by Major Trevathan. He evidently deeming that the whole matter was too "problematic" to send on to the higher command.

I offer this tale to you, Dear Reader, attesting that the events as presented here are true, although, admittedly, hard to believe. As closely as I can remember, it is exactly parallel to my recollections and details of my initial report, filed now these many years ago. I likely would not believe the story myself – had I not lived it. But I also attest that I am a man of honour and that my word has never been doubted, nor my record as a military man impugned. Make of this account what you will.*

*I have since learned, having studied in my retirement the Greek language (my Latin had always been good, and a favorite subject), that a similar creature is recorded in Ctesias the Cnidian's Indica, as the skōlex (Greek: σκώληξ), although the creature we encountered was at least three times the length of that described by Ctesias of only "7 cubits." Later, Philostratus also reported the creature, attesting to its white color and worm-like appearance.

Perhaps also of interest is the report that this worm was reputedly hunted with bait (what baits are not specified, but I fear human sacrifice might have been part of the plan) and a volatile, highly flammable oil was collected from it – such oil reportedly being used by Indian kings in warfare against Alexander. This might explain the weird nature of the creature's remains burning away so totally after its destruction and, perhaps, the seeming inward glow that I perceived.

The reader might likely wish to know what happened to the gallant Sergeant Smythe. He survived his wound, young Doctor Chambers having acted promptly, although the amazingly "clean" incision caused by the giant worm's teeth meant that the bone had to be reduced to allow for folds of flesh and skin to be closed over the stump of his right arm. He was pensioned out of the service and returned to England. Not only did we keep in touch over the intervening years, but Alfred and I remained – and are to this day – fast friends.

I resigned my commission in 1913, having risen to the rank of Major and being then 57 years of age. I was, however, shortly thereafter called back to service, this time with the Lancashire Fusiliers at the commencement of the Great War. I was brevetted to Lieutenant Colonel during the horrendous action of the Somme, finally serving in the Signals Corps. At the end of hostilities, I returned home to my family's estates in Oldham on the Medlock.

I will claim one distinction. I am, if not the only gentleman in the Empire with a one-armed butler, I must be one of the very few.

Lt. Col (retired), Sir R.C.St.J.M., KBE, DSO, VC
The Gables, Oldham, 12 April 1921

SYMPTOM OF THE UNIVERSE

by John Claude Smith

an abyss brimming with seething monsters motivated by black smudge frustration

Martin Crowne placed the cigarette between his chapped lips, ready to spark up and experience one of the few pleasures this life offered. As he raised the flame to the tip, his wife, Diana, said, "You don't want to do that here, honey. Drop the match or a still smoldering butt and you'll start a fire." She said this as if she were reading a movie description from the television guide. Martin knew the act of lighting a cigarette and the possible repercussions to follow did not matter to her. What mattered was that she was stomping on his joy.

The flame died under the heel of his black dress shoe. He felt the ground below his weight squish, as if the ground were wet, though there was no outward indication it was. This was obviously not a place often trespassed by one wearing black dress shoes, though. He slid the cigarette back into the pack.

He rubbed his always aching hands together, the fingers massaging to no avail as he stared at Diana's taut features, a stretched canvas awaiting oils, a dollop of personality. Where had the woman he loved – or at least thought he loved – disappeared to?

a sketch in red sand erased by an embryonic squall that erodes this manifestation of reality

"Why did you bring us here?" Diana asked, as Martin surveyed the mass field of reeds or what-not, he wasn't sure. Botany was not his thing, but then again, what was? He thought survival, yes, that was his thing.

Through the dreadful, soul-crushing malaise of a relationship gone sour, survival was something to behold.

"Sunday drive. I was bored."

As if a Sunday drive could erase the last fifteen years of boredom.

"But why here?" Diana said, ignoring his comment. Their usual tit-for-tat volley of questions without answers.

It seemed neither he nor Diana knew what they were doing. Neither one of them had the courage to face the ugly truth that what they once had was no more – hadn't been for years – so they meandered along, as if walking down a Yellow Brick Road to Oblivion.

Of course, Diana's take on things might be different. She might even be happy.

No, that couldn't be it. So, what were they doing? Why were they here?

As their dog, Sherlock, started tugging on the leash, Martin let it drop from his fingers.

"What are you doing?" Diana was furious. Martin almost wanted to laugh at the rare show of emotion. "He might get lost – Sherlock! Sherlock, honey."

"He probably needs to do his duty, having been locked in the car for the ride so far."

"Doing his duty and letting him run rampant in this meadow are not the same thing. He might get lost out there." The expression on Diana's face was stern, something to add a little color to the usual dull countenance. Mind you, the color was just a different shading of gray, just like the gloomy, cloud-flecked sky.

Such odd weather for the end of August.

Everything about existence was sculpted from oddness lately, thought Martin. It was as if the years that had passed were stuffed in coffins he would drag around until the end of his days, accumulating every birthday or, let's be realistic, mounting with brute intent with every wedding anniversary. They were approaching sixteen years "together", or some semblance of together. Christ, what would twenty-five feel like? Thirty?

Was the anniversary gift for thirty-five bloodshed?

Lost in his thoughts, not sure why he'd decided on a Sunday drive to nowhere in particular. Twenty-seven miles south of San Francisco, where they lived, to some place called Prados Voraces Regional Park, between Union City and Fremont, California. Martin rifled through the brain files, pulled up the rarely used Spanish he had taken for two years in high school, and roughly translated the name of the park as Hungry Meadows or, no, voraces meant "ravenous".

Ravenous Meadows?

He had no plans set when they left San Francisco, no destination in mind as he pulled off the freeway just to get out of the surprising Sunday traffic. He used this diversion as an excuse to have a cigarette, something Diana disallowed in the car. Perhaps the whole intent of the drive was simply to be away from the suffocating confines of the house, but taking Diana and her sad mutt along for the ride meant he brought the reason behind the suffocating sensation along with him.

He felt trapped, with no means of escape. Parole was a joke. This was a life sentence. Till death do us part.

skeletal wasteland architecture that bridges the gap between the gulf of intent and necessity

Martin rubbed his temples, exchanging one means of pain for another, massaging them as if the pressure would squeeze something out of his thoughts. Perhaps an end game strategy. Perhaps a gun.

Just then, Sherlock squealed in an uncommon way, as if something had surprised him. The sound was followed by a gurgling noise that shook Martin from his sweet reverie.

"Sherlock," Diana yelled, then turned to Martin. "Go get him, honey. Something's wrong." She clutched Martin's pudgy bicep. Years away from the gym had turned his muscles into mush. "Go get my dog."

Martin shrugged his shoulders. "Since he's your dog, you go – "

"You love him, too. Don't be an ass. Go get our dog."

Oh, now he was their dog.

Martin shrugged his shoulders again and ambled into the reeds, in the direction he'd last heard her dog, not theirs. He said more than yelled, "Sherlock," as he slogged through the strange soggy but not soggy meadow. He noticed the edges of some of the reeds seemed serrated and almost barbed. Whatever this plant was, reeds or what-not, he was glad he'd worn a windbreaker to at least protect his arms. Otherwise he'd be covered in cuts. Even at that, he had to shield his face as the reeds stretched up to his height in many places.

"Do you see him?" Diana yelled. She sounded much farther away than Martin imagined. Perhaps his imagination was pushing her away, the distance a momentary fulfilled wish.

"If I saw him, don't you think I would…"

But his voice died when his foot stubbed into the dog.

He raised his hand to his mouth in shock. The dog was squirming, trying to break free of the reeds. Many of the green plants were wrapped around the animal, many more coiled around the dog's head and mouth, muffling vocal protest. The dog's left eye, the only one Martin could see, was opened wide with terror.

Martin stepped back and almost panicked. Questions of how the dog had gotten so tangled in the reeds were made moot as he watched the reeds tighten their grip around the dog, pulling it down into the soil. This vision, as well as the fact he was standing amongst the strange reeds, fueled the adrenaline coursing through his body.

What should he do? What could he do? What if the reeds decided he was next? *Decided*? What was he thinking?

His fingers ached for action, to help the dog; or ached because that's what they always did, no matter the circumstances. As if they had a mind of their own.

"What?" Diana yelled. He barely heard her. "What were you saying?"

"I... I stepped on something."

That was all he could think to say as his mind reeled with possible responses. With possible outcomes *to his advantage*.

To his advantage? What was he thinking?

"Come quick," he said. He raised his left hand above the reeds.

"Come quick."

"What's going on? Is Sherlock okay?"

"Come quick, darling." He waved his hand. "Sherlock needs you."

What was he thinking? What was he doing?

He stopped waving his hand when the reeds pulled Sherlock deeper into the soil, and the soil moved in a peculiar way, as if it were ingesting the dog.

"Dear God," he said to himself, as he lowered his hand. Perhaps this was not such a good plan.

"Raise your hand again, Martin. I've lost my bearings."

Martin turned toward her voice, contemplating options: stop her progress, or aid her in her quest. His quest...

foundation soldered from rusted shadows, armored spines, vapor trails left by shooting stars

Without hesitation, though the answer still rolled over and over in his head like a Magic Eight-Ball before it settled on a response, Martin raised his hand up again and said, "Here," just as Diana bumped into him from behind.

She pushed Martin aside and took in the scene.

"Oh, my god. How...? Do something. You have to do something!"

Martin remained still, watching the horror. Sherlock's head was buried halfway into the roiling soil.

"Martin," Diana cried. Their eyes met for an instant. Martin felt a twist of guilt corkscrew into his gut, but remained stone still, a statue of indecision.

But he knew it wasn't true indecision. What frolicked within him knew as much.

"Bastard," Diana said, as she moved forward and knelt down by the dog. "Bastard." She sobbed as she reached toward Sherlock.

A dozen or more reeds wrapped around her wrist. She made a sound that was not a word, more an expression of confusion.

Martin flexed his fingers, but remained frozen in place.

"Martin…" Diana struggled with the reeds, trying to pull her arm away, her strength no match for that of the reeds.

"Help me," she cried, as her other hand was taken by another cluster of the animated reeds. With suddenness, she was yanked down to the churning soil.

Martin's heartbeat pounded in his chest, his ears. When Diana tried to turn her head toward him, reeds wrapped around her neck, her mouth. Futile sounds escaped from the space between reeds and curled lips. When their eyes met, Martin stepped back one, two steps.

Really, what could he do?

Did he really want to do anything?

Was this grotesque, impossible scene an answer to prayers he'd never considered?

A reed covered Diana's eyes, a blindfold cutting into her flesh, the orbs.

a foul genie culled from the sentient void by synaptic tremors wrought from fever dreams

Martin turned and ran as fast as his thick legs would permit. The lashing of reeds against his body, clinging but not grabbing hold, almost tripped him up. He only stumbled as he made it out of the field and onto the unsteady ground beyond. He scrambled to his feet, never fully hitting the ground, not wanting whatever had happened to Diana and Sherlock to happen to him. Within seconds, he was at the car, digging into the pockets of his black slacks for the keys, finding them, and anxiously unlocked the door.

Safely within, his aching, throbbing fingers gripped the steering wheel as he dropped the keys. They landed on the brown rubber floor mat kicked askew beneath his shoes. He noted his knuckles were covered in blood and laced with deeps cuts.

The reeds had done quite a job to his hands. He peered into the rearview mirror and noted less damage to his face.

He attempted to catch his breath, exercise of any nature foreign to him. But as he tried, a sudden jolt of laughter ambushed his intentions.

What was he laughing about? What was he doing?

What had just happened?

He moved his feet to the left as he tried to locate the keys.

Had he just been given the keys to his freedom?

Martin laughed again, but the laughter was accompanied by tears.

What was he doing?

He opened the door, practically fell out of the car, and vomited.

Afterwards, he stood up on shaky legs – or was it the weird ground – and started to walk back into the field of reeds.

"Diana," he said, barely above a whisper. He repeated this at the same volume as he weaved into the meadow.

"Honey," he said, as he sensed she was near.

He was correct, but she was not as he expected. Neither was Sherlock.

Both bodies lay inert on the ground, blood spattered on their swollen faces, abrasions – fingernail cuts, reddened skin – threaded around Diana's neck.

"No," Martin said, his voice rising above the volume he'd used while he'd trod into the meadow. He reflexively flexed his always aching hands.

This could not be real. He must be dreaming. Perhaps if he pinched himself he would wake up. Perhaps it would just leave red, crescent-shaped bruises. Just like what was strung around Diana's neck, with variations on the crescents scraping and cutting into the flesh, forming a bloody necklace.

Still, Martin denied the obvious.

This could not be real.

He was not a murderer.

The word slipped out from a nook or cranny or a widening crack within the fabric of Martin's reality.

Murderer!

He thought he heard the word echo in his head, in Diana's voice.

He closed his eyes, placed his palms over his ears.

This could not be real.

Martin let out a garbled cry, the sound muted by his hands, his always aching hands, as he pressed his palms harder against his ears. Within his head, his breathing sounded like wind rustling through the reeds, whistling and scratched raw by the serrated edges.

Martin inhaled deeply and held it in, fighting for composure.

as the howl of dying eons echoes across neuropathways and throbs along satiated phalanges

Reality is what you believe to be true. Who said that? Aldous Huxley? Philip K. Dick? Dick would know about all variations on reality, wouldn't he?

Despite evidence to the contrary, the reality at his feet did not reflect in any way what he had witnessed. He knew what he had witnessed. Convincing the authorities might take monumental effort, but Martin knew what was true. Martin knew which reality he believed in.

No matter the circumstances, the wasted years, he was not a murderer. There was no way he was a murderer.

The sweat on his brow itched as it made trails down the sides of his face, his cheeks. He pulled his hands from his ears. Silence filled the gaps of space and logic.

There was no way he was a murderer.

There were no bodies at his feet.

(Just don't look down.)

He was standing in a meadow – Prados Voraces – twenty-seven miles south of San Francisco, above the place where the reeds had taken his wife and dog into the ground. It may be absurd – it was absurd – but he knew what had happened.

His hands ached like never before.

He repeated the mantra, calming nerves: Reality is what you believe is true.

Who said that? Did it matter?

All that mattered was what he believed to be true.

He knew he was not a murderer. He believed this with every iota of his being.

Martin Crowne opened his eyes and let out a tiny "Oh" as a reed coiled as a snake around his ankle…

the fantastical boils into life in the salivating maw of the insatiable cosmic wilderness intrinsic to every living creature within the multitude of realities within the universe…

SUSTENANCE OF THE STARS

by Scott J. Couturier

Part I: The Confession

I love the taste of human flesh.

This is not hyperbole – though really, how could it be? Either you have the craving or you don't. I never bought into the whole Freudian/Jungian paradigm, "all humans are cannibals beneath the sheen of civilization", yadda yadda etc. It is not in all men to abduct a small, doe-eyed girlchild from an inattentive parent, to spirit her away in the back of a van to a secluded area where they've constructed a ceremonial altar and a small, rudimentary oven out of stones. It is not in all men to rape a child to death, to sup on her still-pulsing blood, to carve out great furroughs of her flesh with their teeth. And then, the process of carving and roasting, the great gouts of charnel smoke, the final gorging climax… no. I LOVE the taste of human flesh. Young flesh, particularly. It's a stimulant, a drug, a ceaseless and unbounded need with me. I would die without it, and killing for it is bliss.

Now, cunning is a fine complement to craving. Taking a few select victims a year ensured that no one could trace me – I was free to pursue my abominable acts in peace, only twice having to participate in police inquiries. I've never been a suspect, never given anyone any reason to suspect me. I've never been seen – in and out, like a killing wind. I like to fetishize myself sometimes, imagine myself as some nightmare monster out of myth or antiquity. My belly rounded with childflesh, I've sat in my rocking chair and watched the police cars speed past, lights flaring with inchoate, idiot alarm. I always sleep well in the evenings, always rise early with the sun. I'm a farmer by trade, a beast by nature.

Now, I had a neighbor; nice fella, if a bit daft in the head. My land covers a good forty acres, and his near thirty, mostly sown with corn, hayseed and Timothy-grass. I can just see the lights in his kitchen windows from my house. He's a pudgy, ill-tempered sort, blear-eyed and possessed by a ferocious sense of deserving something, be it all the world or merely someone else's supper. Many are the disputes we've had over the property line dividing out fields; hell, it's practically a seasonal ritual by this point. He's a bellicose alcoholic, well-pickled in his juices, and not at all the sort of person I'd want to eat even if he wasn't monstrously unpleasant.

However, he always told some of the craziest stories. He claimed that, since birth, he'd been getting regularly abducted by a race of squamous gray-green extraterrestrials hailing from somewhere in the constellation Ophiuchus. Particularly, he railed about some cosmic junction around Barnard's Star, lips frothing with impotent rage as he recounted the excruciating minutia of endless arcane medical procedures, probes and chip-implantations. He even showed me where one of the chips had been sealed under his skin ("to monitor my white blood cell count," he insisted): I'll admit, I felt a hard bump when I pressed. Also, I'll admit that some of his more outlandish recollections inspired me to freshly depraved heights (though I would never give him any direct credit for my work). Suffice to say that without his quaking, slant-eyed testimony, I never would have attempted a living sternum-to-groin vivisection.

It was delicious and delirious. A hot, seething, pumping red-purple buffet. The trick is to remove the tongue first.

At any rate, I never gave his stories much credence beyond mining them for inspiration. He had no family, no friends to speak of; down at the local pub folks joked about him fornicating with a bewildering variety of animals to pass the time. Funny thing is, I did occasionally notice some odd lights hovering in the sky around his house in the lonely hours, but put it down to tricks of atmosphere and starlight. It's frightfully easy to rationalize away the plain evidence of one's senses: I once watched a cop come within a few feet of a disturbed patch of earth near my porch, moving on total instinct. At the last second, nostrils flaring, he veered away from the crumpled half-eaten corpse I'd so shoddily concealed, bidding me a curt good day. I can only think he didn't really want to find what he was looking for, just like I didn't really want to admit that I ever saw those lights.

Now, we passed a lot of years between us. I am not a young man, and he was even less so. Every so often he'd have a new tale to tell, and I would lean on a fencepost and listen, nodding in polite long-suffering disbelief. Never did he suspect my proclivities. Sometimes I'd see him out wandering his fields at night, shotgun clutched in hand; my response was always to draw down the blinds. I'm a master at avoiding unwanted attention, an Übermensch at sliding snake-like through the tall grass. Never did he trouble me in his delirium. We made good neighbors, even if he did occasionally manage to plug one of my prized barn cats. I once caught him in the act of stomping flat an entire shrieking litter – I don't mind telling you, as much as I love cats it turned me on. He had a special kind of cruelty, this idiot neighbor of mine.

At any rate, one night I was sitting out on my front porch, famished. I'd not claimed a kill in nearly ten months, determinedly keeping a low profile until the most recent police kerfuffle died down. I'd accidentally taken a "high-profile" victim, the daughter of a lower-class family with some esoteric blood-relation to the mayor – in all honesty, it was a real pain. No one had implicated or even questioned me, but there were billboards and crudely-printed signs posted all over town, the little bitch's hideously pixelated face staring out at me whenever I went in for gas or groceries or a drink. Underscoring her perpetual rictus were the words HUGE CASH REWARD FOR INFORMATION printed very large, followed by a hotline number. Needless to say, my palms were sweating just a teensy bit more than usual. Also, I was so hungry. My gut growled and my groin writhed, demanding some form of diabolic release. I thought about going downstairs and watching the tiny supply of tapes I'd made of some of my earliest victims, before I decided the practice was too risky.

Just then, high up in the sky to the east I caught a weird flicker of purpureal light. Looking up, I saw the anomaly resolve itself into the form of a soundless light-studded disc, descending slowly down from the presumed fathoms of space. The flashing glow was answered by a light on the ground, a faint green pulse emanating from a cluster of poplars near to my neighbor's garage. I watched in rapt fascination as this green light gave off several tic-like flares, answered in kind by the lights lining the disc's outer stationary edge. Gradually, the craft lowered until it hovered directly over my neighbor's house, the hypnotic pulse of its running lights extinguishing. It was only discernible as a black blot against the stars, though intermittent green flashes still welled up from the poplar stand.

I have been called an enterprising man. I've always taken this as a compliment, though I doubt those who pay it so frequently and cordially have the slightest inclination as to the true heights of my entrepreneurial spirit. As I saw that green light flickering, I felt a sudden, wrenching twist in my nethers; and, grabbing up a garden spade, I hurtled out the front screen door and down the hill towards my neighbor's house. I was, I admit, wholly bound up in the wonder of what I was indisputably witnessing; and, my nature being what it is, I felt the need of consummation.

I clutched the spade in shivering hands as I crept towards the poplar stand with practiced stealth, gratified to see the green light still flashing undiminished. I had some inkling that this signal was being broadcast by a scout requesting recovery by the fulsome mothership above. I grit my teeth as my ankle twisted in a hollow, pain racing up my left leg to explode redly in my hip; I stumbled, nearly dropping the spade, but regained by feet and trajectory with little more than a faint huff of pain.

Though I specialize in younger victims, sometimes I'm compelled by whim or necessity to go for older marks, often resulting in protracted scuffles. For that matter, some of the kids can be quite a pain, too; their fists are generally at groin level. In the heat of the kill you learn to filter out injury, to overwhelm any pain or human weakness with the roaring need to claim and devour life. So it was as I burst into a small clearing amid the poplar stand, leg throbbing but held rigidly, a predator's poised limb.

I grinned like a madman as I beheld a short, spindly mottled-gray entity clutching a signaling lantern to its rubbery chest. The being turned and perceived me with its wide, gaping pitch-black eyes: just then the lantern flared green, creating a suitably ghoulish funhouse effect. Silently, I swung the spade overhand, felling the creature with a single brutal blow to its oversized cranium. A strange whitish blood spurted out as it toppled at my feet, its willowy body thrashing about in whip-like death spasms. Intrigued, I watched to see if the creature would vent its bowels at death, if indeed it possessed such a faculty; there seemed to be no anal orifice, and no genitalia were visible on its glistening androgynous form. After a few moments thick, pestilent dollops that smelt of waste formed in its armpits, leading me to conclude their race had a very different methodology of evacuation; yet, not really so dissimilar. Apparently shit still smells like shit, whatever galaxy you're from.

I hastily wiped off the still-twitching entity and slung it over my shoulder, my leg sending out fresh waves of painful protestation. Still, my kill was fairly light, and hung limp as a bundle of seaweed against my heaving chest and back. I managed to bound back up the hill towards my house with minimal difficulty, frequently casting glances back over my shoulder at the brooding, lightless alien craft. So far my deed appeared to have gone unnoticed; the night was dark, still and heavy, vibrating with cicada song and sluggish with humidity. As I reached the door to my farmhouse, kicked it open and hauled my prize inside, my mind was whirling with all the attendant wonder a mere human who has witnessed some glimpse of a great and mystical secret experiences. Moreover, I was deliciously, diabolically hungry, my stomach convulsing in knotted cramps, my knees practically weak with a gourmand's anticipation. Tonight, I would dine on the most exotic and sentient of dishes.

As I butchered and dressed the alien, it occurred to me that my erstwhile neighbor wasn't even remotely cracked in the head. He was sane – horribly and perfectly sane. Here was tangible proof that his maniacal ravings were not mere delusions, that indeed some form of extraterrestrial intelligence was abducting him regularly to perform horrendous and seemingly malefic operations – or at least lurking voyeuristically in his poplar stand. As the thrill-haze of killing passed and the difficulties of dissecting a being wholly foreign to Earthen physiology made themselves ever more apparent, I came to wonder at my impulsive act. Surely the creatures would note the sudden disappearance of their scout, and come looking for its murderer? My mind flashed to the cold chambers of studded metal, the great electrode-riddled examination tables and insidiously snaking probes that my neighbor had so often tremblingly described. I wondered if perhaps I desired punishment for this blasphemy, to be taken up into their marvelous shining craft and subjected to every clinically sybaritic torment imaginable. Grinning to myself, I started hacking at the alien's corpse more feverishly, and even allowed myself to sample a few tastes of its blood. Harsh, almost acidic – but frightfully invigorating. I ejaculated into the open carcass before slicing it into rubbery, pearlescent steaks; these I plopped into a massive stew pot filled with boiling water, along with several generous scoops of its brain. The organs – strange frilly gelatinous things, glistening with an inner lambency – I left alone, thinking the flesh less likely to hold concentrations of toxins.

I'll admit, the resultant stench wasn't terribly appetizing. I did what I could with the spices, vegetables and stock at my disposal, opening all the windows in the house to air out the atrocious smell of liquefying rubber. I was pleased to note that the ship had disappeared from over my neighbor's house; furthermore, there was an all-encompassing calm on the evening air, a primal sense that my current debaucheries would proceed unhindered.

Eventually, with a judicious application of culinary wizardry, I managed to turn the seething dish around. Nibbling at the limp gray flesh, I was surprised at the meatiness of the flavor; it had the consistency of calamari, but with a slightly easier give to the flesh. Underneath the expected rubbery-acidic taste was an earthy succulence, savory, almost like spring morels. The brains had dissolved into a potent broth, rich and frothy, near-dizzying to the senses – each sip coarsened my mouth like strong absinthe, and set off tiny explosions of light at the corners of my eyes. Gradually, as I tucked into a long strip of well-boiled steak, I realized that the creature's body was exerting some strong psychedelic effect on me. However, my hunger was too potent to be ignored; voracious, terrible, I set to gorging on my well-earned feast, giddy in anticipation of my first anthropophagous acid trip.

But… is anthropophagous the right word? It wasn't at all like eating human flesh, not nearly as savory or filling. At length I started to feel terribly sick. I threw up several times, my head spinning with a kaleidoscope of massy, pulsing colors. A veil formed over my vision, a screen on which all that I was was projected: I saw my essence entire, a black and loathly encrustation of psychic energy, a shriveled death-dealing canker with a silverish sheen, like the gilding on a cracked and befouled mirror. I recoiled in myself, seeing to fullest breadth the ghastly extent of my psychopathy; for the first time I was able to project myself into the minds and bodies of others, to feel grief at the countless lives my vicious crimes had destroyed by proxy. Under normal circumstances I rejoiced whenever I heard that some grief-stricken mother had collapsed from a stroke in the midst of hunting for her lost child, or that some sorrowing father had passed away mumbling the name of his little lost lamb. Such resonances gave me power, extended me into countless interconnected lives like an omnipotent web-spinner of Death; each soul taken by grief was added to my private tally. Yet now, now I found myself hunched over my knees on the gore-slick floor of my kitchen, hands clutching spasmodically at the back of my head as if to claw inside to my hammering, humming brain. Tears streamed down my face, tears of irreconcilable grief; I became all of my victims, became each shade-haunted member of their families in turn. I felt the piercing knives, both literal and figurative – I ached in my innermost soul, died in horrible drawn-out grieving agony over a thousand distended lifetimes. I was now writhing on the floor, flooded by empathic memories: all the myriad souls I'd collected overpowering me, mutilating me. I screamed aloud at my own monstrous aberration, and biting down dissevered a massive chunk of meat from my own right forearm.

Chewing on my own flesh helped ease the flood of visions. I masticated sedately, falling back against the cabinets in something of a swoon. It was then I felt myself literally leave my body, my consciousness expanding to a degree heretofore unexperienced by any material dweller on this humble chunk of spheroid rock we call Terra. I perceived the massed consciousness of the entity I had devoured: billions of brightly interconnected sparks burning in euphoric unison across untold vastnesses of interstellar space. They were a 'psychic' species, to employ a crude Earthen term; every synapse and soul comprising their race shares a fundamental quantum interrelation. In flashes of ingested racial memory, I saw their blindly-groping ancestors crawl out from a seething protoplasmic mass beneath twin suns, one a swollen orb of dullish cinnabar and the other a small, blue-white dwarf which emitted rapidly oscillating pulses. Their world had no moon, a major shaping-point of their psyche; even from the beginning their racial consciousness was intermingled, though countless millennia of sacral meditation, eugenics and esoteric practices had whittled away at their individuality, until they existed as one near-omniscient hive mind. I saw their civilization rise, fall, rise, fall, and rise again; finally the gleaming towers refused to tumble, shining like pillars of pure hierophanic light. Only then did the species learn to cheat the iron boundaries of space and time, their racial consciousness becoming pandimensional in scope as they spread from star to star over a period of unreckoned aeons.

In glimpses of shimmering prescience, I understood that my vicious killing and cooking of the alien had sent mortal shockwaves through its companions piloting the ship. They had collapsed in a torpor of near-death, and the ship had automatically evacuated them out beyond the moon's orbit, a distance sufficient to resuscitate them without further contamination from my virulent psychic emissions… or so the vessel presumed. I understood in some speechless way that the seed of my abominable bloodthirst had been implanted deeply into the meticulously-preened psyches of the alien pilots. I saw that the creatures were very careful about what they ate, for they invariably absorbed psychic imprints from their food; mostly, they were vegetarians. Also, they often had to deal with violent etheric transmissions whenever one of their own species was eaten and digested, transferring some of its DNA to the consuming animal in the process. Or in this case, me.

I reeled and vomited again, sweat gushing from my pores in foul-smelling torrents. I understood dully that my neighbor, crotchety and sour-faced and stupid, was part of a broad-spectrum breeding program instigated by the aliens several thousand years ago. Frowning through my waxing delirium, I tried to discern exactly why they'd bred such an unpleasant stump of a human being, but my ability to see was already fading. Instead, I watched as my killing lust spread amongst the webwork of alien minds like a psychic fever, infecting each pure-burning node with a sickly hellfire taint. There was a roaring sound, blasting outwards from the center of my brain; it sounded like the great moan of billions of grotesquely-starving bellies. The last glimpse I had before blackness claimed me was of the aliens reviving on their ship, which was still hovering strategically in the moon's spaceward umbra. They looked to each other tremblingly, their tiny jaws yawning open; I saw small incisor-like teeth, opaquely transparent and ridged with minute serrations. Grinning psychotically, I watched as the beings rushed to seize control of their vessel and plot a course back to Earth, their black eyes now red-litten with a magnificent hunger for human flesh.

The rest, I'll admit, is far less interesting. I lay unconscious for several hours, periodically emptying my stomach so that when I finally awoke I lay in a reeking stew of gastric juices and pulped alien flesh. Staggering to my feet, I received in a flash the entirety of what had happened, causing an upstir of manic hilarity that consumed me for several quaking minutes; indeed, I admit I almost took my own life. The bite wound on my forearm had scabbed over, but was still plentifully leaking blood; at length it was this pain that brought me back to Earth, to my husk-like body. Staggering to the window, I peered down towards my neighbor's house, for the first time noting a horrid buzzing sound that filled the air and caused the very marrow of my bones to vibrate disconcertingly.

You can pretty much guess what I saw. The saucer had returned, had in fact landed with reckless force in the midst of my neighbor's fields, obliterating his crop. The sun was just coming up, saturating the whole scene in a monstrously roseate hue, like the emanations of some diabolic birthing canal; transfixed by the nightmare, I watched as the alien beings emerged from my neighbor's house slathered in blood, their supple hands (until so recently bent to the crafting of genomes) squeezing tightly around clumps of organ meat, at which they were tearing with a fervid glee I knew all too well. With a body-and-soul-wide tremble, I understood fully the implications of my astral interjection into the race-mind of their species.

Stupefied, I watched as they concluded their grisly meal, then set about conducting some sort of abstruse mental orgy. The proceedings I only dimly understood, something about the stimulation of non-material reproductive organs vibrating in a dimension beyond matter; needless to say, I didn't stand and watch long. Bolting upstairs, I quickly grabbed the survival kit I always kept prepped against the rare prospect of my crimes being uncovered (I'll admit, it was dusty from lack of attention). I also grabbed my murder tools – no need to elucidate further, I think – and all the money I'd managed to hoard from some of my older victims. Going downstairs, I quickly emptied the contents of my refrigerator into a sack. With a pang I wondered at the fate of my collection of preserved vulvae, kept on a shelf in a secret room in my basement; but, priorities priorities.

Going back to the window, I saw with a shudder that the creatures had concluded their lascivious communion and turned their attentions up the road, towards my house. I saw that some clutched exotic metal implements in their gore-slick hands – doubtlessly weapons of some kind. This was confirmed when I saw a squirrel attempt to dart across their path, only to by scorched to a cinder by a lance of purple-green fury. My mind going blank with terror, I turned and fled out the back door, plunging blindly into the dense woods adjoining my house.

After that, life became a daily struggle for survival. The pith of my perversity had been beamed out across the void, infesting even the noblest of their race with a filthy cannibalistic yearning. Soon the saucers came in dozens, then in droves; the cities burned, reduced to goresome necropoli haunted by the ghoul-like cracking of bones… or so I heard from other survivors, who I often ate in turn. I managed to hide out in the woods for five months, glutting on deer and passing refugees. At last I was picked up by an army sweep and taken unresisting to a nearby retention camp. There, I pled my case as a helpless farmer driven from his land by noisome alien invaders from outer space: admittedly, there was no lie in the words.

Working in the refugee camps, I was deluged by endless speculation about the invaders. Why, after all these millennia, had they suddenly turned on humanity? We know now that our governments were in cahoots with them all along – know, in fact, that Benjamin Franklin was an alien, allowing him sufficient nonconductive properties to perform his famed kite-and-key experiment and emerge not only alive but unsinged. So, why now? Obviously, I found it difficult to keep my mouth shut; I hate to cite a stereotype, but it's true that serial killers are possessed of a certain microcosmic megalomania. Almost, I began to feel proud of the horrific doom I'd inadvertently brought to Earth, proud especially of the disfiguring stain I'd spread on the DNA of our extraterrestrial overlords. Yet at the same time I felt a weird twisting in my gut, and not the familiar cramps of lust or hunger (there is certainly no shortage of victims in the camps). I felt – it's hard to say it really – sorry for my own species. I've always delighted in plucking a few flowers from the mad rush of life, but to think of the Earth as barren, humanless, preyless… it breaks the tiny, jagged and ebon-black splinter I call my heart.

So, here I am. I told my story to a staff sergeant, who took me into custody and put me in touch with a general something-or-other, three stars. Now, five tellings in I'm finally talking to you, to someone actually in control, or at least working directly for those in control. I have no idea if my testimony will help in the fight; word is that the Earth's already mostly stripped. I've heard that the aliens are starting to turn on each other, to devolve and lose their psychic abilities. As I said, I'm compelled by nature to feel a kind of pride at breeding this interstellar travesty – I've spawned a glorious blight, one that may one day consume the stars themselves. But at the same time, I'm still human, and I want – need – my species to survive.

Part II: The Result

Agent Matheson stared at the self-confessed killer in stony silence, right hand settling on the grip of his firearm. There were three other agents in the room, all well-trained and initiated into the Mysteries; still, he could feel the pack-impulse of their tension. They desired to kill this man with such fervor that the room was flooded with a physical musk.

The killer grinned, sniffing at the air. "Ah, I know that smell well. I figured I'd not be walking out of this room, boys, so why don't you go ahead? Believe me, it's long past my time."

One of the agents went for his firearm. "Stop!" Matheson snarled, turning to his subordinate and flashing him a commanding glare. The man backed down, but his limbs were trembling, sweat pouring from beneath his opaque glasses – or was he weeping? With a curt gesture Matheson commanded the trio to leave, telling them to contact Washington and relate the man's ground-breaking testimony. "As for the prisoner... I'll watch over him," he said, the words twisted with a strange unreadable inflection.

Hesitantly, the three men turned and left, leaving Agent Matheson alone with the killer. The man smiled, held up his shackled hands and said, "You don't want to play? That's just fine. I figured you might want to keep me for medical dissection, or something along that line."

The agent pursed his lips. "That was a pretty eloquently-told tale, especially considering the savage you claim to be."

"Noticed that, eh?" The killer grinned. "I'll admit that contact with the alien hive-mind jacked up my faculties somewhat, but I've always been able to spin a good yarn. Often, that's the best way to draw in the kiddies." He chuckled at his own observation, mock-tugging on his chains. "Speaking of which, I want a last meal before whatever it is they're gonna do to me. A young girl, fresh; her name's Lydia Tanner. I've already done the work and staked out her family's camp. Show me a database and I'll pick her out."

Agent Matheson allowed himself a small, hollow chuckle. "Still hungry?" he asked, almost in a whisper.

The killer grinned. "Always." Then, his bliss-transported features took on a darker cast. "So, I've come and told you everything. Now it's time for you to tell me something in turn. Agent Matheson, is it too late to stop the invaders?"

Slowly, meditatively, the agent rose from his chair. Drawing out his gun, he leveled it at the killer's forehead. "Yes," he said, and pulled the trigger.

Blood and brains splattered the far wall, the shot muffled by a silencer. Good, the agent thought, his mind shimmering with distorted psychic contact. Moving hastily, he bared the purple-mottled scar on his right forearm where he had been bitten by one of the Dentrili. He had been wounded in an early battle with the invaders, watched his entire platoon devoured… left alive, he had wondered at his good fortune. However, the rise of certain invasive, individuality-subsuming thought patterns, along with a waxing anthropophagic fascination, had soon revealed the real greater-than-death horror of his predicament. Now wholly infected and absorbed by the hive-mind, the agent had long ago ceased to function as an independent entity.

I have found the Source, the vestige of agent Matheson thought, beaming the revelation outwards. It was received with incalculable joy by the greater collective.

At last, at last! came an obscene chorus of slavering voices in his mind. Now, eat!

The agent shivered as he obeyed. Kneeling down by the killer's splayed corpse, he drew out a hammer and pounded at its skull until a thick stream of brains poured out on the tile. Kneeling down, he began feasting on the lumped gray matter, ecstasy shivering through his body and, by surrogate, through the collective psyche of the Dentrili. Ever since the Great Revelation they had been in manic search of its source… now, the DNA of the killer passed fully into the collective, closing the genetic gap. The gorged husk of Agent Matheson sat back and grinned in stupefied gratification as a Second Great Revelation swept over the Dentrili, instilling a hunger for all life, for the sustenance of the stars themselves.

ALIEN SHORE

by Rob F. Martin

The buttons from the minuteman's jacket ricocheted off my face, nipping my cheeks, as Tlaloc punched through his stomach from behind; then the tightness in my chest broke into a cool flood of relief that rippled through my being. Just before I saw Tlaloc's crimson eyes flicker over the minuteman's shoulder, I was on my knees, gazing into the barrel of his rifle – the acrid smoke of the bullet that'd sprayed Mamá's head onto the desert sand swirling before me, stinging my nose and dancing down my throat.

Tlaloc withdrew his hand, and the minuteman's ribcage collapsed inward. He dropped to his knees and our glances met. In that moment, the hot, churning hatred within me was dampened by a wind of empathy. Something happens in your heart when you watch another person die. You're forced to recognize your shared humanity and grieve for its loss. You see the eyes begin to dim, like buckets pouring out their essence, until they go dark. The body starts to relax as it surrenders to the inevitable. You wonder what he was like as a child. You envision him sleeping in his bed with his favorite stuffed animal poking out from beneath his arm. And as he takes his last breath, you wonder what the purpose was for any of it.

He fell forward, his head grazing my dress and landing at my knees.

Tlaloc loomed over me, standing against the orange wall of the sunset sky, cocking his head to the side like a curious puppy. His skin was made up of tight black scales that had an iridescent sheen, like oil on water. He bent toward me and I recoiled as he extended his hand to my face. Yet his thumb was warm and soft beneath my eyes as it wiped away my tears. Gliding his finger beneath my chin, he guided me to my feet, my legs and neck wobbling – he caught me by the arm and held me steady. My tongue was pasted against the roof of my mouth, and I blinked sweat from my eyes, the desert landscape seeming to stutter about.

With a finger, Tlaloc popped a hole into the air before me, and a splash of water bounced off my cheeks. A pure blue stream, almost glowing against the orange sky, trickled out from the punctured air. With his thumb, Tlaloc rubbed the sweaty dirt from my face. I leaned into the stream, and the water dripped onto my tongue, loosening it. When I finished, I wiped my mouth with the back of my hand, and Tlaloc pinched the hole shut. He then stretched his wiry finger to the horizon.

"The Pyramid of the Ocean?" I asked.

He nodded and began to lead the way.

* * *

"Gabriela!" Mamá called as the black van rolled up to the curb. "Time to go!"

"Okay, Mamá!" I zipped my duffel bag and ran out to meet her in the street, where she was paying the driver. As I approached, he put out his hand, blocking me from entering the van.

"Ten thousand pesos extra for the girl!"

"That wasn't the agreement. I was told a hundred thousand pesos for two people," Mamá argued.

"Extra for teenage girls. They make the trip more dangerous. Attract kidnappers." He nudged an open hand toward Mamá. "Ten thousand pesos more."

"That's all we have."

"Then no ride."

"Mamá," I interrupted, handing her the extra pesos. "We can worry about money when we get to America."

"Yeah, Mamá! When you get to America!" said the driver with enthusiasm, extending his hand toward the van, guiding us through the open rear doors.

Stepping up into it, I tasted the sweaty smell that laced the thick, stagnant air. We sat down on the ratty rug – it reeked of ammonia and was damp with urine. The doors slammed behind us, and a lump formed in my throat. I wanted to look back at our home one last time, but there were no windows. I clasped Mamá's hand.

"Okay, everyone," said the driver, hopping into the cab. "My name is Carlos. And I'll be your chauffeur to the great land of America. Should take about a day n' a half. Two at most. And this is Domingo." He motioned to a tattooed man sitting in the passenger seat, who looked at me from over his mountainous shoulder, straight-faced. I felt myself flash him a timid smile, and he turned away.

"We'll go west and then up the coast," Carlos continued. "When we get to the Sonoran Desert, there'll be a spot to cross over into Arizona. Okay! Let's go!" He threw up his fists and pumped the air. "Mamá wants to see America!"

The van began to pull away, hobbling over the uneven pavement. My back bounced against the metal wall, and my neck whipped forward. I clasped Mamá's hand tighter, winking tears out of my eyes and swallowing the growing lump in my throat. When the ride smoothed out, I rested my head on her shoulder.

From off of the dashboard, a soft blue glow provided some minimal light, along with the occasional quick flash of a passing street lamp. Three other passengers sat across from Mamá and me. A strained silence hung between us as we shared glances and looked away. The air was becoming like wet, constricting tendrils. The wobbling of the van began to tease a sour feeling out of my belly that danced up into my throat. I focused on my thumb until the queasiness subsided.

"You sisters?" asked the man sitting across from us, grinning.

"Excuse me?" Mamá laughed.

"You sisters?"

"No. This is my daughter, Gabriela."

"And your name?"

She looked down, pulling her hair over her ear. "I'm Carmen."

"I'm Zacarías."

"Hello."

"You pretty young ladies traveling all alone? No husband? No father?"

As he asked this, Mamá pushed her dress between her legs, and I could feel her squirming as her knees rubbed against each other.

"Papá! You're being unwelcome!" the woman beside him said with a withering glance.

"I apologize. I wasn't seeking to offend."

Carlos slapped the back of his hand against Domingo's chest. "Old man flirtin' with Mamá Carmen!"

Domingo nodded, making a noise that was something between a deep-throated grunt and a closed mouth laugh.

"Don't worry about it," I said. "We're used to it."

"See Adelita?" Zacarías laughed. "No harm done."

"No harm this time, Papá." She rubbed her pregnant stomach, looking to me with apology.

I nudged my head toward Carlos. "So, did he charge you extra for the baby?"

"Children under three years old ride for free!" He yelled back.

Adelita turned her head toward the cab. "You're full of compassion, Carlos." Then back to me. "Do you two have a plan after you cross the border?"

"Survive," answered Mamá, her hand loosening from her dress.

Carlos looked to us from the rearview mirror. "You just call the number I gave to you free of charge and tell him that I sent you!"

I smiled at Adelita. "We'll figure something out."

"Nico has a brother in Arizona," she continued, touching the shoulder of the other man she was with. "We were hoping to do this the right way and apply for permanent residency after the baby came. But the killings forced us out sooner."

"Teenage boys and girls butchering people in the streets with machetes." Nico shuddered.

Zacarías nodded. "There's more body parts in the dumpsters than trash."

"Things aren't so bad," Carlos said. "Just need lots of big friends. Like Domingo here!" Again, he slapped Domingo with the back of his hand. "And lots of bullets. Blow open their kneecaps and hack 'em to death with their own machetes."

"And here we are," said Nico. "Fleeing to the country that's responsible for creating the red powder that's driving the carnage."

With this comment, the strained silence returned, smothering the conversation. And for a while we sat under the weight of Nico's words, the quiet broken only by the occasional serenade from Carlos: "Going to America!"

Sweat erupted from my brow, ran down my face in hot streams, and dripped off my chin. To keep from feeling sick, I focused on Adelita. She cupped her stomach, shifting with every bump and stutter of the van. Nico repositioned the pillows behind her and kissed the top of her head. She smiled in response and clutched his forearm. He slid his fingers between hers as she nestled against him.

"We'll make it, Baby," Mamá whispered, pulling me close.

Zacarías began to chant some kind of prayer under his breath, eyes closed and grasping the talisman he wore around his neck.

"Papá, stop that!" said Adelita.

"Yeah. Don't be doing that weird shit in the van, Papá Zacarías!" shouted Carlos.

"Just asking for safe passage over the ocean," Zacarías apologized.

"As I've argued with you many times," Nico responded, "if the gods do exist, they clearly don't care about us."

"Maybe," said Zacarías. "But, it doesn't hurt to try and get in their good graces."

"Why did you ask for safe passage over the ocean?" Mamá asked.

"I was talking about the Great Ocean, the one that surrounds all things, existing just behind the veil, yet infusing everything." As he said this, Zacarías moved his hands in a circle. "The entire universe is like a great sponge sitting in the midst of the ocean. Every single space of the sponge is filled with ocean water. And yet, all around, there's still more ocean."

Nico sighed. "That myth was also written in a day when people believed the sky was a body of water held back by a solid dome."

Adelita tapped his forearm. "Forget it, Babe. Just let him go."

"My Grandmamma believed that too," said Carlos. "Told us about some desert lizard man that takes you to a pyramid and then takes you swimming. Or some weird shit like that."

"That desert lizard man is Tlaloc. He's the guide to the Pyramid of the Ocean."

Sitting straight, Mamá stared wide-eyed at Zacarías. "Where is it?"

"The pyramid?"

"Yes."

"It's not in any particular place. And you can't get to it by a fixed route.

"Imagine that you're out on a sunny day. You look down and notice your shadow on the ground. The shadow, while not you in substance, is still a formless, two-dimensional reflection of you. You're the object of that shadow. And if you look close enough, you may see some slight features that resemble you–the way your hair hangs, or the shape of your body. But, no matter how hard anyone looks at the shadow, they'll never be able to fully comprehend the object from which it's cast in all its intricacies.

"Now, think of the reality we experience as a shadow–a flat realm of two dimensions, without any color or clear features. The realm of the pyramid is the object from which the shadow is cast. The realm of the pyramid is ultimate reality.

"Now, think of that ultimate reality as the shadow of another realm, colorless and featureless and flat. The realm of the pyramid is the shadow of the Ashen Shore. And the Ashen Shore is the place from which ultimate reality springs. But, only Tlaloc can transcend this shadow to the pyramid."

Mamá leaned forward. "Then what happens? When you reach the pyramid?"

"Well, after climbing its two hundred and fifty steps, you enter through a narrow threshold. From there, Quetzalcoatl, the feathered serpent, carries you across the Great Ocean to the Ashen Shore. Only, Quetzalcoatl is the ocean, carrying you upon its waves.

"As you roll up onto the shoreline, you're welcomed by a roar of compassion. Thousands upon thousands of voices greet you with a swell of empathy. You're embraced by the sand. You become one with everything. You see yourself as you truly are in the cosmic picture. You're home."

Carlos laughed. "That's some crazy-ass shit there, Papá Zacarías! You been smoking the red powder?"

"But, these so-called sacred texts were written from within this shadow, as you call it," said Nico. "The folks who wrote them were straining the limits of language to describe something beyond their comprehension. So, how we actually envision what they depict could be wrong. I can come across a starving dog on the street and, out of a sense of compassion, kill it to end its suffering. Doesn't mean the dog would see it as compassion."

* * *

As I followed Tlaloc through the desert, I reached for Mamá's hand, grasping only air, and my vision was blurred from tears. Tlaloc patted my head, whimpering.

"Will Mamá be there?" I choked.

The slit that was his mouth bent into a smile. He nodded, and we continued on.

After a while, I began to feel like I was wading through water. Ripples formed beneath my sandals – yet the ground remained parched. Bubbles started drifting up from my nose – but the air was still dry. And I sensed I was walking the boundary between shadow and substance.

Off in the distance, a churning cloud of dust rolled over the sand, backlit by the setting sun. Hues of purples, blues, oranges, and reds swam upon its billows. As it drew closer to us, it increased in size, spreading across the horizon, and a colossal white sphere that was hovering over it came into view. Four wiry appendages dangled from under it, swaying back and forth, stirring up the sand.

Tlaloc held out his arm and moved me back. We stood watching.

The dust cloud stopped rolling toward us, momentarily settling as the sphere floated in place. Tremors rumbled beneath my feet as the appendages began beating into the sand, gyrating and flapping. As they burrowed a cavity into the ground, the dust cloud grew thicker, darker, and wider. Digging deeper, they began to vanish beneath the surface as the sphere descended into the expanding cavity. The trembling increased, and it felt like the ground was trying to shake me off its back. I lost balance, and Tlaloc caught me. The sphere completed its descent, sealing itself within the cavity, and the tremors slowed to a jerking stop.

Tlaloc guided me through the dissipating dust – to the edge of where the sphere met the land. And we stood on the perimeter of a great eye gazing up from the desert floor.

* * *

Mamá gave birth to me in captivity, and I spent my first thirteen years locked in a house behind barred windows. Each room was equipped with thick chains, streaming out from metal beams on the walls. I'd always have one attached to my ankle, with just enough slack to move around. Most of the time, we were kept in the basement, where there was a space for me to play and a room in the back where Mamá would be locked for hours at a time.

I was never sure which of the three men holding us was my father. However, there was one I sort of grew close with – his name was Héctor. After going in to Mamá, he'd come down on the floor and play with me, and together we'd build blanket forts. Sometimes he'd pretend he was a horse, neighing as he let me ride on his back. Occasionally, he'd bring down his virtual reality goggles; I'd peer into them wondering if that's how things really were. On my birthdays, he'd bring me a cake and sing to me.

I had both affection and disgust for him.

I still wonder if I reminded Mamá of them – if she could see them staring behind my eyes or imprinted in the features of my face.

The night before we escaped, she sang me a song I'd never heard. Her voice cracked, and her words trembled.

"Keep the pillow over your head. And sing that song to yourself if you begin to hear any loud noises," she said, trying to hide her quivering lip. "Mamá loves you." She leaned in toward me, and I clutched the grimy fabric of her dress. "Now, get some rest." Her warm kiss pressed against my cheek.

"Mamá?" I squeaked, my fingers slipping from her as she stood.

"We'll make it, Baby. I promise."

She sank into the dark corner of the basement and faded into the back room.

After a few moments, the gliding sound of the deadbolt rang out from the top of the stairs. The door creaked open, and a rapid pattering of boots descended and moved toward her.

I put the pillow over my head, pressed it against my ears, and sang Mamá's song.

We'll meet again on the Ashen Shore… We'll swim together over the Great Ocean…

The next morning, I woke to her sitting beside me. She was running her fingers through my hair, and the chain had been removed from my ankle.

"We're free, Baby. You can play outside now."

She looked different, a ravenous fire now consuming the emptiness I'd always seen in her eyes. And for the first time, I could tell she wasn't forcing a smile and wearing her bravest face. Standing, she slung a duffel bag over her shoulder and extended her hand to me.

We ambled up the basement stairs, and I kept expecting the chain to tug at my heel and pull me down. As we got to the top, Mamá asked me to cover my eyes before she opened the door. I still don't know what she did to them, but there was a thick stench of burning meat hanging on the air as she led me through the house.

"Keep them closed!"

Tasting the burnt air, I envisioned the gruesome scenery around me and choked back a gag. The stench slithered behind my eyes and began punching at them.

"Almost there, Baby!"

My knees quaked, and the floor felt like it was shifting and spinning beneath me. Mamá clasped my hand tighter. A door thundered open, and I stumbled onto a damp pillow of grass.

I opened my eyes to grey clouds swirling upon a glowing blanket of yellows and oranges unfurling into the horizon. A light dawn rain danced upon my face, startling me. I'd always wondered what rain felt like.

"Breathe in deeply and hold it," Mamá said. "Then breathe out slowly."

It felt like the earth herself was blowing her essence into me, welcoming me.

Mamá put her arm around me, and we got into one of the cars parked in the front of the house. She dropped the duffel bag onto my lap, slid the key into the ignition, and sighed as the car sputtered to life. It rolled forward, and we jerked and flopped in our seats as she pressed the brakes.

"Sorry, Baby," she said, the engine revving. "I'll figure it out."

The fire in her eyes blazed up as she taught herself to drive in those few moments. Soon enough, we were stuttering down the stony road, unsure where to go.

"Mamá, where'd you hear about the Ashen Shore?"

"It's from a story I heard about when I was a little girl in the orphanage. I've only just begun to remember it."

"How do we get there?"

"I don't think anyone knows."

"What's in the bag?"

"Their money."

That was four years ago. And I still get startled at the first drops of rain.

* * *

"Okay, here we are," said Carlos as the van limped off the road and rolled onto the sand. "Took a little longer than I said it would." He hopped out and opened the rear doors. "Everybody out that's going to America!"

"What's this?" Nico said.

"It's where you all get out."

"We're not getting out here."

"Yeah you are."

"The deal was that you take us to the border."

"The deal was to drive you to the Sonoran Desert. And I did. Straight ahead, about six miles, there'll be a hole in the fence. You can crawl through it. And on the other side you'll be in America." He motioned to Mamá and me. "Now hurry up. Cause Mamá Carmen needs to get there!"

"You can't just leave us here!" Adelita protested.

"Yes I can!" snapped Carlos. "Now don't piss me off!"

"I should've known not to trust you!"

"Get out of the van! Before Domingo makes you get out!"

Nico began to stand as if to charge at Carlos.

"Everyone calm down," said Zacarías, putting his hand to Nico and moving him back. "I'd be happy to pay you extra if you'd just drive us a bit closer."

"No, Papá Zacarías. End of the line is here. Plus, the van doesn't ride too good through the sand. But, don't worry. People walk across this all the time."

"My daughter's pregnant."

"Not my problem, Papá Zacarías. And I let the baby ride for free of charge. And you better be careful when you get there. The minutemen fight over who gets to shoot pregnant girls. They don't like illegal babies."

"You brought us out here to die!" Adelita snapped.

"I did what you paid me to do!" He drew a gun from his pants and aimed it at her. "Now get out of the fucking van!"

Domingo opened his door, and the van bobbed up and down as he slid from his seat. He came around and stood behind Carlos.

"Please," Zacarías said, holding up his hands. "Don't do this to us."

"You made the choice to have me drive you out here. Not my problem you didn't think things through. Maybe the desert lizard man can help you!"

"Please, Carlos."

"Get. Out. Now."

He aimed the gun between his eyes.

"Come on, Baby," Mamá said, patting my knee. "We'll be fine."

"See! Just follow Mamá Carmen!" shouted Carlos, slipping the gun into his belt as Mamá and I stepped down from the back of the van. "If you get goin' now, you can be in America by sundown." He held out his hand to Adelita and helped her down. "Thank you for your business."

"Bastard," she muttered.

"Hope your riding experience was a pleasureful one," he said to Zacarías. "Enjoy your stay in America."

Nico jumped down and pushed past him. "I don't need your damn help!"

"Remember. Go straight for six miles. When you get to the fence, look for the hole."

"My child's blood is on your hands!" Nico snarled.

At that, Domingo darted toward Nico, his mountainous bulk thundering against the sand. Nico spun around to face him, digging his worn sneakers into the ground, bracing for impact. Domingo reached into his waist and yanked out a pistol. Mamá grabbed my shoulder and pulled me behind her. Peering around her, I watched Domingo extend the gun to Nico.

"Take it," his voice boomed.

Nico didn't reach out, still standing in defense.

"Take it," Domingo said again with a nod.

Nico carefully slid it from his hand.

With sadness in his eyes, Domingo looked to Mamá and me. I felt my face twist into a frown as he turned and headed for the van.

"Why you giving your good gun away?" yelled Carlos, spreading apart his arms as they slipped into the vehicle. "You softy."

Dust erupted from beneath the tires as they spun out. The van rolled onto the road, heading off in the direction from which we came.

"Well," sighed Zacarías. "We better get going,"

We began our six-mile trek across the Sonoran toward the border, stumbling over the sand as if we were entranced and daydreaming, saying as little as possible to preserve our strength. I watched the sky transform from a hazy blue to a cool polychromatic of purples and oranges. We stopped a few times so Adelita could rest. For the final stretch of the journey, Nico carried her on his back.

"There!" Zacarías said, pointing ahead as the fence came into view. As we staggered closer, I could see a slit in the lattice. Nico crossed first so that he could help the rest of us through, Zacarías guiding from behind.

It was like pushing though a curtain of gnarled branches, the frayed ends of the lattice nicking my arms, biting at my face, stinging my back.

"Almost there, Baby!" Mamá said.

The hem of my dress was caught, and I yanked my leg to free it. As I did, it tore, and I fell forward into Mamá's arms.

"We're here, Baby," she said, embracing me.

I took a deep breath, exhaled, and squeezed her tight.

Then, I watched three figures emerge from behind her. "Mamá, the minutemen."

She pushed me away and spun around.

"Early catch tonight, boys!" exclaimed the one in the center, wearing a cowboy hat and snap button jacket.

"Just like fishing! Be quiet and they swim over!" said the second, a red bandanna wrapped around his scalp.

They spoke in broken Spanish, as if to mock us.

"Look! An old decrepit one!" laughed the third, pulling Zacarías though the fence, his face gashing beneath the frayed lattice.

"Please," said Zacarías. "We don't mean any harm."

"Old man, you're nothing to fear. And you can't talk your way out of what's coming!" growled the first. "You vermin sneaking into our home? All deranged from that powder shit! To kill our children! Rape our women!"

"No! Of course not!"

"Yee Haw!" shouted the third minuteman, poking Adelita's belly with the barrel of his rifle. "We got ourselves a preggers!"

"And you smuggle in your vermin offspring?" continued the first. "To infest us like rats!"

The third minuteman pulled back his rifle and then rammed it into Adelita's stomach – she wailed out and fell to her knees. Nico drew Domingo's pistol from his waist and fired it. The bullet caught the third minuteman, and he twisted sideways, toppling over. Another gunshot sounded – from the rifle of the second minuteman – and the side of Nico's face broke open. The sky's orange glow shined through the wound from behind.

"Nico!" Adelita moaned, cradling her stomach.

"He was mine!" yelled the third. "I'm the one the son-of-a-bitch grazed! Now I'm left with the geezer!" He fired into Zacarías' chest–he fell against the fence, arms flailing out.

"Papá!" Adelita cried.

The minuteman with the cowboy hat forced Mamá and me to our knees as the other two stood over Adelita.

"You can have gestating little vermin," said the second minuteman.

"Yee Haw!" yelled the third, setting the barrel of his rifle to Adelita's belly. The second aimed at her head.

"Close your eyes and sing our song," said Mamá, rubbing her palm against my back. "Just like you did when we escaped." There was a shimmer in her eyes – a tranquility I'd never seen in her. "It'll be over soon."

I cupped my ears with my hands and closed my elbows over my face.

We'll meet again on the Ashen Shore… We'll swim together over the Great Ocean…

Two tremors of gunfire rumbled beneath me in succession.

After a few moments, I slid my hands from my ears.

"Yee Haw! Boom! Boom!" shouted the third minuteman, holding up his rifle.

"You see the look on her face?" laughed the second.

"Now that the both of you've had your fun, go get the van and start loading up the bodies!" said the one with the cowboy hat. "I'd like some privacy with these two."

"Yes, sir," they replied in unison and walked off.

He turned to us. "I'm a civilized man. So, I'll let you die with some dignity and won't make a spectacle of you." The barrel of his rifle rose to my face.

Mamá took a deep breath. "Just keep singing."

I saw his finger gliding to the trigger.

"Mamá!" I trembled, walking my fingers over and around her hand, clenching it.

"Mamá?" he said. "Shit, I thought you were sisters!" He pivoted the barrel out of my face and toward Mamá. "A mother shouldn't watch her child die!"

A thunderous boom punched into my ear, rattling my limbs, and my hearing emptied out with an echo. Sparks prickled my cheeks. A wave of heat followed. I turned to Mamá, her head resting within a halo of smoldering clumps.

I looked back to the minuteman. I wanted to jump on him and claw out his fucking throat, but he pivoted the smoking barrel back to me.

My chest tightened.

Then, I saw the crimson flicker of Tlaloc's eyes from over his shoulder.

* * *

I stepped onto the white surface of the great eye, and it felt as if I'd plunged myself knee-deep into an unseen pool of water floating on top of it. Ripples unfurled onto the air around me as I began wading across it. My feet and ankles felt like they were dissolving, becoming one with the water. A warm serenity coursed through my veins. I glided over the iris, now elbow-deep. Warm fingers tickled behind my skin as the pool continued to envelop me. Shoulder-deep, I moved onto the pupil. Its thick blackness swallowed me, and it felt as if I'd melted into the waves and then collapsed in on myself. And, on the back of a massive swell, I was lifted onto a winding stone path.

Ahead of me, a three-tiered ziggurat floated against a curtain of dark purples and blues, bobbing up and down as if on water. My eyes tried focusing on it, but they struggled to comprehend its dimensions – it seemed to cast its reflection before itself, and that reflection seemed to cast its own reflection before itself. This pattern of reflection casting reflection was repeated to the left and right of the ziggurat, below it and above it, and, I assumed, behind it.

"It's the pyramid, Mamá!" I hoped she could hear me.

It looked as if it had been carved out of a single slab of stone, rather than constructed from many. Beads of water shimmered upon its smooth, ultramarine surface, giving the impression of glistening scales. And it was capped with a narrow threshold – an amber glow emanated from out of it.

"Quetzalcoatl," I whispered.

The stone path I was standing on snaked up toward the pyramid and bled into its bottom step. I began my journey toward it. As the winding path ascended, it grew narrower, and there was no ground beneath me, just emptiness. Yet I didn't need to balance myself, for on all sides of me, it felt like a cushion of water was holding me up. When I reached the first step, I glanced up, only to see myself glancing up at myself in an infinite sequence. I looked over my shoulder and saw myself staring back at me.

The steps were warm beneath my feet. As I climbed, the beads of water that coated the pyramid slid onto me; wrapping around me, they formed a single, serpentine coil. As I continued to ascend, it expanded, constricting me like a liquid snake, inviting me to become one with it. Liquefying, I mingled with it. Reaching the top of the pyramid, I splashed through the threshold, embraced by the amber glow.

I could smell Mamá's essence, and we flowed together as one, swirling within the waves of the Great Ocean, riding the back of Quetzalcoatl. I sensed that Adelita and Nico were with us; I even heard the cry of their baby. Zacarías was there as well, along with thousands of others. And we laughed and sang, coursing through the water, never to be abandoned, to exist forever within the compassionate embrace of the Ashen Shore.

Soon, I could feel my essence splitting from the water and churning within it, forming a torso. A pressure welled within me and extended outward to sprout arms and legs, and I began kicking and paddling. I opened my eyes into an eruption of bubbles as I exhaled from my new lungs.

For a moment, my sight rose just above the waterline, and I got a glimpse of the Ashen Shore, before sinking back under. It looked like thousands were waiting on the sand, ready to embrace us. The song of their welcome hung as a muffled, throbbing echo above the surface of the water.

I paddled upward in furious excitement. The waves gave me a gentle nudge and lifted me onto the shoreline. Their frothy fingers danced down my skin, hissing as they receded, diminishing beneath that great, swarming chorus welcoming my arrival – a cavernous moaning that pulsed beneath layers upon layers of frenzied wailing and shrill cackling, mingled with thousands upon thousands of agonized voices weeping with deep-throated groans.

I was on my back with my arms sprawled out to the sides. Rather than a shoreline of sand and shells, I'd been tossed upon a bed of dark ash and charred bone fragments. A hollow feeling arose in my chest as I struggled to move but realized I couldn't. It was as if I were throwing myself against the inner walls of my body, trying to get my arms to flail about – conscious but comatose; alive and locked within a state of unlife. My neck was arched back, and I could shift my eyes between the expanse above and the landscape around me; for a while, I watched as smoldering embers spread across the soot-stained sky like seagulls taking flight.

I was able to get a glimpse of Mamá to my left. She was lying on her side, her wet hair plastered against her face; I wanted to brush it over her ear so we could see each other. Further down the shoreline, to my right, Nico lay on his back, his arms straight above his head. Adelita rested with her cheek on his chest, her arms locked around a baby girl – a turtle with a pink bow on its head smiled up from her ratty pajamas. I couldn't see Zacarías.

I shifted my eyes back to the ember-laden sky. Film cameras glided over and around us, perched upon tentacle-like cranes that appeared to be made of dark red intestines wrapped within thick black metal coils; creaking sounds rang out as they bent and swiveled. From off of the cameras, tendrils of cables dangled toward the ash-covered ground and fanned out like thousands of snakes across the shore.

I shifted my eyes toward my forehead and, from an inverted perspective, saw rows of reclining chairs lining the landscape, stretching out beyond the horizon. Grafted into them with red and blue wires, countless pale white people lay wailing and moaning, looking like ghostly porcelain dolls against the dark ash and soot-stained sky. Virtual reality goggles were soldered across their eyes, each pair fused to one of the cables dangling from the cameras. Pallid, stringy roots grew out from where their fingers and toes would've normally been and sank into the ground. And as they drank from the ash, I began disintegrating into it – my tragedy feeding their compassion, their empathy keeping me alive so that they could live off the spectacle of my dying.

In time, my vision faded with the fizzling of my eyes into dust, and I was a mere outline of reddish powder atop a bed of bone and black ash – until the frothy tide of the Great Ocean rolled up and pulled me out again like shoreline sand, and a light rain began dancing upon the surface of the water.

YE HERMIT'S LAY

by Adam Bolivar

A hermit dwells beside Lake Nod,
Composing lays in ink
Of those who seek the Hidden God,
Whose souls the waters drink.

Within the lake a sapphire isle
Lay cloaked in mists that swirled;
Who finds it must be free from guile,
The purest in the world.

The tale of how Jack reached that place
Is one that's seldom told;
They say his was tricksy race,
Whose blood was strange and old.

The Drakes these kindred so were known,
Who bore an English seed,
Which in a new land they had sown,
New Albion indeed.

There was a mount, an ancient hill,
Old Hex to some it known,
Whose caverns brought uncanny chill,
Which settled in the bone,

For in the mountain's deepest heart,
A beast was bound, enchained,
A devil snared by blackest art,
And now in darkness reigned.

Atop the mount a tower sits
To which Childe Jack was bound,
Devoting to this end his wits,
Until the keep is found.

For at the tower's very top,
A maiden lies in wait;
And Jack has vowed to never stop
Until he'd stormed the gate.

The hermit bides until Jack comes,
And dwells beside the lake;
He listens for the beat of drums:
The coming of the Drake.

BRIDGE

A Tune From Long, Long Ago

by Don Webb

In the late nineteenth century obsessive German minds began the cataloging of all human knowledge. After all, almost everything that would ever be known was already almost known. The wise thing to do was to collect that knowledge and catalog it. Thomas Mueller was an obsessive German who impressed his obsessive comrades as obsessive. Working in the new field of Musikwissenschaft, Mueller began a complete catalog of every Hungarian folk tune. He began his collection in his twenties, and continued into his seventies and the disaster of 1914.

John Spenser paused after typing the above words. He could've done the happy dance in his tiny third floor apartment overlooking Congress. He had found the perfect dissertation topic – fairly well researched (in German), almost unnoticed in English and with a truly spooky ending. Best of all a research assistant at the Harry Ransom Center had found the sheet music associated with the "doomed" concert of 1914 – a collection long thought lost. It even contained the Hexelied or "Witch's Song." He could create popular articles off this for years as well perfectly respectable academic papers. Mueller had worked through decades, and so his work was exemplary in showing the changes from Adler (and even pre-Adler) methodology toward the beginning of modern ethno-musicality. There were grants and professorships and interviews at Halloween for this one. He made himself a glass of hot chocolate from powder and microwaved water. He sat down to type some more. He hadn't noticed that he had also begun to hum.

* * *

Thomas Mueller arrived in the village of Stregoicavar by carriage on a perfect late spring evening, when the air in the mountains bore the scents of a hundred types of wildflower. The sun had retreated behind the mountains leaving the western sky a deep regal purple, and the brighter stars were claiming the sky. The inn had a pleasing goulash, a fine local beer and talkative locals. Mueller had scarcely tucked into his supper when locals were approaching him.

"You are the professor that pays money to hear old songs, are you not?"

After three decades of research, Mueller was accustomed to this. Most of the informants would have nothing new to sing for him. He had encountered songs derived from medieval church music, songs from the Folies Bergère which had somehow made their way into the back country of the Hungarian hills, patriotic clap-trap. But original folksongs were still hidden in these remote villages – and one with as promising a name as "Witch-Town" would surely hold some gems. His offer never varied. A few coppers for each song, but a silver fillér for a new song that he would write down. The first hour gave him nothing new, but was entertaining. Someone sent for the old men and women, who were sure to know. The silver pouch was opened – firstly a ballad of the fight between Count Boris Vladinoff and the Turks, then a creepy tune about the original inhabitants of Witch-Town and how the honest Hungarians killed them off, finally a song about the Devil's Keep where Satan in the form of a giant toad still appeared.

"I could sing you a song that you will never have heard," said a red faced old man, clearly fond of strong drink. "But it will cost you more than a fillér."

Everyone became silent.

Another silver haired man spoke up, "Pay no attention to my brother. He is a drunk who cannot sing."

The conversation in the room shifted from German to Hungarian. Herr Mueller acted as though he could not speak Hungarian. He wanted to know what the villagers said to one another. He kept a quiet smile on his face as he feigned ignorance.

"Stefan, do not sing the witch ballad. We have worked hard to erase it from our village. What if a pregnant woman overheard it?"

"Look around you, do you see any pregnant women? Besides, what do I care if a German professor hears the song? Maybe it will make me forget it. Maybe he can carry it away from here. Even though our grandfathers' grandfathers cleared the land here, we are under the thrall of the dark people that lived here. Let him hear it!"

"Do what you want, Stefan, but don't do it here," said the brother.

The innkeeper had been summoned during this exchange. A younger man, stout with hardly any gray in his hair, he looked like a small bear.

"Stefan Gyori, I forbid you to sing the Witch's Song in my inn. This spot is clean. My grandfather kept it so, my father kept it so, I will keep it so. I have managed my whole life to hear not a note, not a word of the witches' ballad. And I will die clean with no mortgage on my soul."

There was agreement from several of the men and women. Stefan Gyori shrugged, and then addressed Mueller in German.

"Mein Herr, my neighbors are a superstitious lot. They fear that the song I would sing would bring bad luck upon this fine inn much as breaking a mirror."

Mueller replied, "Perhaps you could sing it to me elsewhere? Unless you fear it will summon the devil." He smiled at the last part, he had to fight superstition often in his quest for folk-music.

Stefan Gyori smiled back. "No, mein Herr, I am not as superstitious as my countrymen. I will gladly sing this song anywhere – crossroads, cemetery, you name it."

An old woman, who had set by the fire and said nothing all night, had a challenge for Stefan. "Oh really, Stefan Gyori, would you sing it by the Black Stone?"

Gyori's red face blanched, but in a voice only slighter higher than he had been using, "I fear nothing. I would sing it by the Black Stone."

The silence that had fallen before was nothing compared to the silence that greeted this remark. Mueller could not have been more pleased.

Gyori ended the silence with, "Of course because of the rarity if the song, I must ask for fifteen Krona."

"I could pay you ten." Said Mueller.

"It must be fifteen. After all, mein Herr, no one else will sing it for you."

Certainly the fear showing in the eyes of the room agreed with that pronouncement.

"Fifteen then, but I do I want to hear it sung by this Black Stone."

"I will sing tomorrow in the sunlight."

"I thought you were not superstitious."

"I don't fear lightning either, but I don't carry metal bars around during a thunderstorm."

* * *

John's roommate Jose Wong was fast at work on his laptop. They had a graduate school meal. Two bottles each of local craft beer (Mad Meg from Jester King) and two packages of "Oriental Flavor" top ramen (with margarine for richness). It was Tuesday night; the sounds of a single street guitarist came in their window. John was writing a description of Mueller's methods in dealing with informants. Jose got up and closed the window – perhaps with a little anger.

After a few minutes Jose said, "Can you stop humming? I am trying to write some code, and your humming is bugging the shit out of me."

"Oh I'm sorry. I didn't notice. How's the second level going?"

"The game part is great, the team is really slow delivering the graphics, and I'm stuck with sound."

"Well if you need help with the music –"began John.

"Yes, I know you're a musicology major. You say that every damn time."

They went back to work.

Fifteen minutes later Jose said, "Since you can't be quiet, I'm going to finish this over at the PLC."

He slammed the door on the way out.

Definitely need a new roommate next semester.

* * *

"This village had a very different sort of folk than it has now. It was a dark and bad place once with a different name," said Stefan Gyori as he walked Thomas Mueller away from the inn.

It was a bright day with the sun high in the sky, contented cows munching on green grass, birds busy with nest building in the hedgerows.

"What was its name?"

"Xuthltan. They were not Magyars. They were not Christians. They engaged in dark practices – devil worship, it was said."

"The Witch's Song is about them?" asked Mueller.

"It is from them."

"But I thought the Magyars killed them."

"Most of them were killed in two raids. But some of the women were kept as bondmaids. They raised the children of the noble families and they taught them the song."

"The song teaches a pagan story?" asked Mueller.

"Who knows what it teaches? We don't understand the language. It makes you see things, it makes you know things. And if a woman that is with child hears the song, her children are horribly deformed. Of course it took years to figure this out. We took the servants – old hags by then – and burned them in the village square. But the song lives on."

They arrived a patch of land that knew no green grass. Mueller thought of the "blasted heath" in Macbeth. A spindly black stone monolith rose in the center of the desolation. It was octagonal in shape, some sixteen feet in height and about a foot and a half thick. The surface was thickly dinted as if savage efforts had been made to demolish it; but the hammers had done little more than to flake off small bits of stone and mutilate the characters which once had evidently marched up in a spiraling line round and round the shaft to the top. Mueller disliked the characters at once. He was about to tell Stefan he need not sing, when the man began his eldritch lullaby.

Even though it was full daylight and a warm day, Mueller felt cold as he heard the tones. He stopped Stefan and pulled forth his tablet. He was a man of science, after all. He would record the notes. As he did so, he became dizzy and numb. It seemed that part of him was not standing in his body, but on a vast plane with a darkling purple sky. He stood before a vast pit, and something was moving in the misty depths below. It was going to show itself. There were others around him – strange caricatures of the human form with extra eyes or limbs, or fewer than they should have – as if life here were ruled by asymmetry much as on Earth it is ruled by symmetry. Suddenly the vision stopped, he was covered in a cold sweat. Stefan had his hand out.

"You pay me now."

* * *

Jose didn't come back until seven thirty the next day. John was showering. He was the TA for a music theory course that was early enough in the morning to weed out the less determined underclassmen. He heard Jose slam the door. He stayed in the shower until Jose slammed the bedroom door. He got out quietly and began getting dressed. As he headed out the door, Jose yelled at him, "It's OK. I'm not mad at you. I got inspired and finished the sound for level two. It's OK, bro, I was just grumpy about deadlines."

* * *

It was twenty years later, and Mueller had taken to making long walks in Berlin. The city with its endless smoke and noise and excitement could distract him from the tune which had haunted his thoughts more and more. His hair was shock white, his face wrinkled, his frame thin. That he had been a well-respected Professor as short as five years ago, no one would have guessed. He wore his clothes for too long without having them washed. He was not a frequent bather. He followed crowds and noises – spending late nights in the cheapest of bars, where he paid for his drinks by playing the piano and singing bawdy songs collected over fifty years. He dreaded being alone more than anything. When he was alone he could hear the Witch's Song. It seemed to come out of the black depths of space. It no longer bothered to sound like the all too human rendition that Stefan Gyori had croaked out beside the Black Stone. It no longer even had words. It had become pure tones, almost mathematical in its perfection. With the tones came the pictures – the pictures that told the hidden history of the human race. He knew that if he ever understood the implications of the history, he would go mad – but crowds and beer and bawdy songs were strong bulwarks against thinking too much.

Humans did not come from Earth. They were not the beautiful creatures of symmetry and thoughtful perfection of a loving creator. They were brought from another world where they were creatures of strange form, ruled by strange lusts and stranger religions. They were brought here and mated with hairy simians. They were made to forget their true, yet terrible natures. Some sort of being fed off a spiritual product the humans made – and humans unconscious of their true form produced more of this substance – more of this drug than humans who knew the truth. The Others, they needed the drug. Horrible things that humans once called gods in foul places like Xuthltan, then called demons when humans began making gods in their own images. Lastly they were forgotten, banished from memory, but oddly much stronger in human history. These Elder Gods grew every year, soon the planet would be theirs. When Dr. Mueller bothered to read the paper, and watch the worsening world situation, he saw Their hand at the human throat.

But the song was not about Them. It was about restocking the home world. Some great sorcerer of Ool Athag had written the song to lead human souls back to the world of beast gods who dwelt in pits, where children born with three hands and five eyes were considered lucky, where copulating with demons was a sport. The song affected a magnetic center in the human psyche. It filled the mind with more and more pictures of Ool Athag – of the horrible religious rituals, the strange orgies of sex and blood, the incomprehensible and insane art forms. The soul began to detach itself from the Earth. It would be drawn back to the human home world – a strange and surreal Hell that perhaps a Dore or a Sidney Sime could draw, or a mad poet like Justin Geoffrey could sing of. Mueller knew his soul no longer belonged to him – had in effect never belonged to him. He knew it belonged to some monstrous being on the world of purple skies. He knew his soul would fly there after death. And he knew what was "human" in him would die in strange screams and stranger prayers.

It was winter, and a fine snow had fallen on the city – a terrible grey snow fouled by factory smoke. Christmas would soon be here, but the religions of men offered him no hope – nor could nostalgia overtake the growing dread that filled his being. He passed a beggar in the street. The unshaven man in the thinnest of coats claimed his landlord was about to throw his family out. Could anyone spare a few marks to make sure his family could have a roof over their heads for Christmas?

Suddenly like Scrooge in Dickens' tale – Mueller became a new man. He pressed a five mark note in the beggar's astonished hand.

Landlord! Why hadn't he thought of it before? A landlord doesn't care from whom his money comes, only that it comes. If he could pay off the dark lords of Ool Athag with a handful of souls – they might release his. Blessed sleep and ignorance could be his again. He could teach the song to dozens of men – he still had people who remembered him as a great musicologist. He might look like a drunk, might wander the streets of Berlin – but via post he could seem impressive. He would organize a concert – a tribute to Hungarian folk music. The last tune would be the Witch's Song. He would send the world of Ool Athag the souls of a few musicians; surely if he damned enough he could be set free.

It took a few months for backers to agree to fund the concert. It was January of 1914 and all the papers speculated about the possibility of war. Would the central powers hold together? What did the unrest in Russia mean? Would the reforms in the Ottoman Empire be strong enough to keep the Empire intact? Concerts were not priorities for most Europeans. Mueller's hope to escape his return to the dark world of Ool Athag had finally awakened a long latent Catholicism. He found frequent and long visits to the Church as distracting as bars and public houses. Praying long, hard and loudly could keep the alien song at bay – and transcribing the tune into notes also relived the dark and fearful pressure.

Morality too made a weak return to his life. Surely he could not damn the souls for the magicians? Although most musicians no doubt lead lives that made Hell a likely destination – they had hope of reform. Then Thomas Mueller hit on an elegant solution. There were many Jewish musicians in Germany. He would hire only Jews, whose souls were already forfeit for his concert.

His concert took place on July 4, 1914. He advertised sparingly. He wanted as small an audience as possible. The drafty, ill-lit theater was in one of Berlin's poorer neighborhoods. The first part of the show was lively – it drew great applause from the audience, mainly ex-pat Hungarians. The second part was short. When the Witch's Song played – some left, two or three fainted in the audience, and an old cellist died during the concert. Mueller paid all of the musicians double, suggested they burn their sheet music and closed the show. As he walked into the night he felt empty. Clean. Free. A big smile appeared on his face. He had done it. He had bought his freedom.

Of course, the backers were not pleased. Two newspaper accounts mentioned it as a "cursed" concert – but it was back page news given the state of the world.

It was nearly two weeks later as he walked down the street to buy bread that he noticed he was humming. He went home, opened his straight razor and slit his throat. He left no note, and his landlady had no idea that he was once a respected scholar.

Two weeks after that, the Archduke was assassinated. No one thought of the concert, except for a few Jewish musicians who one by one went mad. The frequency of madness in Jewish musicians of Berlin attracted a few scholarly papers, but it was a small concern. A few deformed births occurred and were duly recorded by the late thirties as example of Nazi racial correctness.

The last of the remaining musicians – mad eyed old men – were gathered by the Nazis and the Witch's Song was played a few times while the workers of Auschwitz changed their shifts. If they dreamed of the purple sky, it was surely better than where they were. The death camps removed the last living traces of the Witch's Song from the Earth. However, a single bundle of sheet music hidden in a Paris garret made its way to the Harry Ransom Center at the University of Texas in Austin, Texas with many other odds and ends in 1966.

* * *

John didn't finish his dissertation. His friends, who were few in number, said he was overcome with depression. His enemies, even fewer in number, claimed that drug abuse had caught up with him. His suicide note was melodramatic and literary, misquoting Dickens from A Tale of Two Cities: "It is a far, far better thing that I do now than I have ever done; it is a far, far worse place I go to than I have ever gone." He left a second note to his ex-roommate Jose Wong. "Hey man I hope you didn't listen to me. I'm really sorry."

The later drew the attention of the Austin Police. They tracked Jose down, which was easy; he was a famous designer on his way up in the gaming industry working for Electric Anvil in Austin.

"I have no idea what he meant. He was shit to live with the last few months. All of the time humming some spooky ditty – I think it had to do with his research. He stopped bathing, just lay around the apartment and stopped forking over his share of the rent. I had to split."

"I didn't have anything to do with him after I moved out. I tried calling his Mom, a drunk that lives in San Diego. I told her he had flipped out. She said it wasn't her problem. You know, I didn't realize it at the time, but that tune he hummed really got under my skin. I put in my Master's project, I'm sure you've played it. It's the spooky song you hear when you're on the second level of Planet Revenge. That game got me this job. It's the hot item this Christmas."

"My moods? Well, I've been preoccupied since I heard of John's death. Like, could I have done more, you know? I've been working on Planet Revenge II – it's about this other world with a dark purple sky where you fight monsters in pits. It uses John's song more fully – kind of my memorial to him. So I guess his music will wind up in thousands of households."

For Dan Clore, fellow Lovecraftian

BALLS

by Russell Smeaton

On the last day of humanity, Dave and Paul were travelling across the Pennines. A light rain slicked the roads, mist slowly creeping down from the hills. Conversation inside the car had lulled to a brotherly silence, the only sounds being the swish of windscreen wipers and the hum of the engine.

"I do believe I've got to drop the kids off," announced Paul, breaking first the silence and then wind to prove his point. Dave wound down the window and dutifully pulled into the next petrol station they came to. Paul headed off to find a toilet; Dave went to fill up the car.

"Mate!" Paul shouted across the parking lot, "I need you to come and stand by the door. There's no lock!"

"Alright," sighed Dave ambling over, "but be quick. I don't want to look like a pervert or something."

"Too late for that, bender," Paul grinned and closed the door behind him.

Minutes later Dave heard a loud splash from inside.

"Dude! Courtesy flush," laughed Dave, but to no reply. Minutes passed, silent but for the increasing patter of rain. Dave knocked, calling out to his brother. Still no reply. Frowning, he gently pushed open the door and peered inside. The room was empty except for a buzzing fly and a single bulb casting flickering light. Frown deepening, he edged into the toilet and checked behind the door but Paul was nowhere to be seen. As Dave stood, scratching his head, he spotted the large metal ball in the toilet bowl.

Walking slowly to the toilet, Dave bent down to get a closer look. It was smooth apart from what looked like a red button. Underneath the button he could just make out some writing obscured by the toilet water. After one last look around, Dave picked it up and dried it with tissue. The writing said:

PAUL NOBLE
23.1.1974
BASS PLAYER

Scalp itching, Dave stood up, confused. Still expecting Paul to jump out from some hidden spot, he left the room, cradling the metal sphere, and went into the petrol station. Empty and silent, apart from the gentle tapping of rain. He peered behind the counter and there were two metal balls, identical to the one he was carrying. Both had a red button and inscriptions:

KEITH JONES
4.9.1956
ADULTERER

And:

SAMANTHA BENNET
14.3.1984
ATTENDANT

His head spun. Wondering if this was some elaborate joke, he looked around to see if there was a hidden camera crew waiting to pounce. Pressing the red button did nothing. He shook the ball but it was silent. Taking out his mobile phone he rang home. There was no answer, and Dave felt ice freeze his stomach and crawl up his spine.

In a daze, Dave left the building. There was another car he'd not noticed previously at the pumps. As he walked over through the increasing rain he fought the urge to run. His heart sank when he spotted another ball in the driver's seat.

LESLEY CARTER
11.7.1971
DOCTOR

Shoulders sagging, Dave went back to his car and slumped into the driver's seat. He carefully placed the ball with his brother's name on the passenger seat. Tears threatened to burst free as his throat thickened.

None of this made any sense. After staring blankly out the window Dave started the car up. The rain was coming down harder now. His mind raced and skittered inside his head. It felt like he'd drank too much coffee, his brain refusing to sit still and process what was happening. The only thing he could think of was home. Back to his Mum and Dad, back to cups of tea, toast, and fluffy towels. Back where life was normal.

He pulled out of the petrol station. As he drove back the way he and his brother had just come, Dave's last thoughts were about his family. Seconds later, the car veered off the road, crashing into a small bank. Two metal balls rolled out of the wreckage. They bounced and clanked down a hill before finally coming to rest in a mossy gully.

* * *

Time passed. The Earth rotated around the sun. With no humans left, buildings quickly decayed, choked by ivy. Roads crumbled and cracked. Cultivated fields became overgrown with weeds and livestock were eaten by ever wilder wild life. Dogs moped after missing owners before eventually forming savage packs. Cats instantly reverted back to their natural feral state and prospered. Forests once more reclaimed England and the air became dense as spores spurted into the ether, unchecked by humanity.

Metal spheres littered the world. Some were buried in the collapsed entrails of houses. Others lay on the ocean floor, submerged in the rusting carcasses of crashed airplanes. A few escaped unscathed, and lay glinting in the sunshine.

Exactly one million years later the red button on Dave's sphere started to flash. A squirrel shuffled up, attracted by the flashing light. Evolution had thrust the creature up the food chain. They were no longer the cute furry animals of the 21st Century. The common squirrel now reached just over a meter tall, covered in thick fur with large canine teeth. It picked up the sphere, shaking it, accidently pressing the flashing button as it did so.

Blinding light erupted from the ball causing the squirrel to run for cover.

Seconds later the light subsided, and there stood Dave. He rubbed bleary eyes and looked around. The first thing he saw was the squirrel, staring with hungry eyes as drool dripped from its snarling maw. Panic rooted Dave to the spot. The squirrel crouched, all the while staring at Dave. Dave was no expert, but that crouch looked like the squirrel was getting ready to pounce. Instinct kicked in, telling him not to break eye contact, and he slowly stepped back, tripping over a shiny ball as he did.

The squirrel stood up, head cocked to one side, as Dave floundered on the floor. As he squirmed in the mud his attention was momentarily taken by the flashing light on the ball. Without thinking he slammed the button down, white light exploding from the ball. After his eyes recovered there stood his brother Paul, as if he'd never been away. The squirrel had seen enough and ran, leaving the brothers to reunite.

They stood facing each other for a moment before hugging. At once, they both started talking, bursting out with laughter. Neither could explain. The last thing Paul remembered was going to the toilet, and that was that. Dave remembered seeing the shiny balls, remembered setting off for home, and then nothing. Neither had any answers, only questions. As they looked around the questions only increased. Where was the road? Where was the petrol station? What the hell was that thing just now?

With nothing else to do, they decided to walk up the nearest hill, maybe try and recognize some landmarks. The long, dense grass made the going tough and soon they were huffing and puffing. Unseen things scurried away as they stomped up the hill. As they climbed they spotted an outline of what might have been a building. Exchanging glances, they strode towards it. As they got nearer they could see several flashing red lights.

The brothers collected a total of 3 balls together. The three that Dave had seen in what seemed like another life: Keith (the adulterer); Samantha (the attendant) and Lesley (the doctor).

"You know," started Dave hesitantly, "there was one of these balls with your name on it."

"You what?"

"I dunno… I mean, when I pressed that button there was this flash of light and there you were," replied Dave.

They both looked at the three balls, brows furrowed. After a moment, Paul shrugged and walked up to the ball with Keith's name on it. Picking it up, he was about to press the button when Dave stopped him with a cough. Frowning, Paul looked over at his brother who shook his head in way of response. Neither said a word as Paul's hand hovered over the flashing button. Slowly Paul's hand moved away from the button. He gently put the ball back down next to the others and moved away, as though the balls were bombs, about to explode.

As soon as the ball was back with the others the brothers started babbling to each other. Did they want an adulterer with them? Maybe just the doctor? Why not the attendant? Was an adulterer a bad person? Backwards and forwards they went, conversation rattling round and round as the sun started to go down.

A light wind picked up, cooling their sweat and rippling the grass like the sea. A bird tweeted overhead as insects chirped, hidden in the green ocean. In the dying light Dave looked at over the fields. In all directions he could see flicking lights, like swarms of fireflies. It took a minute or two to register they were in fact the flashing lights of more balls – thousands of them, stretching out in the distance.

Turning to at his brother, he could see that Paul had also noticed the flashes, mouth open.

Closing his mouth, Paul turned slowly to Dave and said with a sigh, "Oh balls".

CALL ME COREY

by Matthew M. Bartlett

Corrine sat primly, one arthritis-hooked hand crossed over the other in her lap, and watched the rain-blurred city roll by beyond the expansive windows of the Senior Van. She sat where she always did when the seat wasn't taken: two seats behind the driver, facing the center of the van, purse at her side, walker in front of her like a rickety shield. Today she had the van mostly to herself, a rarity. One old coot in a trilby and a woolen paletot sat in the very back, holding a black cane between his knees, both hands gripping it at chest level. Dark glasses obscured his eyes. Normally the van was crowded with stooping men with cinched belts and old biddies clutching pocketbooks, chattering inanely, off to medical appointments and markets and who knows where.

Getting here had been an ordeal, every piece of it. Swinging her legs out of the warm bed, throwing the covers back. Relieving herself. Bathing her old body, a tedious and dreadful chore, drying off in the steam filled bathroom, stepping into the chill of the bedroom, pulling on her old, familiar dress and sweater. She had done all those things and she had pushed her walker through the carpeted halls, past the institutional art and the bulletin boards and half-finished jigsaw puzzle on the big table, past the shelves of large-print books, out to the porch, where a rickety elevator shuddered and creaked down to the walk where the van waited, exhaling impatient puffs of cobalt blue smoke.

With no one blocking the windows, they served as a movie screen; today's feature was a smeared and blurred montage of neon-bruised storefronts, empty lots, apartment buildings with barred windows, city buses, figures in coats and hats caught up in the rush of a mid-morning weekday. She looked down at her shoes, lined up her feet neatly, one aside the other. Today was Dr. Grant. His name was there in her day book, in her spiky, blocky hand, ball-point blue, pressed hard into the paper. He was to look at her feet, which had of late begun to swell in the evenings, to ache when it rained, propelling needles of pain up into her knees.

The van turned off the main street, passed still and silent tenements, three-story houses with plywood for windows. On a weedy sidewalk a thin, long-bodied dog walked unsteadily on its hind legs, teeth bared, ears up like toast points, determination in its eyes. It held out its front paws like a tightrope walker. Good boy, she whispered, unaware that she was speaking. Good, good boy. She watched the dog's procession for as long as she could before the van turned onto another road of decrepit houses and overgrown yards. She saw a rat on a windowsill chewing out the stomach of a rag doll. She saw a little girl in jeans and a smudged green raincoat sobbing into her fists in a fenced-in front yard. She saw a billboard above the highway advertising caskets made of hard candy.

The driver's face in the mirror was porcine and expressionless, his lips pursed in a silent whistle. He pulled the van over at a disintegrating curb in front of a boarded-up gambrel-roofed house. A rusted tricycle leaned, half sunk, in the mud of the front yard. A candy bar wrapper flapped like a winged thing trapped in the leaning chain-link fence. A muted buzz started, grew louder, like that of a hornet, and a power-wheelchair toting a twisted up white-haired lady appeared in the driveway, buzzed up to the van. The driver activated the lift, and in a flash the old lady was on board and seated across from Corrine. As the driver pulled away from the curb, the newcomer smiled. It looked like a grimace of pain.

"Good morning," the lady sang. Her eyebrows were painted on a touch too dark and a touch too low, lending her a comically sinister aspect. Her cheeks sagged and her hair, white as the snow in the eaves of a church, shone under the LED lights. Two small Band-Aids locked arms on her cheek.

Corrine nodded, looked past the woman at the houses, the trees, the squat little school, the overgrown shrubs, the garages and sheds.

"Can't talk or won't talk?" the lady said, her sugary tone gone sour.

Corrine smiled, but it didn't touch her eyes. "I'm not much for chatting," she said.

"Oh, that's fine," the lady said. "I'll do all the heavy lifting." Her tone shifted from kindly old lady to schoolmarm. "I am Arlene and I'm from Chelmsford. My son never calls me, I hate cats, and my doctor tells me I'm more cancer than woman. I am 89 years old, not 'years young', and they say growing old is not for sissies, and so I'm no sissy, because I'm growing older by the second."

She paused. A shadow crossed her face, then she grinned a hard grin. "Statistically, I'm dead."

Then she brightened again, scratched at her knee with a crooked, long fingered hand. "I used to be a brunette, I used to be sex-mad, and I once knocked a woman out cold for touching my husband's shoulder at a cocktail party."

Corrine said, "You're a real firecracker."

"She speaks! Heh. Not anymore, lady. Maybe a stepped-on old bottle-rocket in the dirt of a public park. But I had a good time. I surely did."

The bus turned again, passed Turnbush Elementary School. A jungle-gym, its colors faded, glistened in the rain. Giant metal animal heads with handlebars for ears nodded to-and-fro, to-and fro behind a rusted chain-link fence, their oval eyes mournful, weary from decades of silent acquiescence. Birds lined the roof in a companionable row, some flying off to the powerline and back, reporting to the others what they saw from that superior vantage point. The van turned onto a rutted road of winter-torn concrete and gravel. Above the interstate traffic seethed under a looming billboard that depicted a cartoonish devil running toward the viewer, reaching out with a three-dimensional claw. HE'LL TAKE THE HINDMOST, the billboard claimed in a lightning bolt font. Somewhere someone screamed.

Corrine leaned forward in her seat. The bus driver honked his horn and swerved slightly. "Arlene," she said, "My name is Corrine, or Corey, that's what everyone used to call me. When I was a girl, I was abused by my father and his friends from the Knights of Columbus. They took me each in turn, and then two or three at a time. They smelled of cigars and sweat. They tore my flesh, and broke my spirit. I was a toddler, Arlene. They tried to break me, to ruin me for men, and for women. But I'm not milquetoast, Arlene, and don't you ever mistake me for milquetoast.

"I've lived eighty-five years in service to Satan."

Arlene's painted-on eyebrows rose an inch and she opened her mouth to speak.

"I'm not done," said Corrine. "I've caused mighty trees to grow from the ground and subsume the bodies of violent men. I've seen the fabric of this world pulled apart like skin, looked into the illimitable. I walked through savage blood orgies in certain houses in a certain city, my hair soaked with breast milk from the devil's handmaidens, my feet sloshing through God knows what. I've danced in midnight mausoleums with the dusty dead."

The bus jounced twice, as the driver rode up onto the curb at the edge of a great field, beyond which a river snaked and mountains rose like the haunches of half-buried gods. The van bounced along over hillocks and wheat stalks and catchweed and thistle. The ladies gripped the posts nearest them. The driver hit the radio, and ragtime music filled the van.

"I've been a good old wagon, but I done broke," the driver shouted.

"Yes indeed, yes indeed," said Corrine. "Oh, Arlene, you dear thing. Have you ever tasted the boiled flesh of infants? Rutted with red-fleshed devils in fang-lined caves on islands of muscle? Would that you could hear their screams of pleasure. It was like your fingernails torn off and dragged across all the chalkboards in the classrooms of Hell. You want to talk about cancer? I eat cancer for dinner and shit out the common cold."

"Okay," said Arlene.

"Okay what?"

"Okay, Corrine."

"Call me Corey."

A bell dinged once. The ladies looked back at the old coot in the trilby and the overcoat, who had just pulled the stop indicator. The van shuddered to a halt and the man rose, checked on and around his seat for personal belongings, exactly as the sign behind him directed.

"Creeping Jesus," Corrine said.

Arlene said nothing.

The man shuffled up to them, lifted his hat. The top of his head was bald, scorched, torn away in places. Something was feeding in there, or many things. The chewing was audible over the ragtime music that still bubbled around them like fizzy pop. "Ladies," the man said, and stepped off the van. The sewn-in belt of his coat caught in the door and he was spun around, grabbing at the side of the van for purchase, finding none. As the driver rolled off, the man was crushed under the back wheels. The driver backed up over the man, then rolled forward again, then back.

"I'm terribly sorry for the delay," he said with a voice like top-shelf rye. "If you have any complaints, you may call the customer service number and utilize our feedback system. It's in the book!" Then he pulled from the front pocket of his vest a tube of paint and an artists' brush. He squeezed a glistening glob of black paint onto the bristles and daubed it onto the rearview mirror, swishing the brush back and forth, back and forth as Corrine and Arlene watched. Then he turned a lever and the side mirrors folded inward.

"There is no sin," he said, letting the tube of paint and the brush fall to the floor of the van, "and all is as it seems."

Arlene said, "I'm going to be late, damn you, damn it all."

Corrine said, "Ride it out, honey. We're in the hands of the devil now, in his infinite pride, under his watchful gaze. We're not late. We're early."

"All," said the driver, "is as it seems." He started up the engine, pumped the gas, and continued through the field, speeding up now, the van jouncing and jolting mightily. Thunder stuttered in the darkening sky. The riverbank approached, rocky, lined with benches. The river was orange murk, bubbling. The van filled with the reek of blood and alcohol, ammonia and charcoal. The ragtime music fell away into static.

Corrine pictured Dr. Grant's waiting room, people flipping through magazines, the young blonde at the desk calling her out name, no one answering, calling it out one more time. The smell of the office, carpet cleaner and anxiety. The shelves of file folders, tabs of red and blue and green. The bleating telephone. The tiled ceiling and the easy listening music. Dr. Grant's swollen hands and his disarming, tight-lipped smile. "Yes," she said. "I'm ready. I'm here."

The driver piloted the van between two of the benches, over the rocky edge, and into the river. For a while it floated along. Then it began to sink.

HERO MOTHER

by Cody Goodfellow

I wake to her voice confirming in that half-maddening, wholly comforting way that the wetness I'm lying in is only natural. "Broke just before midnight. I won the bet."

I get the nativity kit and the scrambler and the Other Mother's Manual binder (possession of which is, itself, a felony) and the cumbersome Italian semi-automatic shotgun that was a gift from her parents.

The gestation cycle's supposed to be thirty-nine weeks, but even with the suppressors, Barb is clearly done with this one. "She doesn't make the rules. Mama makes the rules."

She needs help getting out of bed. A bad episode yesterday in the shower – she leaned on a rail and it collapsed under her weight. I can't show it to the super.

I page the elevator and send it down off our ID to check the lobby with my spy camera on the wall. Security cameras down there are all trashed, and anything could be down there. Random street freaks, or something less random.

Nobody there but a contract exterminator, spritzing poison on the couches and the snack machines.

She says I'm paranoid, but this exterminator, I swear I saw him the last two times, and he was a trash collector. She doesn't see. She can't imagine why they would want to stop us. She thinks the ones on top would fix it all, if they could. She has to be protected from everything. I have to hold my tongue, but for her peace of mind, she hasn't read the news since the implantation procedure, nearly eleven months ago. She doesn't know how bad it's getting.

"Now," she says, now, now now, and I call back the elevator, and it takes forever to climb to our floor and my camera in the street is hinking like it might be playing a loop of an empty street.

When the door opens, I almost shoot my reflection. The exterminator is gone when we come into the lobby.

She wears her mask and hunches forward in her wheelchair, but she wouldn't fool anybody. This time, the nutritionist had her pounding so much fish oil and dairy that she got gout in her feet and hands, and the immunosuppressors meant she couldn't go outside the sterile bubble of our apartment, to say nothing for the hormone treatments required to accommodate the longer gestation period.

Our state allows everybody to have one. Second pregnancies get collected and put up for adoption, but more likely sent to the orphan farms. When my wife miscarried, she was arrested but then summarily exonerated for murder. If something happens to your baby, the state and your church can get you an easement to try again, or to adopt from the ones clearly unfit for a lifetime of public service. There are worse states.

We decided to do this, instead.

They can't implant in the artificial wombs anymore after what happened in Arizona. The cops flushed out three hundred viable fetuses in a warehouse outside of Tucson. It hardly made the news at all, and they called it "a black market stem cell research lab."

So they need people like my wife.

The midwife meets us at the door with a taser stick and a shot of Demerol. I wheel my wife into the clinic, jolted by the sight of all the familiar equipment in this strange new place. An abandoned insurance office on a dead business loop ten minutes out of the dead metro center. Last time it was an old muffler shop; the time before that, they still had the facility in the old zoo, before it became an immigrant detention center.

We had surgery on her pelvis for this one, but it's still going to be a difficult, dangerous birth. We're worried that the fetus is putting pressure on her arteries and impairing bloodflow to her legs.

After the second one, we put in the Caesarian zipper, but it kept getting infected. This is her eighth.

I love the way she looks at me now. It fills my heart to overflowing, so much I don't even care it's not for me. Did she ever love me? Does it matter? We were brought together for this. When she looks at me like this, it's not her at all. She's Mother Nature.

The nurse guides her breathing exercises as she lays back in the cradle and lets her majestic bulk be lowered into the tank of blood-warm saltwater. The monitors chirp busily, twin heartbeats. The midwife takes me aside, tells me there's a complication.

I look at the monitors and shrug, would they switch them over to a false output to keep us from getting alarmed? But no, the nurse murmurs in my ear, leading me out of the delivery room.

Our obstetrician, Dr. Arbogast, was killed in a single-car accident on her way to the clinic tonight. In her own garage.

"Were you followed?" she asks. "Because there are people outside."

Last time, they had two women with guns for ad hoc security, but this time, there's just us. I take the shotgun and go to the door, but I know what I'll find, and I'm not wrong.

Three of them in a shitty Chinese solar hatchback, watching our makeshift clinic's strip mall from the abandoned McDonald's parking lot across the street. Too many to be cops, but they had learned to act like them. Instead of kicking the door down like they used to, but would wait for the unmarked ambulance that would come to evacuate the midwife and our new baby to its new home. But the police wouldn't go far enough for them, so they're out there, watching.

Funny how these same people used to haunt Planned Parenthood, shaming women getting abortions. I want to go across the street, sometimes without the shotgun but mostly with it, and ask them why they're so dead against this.

But I already know.

It's because the world can't end soon enough for them. They can't stand for anyone, in their arrogance, to try to find some way for it to go on, to replace what was lost and admit we made a mistake. But lately, they're armed a lot better than I am, and a lot more willing to use them.

I'm sure I can't do it. That's when I do it. Holding the shotgun across my chest, pistol grip riding my belt buckle, I cross the street forcefully. They sit staring straight ahead, as I come abreast of the car, I notice all the passenger side windows are kicked in, cobwebs of safety glass mirroring the ruin visited upon their faces.

The driver, a heavyset woman, slumps against the steering wheel. The passenger, a man with a dignified silver beard, leans back against the headrest, marveling at the contents of his character, the better angels of his nature, in an aerosolized smear across the windshield. The one in the back, tucked in between bundles of church pamphlets and protest signs, is young enough to be their daughter, but she's the biggest. Under a Wonder Woman raincoat, she's wearing a vest with enough bricks of plastique to take out the whole block. Perhaps as a mercy, she was taken in the back of the head, so her eyes still stare at me though the hole in her head is big enough for the streetlight to shine through it.

She was prepared to give her life to end our blasphemy. But someone beat her to it.

I back away from the car, looking all around with the shotgun I will never use above my head. About two blocks away on the roof of a burnt-out office tower, a green light blinks once, then cuts out.

Something tingles in my chest. It's my phone. SHE'S HERE.

I go back inside. The nurse takes the shotgun and smocks and scrubs me down before I can see her.

She's lost a lot of blood, fighting the sedative to hold on long enough for me to see her. When she wakes up, the baby will be gone and we'll probably have to move again, and this time, maybe even leave the country. I know that's what she wants most, to go where they have better surgeons who're more committed, who understand why we're doing it this way, why we're taking it onto our own bodies to restore what's been lost.

She lies back in the cradle as the nurse works the hydraulic lift, a cloud of bright scarlet placental blood swirling between her legs. The baby swims comfortably around her feet, nosing the perimeter of the tank. The replay of the video plays on the monitors, the twitching scythe of the tail emerging from my wife's partially evulsed vagina, then slips out of the midwife's gloved fingers to dart to the surface, expelling the mucus plug and fluid blocking her blowhole to take her first breath.

My wife points at the vital statistics. Birthweight is twenty-eight pounds—a tad low—but from bottlenose to the tip of her flukes, she's forty-three inches long and extinct from the world's oceans for going on eleven years.

I give her hand a squeeze and kiss it. She's still holding on, she wants to touch the baby one last time, but the couriers from the institute are here, wheeling the tank out to the truck parked outside.

I know this will be the hardest part for her, the emptiness inside as she recovers, the schemes to get back into that golden, glowing ordeal all over again before the pain becomes too much.

In the Soviet Union at the ragged end of World War II, Josef Stalin ordered a unique class of civilian award, the Order of Maternal Glory, which was presented to mothers who successfully bore and raised seven or more children.

My wife wipes tears from her eyes as the nurse staples the tearing of her birth canal. Nobody pins a medal to her chest.

She pulls me close and whispers in my ear, and the urgency in her eyes makes me do it.

I go after the couriers, out into the back. Two women, they look like substitute teachers, even pointing their rifles at me. One of them has a flashlight clipped to her parka with green cellophane taped over the bulb.

I invoke our right by the contract we signed and burned, invoking our rights as surrogate birth parents. I tell them our daughter's name and I make sure they remember it, before the truck takes her away.

REDEYE

by Stephen Mark Rainey

"Bucharest to London Heathrow, leaving after sunset and arriving before midnight. Let me see what I can get for you."

Adam Lang pulled up a list of available direct flights on his monitor, already knowing the commercial carriers wouldn't meet his client's demands.

"I don't have any evening flights into Heathrow. There is one into Luton, on Skorzeny Air, leaving Bucharest at 7:35 PM and arriving at 9:55 PM. Oh, of course, I understand. I don't like Luton either. Who does? Now, if you don't object to a slightly later arrival, with a connection in Zurich or Frankfurt, we could get you in around 1:30 AM. No? Certainly, I realize time is of the essence. I may have another option for you. Let me check it out. Since it's wintertime, we have a little more latitude on departure times. I know, I hate those long days as well. Bad for the complexion."

Lang logged into his account on the exclusive Redeye Network, certain he could accommodate his client's request – if the gentleman were willing to pay the rate for a specially chartered flight. Like all of Lang's clients, Mr. Dalca could certainly afford it, but with some of these referrals, even from such a trusted client as Baron Krilencu, you never knew how miserly – or plain eccentric – they might turn out to be. Funny how few of them ever just booked their own flights online. For that matter, most of them didn't seem to know or care what Google was, much less any of the online travel services. But, for him, these peculiarities had opened a unique and highly lucrative business opportunity.

"Now, Mr. Dalca, with this option, I can guarantee you will get to your destination within your specified time frame. It's a private charter, and it is a bit more expensive. But satisfying requirements such as yours are Redeye's specialty."

He entered his client's information into the company's system and checked "referral". When he saw the price of the charter, he still cringed.

"Okay, I have that information coming up," he said. "Now, since you've been referred by Baron Krilencu, I can offer you a ten percent discount. With that discount, your price will be – " He paused a moment before reading aloud the amount shown on his screen.

He breathed a sigh of relief when no expression of dismay came from the other end of the line.

"Yes, sir, that is the base price. There are any number of premium features we can add, especially since we have a couple of days before you're set to travel. Absolutely, I have plenty of experience with these kinds of arrangements, and discretion is my top priority. Just so you're aware, I have a ninety-nine percent success rate fulfilling my clients' needs. Why, yes, thank you. Now, I'll need to get some information about your particular preferences. Is that all right? Very good."

Lang opened a new window under the "Premium Services" heading, scanned the options, and began to go down the list with Mr. Dalca.

"Now then. Do you prefer male or female? Female it is. Age? Twenty to thirty. Any preference of hair color? No? All right. Petite, medium, tall, extra large? Medium, then. Any specific race or nationality? How about blood type? Good. Okay, we're almost done. Hey, here's something for you. Redeye already has a couple of selections in stock that match your criteria. If you choose to go with one of these, I can knock twenty percent off the premium rate, since it means there's no need for new acquisitions. Yes, sir, one is Belgian, the other German. Very good, Belgian it is. I understand Redeye has received many compliments on that vintage. I think you'll be pleased. Now, do you have any other personal requirements the carrier should be aware of? Any baggage needing special handling? No? Very good."

Lang completed the form, submitted it, and pulled up the final page. "Now, as for your payment, we have a few different options. Direct transfer of funds to a special international account is our preferred method, but there are alternatives if you wish to – oh, the transfer is fine? Excellent. All right, give me just a moment, and we can get things going here."

So far, so good. Although he welcomed new clients, the initial transactions often made him a little tense, sometimes even nervous. These were not ordinary people, and they could be testy, intimidating, or – as on a couple of occasions – menacing, even when the arrangements proved satisfactory in the end. Mr. Dalca's manner was terse and cold – very typical of the eastern European sort – though he seemed pleased enough by Redeye's upgrade options. He didn't balk at the expense, either, so he might prove to be an account worth courting in the future. Hell, Lang's percentage from this transaction alone would be nothing to sneeze at.

The transfer cleared, and the reservation was made.

"All right, Mr. Dalca, everything is set. You are confirmed on the special Redeye charter, departing Bucharest at 7:05 PM and arriving Heathrow at 9:30 PM. Your in-flight service provider is a twenty-six-year-old blonde Belgian female, medium stature, blood type listed as AB positive. In the event this individual cannot provide service as requested, Redeye guarantees a replacement with matching or near-matching attributes. The carrier does request that you arrive at the private terminal at least ninety minutes prior to departure. Now, if for any reason your plans change, you have until four hours before departure to receive a refund, minus a thirty percent service charge. Do you have any questions about your itinerary? Very well, Mr. Dalca, is there anything else I might assist you with today?"

The slow, hollow voice on the other end of the line replied: "I am satisfied."

The golden words. Lang gave his client his confirmation number and hung up. Excellent, he thought. Tonight, he could break out the expensive wine. A few days earlier, he had set up a regular weekly charter for a client in Indonesia, and the rewards from that deal would put a fair dent in the mortgage on his summer house in Newport. Still, while he enjoyed the challenges and rewards of his particular occupation, he didn't want to do this forever. If anything, he would most appreciate the opportunity to visit many of the locations to which he often booked his clients. While he considered himself well-traveled, he had never been to Switzerland or Austria, two of the places he most wanted to visit. All his life, he had dreamed of snow skiing in the Alps. He could afford it now; he lacked only time enough to fit in all the things he wanted.

Yes, business was good. Far better now than it had ever been. That his reputation in this rarest of industries preceded him counted for a lot, to be sure. However, the somewhat unsettling reality was that there were simply more of them than there had been only a few years earlier. While they mostly remained in the shadows, as their kind had for centuries, they seemed to be proliferating at a rate unprecedented in his lifetime. Disconcerting to some extent, but still a boon to business, and, for the foreseeable future, devotion to business trumped personal unease.

For today, his work was done. He logged off his computer, gathered his coat and hat, and prepared to lock up his office, a small cubby at the end of a row of shops on the outskirts of Arkham's business district. Lang Travel's more conventional business made sufficient profit to keep two agents and an office manager busy by day, and since they ran it capably enough, he did little more than check over the books from time to time. His staff knew he "dabbled" in other ventures, but of course they had no inkling about the true nature of his specialty. Even among the more well-informed members of the business community, he limited his interaction to the barest necessity, for while he rarely gave them much consideration, there were dangers beyond mere competition in his particular field of endeavor.

This end of the tree-lined street was brightly lit, but his car – a purposefully nondescript Toyota Camry – was parked just around the corner, on the darkened side street, which was generally the closest available parking when he arrived in the afternoon. His was now the only car left, half a block down. He would love to have a private parking lot, he thought, but there simply wasn't enough need to justify the expense, since few of his clients visited the office in person. Besides, this little walk twice a day was about the most exercise he got anymore. He needed to do something about that, for sure. It wouldn't do for his heart to run down before he hit fifty – an unwelcome milestone only a couple of months away.

He had barely turned the corner when a rush of anxiety hit him like a frigid, wet wind. He hadn't heard anything, hadn't seen anything – he didn't think – but something had triggered his internal alarm system. He picked up his pace a little but then detected a vague stirring sound behind him, felt the burning stare of unseen eyes. He spun around and – there it was – a very tall, very dark silhouette standing on the sidewalk at the street corner.

No, not standing.

Hovering.

The figure's feet hung a good eighteen inches above the concrete pavement. Lang had to angle his head upward to focus on the faintly luminous eyes glaring at him with laser-like intensity.

He hadn't breathed a near-silent "Oh, my God" and turned to sprint for his car when he collided with something whose surface yielded slightly but whose mass remained as unmoved as a stone wall.

"I beg your pardon," came a deep voice, as hollow and cold as if it had echoed from a tomb. "I have been anxious to meet you, Mr. Lang."

Lang drew a deep, careful breath and tried to appear composed. "Excuse me," he said, unable to keep his voice from quavering. "You startled me. Yes, I'm Mr. Lang. Do we know each other?"

"We have done business."

"I see. You are?"

"I am Mr. Rathburn. This is Ms. Alexi." The first figure he had first seen materialized beside the tall man, and he now realized it was, in fact, a woman. Billowing black hair partially covered her face, and he felt a knifelike gaze from beneath her shadowed brow. Both of them wore long, dark overcoats, and the brim of a black fedora hung low over Rathburn's features. Lang groped through his mind, delving farther and farther in, trying to recall the "business" between them, and after a few moments, the name "Rathburn" struck a familiar chord. At the moment, though, he felt too rattled to quite apprehend the memory.

"Is there something I can do for you? I mean, if you need to set up a reservation straight away, we can go back to my office. It's right over – "

"That won't be necessary," Rathburn said. "However, there is a matter between us never resolved, and we would like you to accompany us on a little trip. It shouldn't take very long."

"I'm afraid I can't," he said, stricken with a fear unlike any he had ever experienced. He had met members of their kind only once before, and under very different circumstances. He had always known that, given his profession, he might encounter them again face to face, but somehow he had never anticipated anything so unnerving as this. "I have a late dinner date in a short while, and I really do need to get home beforehand."

"We have a dinner date as well," the tall man said, "so I understand your concern. As I said, this won't take long. Let me ask you, Mr. Lang, do you remember working with me some time ago?"

"Your name is familiar, but I'm afraid I can't place the exact circumstances. I do have a rather booming business, I must tell you."

"I am aware of this. You boast of having a ninety-nine percent success rate for your clientele, is that not correct?"

"It is," Lang said, feeling simultaneously wary and proud. "I do."

He glimpsed a luminous green flash beneath the brim of the fedora. "That is commendable," Rathburn said. "However, I must tell you, Mr. Lang – and this makes me very sad – that we, Ms. Alexi and I, are the one percent."

* * *

As consciousness crawled back from the depths of some unfathomable abyss, Adam Lang began to understand, for the first time in his life, the meaning of pain.

It was everywhere. In his head, his chest, his arms and legs, his neck. Sharp, burning daggers that seemed to be slicing him apart from within. He wanted to move, to escape, to roll or writhe away from the blaze inside him, but he had no control over his muscles. Somewhere beyond the keening shriek inside his head, he could hear a lower, rumbling thrum, harmonizing with a thin whining sound.

He knew it instantly. He was inside an airplane. A prop plane.

In the air.

After some time, when he began to explore sensation beyond the pain, he realized he was sitting upright. The lighting, which he perceived through a translucent mist, was warm and – thankfully – not very bright. There was a patch of darkness amid the light, and it moved. A human figure, he thought, just a few feet away.

Or perhaps not quite human.

"Welcome back, Mr. Lang." He recognized Rathburn's hollow voice.

"Don't try to move, as you'll only cause yourself more pain. Just relax. Can you speak?"

When he attempted to open his mouth, it felt as if his jaws had been wired shut. But his lips parted and a raspy sound escaped his throat. "Hurts."

"Of course it hurts. That was my intention. Just so you know, you're inside my Beechcraft Baron. In a way, I actually have you to thank for it. After that little debacle you caused last year, I decided managing my own transportation was in my best interest. This plane is for short hops. I also own a Gulfstream G550 for when I wish to take longer trips."

Lang's vision cleared enough that he could see Rathburn seated across from him. When he managed to roll his eyes to his left, he made out Ms. Alexi next to him, her luminous eyes peering from beneath her thick black hair. She might have been attractive but for her blue-white flesh.

"Don't understand," he said. "Don't know of any debacle."

Rathburn leaned forward and gave him an appraising stare. "You don't remember a certain Ms. Edmonds? Out of New York? You made special arrangements for her to fly to Paris via charter. But you used a rather less-than-reliable company – not the one you typically choose. The flight was delayed several hours due to some internal bungling of theirs. Perhaps you'll recall how that ended."

He shook his head, and a bolt of pain shot down his neck. "No, I don't know. All I know is it was too late to make arrangements with Redeye. I did the best I could, and I got her on a charter. I never heard from Ms. Edmonds again. She never offered any feedback. I assumed she took up any issues with the carrier itself."

"You used a budget charter, but you charged her your usual fee. And this carrier failed to provide any of the necessary protection against such delays. So, Mr. Lang, Ms. Edmonds was caught in sunlight. And she perished."

"No," he said, scarcely believing what he was hearing. "No, I didn't know anything about that."

"No? Your cut-rate carrier didn't inform you of such a dire departure from 'routine'? That one of your clients was actually a casualty of your carelessness – or greed?"

"They never did. But I made a good-faith effort to get her to her destination. I did." He tried to meet Rathburn's glare, but his eyes failed him. His gaze fell, and for the first time he realized his shirt was covered in blood.

His blood.

He nearly choked. "Who was Ms. Edmonds?"

Ms. Alexi finally spoke, her voice like the chime of a cracked iron bell. "She was our protégé."

"We are deeply unsatisfied," Rathburn said and rose from his seat. "And now that we both have our answers, our business is almost concluded. Please stand up."

Lang felt his muscles, which would not obey his commands, obeying the voice of the other. He struggled to his feet, wobbled, and nearly fell backward, but Rathburn's will held him upright.

He felt a new stab of fear as Ms. Alexi also rose from her seat, her gaze locking on his already bleeding throat.

Rathburn said to her, "Would you like to do the honors? I will get the door."

* * *

AP Dateline – 23 January, Arkham, MA

In a town known for unusual and sometimes inexplicable events, a new mystery is unfolding in Arkham, Massachusetts. The body of Arkham travel agent Adam Lang was found just before dawn this morning, lying in the middle of the town common, apparently having fallen from some considerable height. A geocacher visiting from out of state indicated he had left his hotel room before sunup and was on his way to the common when he came upon what he took to be a full set of men's clothes on the ground. On closer examination, the geocacher, who preferred to give us only his gaming alias – "Damned Rodan" – determined that there were, in fact, human remains among the clothes. Investigators have now confirmed that Mr. Lang's body had fallen or been dropped several thousand feet, almost certainly from an airplane. All the more mysterious, however, is the fact that the body, before falling, had been completely drained of blood. At this time, there are no further details about the body's condition, and only speculation regarding the actual cause of death.

More information will follow as it becomes available.

SÉANCE

by K.A. Opperman

The crystal ball reveals an eerie face,
And all the candles flicker, glowing low.
The scarlet curtains flutter with a trace
Of something more than midnight winds that blow.

The tarot cards are scattered – only Death
Remains upturned amid the stars and moons.
The pretty sibyl, chilled by spectral breath
Upon her swan-like neck, so nearly swoons.

The ouija board is brought before the host,
And fingers push the planchette here and there.
A message forms, transmitted by a ghost –
The fetching psychic blanches in her chair…

The skull upon the parlor bookshelf grins
Amid the grimoires, in the gloom unseen;
It knows its mistress and her secret sins,
Revealing all this night of Halloween…

LOOKING FOR GHOSTS

by Duane Pesice

"It's a Good Life," said Al McAdam. "I wish I were in a cornfield."

And he polished the tumblers and highball glasses and flutes and schooners one more time, setting them back precisely so that everything fit the way it was supposed to, and he went on with his day.

The television in the corner played MeTV all day long, every day, when it wasn't playing TMC or, very occasionally, the SyFy network. This being the end of the holiday season, the tube was tuned to the latter.

The annual Twilight Zone marathon.

The nightflies didn't mind, as long as the beer was cold and the AC was on. It was a warmer winter than usual, with the temperatures during the day well into the high 80s and early 90s, 25 or 30 degrees above the norm. Even at night it was 60s and 70s instead of the usual 50s.

"He was on Lost in Space," said Diane, pointing out Bill Mumy.

"Yes," Al replied. "He also wrote 'Fish Heads'. Roly poly fish heads…"

"Yum," she retorted. "Speaking of yum…" She gestured with a well-manicured hand, one finger extended.

Al made another mango margarita. "On the house," he said, placing the glass in front of her, being careful not to spill it as he looked down her blouse surreptitiously, like he was supposed to. "Last one."

"Last Call!" He hollered through cupped hands.

It was a slow night in Old Fort Lowell. Hipsters didn't know from Kerouac and most people drank at home anyway.

"Probably was slow in 1949, too," he said to the air as he busied himself once more with the cloth, imagining himself in the scene in On The Road with Kerouac and Cassady and the Harringtons, listening to cool jazz in the evening while clutching his preferred gin and tonic and occasionally accepting a hit from some mojo that someone had thoughtfully brought.

His father had been on the scene, and he had provided Al's means of subsistence, this building, which had been a dive bar, Mexican restaurant, pizza joint, and burrito drive-through before once again assuming its rightful identity as a gin mill. Al Sr had purchased it from the original owners sometime during the early 60s.

Al filled the glasses that needed filling, cracked open a few beers, and started tabulating the day's take while the patrons watched William Shatner through the bottom of their glasses. He thought about the Warner Brothers gremlin and the war effort it represented and had a brief sad.

"Always thinking, that's the trouble with you," he said under his breath while washing pitchers.

He said his good-nights and good-byes, bleatings and salutations, Happy New Years, closed the door behind the crowd.

"Bill, I need some mopping music. Excuse me…" and he hit the remote. Warren Zevon was the first choice on YouTube. "Warren it is."

The song unreeled while he filled the mop bucket and swept the bar area. Al listened intently, though he knew it well. The song held some of his own ghosts.

"'Excitable Boy'," he agreed, sweeping. "Just an excitable boy."

The cash register pinged, letting him know that it had done the math. Al eyed the bottom line with distaste, cast stink-eye at the joint across the street that was killing his business.

"The regulars ain't gonna make this work," he intoned.

The neon lights across the way started blinking off. A minor traffic jam was the result of customer egress, temporarily blocking Randolph Lane.

"I can see the yellow bulldozers lining up," Al said under his breath. "This place is a relic of a different time." He tore off the register receipt and went into his tiny office to enter the numbers into his venerable computer.

From the East side of the building, where his cubbyhole was, Al could see his competitor's parking lot, still a quarter full of cars as the employees went about closing duties. He could also see his lonesome vehicle. He had sent the Jim the cook and Dee the waitress home hours ago.

"I can see when they won't be coming in any more," he said, referring to his employees. "Good thing Bill Callahan has a stake in this thing." Bill was the daytime bartender and manager.

In Al's peripheral vision, a fellow tossing a hammer up into the air appeared.

"Heads or tails, I lose," he said. "If I close, I have no source of income at all. If I stay open, I stay in the red, forever. Stop, talking to yourself, Al. It's not helping."

He shut down the computer, ran a hand through his red-blond hair, got to his feet.

Back in the bar, he mixed himself a small Jack and Coke, changed the tv channel. Another Rod Serling production was on that one. He recognized the scene, an exterior shot of Tim Riley's Bar and Grill.

"My favorite," he said, taking a healthy slug of his drink. "And sooo timely." He went over and turned on the oscillating fan, turned off the air conditioning.

Actress Diane Baker, the female lead, appeared onscreen. "I always thought she was Joan Hackett. Still get them mixed up sometimes," he said. Sometime game-show host Bert Convy joined her as the story unrolled.

"That wrecking ball," Al mused, draining his glass.

Shapes moved, in the corner of his eye. The hammer-thrower, the sallow scribe, a black man with a horn, the shade of his father, dead these many years. His ex-wives, his one child who died young, his regular customers, some of whom had been coming to McAdams' for decades.

He mixed another drink.

The phone rang.

"Hey boss," said the voice on the other end. "I saw the lights on. You okay?"

It was Bill Callahan. "Hi Bill. Yeah, I'm just closing up. Doing some thinking."

"That's dangerous," Bill replied. "Just checking. See you about three." And he hung up.

Al turned the lights off and sat for a bit, finishing his drink and steeling himself for the short drive to his empty house.

"My whole life is empty," he said, washing the glass. "Repetitive motions, a dance with the same steps. The song goes on forever but the words remain the same. It's like I don't even live if I'm not here."

He locked the front door, went out the back.

Home, he microwaved a burrito, turned on the tv, put his feet up. He watched The Lucy Show for a while, sat through an episode of Car 54, Where Are You?, part of an episode of McCloud, starring Tucson native Dennis Weaver, who used to drink at his bar.

"I'm not sure that test patterns weren't better than this," he said to the set.

"There is nothing wrong with your television," was the reply.

"Wait, what?" Al said.

"You are about to participate in a great adventure," the set said.

"That would be great. What do you have in mind, given that you control the vertical and the horizontal?"

The National Anthem began playing onscreen. Then Ralph Edwards and Groucho appeared, followed by footage of Al's deeds and misdeeds.

There was the time he stole a comic book from the drugstore and got caught. The time he put a cigarette out in the ciborium. The moment when he said his I do's, echoed three times. All of the lies that were his life, the good and the bad.

His father's face appeared. "I just want you to be happy, son," he said. "You do what you think is right."

"Say the secret word," Groucho rolled his eyes. A duck appeared onscreen.

"Am I dreaming?"

"Does it make a difference?" asked Groucho.

"No, not really," Al admitted.

"That's the right answer. It's like this, Al. Your values come from a different time, and that time has passed. You're not alone in this. You and the others like you are looked at as dinosaurs, relics of a bygone era, clinging to the remnants of the past. And rightly so.

"Nostalgia won't bring those times back. Raise your sights a little, get in step with the times. Or perish. These are your choices, yes?"

"Yes," Al admitted.

"You've been considering that latter – don't lie to me, I know. I know about the blue-steel revolver in your nightstand. I know about the measured dose of sleeping pills in the little envelope in the medicine cabinet. Say the secret word."

"Twonky," said Al.

"That isn't it, either. This word can explode the planet, et cetera, et al, ad museum." Groucho twiddled his cigar.

"I left my little black bag in my other suit."

"Now we're getting somewhere," Groucho exclaimed. "Look, you weren't even born when all of this stuff was happening. So how can you feel nostalgia for something you never experienced in the first place? Move on, Al. Go with the flow. Be part of the in-crowd."

"That's very strange for you to say," Al replied. "But what if that club wants me as a member?"

"Ah, there's the paradox. That's the part you need to figure out. You're a member of the human race by default. Ralph and I are gonna go now. Sleep on it, and maybe you'll have the answers in the morning."

The test pattern showed on the screen.

Al thumbed the remote, got up, and went to bed, fully-clothed, and fell asleep instantly.

The next day, he arrived at the bar. Ray Meijer, the teacher/poet, and Bill Callahan were playing Scrabble while waiting for Jeopardy to start. The parking lot across the street was full.

Al walked behind the bar, got himself a coffee.

"Gentlemen," he said. "Anybody know a cook?"

The two looked at him, clearly not understanding.

"Bill, unless we get with the times, we're gonna sink without a trace. I want to swim. What that place has…" He swept his arm toward his competitor. "…is food service. We have a perfectly good kitchen that we never use. And they have music. We can do that, too."

"I've been waiting for you to say that," Bill exclaimed. "I'll put an ad in right away."

"You do that. We're gonna dodge the wrecking ball. No sense in repeating the same mistakes, over and over," Al said, the ghosts in his peripheral vision diminishing. "Yog bless us, every one."

Prosaic

by Duane Pesice

You can see the first purple rays of the coming dawn as the test patterns wane and the farm report begins to play onscreen. Unsure if you wake or are dreaming, you stumble into your bedroom and lay your head on the pillow.

The visions of the night still consume you. Whether they be dream or no, your fondest wish is that they continue, but the ghosts fade with the night, to be replaced by the mundane specters of another tricky day.

In the back of your mind, you dream, perchance to sleep.

There's a pattern to everything. You just need to look hard enough, and it will emerge.

Acknowledgements:

We would like to thank again the members of the Weird community, our writers and aides, and specifically thank the members of the original Test Patterns community, without whom we would never have gotten here:

J.D. Busch, Arinn Dembo, Calvin Demmer, Douglas Draa, Jordan Gallader, Mike Griffin, Mike Hel, Sean Hoade, Alex S. Johnson, Scott R. Jones, Ann S. Koi, Jordan Krall, J.B. Lee, Ross Lockhart, Russ Parkhurst, Jim Richardson, Betty Rocksteady, Christopher Ropes, Jayaprakash Satyamurthy, M.J. Sydney, Jeffrey Thomas, Shannon Watkins, Michael Wehunt.

J.B. Lee and Sarah Walker provided excellent artwork for the Test Patterns Teaser chapbooks. Sean M. Thompson distributed those at NecronomiCon 2017.

We would also like to thank Garret Cook and David St. Albans for their continued support of the project and their understanding.

And we would like to thank YOU for reading.

DP – 10/10/2017